Praise for David J. Williams's
THE MIRRORED HEAVENS

DISCARD

"Calling to mind Clint Eastwood and Dirty Harry . . . *Mirrored Heavens'* action is wild and relentless. . . . Cleaves closely enough to the cyberpunk canon to be clearly identified with it, while departing from it sharply enough to refresh and renew its source." —*The Seattle Times*

"Slam-bang action and realpolitik speculations."
—*Sci Fi Weekly*

"A crackling cyberthriller. This is Tom Clancy interfacing Bruce Sterling. David Williams has hacked into the future."
—Stephen Baxter, author of the Manifold series

"Explodes out of the gate like a sonic boom and never stops. Adrenaline bleeds from Williams's fingers with every word he hammers into the keyboard. The razors of *The Mirrored Heavens* would eat cyberpunk's old-guard hackers and cowboys as a light snack."
—Peter Watts, Hugo-nominated author of *Blindsight*

"*The Mirrored Heavens* presents an action-jammed and audacious look at a terrifyingly plausible future. . . . Highly recommended."
—L. E. Modesitt Jr., author of the Saga of Recluse series

"*The Mirrored Heavens* is a 21st-century *Neuromancer* set in a dark, dystopian future where nothing and no one can be trusted, the razors who rule cyberspace are predators and prey, and ordinary human life is cheap. It starts out at full throttle and accelerates all the way to the end."
—Jack Campbell, author of the Lost Fleet series

"*The Mirrored Heavens* is a complex view of global politics in time of crisis. Williams understands that future wars will be fought as much online as off. It's also a rousing adventure with breathless, nonstop action—Tom Clancy on speed. And you will NOT be able to guess the ending."
—Nancy Kress, author of the Probability trilogy

ALSO BY DAVID J. WILLIAMS

THE MIRRORED HEAVENS

THE BURNING SKIES

DAVID J. WILLIAMS

BALLANTINE BOOKS  NEW YORK

A Spectra Trade Paperback Original

Copyright © 2009 by David J. Williams

Published in the United States by Spectra, an imprint of The Random House Publishing Group, a division of Random House, Inc., New York.

SPECTRA and the portrayal of a boxed "s" are trademarks of Random House, Inc.

LIBRARY OF CONGRESS CATALOGING-IN-PUBLICATION DATA
Williams, David J.
The burning skies / David J. Williams.
p. cm.
ISBN 978-0-553-38542-7
1. International relations—Fiction. I. Title.
PS3623.I556495B87 2009
813'.6—dc22
2009011252

Printed in the United States of America

www.ballantinebooks.com

BVG 1 2 3 4 5 6 7 8 9

Book design by Carol Russo

Dedicated to the memory of
George Cotton, S.B.St.J., QFSM
1913–2003

CONTENTS

THE EUROPA PLATFORM

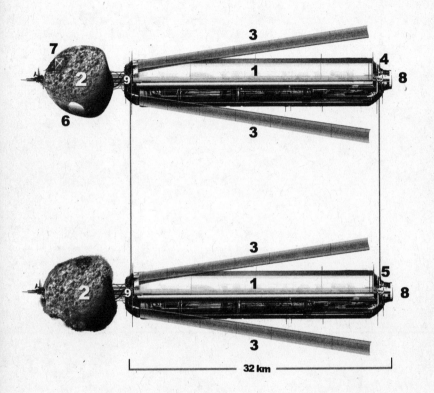

32 km

1	**O'Neill cylinders**	**5**	**New Zurich**†
2	**Aeries**	**6**	**The Window**
	(asteroid habitats)	**7**	**The Hangar**
3	**Mirrors***	**8**	**North Pole**
4	**New London**†	**9**	**South Pole**

*Though only two are shown here, each cylinder has three mirrors.
†Contained within northern end of cylinder.

Art by Randall MacDonald

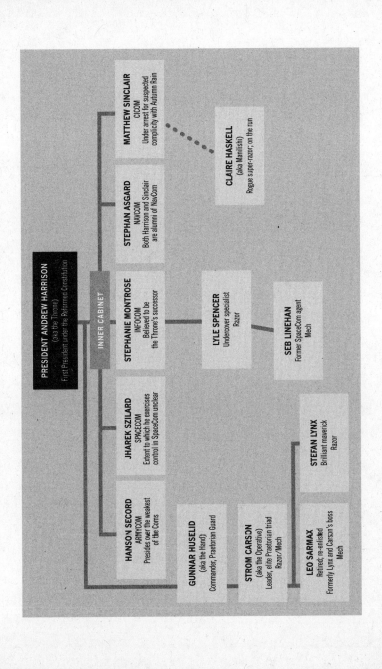

PRESIDENT ANDREW HARRISON
(aka the Throne)
First President under the Reformed Constitution

INNER CABINET

HANSON SECORD
ARMYCOM
Presides over the weakest of the Coms

JHAREK SZILARD
SPACECOM
Extent to which he exercises control in SpaceCom unclear

STEPHANIE MONTROSE
INFOCOM
Believed to be the Throne's successor

STEPHAN ASGARD
NAVCOM
Both Harrison and Sinclair are alumni of NavCom

MATTHEW SINCLAIR
CICOM
Under arrest for suspected complicity with Autumn Rain

CLAIRE HASKELL
(aka Manilishi)
Rogue super-razor; on the run

LYLE SPENCER
Undercover specialist
Razor

SEB LINEHAN
Former SpaceCom agent
Mech

GUNNAR HUSELID
(aka the Hand)
Commander, Praetorian Guard

STROM CARSON
(aka the Operative)
Leader, elite Praetorian triad
Razor/Mech

LEO SARMAX
Retired; re-enlisted
Formerly Lynx and Carson's boss
Mech

STEFAN LYNX
Brilliant maverick
Razor

THE
BURNING
SKIES

PART I
SUN'S MESSENGER

2110 A.D. Maximum security doesn't even begin to describe it.

No one talks to the prisoner. No one enters his cell. No one sets foot in his cell-block. No one else is confined within. The guards charged with carrying out these directives stand outside the cell-block doors in powered armor. The presidential seal has been placed upon those doors. Only one man can break that seal. And he's not taking calls.

The cell-block is located at the far end of one wing of a massive space station that's the aggregation of several smaller ones, each one capable of operating autonomously should the need arise. But none of the crew have ever witnessed such a moment. Nor do they expect to. Nor, if truth be told, do they think of themselves as a crew. They consider themselves a *garrison*. And the space station they man is one of the largest fortresses ever built.

The structure is situated at L5, the libration point that's been an American possession for almost a century now. Its defenses are organized into several orbiting perimeters. Clouds of mini-sats and space mines begin a hundred klicks out. They comprise the first perimeter, stretching as close to the center as sixty klicks in places, forming a continuously shifting pattern that only those kept current with the correct routes can navigate through.

Fifty klicks out, the directed-energy batteries begin to appear: a variety of sats equipped with lasers, particle beams, and microwaves capable of lacerating targets at the speed of light, arranged in several layers, intended to both maximize crossfire capability and ensure maximum redundancy of hardware. Most of those weapons are optimized to hit targets in vacuum, but some of the larger ones are intended for planetary bombardment.

Twenty klicks out the manned defenses begin. Some are troopships designed for rapid deployment to the lunar or terrestrial theaters. Some house still more guns. Some contain the razors who defend the U.S. zone against net in-cursions. Many are just decoys, intended to eat up the enemy's shots and give the real weapons a chance to do some damage.

Ten klicks out are the giant slabs of rock—chunks of asteroids that have been towed into position to orbit L5 like fragments of some incomplete sphere. Five klicks out is the second, inner layer of slabs. Each rock has more weapons racked upon it, including more directed-energy cannons, along with rows of mass-drivers that can take advantage of a ready supply of ammunition.

At the center of all this sits the L5 fortress—half a kilometer across. It's manned by razors, logistics-masters, and AIs intended to direct L5's defenses in the event of war with the Eurasian Coalition, ready to make adjustments as enemy fire degrades the libration point's assets and enemy targets are reprioritized. Scenarios are constantly played out, assessed, and reassessed. The men and women of L5 train daily for the day of final reckoning.

But national security takes many forms. Not all of it involves planning for the next war.

Some of it involves the war that's going on right now.

The prisoner is in his sixties. He wears the regulation uniform that everyone in American military custody wears. His cell contains no furniture, just toilet facilities and a small hatch through which food and water comes.

The man drinks the water, but he barely touches the food. He doesn't seem to sleep either. He just sits cross-legged on the floor, staring at the locked door opposite him.

But then he notices a screen on the wall where there's no screen he knew of.

Even as he hears a voice he thought he'd never hear again.

Hacking L5 is impossible. Not just for all the usual reasons—interlocking firewalls, elite razors, guardian AIs, uncrackable codes, systems switching on and off randomly so that even were hostile razors to get inside they'd still be kicked back out into the cold—but because of L5's location, almost four hundred thousand kilometers away from both Earth and Moon. Any razor based at either of those points would operate at a decisive disadvantage, working more than a second behind the razors based at L5 due to the limits of light's speed. A razor could operate out of a spaceship closer in—but for that very reason L5 accepts no signal traffic that hasn't traveled a certain distance.

All of which makes a hack on L5 *almost* impossible. Unless the attacking razor is based at L5 itself.

Or unless that razor's something more than razor.

• • •

The face now appearing on the screen opposite the prisoner is that of a woman. She looks like she's about thirty. She's got brown hair and freckles. She looks like she's neither slept nor smiled in a long time.

"Matthew Sinclair," she says.

The man smiles. "Nothing's beyond you now," he says.

"You knew all along."

"I'd put it no higher than *hoped*."

"Which doesn't mean you didn't plan it."

"But you're the one who's gone and done it." His voice is lit with a strange sort of pride. "I assume that the ones who watch this room are seeing the same footage they've been too bored to watch for days now?"

"It's like I'm not even here," she says. "I'm a long way out too."

"Oh? Where are you, Claire?"

She smiles: *right*. "Right here, Matthew."

"No one's called me that since my wife died."

"I didn't know you were married."

"She killed herself."

"I'm sorry."

"Why have you come here?" he asks.

"To see you."

"To learn, you mean. But I fear you've chosen a man sadly out of every loop. You have the advantage of at least knowing that I really am Matthew Sinclair. I don't even know if you're really Claire."

The screen changes slightly. The man watches.

"Ah. Codes I gave you. And footage from within the plane Morat jacked. Taken by your ocular cameras, I presume—is he dead, by the way?"

"Yes," she says. "He's dead."

"Did he die well?"

"Not particularly."

"Did you kill him?"

"Yes."

"With news like that, you're welcome here anytime. With or without those codes establishing that you're *probably* Claire. But even if you're not her, you're still welcome to anything I have to say. I've told the Throne everything anyway. I'm finished, as you can see. My life is over."

"Then why are you still alive?"

"Because Andrew has yet to use that laser—the one through which you're projecting your face—as a blowtorch against my head."

"That's not an answer."

"That's too bad."

"You call the Throne by his first name."

"And I daresay I earned the privilege. I've known him for fifty years. Long before he became president. We used to be midshipmen, you know. Back in the final days of the old navy. Back before we laid the foundations of what was to become NavCom. I remember when—"

"Do I look like I came here to listen to an old man reminiscing?"

"You'd deny me my memories?"

"You denied mine."

"Only so you could become what you are."

"And I'll never forgive you for it."

"I don't ask for your forgiveness, Claire. All I require is what's beyond your power to preclude: my own recollections. The foundations of NavCom—I remember so well the blueprints of those ships, the likes of which the world had never seen. Floating fortresses to replace carriers. Submarines that could ride supercavitation at hundreds of klicks an hour. I tell you, Claire, when I was the nation's chief spymaster, I often yearned for those simpler times."

"Why did the Throne make you head of CICom?"

"Because he and I could practically complete each other's

sentences. And because he wanted at least one source of un-wavering support in the Inner Cabinet. He knew I'd never betray him."

"But you *did* betray him."

"I was the only one who was true to him."

"Is that how you rationalize it?"

"He used to have such dreams, Claire. He alone understood what was required. Ironic, isn't it? The military is acknowledged at long last as the only force that can save the country—and promptly finds itself undone by its own straitjacketed imagination. Only one man was capable of rising above that. Andrew Harrison opened my eyes. He showed me that the problem wasn't how to win a second cold war. The problem was how to transcend that problem. How to channel human energy into goals worthy of humanity. How to solve Earth's energy and environmental crisis once and for all. Thus the repurposing of our military machines. Détente was a mere stepping stone along the way. Andrew's ultimate agenda was to lay the groundwork for a new civilization."

"That sounds a lot like what the Rain claimed to want."

"That's no coincidence. It's the inevitable goal of any mind able to break free of the cage that passes for conventional thinking. The real question lies in the new world's contours. And the Rain is precisely where Andrew went wrong."

"But he created them."

"No, Claire. *I* created them. He merely signed off on them."

"And the order for their termination."

"Indeed. He'd become convinced that the elite commando unit we'd built to hit the East's leadership in the event of a final war was about to target him."

"And was he wrong in thinking that?"

"You know, you really *are* Claire."

"What makes you say that?"

"Because this conversation is proceeding exactly as you would conduct it. The oblique probing about the past. The gradual revealing to me of what's going on outside this room. The gradual closing in upon the question you're really dying to ask."

"After the Throne had the Praetorians eliminate Autumn Rain, did you maintain a link to the surviving members who later downed the Elevator?"

Sinclair's mouth creases upward in something that's well short of smile.

"Yes," he says. "I did."

"You'll just come right out and admit it."

"As I've told you, I have nothing to hide. Not anymore."

"So tell me why you—"

"It's strange, Claire. We thought that the world was ours. He was president, and I was his right-hand man, and we were only in our forties. We would either defeat the East or reach accommodation with them, and then move on to greater things. But when he ordered Autumn Rain's destruction I came up against the limitations of his vision. I saw that I had surpassed him, that he would never green-light humanity's successors. I realized that the sooner I ruled in his place, the quicker I would be able to finish the task he started."

"But you'd *already* turned on him, Matthew."

"Meaning what?"

"Meaning Harrison was right: Autumn Rain *was* targeting him all those years ago. What he didn't know was that it was on *your* orders. Right?"

Sinclair says nothing. She laughs.

"Though I bet he's figured it out since. So, in other words, you tried to assassinate him back then—after which you helped what was left of the Rain go underground, rebuild, and then try to take him out *again?*"

"Assassination is such a nihilistic word."

"Call it what it is."

"Ah yes," he says. "Definitely Claire. The anger in you runs so deep. Such a shame it still outpaces the insight. Let's clarify terms: *assassination* is a word that can only be used if people know the target is *dead*. The Rain destroys their target, assumes that target's position, gives orders in that target's name. The perfection of subversion from within. Turning paranoia in upon itself, no? Fear of coups and assassinations drove leaders into seclusion. The Rain capitalize upon that. No one sees the Throne anymore. No one even knows his location."

"I do," she says.

"Do the Rain?"

"I don't know."

"So you've chosen to fight them."

"Yes."

"Why?"

"Do you even have to ask?"

"What about Marlowe? Surely he could have persuaded you that—"

"Jason's dead."

"Oh dear."

"You bastard."

Sinclair raises an eyebrow. "I assure you my distress is no subterfuge. Jason was intended to be your consort when you and the rest of the Rain ruled across the Earth-Moon system. He was the catalyst for your true memories. Don't let your anger blind your logic, Claire. How could I *not* feel pain at such news? Who killed him?"

"Me," she says.

"You could kill me too, if you wanted. You broke in here on light. You can break me with light too."

"All I want to do is talk."

"Same as Andrew. Figure you may as well keep me around, eh? Never know when you might find something I say useful."

"I don't anticipate you being of any use to me ever again. I just know that if I kill you—"

"—the Throne will know somebody penetrated the L5 fortress. Claire, I'm so glad it's you. Why *didn't* you join Autumn Rain?"

"Because they would have perpetuated the problem."

"You need to tell me what you mean by that."

"They want to rule humanity."

"And that's a sin?"

"They turned Hong Kong into a charnel-house."

"Our world's a charnel-house. The only question is what to do about it. They at least have a plan."

"The plan you gave them."

"The plan I *bred* them for. They weren't just born to seize power. They were born to wield it."

"So it *was* to be them that ruled?"

"You as well."

"But not you?"

He shrugs. "Of course I would have."

"For a moment there, I thought you were letting me down."

"They're still children, Claire. So are you, for that matter. They'd need guidance. But I wouldn't have stood in their way for very long."

"Didn't stop them from trying to hurry up the process."

Sinclair says nothing.

"Because that's what happened, right? They sent the Throne the proof of your communications with them, didn't they? Right at the same time they were jacking my spaceplane to get at me? That's why the Praetorians arrested you when they did."

"I can't say I fault your logic."

"Did you order the destruction of the Elevator? Or was that them striking out on their own too?"

"Why would I order the senseless destruction of such

valuable hardware? No, that was their idea. And even if it *had* been mine, I would never have let it happen when you were in the middle of that inferno in South America. They clearly didn't know you were there either."

"I thought Morat was reporting back to them."

"I'm assuming they got to Morat pretty much immediately *after* that."

"Turned him right under your nose."

"I made mistakes."

"That's all you can say?"

"What else would you have from me?"

"How about how the fuck did you let it happen? It really came as a surprise to you that a group that had *already* turned the tables on their executioners would betray their would-be grey eminence?"

"Who said it came as a surprise? Deal with something like the Rain and you never know quite where you stand."

"That's for sure."

"I admit it—I thought I could control them. I thought they saw me as a father figure. I didn't realize that there was only one thing I had that they wanted."

"Me."

"The Manilishi herself." He pauses. "How's that working for you these days?"

"I'm still trying to figure out just what the fuck I am."

"The culmination of the Autumn Rain experiment."

"I know that. But what does that—"

"Mean?" He waves a hand languidly. "Autumn Rain was to be backed on its combat runs by a unique type of razor capable of running zone in a whole new way."

"I'll say."

"Intuition lets you fly, child."

"But how the hell did you engineer—"

"A great question."

"You don't *know*?"

"We designed something in which every cell computes—molecular computing taken to a new level. We foresaw there'd be synergies we didn't plan for. We eventually realized we were dealing with a violation of locality that allows the subject—"

"Don't *subject* me. I broke beyond those labels."

"—to evade the penalties that a razor pays when hacking a remote target. You don't have the split-second disadvantage that any normal razor has during off-planet hacking. Your reaction times outpace the stimuli your brain receives and nobody knows why. No wonder you're running rings around L5's razors."

"I'll do the same to the Rain."

"Claire, you're not invincible."

"Without me, neither are the Rain."

"They'll have the advantage."

"Once it became clear they'd had turned against you, why did you send me to the Moon?"

"I wanted to get you someplace safe."

"Safe?"

"Relatively speaking."

"The Moon wasn't even *vaguely* safe. The Rain were up there. To say nothing of the SpaceCom cabal that the Rain was using to try to ignite war."

"Once you were on the scene and activated as Manilishi, none of that would have meant much. The Rain's primary force was on Earth, preparing to hit the superpowers' leadership. They had one team on the Moon beneath Nansen Station pulling the strings of the SpaceCom conspiracy, and another preparing to hit Szilard on L2. You would have cleaned up the Moon pretty quick."

"Maybe."

"Besides, you have to be awake to all contingencies. If war with the Eurasians breaks out, the Moon is going to look all the better. It's the high ground of the Earth-Moon system."

"Except the libration points. Except this fortress."

"Technically that's true. But I'm willing to bet that the Moon can sustain a damn sight more damage than this place."

"But why didn't you activate me as Manilishi *before* I left for the Moon? Why wait till I got there?"

"Because activating you meant restoring your true memories."

"My true memories?" Her voice is taut.

"Once they were restored, your loyalty would have been a wild card without the proper precautions. As the Rain found out the hard way. What's wrong?"

Tears are running down her face. "You *know* what's wrong, you sick fuck. How can I tell what my real memories are?"

"Because that's what we linked your activation to."

"Fuck you and your sophistry! *How do I know they're real?*"

"How do you know anything's real? Claire, you need to get past the past. You're beyond the range of ordinary definition now. What happened to you back then doesn't matter. All that matters is what happens now."

She takes a deep breath. "What happens now is you keep talking."

"About what?"

"About how I can beat them."

"You'll have to find your own way through on that."

"You don't care who wins?"

"All I care about is perfecting my role as voyeur."

"But you're blind in here."

"I see the crisis of the age in you, Claire. I can see what's going on out there all too well. I know the capabilities of the respective players better than anyone else. All the scenarios that might have gone down after that spaceplane, after the

Praetorian agents arrested me at Cheyenne and began the purge of CICom, all the ways in which the game might have played out across these last four days—it *has* been four days, hasn't it?"

She nods.

"I should imagine that things happened very quickly once they downed your plane, didn't they?"

She nods.

"So . . . the Rain is clearly still a factor, or you wouldn't be so desperate to talk about them. But they haven't won. Otherwise they'd be opening that door, laughing at me."

She nods.

"This base has yet to see major combat—I think I would be aware of that much at least. So the third world war that the Rain were trying to bring about didn't happen. They *did* try to bring it about, didn't they?"

"They tried. But—"

"So inevitable, given the way they think. They set it up so beautifully with the downing of the Elevator. Each superpower would naturally suspect the other side—and those on its own side. The escalation toward war, the increasing tension, the lockdowns—all of it allowing the Rain to move in toward the Throne and the East's leaders. Again the paradox, no? Security specialists think they're creating multiple levels of access, while they're really building labyrinths within which minotaurs can hide. The less you see of the deeper recesses of whatever bunker you're guarding, the less likely you are to know what's really going on in there."

"And the Rain—"

"Their commandos would have torn their way through the president's outer defenses like a scalpel. But without your support, it doesn't surprise me that they failed. Particularly in the president's bunker, where they would have met the

Praetorian Core, the best soldiers the world has ever known. Until the Rain, of course. But the president always chooses redoubts within which he can bring numbers to bear and within which he can evade pursuers. Something the Rain didn't know. Something *I* did. Without my help—without yours—it would have been touch and go. My guess is the Rain hit teams went down on the very threshold of their targets. They would have hoped to try again, during the war itself. But what I don't understand is how war was averted."

"Because of me. And because forces loyal to the president broke up the attacks of the Rain's proxies."

"Ah yes," says Sinclair. "The proxy strategy. How high up *did* the rot go within SpaceCom?"

"I don't know. Very close to the top. Maybe all the way."

"Was Szilard killed by the Rain? Or implicated by the Throne?"

"Neither."

"Neither?" Sinclair's face creases. "The Rain *did* storm his flagship, didn't they?"

"They did. He was on a different ship."

"Selling them a counterfeit—not easy. They wouldn't have missed him if they'd had another team up there in reserve. Well, congratulations to Jharek. He's not known as the Lizard for nothing. So he wasn't placed under arrest by the Throne for all of SpaceCom's indiscretions?"

"Not yet."

"Not *yet?*"

"Even if the Praetorians don't find concrete evidence of Szilard's specific involvement—even if it was just one of SpaceCom's factions—it seems to me the Throne would be well advised to just execute the head of SpaceCom to be on the safe side."

"Andrew prefers to keep his enemies close at hand, Claire. That's one of the keys to his success. Yet now he's maneuvering between the Rain's remaining hit teams and the continual pressure from his own hardliners to attack the Eurasians. Not to mention the possibility that the East may go ahead and strike anyway. His only stalwart supporters are Stephanie Montrose and the rest of InfoCom. True?"

"True. But then again, he thought you were loyal too."

"Stephanie's all data and no imagination. She's reliable. But even with her help the Throne remains very much embattled."

"I agree."

"How much of the Rain is left?"

"I think they're at about half strength."

"Probably more than that, if you consider that they almost certainly held back their best triads. Their strategic reserve. They'll be deep into their next move by now. Are you deep into yours?"

"Yes."

"Gazing upon your face again is such a joy, Claire. But this is the first time you've ever truly seen me. Am I a disappointment?"

"No," she whispers. "No, you're not."

"The initial attacks on the Throne will have told the Rain all they need to know about how he thinks and moves. The other players in the Inner Cabinet will be like dogs when the leader of the pack is wounded. The Throne's options are narrowing."

"They are."

"What he's facing is the Rain equipped with the knowledge they need to win, while he has no safe ground to fall back on within the U.S. zone."

"Leaving him with only one real option."

"I agree." Sinclair pauses. "And yet, what an option. Will he rise to it?"

"He's already set it in motion," she replies.

Sinclair nods his head. "Ah, Andrew. Do you know— he may yet prevail. Odd how so powerful a man remains so daring tactically. Despite all his limitations, he remains in my estimation the greatest figure of our time. If you'd ever met him, Claire, you'd understand that."

"I may yet."

"Meet him?"

"Who knows?"

"Will you join him?"

"I don't know."

"You should join *me*."

"You'd enslave humanity to things that aren't human."

"*You're* not human, Claire."

"More so than you."

"You still don't understand what you've become. Nor do you understand what you're taking on. Autumn Rain has no single razor as good as you. But they are *far* more skilled at taking down prey. They'll maneuver you into a position where you can't bring the full range of your powers to bear. They'll turn your own designs back upon your face."

"Let them try."

"Then let it happen," says Sinclair. "Let the Throne play his last card. Let the last of the Rain strike for the center one last time. How I wish I could witness the clash that's about to occur. To hear the very rafters of heaven shake—if you survive with your mind intact, you would do an old man a very great favor in returning to tell me all that transpired."

"I'll never see you again," she says.

"If only you could see that far into the future."

"Good-bye, Matthew."

"Good-bye, Claire"—but the screen's already gone blank.

• • •

Blankness suddenly gone—and the Operative's waking up to find himself laying inside his suit. He's staring past his visor at a ceiling that's half a meter from his face. He's in some enclosed space. He doesn't know where.

He knows why he's awake, though. He can thank his armor for that—can see it's on a prearranged sequence. It's coming to life around him now—a suit that looks to be better than anything he's ever worn—powering up per whatever instructions it's got, letting parameters stack up within his skull. Those parameters tell him all about his armor. They tell him nothing about his mission. Save that *it's begun.*

Which is why he's sitting up—why he's pushing up against the ceiling, which is really a lid. It swings open, and even as it does so, the Operative's leaping out of his coffinlike container, vaulting to the floor of the larger room he's in, looking around.

Not that there's much to see. Just more containers. And three doors, one of which now slides open. The Operative keeps an eye on the revealed passage while he preps his weapons and scans the containers. The readout says *industrial plastics.* But the Operative's got a funny feeling that's what a scan of his own container would have said. He walks to one of the other containers and extends an arm—igniting a laser, he slices through in nothing flat. All he gets for his trouble is some melted plastic.

And the knowledge that he's just wasted five seconds. Because something in his head is telling him not to worry about these containers. That same feeling is telling him to go through the doorway. The Operative knows better than to doubt it. Posthypnotic memory triggers are unmistakable. He exits the room and walks down the corridor, eyeing every meter of those walls and ceiling. The door at the end of the corridor looks just like the one he just passed through. He waits a moment, wondering if this door is about to open too.

Sure enough, it slides aside. The Operative finds himself staring straight down the barrel of what looks to be a heavy-duty pulse rifle—a model he hadn't even realized was in production yet—held by another figure in powered armor. The Operative sees his own image in the visor. He looks past the reflection to behold a face he knows.

And then he hears that voice.

Take a man. Take his world. Turn it upside down. Tell him he's the very thing he's fighting. Give him memories you've manufactured. Let your enemies dose him with drugs that open doors within him. Let the edges of the zone drip like liquid through him. Let him see his own mind melting on every screen. Let him know time as some blasted fiction.

Then bid him open his eyes.

But all Lyle Spencer can see is blur, and all he can feel is cold. He seems to be floating against the straps that hold him down. He's in zero-G; he hears murmuring around him, along with the thrumming of remote engines. And a voice cutting through all of it.

"Sir. Can you hear me, sir?"

"Yes," replies Spencer.

"Move your right foot."

Spencer does so—even as he gets it. He was in storage. He's opening his eyes. The walls are lined with cryo-pods like the one he's in. Most of them are open. Those who can are getting out, pulling on uniforms. Those who can't are waiting, gathering their strength. Technicians are drifting around the room, facilitating the awakenings. The face of one such technician looks into Spencer's own.

"Sir," she says, "how do you feel?"

"Like shit."

"We need to test your reflexes, sir."

"Go for it," he says.

She offers him clothing and a wire at one end of which is a zone-jack. There's something weird about her uniform. He struggles to clear his mind, reaches for the jack she's handing him, glances back at her.

"Where are we?"

She stares at him with an anxious expression. "You don't know?"

And suddenly he *does* know. And wishes he didn't. Her uniform's Praetorian. So is the one she's offering him. He has no idea what he's doing here. But he knows damn well what these soldiers will do with him if they wake up to the fact that he's woken up among them.

"Of course I do."

"Sir," she asks, "what's the name of this ship?"

"The *Larissa V*," he replies.

He has no idea where that came from. But apparently it's the right answer. He takes the jack, slots it into the back of his neck. Zone expands all around him. It contains many things, one of them being the face of Seb Linehan, Spencer's erstwhile partner. A man who should be dead. He doesn't look it. Though he looks like he wishes Spencer was.

Claire Haskell sits within a container aboard some ship, and darkness sits within her. The conversation with Matthew Sinclair has left her feeling sick. She thought she would have left the wreckage of her past life behind her by now, but it's only growing ever more insistent—Jason's face in the throes of passion, Jason's face as she killed him, his body contorted on the SeaMech's floor—all of it keeps replaying in her mind, and she wishes she could undo all of it.

Her own weakness appalls her, but she can't deny that she'd sell out the whole world just to put the clock back four days. She'd throw in her lot with the Rain just to keep Jason alive.

But now he's dead. And she's thankful, because it means the key to her heart's been thrown away forever. No one can hurt her anymore. No one can second-guess her while she takes stock of the whole game—the superpowers as they shore up their defenses, the endless gates of both those zones, those endless eyes scanning endlessly for Rain.

And for her. She can't see the Rain, though. She hasn't seen them since their defeat four days ago—in the minutes after that defeat, she got a read on them receding into zone like a leviathan fading beneath the waves: just a quick glimpse of scales and teeth, and then it was gone. She saw enough to realize just how much of a threat they still were. It worries her that she hasn't seen them since. It worries her even more that they might have seen *her*. That they might have found some way inside her, and she might not even know it. Even if she *is* Manilishi, that doesn't mean she can't lose.

So she takes what precautions she can. If the Rain retain some secret thing inside her—some secret key to her, in spite of all her precautions—they might see what's in her brain's software. They might see what's in her mind.

But they won't see what's on her own skin—what she's drawn upon it. Across the hours, in the oily darkness of the holds of spaceships, surrounded by the clank of machinery, she's pricked maps upon that skin, scarred that skin, painted it all in her own blood: all her calculations, all her strategy, whole swathes of blueprint of zone upon her limbs and chest—*both* zones, and the neutral ones, too—endless geometries of virtual architecture, endless coordinates in no-space. Insight's a myriad bloody slashes all across her. Knowledge is no longer fleeting now that it's etched upon her.

She studies endless patterns, looking for what all the others may have missed. Twenty-four hours since thwarting the war, and a nagging disquiet is stealing through her. Forty-eight hours, and that disquiet has become a fear unlike any she's ever known.

Now it's been ninety-six hours. The conversation with Sinclair has confirmed what she's been thinking. She's so scared she feels like her mind's coming apart. Worse, as long as she was slicing herself, she was forgetting Jason. But now she's got nothing more to cut.

She's got nothing more to learn either. She knows exactly where she needs to be: right where she is now. Crosshairs slide together in her mind. She feels herself start gliding forward.

The chamber in which Leo Sarmax awoke is almost identical to the one that the Operative just left. The difference is it contains only a single additional door.

And a phone.

"A what?" asks Sarmax.

"A phone," says the Operative, gesturing at the small device that's set into one wall. "Archaic communication device phased out by the middle of the last century."

"Carson. I know what a fucking phone is."

"Then why'd you ask?"

"Because that's not a phone."

"Yeah?"

"That looks like nothing I've ever seen."

"That's because it's a real antique."

"Yeah?" asks Sarmax.

"Ma Bell, baby. Twentieth century."

"So what the fuck's it doing here?"

"I'm guessing somebody rigged it."

"Why?"

"Well," says the Operative, "that's the big question, isn't it?"

"And you don't remember the answer?"

"No, I don't."

"You don't remember *anything* about why we're here?"

"That's a negative."

"Those fucking *bastards,*" says Sarmax.

"So what's new?" replies the Operative tonelessly.

"Would have thought you'd have been promoted above this kind of bullshit."

"Career trajectory's a bitch."

"Would have thought the handlers would be showing me more gratitude for walking back in their door."

"*Gratitude's* not in their vocabulary, Leo. We need to figure this out from first principles."

They stare at each other.

"You first," says Sarmax.

"Okay," says the Operative. He gestures at Sarmax's rifle. "For a start, we've got some new tech."

"Not just my rifle. My armor. *Your* armor."

"Straight off the Praetorian R&D racks, I'm guessing."

"Let's hope so," says Sarmax.

"And we were placed in rooms in close proximity to one another."

"But not in the same room."

"Presumably to allow each of us some warning time if the other got nailed. Have you tried that door out of here?"

"It's sealed," says Sarmax. "Could blow it open, but I'm not sure that's a good move. Have you tried the zone of wherever the fuck we are?"

"The zone's off-limits."

"Meaning what?"

But the Operative's not sure he has the answer. All he's got is the fact that the zone-interfaces in his armor are switched off, as are those within his head. He could switch them on, but he doesn't. Because a certain feeling's brewing in him. He's starting to piece together what this all must mean in aggregation.

"We're on a stealth mission."

"Which makes no sense," says Sarmax.

"Doesn't it," says the Operative mildly.

"Obviously. How the *fuck* can we be stealthy if you can't cover us in zone?"

The Operative mulls this over. He understands Sarmax's anxiety. All the more so because he shares it. Hacking an enemy's systems is how one stays undetected. It's how one stays ahead of the eyes. But these last few days have witnessed the death of a lot of assumptions. And the current situation is setting in motion some nasty questions.

"The Throne's handlers are changing up the game," says the Operative carefully. "They're reversing the normal procedure. They're terrified of Rain penetration of the zone. Clearly whatever terrain we're in—"

"And we don't know where that is."

"—clearly it's vulnerable. But as long as we're off the zone we're probably running silent."

"Silent? We step in front of *one* camera with the wrong camo settings and we're *fucked*."

"Have you seen any cameras, Leo?"

"What?"

"Have. You. Seen. Any. Cameras."

"No. I haven't."

"Maybe there's a reason for that."

"I don't like this one fucking bit."

"Wish you were back administering your little corporate empire?"

"Not with the Throne unwilling to leave me the fuck alone."

Not with my lover dead, he might have said. *Can't beat 'em, join 'em,* he could have muttered. But he doesn't. And the Operative knows better than to press the point.

Suddenly there's a jangling noise. It's coming from the vintage phone.

"Pick it up," says the Operative.

"You must be joking."

"That's our connection with whatever's going on beyond these rooms."

Apart from what's happening in the Operative's skull. For even as the phone rings, something's expanding within his mind. Some kind of heads-up display—set on automatic release?—he doesn't know. He suddenly realizes who's on the other end of the line, gets a glimpse of what's really going on. He picks the receiver up, holds it between himself and Sarmax while the helmets of both men amplify the sound.

"Carson," says the voice of Stefan Lynx. It sounds tinny. The Operative wonders how the twentieth century dealt. "That you?"

"Of course it's me."

"Don't suppose Leo's with you?"

"He is," says Sarmax.

"Hey Carson," says Lynx, "did something strange just happen in your head? Like, right when you picked up the phone."

"You too, huh?"

"*Fuck,*" says Lynx. "They've hung us out to fucking dry."

"Don't jump to conclusions."

"All I need to do is fucking *step.*"

Cold storage has an expiration date: right now. Usually it's used for long-range trips, like Mars or the rocks. But Spencer's instruments show he's only been out for about two days. Meaning that the normal rationale for cryo doesn't apply.

Spencer can think of other reasons, though. He's mulling

them over as he listens to Linehan rant on about getting fucked over yet again. More of the personnel in this room are up and moving about, floating through the zero-G, climbing rungs along the walls, dispersing to their various duties. Some of them are still recovering. Among them's Spencer, reclining in his cryo-cell, stretching his muscles. He's handed back the jack that the technician was using to calibrate his zone-reflexes. As far as that technician knows, he's off the zone.

The reality's a little more complex.

"You're in the rear troop areas," Spencer says—though his lips aren't moving. His neural link broadcasts silently, bracketed along limited range, aimed at where Linehan has indicated he is.

"And you are?"

"In the forward cryos."

"Who's up there?" asks Linehan.

"Mainly crew."

"What kind of crew?"

"Gunnery personnel. Bridge personnel. Various other hangers-on. What's back there?"

"What's back here is a shitload of Praetorian marines. I've never seen anything like—"

"Is that what you are?"

"Sorry?"

"A Praetorian marine—is that what you are?"

"Meaning *is that what I appear to be?*"

"Just answer the fucking question."

"Sure, Spencer. I'm decked out as a Praetorian marine. I'm surrounded by the motherfuckers. We're all just hanging out. Awaiting orders, apparently. Christ man, if you weren't even briefed on *me* then we are fucking *dead*—"

"Just *tell me what you remember.*"

"They fucking reconditioned me!"

"Who?"

"Your own team. InfoCom. Orders from that whore

Montrose, I'm sure. Trance, drugs, the works. They said I'd be loyal to them from now on. Loyal to *you*. They said I'd be the perfect bitch for you, you fucking bitch—"

"Will you calm *down?* All they told me is that it was going to be some off-Earth operation. Next thing I know I'm waking up from cryo-sleep with the identity of a Praetorian razor."

"That makes me feel so much fucking better."

"How long were you trying to find me?"

"I wasn't. You know I'm no razor, Spencer. First thing I knew of a zone connection is when you suddenly activated it."

"How long had you been awake before I called you?"

"About twenty minutes."

"Looks like they're waking up this ship in batches," says Spencer. "What do you know about this craft?"

"From the inside, it looks like a Praetorian warship."

"And from the outside?"

"Who the fuck knows?"

"Based on what you've seen so far, what class of warship?"

"Been trying to find out. It doesn't conform to any specifications I know. What are you seeing on the zone?"

"Not much," says Spencer. "All I can see are parts of this ship's microzone. Nothing outside a very local firewall."

"And what you can see doesn't help?"

"Not really. The ship's obviously in lockdown. And specs on the interiors of these things aren't exactly a matter of public record—"

"And your side doesn't have them?"

"My side's your side now," Spencer reminds him. "And the answer's no."

"The list of bosses I'm gonna fuck over before it's all over just gets bigger and bigger."

"I'm sure Montrose is quaking in her boots."

"But she didn't give you the specs of this ship."

"Goddammit, Linehan! She didn't give me *shit*. We're going to have to figure this one out for ourselves. Working with what we know. We're InfoCom operatives—"

"You're taking that on faith."

"If we're no longer InfoCom then we may as well give up trying to figure out anything."

"Have it your way," says Linehan. "We're InfoCom operatives. We're on board a Praetorian ship. A ship that must be getting close to wherever the fuck it's heading because everybody's getting woken up. Maybe we're part of some Montrose power play aimed at setting the Throne back a notch or two."

"Montrose has been the Throne's most loyal supporter," says Spencer.

"Who better to fuck him over?"

"If we're a weapon aimed against these Praetorians, then—"

"We're meat," says Linehan.

"Probably," replies Spencer.

"Can you think of any *other* reason we're here?"

"Don't know if this is just me rationalizing, but we could be a hedge."

"A what?"

"The Throne might be using InfoCom the way he used to use CICom. As a hedge against potential disloyal elements."

"You're saying that the Throne might suspect his own guys."

"I'm saying I don't know."

"Damn right you don't. Keep in mind that the Throne dumped CICom's whole crew into the furnaces."

"No one ever said this game wasn't twisted."

"Twisted enough to make me wonder whether there might be someone *else* on this ship who isn't a Praetorian," says Linehan.

"Can't rule it out," replies Spencer.

"I'd say it's one of the more likely scenarios—that we're the monkey wrench."

"To fuck with someone who thinks they've beaten this ship's defenses—" But as Spencer transmits these words, he notices one of the technicians approaching his cryo-cell. Notices, too, that he's one of the only ones left in his cell. "In any case, we need more data."

"And we need to make sure we don't get *caught*," says Linehan.

"I couldn't have said it better myself." Spencer looks at the technician, who starts to speak—only to be cut off as a siren starts wailing at full volume. The noise is almost loud enough to drown out the shouting that it's triggering. Panels start sliding open in the walls. Suits are sprouting from them. People are clambering into them. The ship's engines are changing course.

"Call you back," says Spencer.

The container that Haskell's in is moving along a vast maze of railed corridors that exist solely to propel containers like hers through the bowels of the spaceport where they've been unloaded and out into the depths of the city. She's working the levers of the zone to make sure her container makes all the right turns. She's flung this way and that, her suit's shock absorbers cushioning the impact on her body.

So far everything's going like clockwork. She's running sleek and perfect. The zone around her can't touch the tricks she's playing on it. A million eyes are no match for feet too quick to catch. She's cutting in toward her target like a torpedo.

And all the while she's trying to restrain the fear that's

rising up within her, ignited by the patterns on her skin, fanned into full fury by the patterns all around her. She can fucking *see* them now, coming into focus, patterns that extend from zone and out into the universe beyond. She's terrified of what she's becoming—scared shitless of what she's heading into. It's like a wave that's swelling up to swamp her—like the crossroads of fate itself. A nexus upon which all possibilities converge.

And from which none emanate.

W e're right in the middle of this," says Lynx.
"So what's new?" says the Operative.
"What the fuck are you guys going on about?" asks Sarmax.

"You tell him," says Lynx.

"My armor's tracking something right now," says the Operative.

"So's mine," says Lynx.

"Why not mine?" asks Sarmax.

"Because you're not a razor," says Lynx.

"Neither's Carson," says Sarmax.

"Carson's a *bastard*," says Lynx. "And don't play stupid with me, Leo. I know you know damn well he's not just a mech."

"Didn't know you knew that," says Sarmax.

"Didn't have the chance to tell you," says the Operative.

"Well," replies Sarmax, "who cares? Christ, Lynx: Carson was holding out on both of us at one point. I'm over it. Are you?"

"Not even vaguely," says Lynx.

"Because you thought you were pulling my strings," says the Operative. "And all the while I was pulling yours. Listen, guys, I hate to break this up, but we've been thrust way beyond the front lines and the clock's ticking. We've got a target that we need to catch. We've—"

"—got to start making sense," says Sarmax. *"How do you know there's a goddamn target if you're shorn from zone?"*

"Apparently we're not," says Lynx.

"Christ," says the Operative, "you haven't jacked in, have you?"

"Fuck no. My head keeps screaming that's a really bad idea."

"Probably because it is."

"But there's some kind of interface in my armor that's just switched on. That's working on the zone all the same."

"Same here," says the Operative.

"Though it's like no zone interface I've ever seen."

"Same here," says the Operative. "All I've got is a local map and something marked incoming."

"Something's tripped our fucking perimeter," says Lynx.

"And it's heading this way."

"Probably because it's coming for us."

"This map of yours," says Sarmax.

"Yeah?"

"Give it here."

"It's local," says the Operative. "It only shows a fraction of wherever the fuck we are."

"That's a damn sight more than I've got."

"Here," says the Operative, sending the map whipping into Sarmax's input jacks. Sarmax stands there for a moment. And blinks.

"Fuck," he says, "we are in some *fucked-up* terrain for sure."

"In both real and zone," says the Operative.

"And you can't hack the target?" asks Sarmax.

The Operative shrugs. "Apparently all we can do is track it."

"And catch it," says Lynx.

"We've got limited options," says the Operative. "We're

clearly trying to remain as invisible to the rest of the zone as possible. Presumably that's why we're not supposed to run any comprehensive scans on it."

"So we're pretty much blind," says Sarmax.

"No," says Lynx, "just very specialized."

"Sounds precarious," mutters Sarmax.

"You think?" The Operative sounds more amused than he is. "Think about it, guys. We're sitting in the equivalent of a zone Faraday cage. We're using black-ops tech. We're way past the point at which we'd normally remember whatever the fuck we were told in the briefing-trance. Someone's really pushing the envelope here."

"Agreed," says Lynx. "The whole thing points to only one conclusion."

"Rain," says Sarmax.

"Bingo," says the Operative. "Let's prep tactics."

The door slides open.

Klaxons keep sounding. Lights keep flashing. Spencer's cut off contact with Linehan. He's got his hands full just keeping up with events around him. He's in his suit, holding onto a handle that's sliding along the wall of a metal-paneled corridor—one among many handles sliding in that direction, with the opposite wall containing those going the other way. One in every three or four of those handles are gripped by a crewmember. Everyone's going somewhere. Everyone's racing to his station.

Including Spencer. He can see he's been assigned to the bridge of the *Larissa V,* which is going to place him under the microscope for sure. But maybe that'll let him figure out what the fuck's going on. He hopes things will be a damn sight clearer when he gets there.

If he gets there. He's now heading into the ship's restricted areas. The crew's starting to thin out. He's being subjected to extra scans. Retina, voiceprint, zone-signature, the works—but whatever responses he's giving must be working, because doors keep opening and green keeps flaring and nothing's stopped him yet. He leaves the moving walls behind and climbs through a series of access-tubes. He comes out into some kind of antechamber. A marine floats on either side of a formidable-looking door. Spencer fires compressed air to come to a halt in front of them.

"Your codes," says one.

Spencer doesn't reply—just beams them to the marine, hopes they work. Turns out they do. The marine stands aside as the door opens. Spencer goes through onto the bridge.

And takes in the view.

Haskell's left that container behind. She's pulling herself through a chute. Zone flickers in her head. Her breath sounds within her helmet, echoes in her consciousness in endless fractal patterns. She's left the basement of the city behind. Her weightlessness is starting to subside. Occasionally the chrome tube she's in splits: two-way forks, three-way forks, right-angle intersections. But she never hesitates. She's just climbing onward as gravity kicks in, pulling herself up via those rungs that have now become a ladder, which ends in a trapdoor. She presses against it, pushes it open.

And emerges into light. She's in a forest. Trees tower up around her head, late afternoon sunlight dancing through the branches. She turns, closes the trapdoor—noticing how perfectly it blends in amidst the undergrowth. She starts making her way through the woods. She's not surprised to find that it's really more of a grove, that the trees ahead are

thinning out. She catches a glimpse of distant mountains—
and sights buildings much nearer. She pushes her way
through the last of the undergrowth and emerges into the
space beyond.

Lynx has disconnected. And whatever's out there
is still closing. Sarmax and the Operative proceed through the doorway, heading out into a corridor buttressed by bulwark-rings every ten meters. It looks like
they're inside the rib cage of some enormous animal. Sarmax
is on point. The pulse-rifle he's carrying is capable of knocking a hole through metal a meter thick. The Operative has his
wrist-guns ready and his shoulder-racks up. The two of them
move down corridors and up stairways. Gravity fluctuates as
they turn this way and that, varying from normal to about
half Earth strength. The target keeps drawing nearer. The two
men continue to communicate on tightbeam wireless. That's
as far onto the zone as they're going to venture. Except for
the single screen within the Operative's head, projected by
software within his armor. Software he doesn't understand
and clearly isn't supposed to. All he's supposed to do is obey
orders.

But he can't stop himself from thinking about all the
things that might lie behind those instructions. The margin of
victory in the secret war is clearly coming down to zone.
Autumn Rain's ability to penetrate that zone is the reason the
world was forced to the brink four days ago. It's the reason the
world remains on the very edge. How do you stop an infiltra-
tor with the ability to turn defenses against those they would
protect? How do you shield yourself against those who may
already be inside your shield?

The Operative doesn't know. But he's guessing he's caught
up in somebody's attempt to answer. And now suddenly more

pieces of the puzzle are bubbling up, rising into his mind like a submarine surfacing—recollections of what they told him when he was in the trance. The larger map of the place they're in clicks on within his head. He gazes at the blueprints and feels his heart accelerate as he realizes what they're caught up in. He signals to Sarmax that they're turning as he opens a door.

The far wall of the room within is barely visible through a mass of conveyor belts. Freight containers are stacked along those belts—containers like the ones in which the two men woke. The Operative moves past Sarmax and leaps onto one of those pallets. Sarmax does the same. They start moving at speed along that belt, keeping their weapons at the ready.

"I give up," says Sarmax. "Where the fuck *are* we?"

"In neutral territory."

"In space."

"Obviously. We're in the Platform."

"We're inside the *Platform*? But that's—"

"Insane? I think that's the point."

The bridge of the *Larissa V* isn't small. Its crew attends to two levels of instrument-banks. A large window cuts above those banks, sharpens to a beak where the room protrudes farthest forward. And in that window . . .

"Spencer? You there?"

"Shut up."

"You wouldn't believe what's going on down here."

"Shut *up*," replies Spencer, and disconnects. Looks like his integration with the bridge's wireless node reactivated his link with Linehan. Which is a really bad idea right now, particularly since another voice is whispering in Spencer's head, telling him to sync with the primary razor.

Which must make him the secondary razor. The one no one here has seen yet. The one who's been shipped in special—part of the larger crew that's been assigned to this ship, woken up in preparation for the start of active operations. Spencer takes his seat near the room's rear, next to that primary razor. He reaches for the duplicate ship-jacks, leans back, and stares straight ahead as he slots those jacks in. He feels the razor watching him. He feels like the whole bridge-crew's watching him—the captain and his executive officer on the second level, the gunnery officers on the room's left side, the telemetry and navigational officers on the right. He wonders how much of what he's feeling is paranoia and how much is real. He resolves not to let such questions show on his face. He gets busy running zone-routines, trying to act natural.

Which isn't easy, given what's in the window.

The largest space station ever built shimmers in the sun. The Europa Platform consists of two O'Neill cylinders and their attendant infrastructure. Both those cylinders are clearly visible, connected to each other at both poles, slowly rotating in opposite directions to maintain a stationary position vis-à-vis one another. Each is just over thirty klicks long.

The nearer cylinder's about five klicks distant, taking up most of the view, one of its outlying mirrors glimmering alongside it. Part of one of the cylinder-windows can be seen just beyond that mirror, a slice of green shimmering within translucence, but most of the visible structure is grey shading into black—though on the zone it's lit up in every color, shot through with data overlays. The cylinder-ends that are nearest to Spencer are designated NORTH POLE, and the walls that curve out from each point house the cities of New London and New Zurich, respectively, along with their accompanying spaceport-freight yards.

But it's the opposite ends that really get Spencer's attention. Beyond the point labeled SOUTH POLE on each cylinder is a massive sphere—each as wide as the cylinder against which they abut—mostly rock, but studded with a great deal of metal as well. From where Spencer's situated they look like moons rising above some strange metal landscape. They're habbed asteroids—and the zone within what have been labeled as AERIES is dark, concealed behind the ramparts of the firewalls of the Euro Magnates. Five years ago the Treaty of Zurich confirmed L3—the most isolated of the libration points, the Earth directly between it and the Moon—as a neutral possession. The Euro Magnates have made good money from it. Ten million people make the Platform one of the largest off-planet settlements. But the Rain co-opted the neutrals on Earth. So why not here?

At least, that's what Spencer is starting to wonder. He can see now that the specs of the ship he's in are those of a European freighter. He can see, too, seven more such ships— also in close vicinity to the Platform, also manned by Praetorian crew, all decked out in neutral colors that allow them to blend in with the other freighters nearby.

Of which there's no shortage. Another screen in Spencer's mind shows the larger view around him. The Europa Platform is at the center of a grid. Ships are lined up for approach into its spaceyards for hundreds of kilometers out. Several mass-catchers are about fifty klicks away, receiving ore from asteroid-harvesting operations farther out. Processing stations float nearby, along with a number of mass-drivers. More than a hundred klicks off the "north" end of the Platform is Helios Station, several kilometers of solar panels clustered around microwave and laser projectors that beam power to the Europa Platform and the other structures. Spencer notes that Praetorian units have covertly taken custody of the Helios's control center, along with that of the mass-drivers. He can see quite clearly that all such deployments are aimed at the Platform—that the heart of neutral activity is now under the watchful eye of the Praetorians.

He shifts his focus back to the Platform itself. He's guessing that the ultimate aim of this operation is one of the areas on the Platform that's opaque on his zone-view—the farther cylinder or the two asteroids. According to the blueprints, the farther cylinder's pretty much like the nearer. So Spencer's focusing on that nearer one now, staring at the zone compressed within it—the tens of thousands of cameras that show the bustling streets of New London, along with all the landscape that lies beyond.

Which suddenly *clicks* in his head.

"Confirm contact," he says.

The merest splinter of a second has passed since Spencer's jacked in. The prime razor nods, looks satisfied. Spencer has just ratified his sounding the alarm—has just confirmed that the signal coming from the first cylinder is, in fact, the real thing. But the satisfaction starts fading from that razor's face as Spencer starts describing far more detailed coordinates than the prime razor had been able to obtain. Spencer displays the data on a screen, lets everybody see the light that's now moving at speed away from the north pole of the nearer cylinder, away from the city of New London and out toward the cylinder's southern end.

"We have a definite live target," he says.

"Definite incursion," says the primary razor.

"Track and report," says the voice of the executive officer.

Spencer opens up another channel in his mind. "Linehan," he says.

"About fucking time," says Linehan. "What's going on up there?"

"Jesus Christ," says Spencer, "what isn't?"

• • •

Haskell's come through into the cylinder's main interior. Valley is stretching out before her. Two more valleys are ceilings far overhead. The mirrors outside the cylinder's windows are angled to give the impression of day dimming into twilight. Haskell's mind is practically shoved around the corner of a million impending futures, flickering like ghost-static through her, superimposed against her parameters in the here and now. On the outside, she's just a woman in a light vac-suit fresh off one of the off-Platform shifts. Just a normal worker heading home on one of the maglev trains.

Though she must be doing pretty well to have a residence in the countryside outside the city that's now receding behind her: streets and rooftops curve across the entirety of the North Pole region, stacked upon one another like some kind of Navajo cliff-dwelling on steroids. New London's quite a place. The only thing that's in the same league is New Zurich, right next door. Not that Haskell has the slightest intention of going anywhere near it.

Nor does she need to. Because her next objective's plainly visible in the distance. The South Pole mountains aren't like those of the North. They're unadorned by any city. Those few structures that cluster upon the peaks are security installations perfectly positioned to keep a watchful eye on the city opposite them.

Though Haskell knows full well that it's behind those mountains that the real security starts. Particularly within the zone: the firewall of the asteroid that's latched to the cylinder's southern end is one of the steepest she's ever seen. Even *she* can't see within without alerting everybody in there. The only way to get a view is to get inside.

This is precisely what she intends to do, though she hasn't yet decided how. She's improvising. And now that she's left New London behind she can see she's moving toward the first of the lockdown areas. It's largely farmland strewn with lakes and forests. It looks idyllic, but it doesn't fool Haskell in the slightest. It was declared off-limits to civilians about twenty-four hours ago. Something about a potential chemical leak—something that's bullshit. Haskell can see the way it's all been set up. She's planning on giving the defenses something to chew on. She's got her decoys out, wreaking havoc on the cylinder's zone. Her train drops beneath the level of the valley-surface as tunnel walls close in around her.

"Closing fast," says the Operative.

They're past the freight-conduits and into an area that's still under construction. Robots are working everywhere. None of them pay the slightest attention to the two men blasting past them. It's as if they don't even see them. The Operative beams the latest readouts into Sarmax's head.

"It's splintered into multiple signals coming in toward us. But they're distorted, like they're running interference on each other—"

"There may be only one signal."

"Or maybe that's what they want us to think."

"So are we hunting it, or is it hunting us?"

"Looks like it might be both."

Making this a tough call. The Operative knows there comes a time in every run when you make your break. When you change directions sharply and go flat-out. But the timing's a little suspect on this one.

Or else whatever is causing this signal is just really good at guessing.

"Closest one is moving in fast," he says. "On one of the core maglevs."

"How can you tell it's genuine?"

"I'm not sure I can."

"Let's hope Lynx is getting this."

"We need to coordinate with him," says the Operative.

"By breaking radio silence?"

"There's another dedicated landline just ahead. If he's got the same signal we've got he'll be waiting for us."

"*Another* landline?"

"For sure."

"How do you know this?"

"Because the coordinates are sitting in my fucking head."

"They were put there?"

"No, I was born with them," says the Operative. "And so was Lynx. And we knew a priori from the fucking *cradle* that we had to pursue a certain target along certain trajectories and if that target deviated suddenly we'd need to coordinate in a way that couldn't be detected by anyone on the zone." The Operative is pretty much ranting now. "*Obviously* they were put there, asshole!"

"I get that," snaps Sarmax. "And get this: *this* is why I fucking left. Because these runs always end up with us like rats stuck in some custom-built maze."

"Though usually not this intricate," says the Operative.

"Too right," replies Sarmax. "This whole terrain has been *prepared*. Like some ancient battlefield where they dug the goddamn elephant traps in advance. I mean, that's what, the tenth camera we've seen that's been ripped out at the wires? God only knows how we fit in. All we're doing is running against some fucking *program*."

"Speaking of," says the Operative—he brakes to a halt, turns and pivots onto the wall, and rips a panel aside. The phone that's revealed is more modern than the last one. It's already flashing. The Operative pictures the wires that lead away from that phone, wending through walls to wherever Lynx is crouching, completely shorn from all the others in here. Or so he hopes. He picks up the phone.

"Carson," says Lynx.

"Yeah," says the Operative—and once again feels something light up within his skull. It's a sensation he's almost starting to get used to. This one's some kind of response to the data he's been accumulating about their target. Something he needs to tell Lynx.

Right now.

"This just got a lot more difficult," he says.

"I'll say," replies Lynx.

"You just got a newsflash in your head too?"

"What are you talking about?"

"Simple," says the Operative. "We need to take this thing alive."

"Like fuck we do," says Lynx.

Lights upon a grid, converging on an area about ten klicks south of New London. Tension mounts on the bridge and not a word's being spoken among the crew. Everything that needs to be said is going down within their heads.

Which can have its drawbacks.

"This is getting tight," mutters Linehan.

"Tell me about it," says Spencer.

"Can you see the Platform from up there?"

"I'm on the goddamn bridge, Linehan. Of course I can fucking see it. Where the hell are you now?"

"Sitting in a drop-ship."

"Doing what?"

"Getting ready to drop, you moron."

"To the Platform?"

"They're briefing us on its layout right now."

"Have they set a countdown?" asks Spencer.

"Not that they've told us. Are you seeing one up there?"

"Not a goddamn thing. This whole thing's compartmentalized pretty tight."

"They may still be deciding whether to deploy us. Send me downloads of the view from the bridge, will ya? And the camera footage of how that view's changed since we started orbiting."

"Done," says Spencer. "What are you thinking?"

"A lot. What are you seeing up there?"

"There's some kind of shit going down on the Platform. We've got at least two units down there, with multiple signals closing on them."

"Way too late to tell me *that*," says Linehan. "Get me the coordinates."

"Done."

"Any more data about this thing we're in?"

"We're tarted up as a Harappa-class freighter. Registered to a firm in Paris, left the Zurich Stacks in low-orbit two days ago and came straight here."

"And before that?"

"There was no before. This is our maiden voyage."

"How convenient."

"Especially because we've been built with a few modifications."

"Like what?"

"Like the one you're sitting in. Fast dropship deployment capacity. Looks like there's four more down there in addition to yours, each full of marines."

"Packed in like sardines," says Linehan. "What about the ship's weaponry?"

"Four heavy directed-energy batteries and two kinetic-energy gatlings. All of it locked away and out of sight."

"But once they extend those barrels it's going to be pretty fucking obvious that we're not a bunch of Swiss carrying second-rate tungsten."

"It may already be pretty fucking obvious. We're tracking the Rain and the Rain may be tracking *us*."

"Don't I know it, Spencer. The officers down here are going on about how we're going to stop the Rain for good. But the rank-and-file's saying something else."

"Don't put too much stock in rumors, man."

"You ignore them at your peril, Spencer."

"So what are they saying?"

"That we're out to bag ourselves a *witch*."

Haskell's now off the train and onto another one that's drawn up alongside—a railcar that's as off the zone as she can make it, even as the train she's stepping from hurtles on with one of her decoys enscribed hastily upon it. She's just over twenty klicks north of the South Pole. She feels like she's falling in toward it, towed in by the weight of the future. She's about to break through another defensive screen, but her decoys are going to drop behind her, hang back a little, lead the defenders on a merry little chase that goes exactly nowhere.

Problem is that those defenders are exhibiting some strange behavior. They were starting to respond at first—they looked like they were scrambling. But now they've stopped altogether. Have they lost track of the decoys? Are they awaiting orders? Or is there something else that's going on? Maybe she's missing something. Because she's perfectly aware that these aren't normal defenses. Not down here. The disabled cameras and sensors testify to that. The only working cameras she's seeing look like they're newly installed. She's got her camouflage cranked—she's hoping that all anyone who's watching is going to see is just a redeploying railcar. And maybe not even that. Because now her mind's leaping in to hack those cameras.

And failing. Turns out they're totally bereft of wireless interface. Haskell wonders where their wires lead. She's got no access to them—meaning they're not connected to the Euro zone. And their feeds aren't viewable by the Euro police forces, most of which seem to be back at the city anyway. She's seen the occasional robot sentinel in these tunnels. But she knows that most of the Euro forces that aren't in New London are stationed at the South Pole mountains, to stop intruders from getting through to the cylinder's Aerie—in theory. But in practice, she's got a feeling that the forces controlling the approaches to the asteroid have been *co-opted*. She wonders if the defenders she's running rings around know that. She accelerates her railcar, skirts past the defenders halted in their tracks, and streaks into the sections of underground that lie beyond.

"Look," says the Operative, "it's really quite simple."

"This I'm just dying to hear," says Lynx.

"You already heard it. My orders say targets with this signature get taken alive."

"That's not true, Carson."

"What the hell are you talking about?"

"I mean my orders say all targets get wasted."

"Your orders come from me!"

"*And* the handlers, Carson, who told me this thing dies."

"They told me to spare it."

"When?" asks Lynx.

"It's on memory trigger. How the fuck should I know?"

"Well, my orders say otherwise."

"Or so you remember."

"So? That's the way this whole thing's been working."

"Yeah," says the Operative, "but now it's *not* working, is it?"

"While we talk, this thing's getting away from us!"

"At least it doesn't seem to be hunting us now."

"Because it's probably after something else. Shit man, they *really* told you to spare the target?"

"They really did," says the Operative.

"Jesus, this isn't good."

"You've been fucked with."

"I think it's the other way around, Carson."

"Are you really Lynx?"

"Are you really Carson?"

"Of course I'm Carson!"

"Of course you are. The same Carson who pulled my strings so adroitly back on the goddamn Moon. The same Carson who's had the opportunity for endless off-the-record bullshit. The same Carson who's got all the higher-ups eating out of his goddamn hand."

"If they really were, you think I'd have to put up with *this* shit?"

"You think I can't see what's going on here, Carson? You think I haven't figured out your little secret?"

"*My* little secret?

"About which I have a theory."

"What's your theory?"

"That I'm going to reach this target *first*."

The voice cuts out. The Operative disconnects.

"Sounds like that didn't go so well," says Sarmax.

"Why are you pointing that pulse-rifle at me?"

"Like you can't guess," says Sarmax. He keeps the weapon trained on the Operative—primes it. There's a low humming noise.

"This just gets better and better," says the Operative.

"Shut up," says Sarmax. "Here's what's going to happen."

• • •

"What do you mean, *witch?*"

"Knew you were gonna ask me that. I've got no fucking idea. And neither does anyone else down here."

"Well, what else are they fucking saying?"

"Nothing coherent. Just that it's not just the Rain we're after. That we're also gunning for some kind of Rain witch or something. They've also used the word *queen*. And some of them are saying it's not Rain at all, that there's something else on the loose."

"Maybe one of those Rain-type creatures we keep hearing about."

"The cool kids don't talk to me, Spencer. What have you heard?"

"Apparently the Praetorians tried to copy some of the Rain's tech. Which the Rain then tried to steal right back. There was a rumor some kind of robot was on that spaceplane that—"

"The one that deep-sixed in Hong Kong four days back?"

"Yeah. And I heard that some kind of supercomputer ended up on the Moon, but it was autonomous, so that—"

"God only knows what the fucking truth in all of this is," mutters Linehan. "That's probably what they want: to keep us guessing. We gotta go back to basics, man. Because we're not the only gang of assholes that's camped out on the Platform tonight."

"You mean the Rain?"

"Never mind the fucking Rain. Of course they're in this somehow. I'm talking about the *other* lot that's somehow managed to get themselves dealt into this lousy game."

"Oh yeah," says Spencer, "those."

• • •

Haskell's leaving the equator behind. She's changed it up again, too, partially out of respect for those strange cameras, but mostly she's just running on intuition. She feels the scratches on her skin flaring as though fire's dripping over them. She feels those symbols turning within her brain. She's dropped through additional layers of infrastructure and is almost at the outer layer of cylinder-skin while she leaves the equator behind. Gravity's now in excess of normal. Walls are surging past her. She's left the domain of maglev behind. She's in what's essentially a giant conveyor belt. One that's designed to haul exactly one thing.

Ice. Haskell has melted partially through the chunk upon which she's riding, and let that ice refreeze over her armor, making her that much harder to spot, especially given how much of the cylinder's infrastructure is dedicated to the processing of water. Haskell feels the pressure build around her. Everything's coming down to this, a woman become bullet about to crash through to the world beyond the South Pole. The howling of her sixth sense has reached fever-pitch. Her skin's burning like a sun's coming to life within it.

Strands of light whip past the roofless two-person railcar as it shoots through the tunnel. The man who's driving is standing up front. The other man's sitting at the back. He keeps his pulse-rifle pointed at the driver.

"So," says Sarmax, "now that we've got some speed, let's talk."

"About fucking time."

"We've got a real problem."

"Lynx has overdosed again."

"It didn't sound that simple. One of you is being fucked with, and neither you nor I is in a position to determine who's the lucky guy."

"Which is why you're pointing that gun at me."

"It seems like the prudent option," replies Sarmax.

"Does that mean you have a plan?"

"It means I'm still thinking of one."

"If you shoot me you won't have a hope of finding the target."

"Your *armor's* what's tracking the target, Carson. Not you."

The Operative shrugs, shifts slightly left as the tunnel undergoes a slight bend. He's providing Sarmax with the real-time feed from his tracking—factoring out what he's decided are decoys. Sarmax has made it clear he'll shoot if that stops. The Operative's tempted to hit the brakes way too hard. But he knows that's the oldest trick in the book—and that there'd still be an opportunity for Sarmax to get off a shot, with a weapon that—when it comes to survivability at point-blank range—may as well be a heavy laser cannon.

"You're not that dumb, Leo. It's my *interface* with the armor that's doing the tracking."

"And that possibility is why I haven't put one through you yet."

"It's a possibility you're going to have to get used to."

"Until we reach the target."

"You're really putting pressure on me to make a move in the meantime."

"Go for it," says Sarmax. "You'll die before you can even turn around."

"Have to admit you have the advantage."

"The *Rain* have the advantage, Carson."

"To which I can only agree."

"They're totally inside us."

"There's still the chance to beat them yet."

"Sure there is. And it starts with me killing you *and* Lynx."

"You mean to be sure."

"Sure. Shit man, what would *you* do?"

"Exactly that—*if* I was sure I wasn't being fucked with myself."

"I'll take my chances," says Sarmax.

"Not that it matters," mutters the Operative. "Lynx will still be way ahead of us, even with our taking this train."

"So we make up for lost ground with a new route," says Sarmax. Coordinates light up on the map within the Operative's head.

"That dotted line means it's still under construction."

"But near completion," replies Sarmax.

"Even you aren't that insane."

"Twenty seconds, Carson. You make that turn or I'll blast you into the next world."

"The one where your Indigo is waiting?"

Sarmax doesn't reply.

"You killed your girl," says the Operative. "That's okay. She was Rain. She had it coming. But now you've got a death-wish and you want to nail us all to your fucking ferry."

"Who are you, Sigmund fucking Freud? Ten seconds."

"You've gone crazy."

"I'm the only one who's definitely sane."

"Which won't matter if this railcar bites it."

"Carson, I've got to be the one who makes the decision about the target. I can't trust you or Lynx to do it. Two seconds."

"I see it," says the Operative—and with that he sends the car hurtling down a much narrower tunnel. There's only one other rail besides theirs. But then that other rail cuts out.

"Faster," says Sarmax.

"Can't," says the Operative. "Not without fucking with the zone to get this bitch beyond capacity."

"Fuck that," says Sarmax, "zone's a party everybody's gate-crashed."

Gravity increases. The walls start to flicker on either side.

"Hello," says the Operative.

"Jesus," says Sarmax. "Is that what I think it is?"

It is. It's space. They speed out of the tunnel and into the construction area. There's nothing below their rail save vacuum. Scaffolding's all around. The completed hull of the cylinder stretches right above them like some impossibly massive ceiling, sloping down to where their rail enters still another tunnel . . .

"This rail's really starting to vibrate," says Sarmax.

"That's because it's about as stable as you are," says the Operative—and ducks his head as they rush into the tunnel. It's narrow. There's barely enough room for this single rail.

"Sure wish we had a better map," says Sarmax.

"We're through," says the Operative.

And now gravity's lessening slightly as they race out into a broader tunnel. But even as they do, something unfolds within the Operative's head. He stares at the pattern that's revealed. He traces all the implications.

And then suddenly he gets it.

"Leo."

"Yeah?"

"I just woke up to what's so critical about this target."

"So talk fast."

The fucking Eurasians," says Linehan. "They're here too."

"Is that what the rumor mill's saying?"

"That's what the *officers* are saying! What the hell's going on?"

"Sounds like you already know it."

"You *were* going to tell me, right?"

"I only just found out myself," says Spencer.

And it's all he can do to keep up. To say this operation's need-to-know is an understatement. But the data overlays now lighting up across the bridge are nothing if not precise. On the opposite side of the Platform's orbit are eight Eurasian ships, spread out the same way the American ships are, able to support each other and cover the Platform simultaneously.

"They're with us," says Spencer. "Not against."

"You sure about that?"

"Do I sound like I'm sure of fucking *anything*? I'm just saying what they're telling us up here."

"Down here, too. This is a joint operation."

"Aimed at Autumn Rain."

"Or the Euro Magnates," says Linehan.

"Who may be the same thing by now."

"Who may have always been."

"You really think they've been pulling the Rain's strings?"

"I think you've got it backward, Spencer. What's the story with that chase you're monitoring?"

"Getting weirder by the minute."

Ice and tunnels and speed and it's all falling short. They've got her number, suddenly springing to life, sweeping past her decoys, closing from both sides. Haskell shunts her ice-chunk off the main belt, sends it racing down an ancillary belt as she tries to figure out how the hell they're tracking her. And while she's at it, she's trying to hack them directly.

But she's unable to. She can't seem to come to grips with them and has no idea why. It's almost as though they're not actually there, as though she's clutching at illusion.

It's like they're ghosts.

Which makes no sense. *She's* the ghost. The one who slips through perimeters like a phantom. But not this time—she's bringing all her force to bear upon the problem and she's still coming up short.

Leaving only one possible answer. Her pursuers have found a back door to her. One that she needs to neutralize fast. But first she needs to find it. She starts racing through the code of her own brain even as her mind races through the Platform's zone. She's sending the ice she's in forward through a tube whose heated walls start to liquefy what's encasing her, causing water to pour across her visor. She's caught up in that surge now, charging out beyond the frontiers of her own brain, closing in on the door that's out there in that limbo—but everywhere she turns is dark. She sees exactly what she's going to have to do if she can't find the route they've found to her. Bailing out of zone is an act of desperation, but her pursuers are closing in. Before she pulls the plug, she tries one more thing—amplifies her decoys, sends them hurtling out in new directions.

But one of them isn't listening.

She sends more commands. It's not responding. It's just circling in toward her, on a course to intercept both her and her pursuers, only a couple of klicks distant now. She stares at it. Realization hits her like a meteor smashing into a planet.

⊕ F*uck,*" says the Operative, "lost it."

"What the hell do you mean you lost it?"

"I mean I fucking lost the goddamn signal!"

"How the fuck did you manage to do that?" asks Sarmax. He's no longer pointing his gun at the Operative. But he looks like he wouldn't mind shooting him anyway.

"Maybe our equipment fucked up."

"Maybe *you* fucked up," says Sarmax.

"What's fucked up is this whole fucking scene."

"No shit."

The Operative shakes his head. He's starting to feel like a pinball getting flung around inside a machine. He and Sarmax are still roaring through the bowels of the cylinder, still watching wall shoot past them. Still trying to make sense of the data that's streaming through their skulls.

"It dropped off the zone," says the Operative.

"That's your fucking excuse?"

"That's my fucking explanation."

And it'll have to do. Because the Operative can't think of any others. Not without taking apart his armor and trying to see what makes that zone interface tick. Besides, that interface couldn't *really* be malfunctioning. Because now it's detecting something else, back in the area they started in. It's very faint, and it quickly disappears. But for a moment there it was unmistakable. The Operative mentions this to Sarmax.

"What?"

"You heard me," says the Operative.

"Where?"

"Closing."

"So what are you waiting for?"

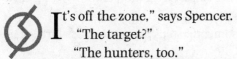 t's off the zone," says Spencer.

"The target?"

"The hunters, too."

"Because something's hunting them."

"Starting to look that way."

"More than just starting," says Linehan. "Textbook setup, man. We're the reserves. Out in space. We're flying cover while our forward operatives—whoever the fuck *they* are—cover the area through which we know hostiles have to pass."

"You've got me, Linehan. How do you know hostiles *have* to enter the cylinder?"

"I don't. Can you get me a readout of the shipping activity across the whole Platform across the last four days?"

"Define shipping activity," says Spencer.

"Times and locations on the Platform at which ships have landed or departed. Normalized against historical activity across the last three months."

"Easy enough." Spencer pulls it up. "Here." But as he's sending the file over to Linehan he's taking a look himself.

And drawing some quick conclusions.

"*Fuck,*" he says.

"Fasten your seat belts," says Linehan.

Greenery's everywhere. Haskell's standing on the stairs one level above the floor of a much larger chamber. She can barely discern its contours. A translucent roof stops just short of the cylinder's hollow interior above her. Light's dribbling dimly through. Greenhouse structures are stacked along its edges. The floor's partitioned into giant squares, given over to different types of crops.

Haskell leaps from the stairs, dropping into the plants beneath her. The tall grasses close in over her head. She brushes through them, finds the closest irrigation channel, and starts running along it in a crouch.

Which is when someone steps from the grass farther up ahead.

Someone in a suit of armor that's completely beaten her own suit's camo. A nasty-looking minigun's mounted on its shoulder. The gun's barrel swivels toward her, even as she springs back onto the zone and finds that whoever's in the armor has isolated himself from all nets—presumably to deal with the likes of her. She stares into that barrel, and it's as though it's already fired. As though she's already gone.

But she's not. She's still frozen in that moment, still watching existence freeze about her. The suit holds up a hand, gestures at the side of its helmet. As though it wants to talk. She obliges, activating a tightbeam channel, and a voice crackles in her head.

The habbed asteroids," says Spencer.

"The Aeries. Yeah."

"*Nothing's* landed there since this whole thing started."

"And nothing's going to either. Like I said, targets have to pass through the cylinder."

"But why would targets even come to the Platform in the first place?"

"It's not like either of us is a stranger to this type of drill, Spencer. There are only two ways to bag a target, right? Either you go get it or—"

"You make it come to you."

"Yeah."

"So what's the bait?"

"I'll take a wild guess: something impossible to resist."

Going somewhere?" the voice says.

Haskell doesn't reply. Time spirals slowly sideways. Cosmic background static pours through her. She feels herself drowning in it. She feels herself rising past it. She hears the voice continue.

"Take off your helmet. I want to see you."

Her body's so full of adrenaline she can barely move her hands from where she's got them above her head. But she does: lowers those hands against infinite resistance, unclasps the helmet's seals, lifts the helmet off, tosses it aside. The suited figure moves forward with all the purpose of a predatory insect—so close now she can see ebony skin through the visor. She can even see what looks like silver hair.

But she can also see that gun—adjusting minutely on its axis as it aims directly between her eyes.

Ø Flame and motion in the windows of the bridge: two of the other Praetorian ships are firing their motors. They're dropping out of orbit, toward the cylinder.

"They're sending a couple of ships in," says Spencer.

"Drop ships?" asks Linehan.

"No, entire fucking ships. Decked out as medium-grade freighters, American, same as this one. Guess the rest of us are providing cover. Along with whatever they've got mounted on the Helios power station."

"That Helios is quite a structure. Ten klicks of lasers and microwave—"

"I'll say. Talk about directed-energy capability—"

"How soon till the ships hit the Platform?"

"About a minute."

"Which end are they heading toward?"

"North Pole. The spaceport end. You called it."

"Damn right I did," says Linehan.

"So what the fuck's in those asteroids? The Euro Magnates?"

"I think they've been taken off the board, Spencer. I think the thing that's in that cylinder's Aerie is the same thing that's directing this whole operation."

"While simultaneously doing everything it can to convince its prey that it's ripe for the taking?"

"I see you see where I'm going with this."

Y ou're a woman," says the man within the suit.

"And you're Stefan Lynx."

A momentary pause. "What the hell makes you say that?"

"I've seen your file. I recognize your face. You dye your hair silver. You're not that hard to pick out of a crowd."

"You've hacked through to the heart of our systems."

"I'd hardly say your file is at the heart of the Praetorian systems, Stefan."

"Shut up," he snaps. "All your zone tricks can't save you now. Because I'm the one who's got the gun—*don't* move your hands. Keep them *right where they are.*"

"I'm not moving."

"Good."

"What do you want?"

"To gaze upon the face of Rain before I obliterate your face."

"I'm here to fight the Rain, Stefan."

"You *are* the Rain, bitch."

"You'd better check your orders. Your Throne wouldn't want me killed. Your Throne would have ordered me taken alive. And I can assure you right now he'd be pretty fucking livid if—"

"Shut up!" She stops talking. "Don't try to twist my mind!" But she realizes there's some doubt in his head. That he's trying to psyche himself up to kill her.

Or else he's just savoring the moment.

"Start begging for your life."

"What?"

"You heard me, Rain whore. Let's see you fucking *plead*."

"You'll kill me anyway," she says.

Near-instantaneous swivel: the gun fires. A shot streaks past her head. "Not good enough," he says.

"Strom Carson," she says. "Where is he?"

"Who?"

"The leader of your triad."

"Say that name again," he says.

"He's got different orders, doesn't he?"

"What the fuck makes you say that?"

"Your team's been fucked with, Stefan. *Where's Carson?*"

And for a moment she thinks she's gone too far. Lynx takes aim at her chest—and then suddenly leaps toward her, grabs her by the neck as he pulls out a pistol, and shoves it up against her temple. And now he's switched to audio piped from his suit's speakers. "*He's right behind you.* Come out asshole! *Right fucking now!*"

She's staring in the same direction he is, across the fields at the nearest wall. She still can't see it. But then they switch off their camo and she does: two figures in two doorways. One of them is advancing. The other is staying put. Haskell notices that they've got their camo patterns adjusted so that they're only visible along the line of vision in which she and Lynx are standing. The figure that's still standing in a doorway is covering the whole area with a pulse-rifle. The other figure's still closing.

"That's far enough," says Lynx.

"Deactivate your weapons."

Lynx laughs. "I got a better idea, Carson. *You* deactivate *yours*. Before I do your Rain girlfriend."

"That's not the Rain. That's the Manilishi. Which belongs to the president."

"Don't think you can make up words and impress me, Carson. She's Rain. She's pulling your strings."

"No," snarls the third man—whom Haskell figures to be Leo Sarmax. "The Rain's pulling *yours*."

"Shut up, Leo," says Lynx. "You don't know shit."

"*None* of you do!" screams Haskell. Lynx's arm tightens around her, but she keeps talking anyway. "We don't have time for this! The Rain are closing on us even now!"

"Don't think I don't know that," says Carson.

 T his could kick off at any moment," says Spencer. "It may already have," says Linehan. "Are you armed?"

"Just sidearms. Nothing as fancy as you've got."

"If the shit hits the fan on this ship—"

"It's more likely to hit it down there."

"It's *definitely* about to fucking hit it down there. The Rain are in that cylinder for sure. They're betting they can beat whatever trap's been set."

"And reach the asteroid in which the Throne's sitting."

"The Aerie where he's waiting for them. Daring them to come and fucking get him."

"It's a magnet," says Linehan. "A fucking magnet."

"Look at the size of those Aeries." Spencer transmits the dimensions of the rock that's attached to the cylinder in which the action's going down, lighting up the sphere in 3-D false-color. "The Praetorian Core comprises an entire *division*. Every last one of them could be packed in there with him, with this fleet that we're a part of just waiting to swoop down at the first sign of trouble—"

"And the East's ships, too."

"Who've got that other cylinder covered."

"But if *he's* involved then that means the Eurasian leadership—"

"It might," says Spencer.

"Might? It must."

"Why?"

"Because there's no way he would allow Eurasian troops to be a part of this under any other set of conditions."

"Double or nothing?"

"Anything you want to bet, Spencer. It's everything. It's the only way *any* of this makes any sense. He's in one of the Aeries; the Eurasian leadership's in the other. Along with their own Praetorian equivalents."

"Maybe."

"Jesus man, think about it. Both sides know Autumn Rain has been playing them off each other. That they've gone to ground within the East's zone to escape ours, and vice versa. The leaderships intend to squeeze the Rain between them, and if they can achieve enough integration between the two executive nodes—"

"They'd stand a good chance of bagging Rain," says Spencer.

"Which means the Rain has to strike them first."

"At a place of the leaderships' own choosing."

"That place being here."

"And here we are right in the middle."

Y̶ou have to take me to the Throne," says Haskell.

"Yeah," says Lynx, "fucking right."

"Lynx," says Carson, "this is your last chance—" but as he says this, a tiny hatch in Sarmax's knee opens and fires two quick shots. Haskell feels heat on her face as the blast sears past her, feels debris pepper her suit as the barrel of Lynx's minigun disintegrates, along with his pistol—and his hand. He's knocked sprawling on the ground screaming as

Carson and Sarmax fire their suit-thrusters. In an instant, Carson's crashing into Haskell, knocking the wind from her, shielding her with his body.

For a moment all's still. Haskell clears her throat.

"Mind if I get up?" she asks.

Carson says nothing—just stands up and hauls her to her feet. Lynx is sitting on the ground, cradling his arm. His visor's up. Sarmax has landed halfway between her and the door, covering Lynx with his pulse-rifle—covering the rest of the ag-complex, too. She sees Carson shake his head within his suit, realizes that Sarmax was probably asking Carson on a private channel if he should finish Lynx off. But apparently Carson has declined. Though it seems he's not done yet.

"Lynx," he says aloud. "You're under arrest."

"Just shoot me now," mutters Lynx.

"I *would* shoot you now, you stupid fuck, except for the fact that you thought you were serving the Throne. But believe me, if you *had* killed her, this would have been your grave."

"And if you try broadcasting anything, it still might," says Sarmax. "How's your arm?"

"Cauterized," says Lynx. "Suit sealed. Fucking bas—"

"Shut up," says Carson. "Claire Haskell: we're Praetorian special ops. We're here to protect you. Get your helmet back on. We have to get—"

"Save the speech," says Haskell. "If you're Praetorian, take me to the Throne. *Fucking now.*"

"Actually," says Carson, "I have orders not to."

Haskell stares. Lynx laughs.

"Orders from the Rain, huh?" he says.

"Orders from the Throne," replies Carson.

"I guess I can't blame him," says Haskell.

"You really can't," says Carson. "Let's move."

• • •

 We're caught up in the fucking day of judgement."

"Calm down," says Spencer.

"I *am* calm."

"You probably shouldn't be."

"It all depends on how far the Rain have infiltrated. Whether they've managed to get into the Aerie."

"Whether the Throne has been successful in confining any infiltration to the cylinder."

"The Rain might just nuke that asteroid."

"And that asteroid could probably take it. Besides, it's not enough to just obliterate the Throne. The executive node switches in that eventuality."

"How the fuck do you know *that?*" asks Linehan.

"I've no idea."

"That makes me nervous."

"Yeah," says Spencer. "Me, too."

"You could be the Rain."

"We both might be."

"Christ, this is fucked up," says Linehan.

"I noticed."

"So what else do you know about the executive node?"

"That it's transferred to the president's successor in the event of his physical destruction."

"And who's the successor?"

"I'd guess Montrose."

"I'd guess that too. And I'm thinking she's nowhere near here."

"Not much is."

"Which is why the Throne picked this place," says Linehan. "L3's out of sight of the Moon and all the infrastructure around it. Only about twenty percent of our strategic weaponry has the angle and range, and—"

"Right. More than enough backup to bail the president

out of whatever goes down here at the same time minimizing the assets he has to keep track of. This dump's perfect."

"I wouldn't go *that* far."

"Best among some shit options?"

"The logic's clear enough," says Linehan. "The two leaderships have to be in direct contact. But they had to pick neutral territory, since neither leadership is about to send its executive node into the other's terrain. And it has to be in space, because this way they can control every last approach. And then, when the Rain moves in, they can hit them in that cylinder from all sides, with overwhelming force."

"And emerge and declare that they've destroyed the Rain and forged a new treaty while they were at it—a second Zurich to divide the world anew." Spencer shakes his head. "They can absorb what's left of the neutrals and then get on with whatever the fuck they like."

But now something's happening on that nearer asteroid. Nothing that's visible physically. In space the Aerie remains the same as it's been this whole time: partially occluded by that cylinder, partially glinting in the sun, a metal-studded rock that keeps its own counsel.

In the zone, though, it's a different story. Something's happening on the asteroid's firewall. On the part of the sphere that's blocked by the cylinder.

"On the rock," says Spencer.

"Yeah?"

"A door's opening."

They're going lights out and hell for leather. No zone presence now, and they're hoping nothing can see them on board the special train of the Euro Magnates. They've traveled three levels up—into a corridor that isn't supposed to exist—through a door and into the transit-tube where the train was sitting. No sooner were they aboard than it took off at full speed—back toward the city-end of the cylinder. Sarmax is keeping an eye on Lynx, whose armor's sensors and weaponry have been deactivated. The Operative's keeping an eye on Haskell. Both men keep an eye on everything else as well. As far as they know, this train's empty. But there are nine other cars beside theirs. And they're not about to make any assumptions.

"So where exactly are we going?" asks Haskell.

The basements of New London," replies Carson.

"For the greater glory of the Rain," says Lynx.

"Shut up," snarls Sarmax, but Lynx just laughs. And keeps on talking. "Can't you think for yourself, Leo? Don't you see what's happening? Carson and this—this *thing* here—have got this all worked out. We're heading straight into the hands of Rain."

"I don't think so," says Sarmax.

"How do you fucking know?"

"Enough with the mind games," snaps Carson. "The Rain could be on us any moment. Here's how it's going to work. In about ten seconds, this train is going to stop. When it does, Lynx is on point. Leo's next. Then the Manil—I mean Claire. I'll be covering her and guarding the rear. Got it?"

"So that's why I'm still alive," says Lynx. "Another target."

"Basically," says Sarmax.

"You must be enjoying this, Leo."

"Am I that transparent?"

The train slides to a halt. The doors open—but Sarmax is already shoving Lynx through them, stumbling onto a narrow platform. Everybody follows. There aren't many ways out of here. Just a stairwell and an—

"Elevator," says Carson.

They press inside. It's a tight fit. Haskell feels Carson's suit press against hers. She feels as though she's in a dream. It's like she's seen all this before—she feels the floor press up beneath her, level after level, they flick upward into the rafters of the Euro city. Gravity starts to subside. When they finally stop, there's not much of it left.

"Ready?" says Carson.

"Let's do it," says Sarmax.

They hit their suits' thrusters as the door opens, heading out into an empty corridor, then through what seems to be some kind of antechamber. Beyond it is a door so thick it looks like it was pried out of some bank vault.

"You got the key?" asks Haskell.

"I'd better," replies Carson.

He triggers the necessary codes. The massive door starts to swing open. As the door gets past forty-five degrees open, Sarmax shoves Lynx forward, through that doorway and to the left, while he hits his own thrusters and heads to the right. Carson and Haskell wait.

But only for a moment.

"Clear," shouts Sarmax.

Carson gestures at Haskell. She shoves off the floor, floats into the room alongside him as the door swings shut behind them.

"Not too far," he says. She fires compressed air, stops—looks around to see that the room's on two levels. She and Carson and Lynx are on the deck that constitutes the outer level, a circle around the sunken inner one, where Sarmax hovers, scanning surfaces. The walls curve between two windows situated opposite each other, each one cutting across the outer level. Space flickers in one of those windows—lights of ships and stars set against an all-consuming black.

The other window shows the interior of the cylinder. The lights of twilit city stretch away on all sides, descending to three valleys that look like the sides of some vast equilateral triangle whose segments have been thrust apart. One of the gaps between two of the valleys shows a sun on the point of setting. The other gaps contain largely darkened mirrors. Night's almost fallen on the land.

"It's almost here," says Haskell.

"What?" asks Carson.

He looks at her, and she knows she can't explain. How could she? Everything's turned around her. She was going south and now she's been slung back north, back into the heart of the city. Sixth-sense pivots within her head; the maps upon her skin take on new meaning. All this time she thought she was looking out through the lens of intuition and all the while it was looking in at her. Everything was leading here. She tries to speak, muttering something about how the view's not cheap.

"It wasn't money that bought it for us," says Carson. He floats near the door, closer now to Lynx than to Haskell. He nods in the direction of Sarmax—more one-on-one coordination, Haskell presumes. Sarmax makes a return gesture.

"Shouldn't I get away from these windows?" she asks.

"They're one-way," says Carson.

"So now we wait for your masters?" asks Lynx.

"Yours too," says Carson. "Have a seat."

He shoves Lynx into one of the chairs that ring the outer level of the room. Lynx sits there, stares at what's left of his wrist. Haskell feels his amputation as though it's her own. She doesn't know why. But he has the demeanor of someone who owned the universe only to lose it. She senses much history among these three men. History it seems the files only hint at.

"It embarrasses me for you to see us like this," says Carson, as though he's read her mind.

"Why?"

"We've seen better days."

"It gets better than this?"

He laughs. She realizes that he doesn't do that often. That he has no idea what to make of her. Then suddenly his head snaps to regard an instrument panel next to the door. He shouts down to Sarmax that they've got company. Sarmax hits his thrusters, vaults up to the outer platform.

"Approaching the door?" asks Carson.

"Yeah. Camera's out, of course."

"Who took it out?" asks Haskell.

"We did," says Sarmax.

"We hope," says Carson. "All we've got is heat and motion coming toward that door."

But Haskell can sense far more than that. This room she's never seen before is aglow in every vision. She can see all too clearly the logic that led to its selection: any team that bagged her or Rain would come here without any footprints on the zone, on an unmonitored route that's not on any chart. This is the ideal point for rendezvous, with escape routes in both directions. The fleet's outside. The interior's covered by snipers. If whoever's outside the door isn't who they're supposed to be . . .

"So which is it going to be?" she asks.

"For me, space was always the place." He gestures. They fire their suits' thrusters, move toward the window facing out into vacuum. Sarmax remains where he is, covering Lynx and the doorway. Carson tosses something onto that window, then pulls Haskell back from it.

"They've got the right access codes so far," says Carson. He grasps one of her arms, turning her around so that both of them are facing the door. "I've placed a charge on the window. Explosive decompression will give us a good start in the vacuum. You'll have to excuse me, but I don't intend to let go of you."

"It's what you're paid for," she says.

The door starts to open.

. . .

⊘ "The guns on this ship are tracking on something," says Spencer.

"Where?" says Linehan.

"Looks like they're reorientating some of the KE gatlings onto the New London spaceport," says Spencer. Right where the two Praetorian ships just landed—he stares at the surrounding topography, but it looks normal enough. Just more ships lining up for approach and pushing back from the Platform. He shifts his focus back to the far end—

"We might be about to see some shit," says Linehan. "If the Throne's starting to feed reinforcements into the cylinder from his Aerie—"

"He's not," says Spencer.

"You seem really sure of that."

"C'mon, man. Those ships that just landed on the cylinder's other end, at New London—*they* were the reinforcements. Along with the rest of us still out here. The Throne needs a better reason than that to open up a door in his citadel."

"So then they took something inside the asteroid—"

"No way."

"What makes you so sure?"

"I'm sure of nothing. But logic seems to preclude it."

"Go on," says Linehan.

"The operatives we were tracking in the cylinder went lights out. So did the target. Here's my hypothesis: they got whatever they were chasing. They either captured it or they killed it. Now they need to do something with it."

"If they killed it, what the fuck else can they do to it?"

"Inspect it. Dissect it. Use its codes to triangulate on the live ones. Rain corpses don't come cheap."

"You're not making any sense."

"I'm just speculating here, Linehan. It's all I can do. But I'm wondering whether that thing's now driving the timing of the whole operation. We got put on alert when it got detected. And the tension's still getting cranked. Hostiles are still out there."

"Where are you going with this?"

"To the logical place one ends up if one assumes that this thing or its carcass can be used against the rest of the Rain. Whether or not it's some Rain witch—whether or not that's all bullshit—the point is that if it's something the Throne needs—what happens then?"

"He brings it inside the Aerie—*oh.* No."

"*No,*" says Spencer. "The Throne *can't* bring it inside."

"Because it could be trojan."

"Yeah. Exactly. On the zone or physically—doesn't matter. The whole point might be to use this to get to him."

"Which puts him in a tight box."

"Yeah," says Spencer.

"Because he can't go *to* it either."

"No way. If he leaves that asteroid, he forfeits his whole fucking strategy."

"So what does he do?" asks Linehan.

"Sends something in his place."

"Got something in mind?"

"All depends on how important this asset they've bagged is."

"And if it's critically important—"

"—then the Throne has to send in something he trusts totally."

Static. Then: "I didn't realize there was such a thing."

"That's all there is," says Spencer. "A single thing."

The far edge of the door passes the near the edge of the wall.

"Stop right there," yells Sarmax, his voice blasting through the room on amplification.

The door stops moving.

"Stand by to receive primary code," says an amplified voice on the door's far side.

"Standing by," says Sarmax. She realizes he's beaming the code to Carson. Who nods.

"Get in here," yells Sarmax.

The door gets moving again. Suited figures start to sail into the room. Haskell notices that Carson continues to wait where he is, one hand on her arm, his back to the window, poised to blow that window and blast them both into space. Though once he sees their uniforms he relaxes almost imperceptibly.

And once he sees how many of them there are, he relaxes visibly—but still at the ready, facing the first of the suited figures, who's now almost reached him.

That figure wears Praetorian colors. She wonders at that but decides that somebody probably figures that if *these* troops see combat, it no longer matters what makes the news. But the colors they wear aren't the usual Praetorian ones the news-channels feature: slashes of dark blue set against a darker grey. The ones she's looking at have replaced that blue with an almost reddish purple. But everything else about these suits—the shape of the helmets, the weapons configurations sported by the armor, the way in which insignia are displayed, all of it—is classic Praetorian. Haskell realizes that she's looking at something she's never seen—the uniform of the Praetorian Core. And now the soldier in front of her is saluting Carson.

"Sir," he says.

Carson returns the salute. "What's the situation, Lieutenant?"

"Under control, sir."

"And his ETA?"

"Within the minute, sir. Via max-speed maglev."

"See this lady?" says Carson.

"Yes, sir," says the lieutenant.

"Her life is more important than yours. You'll die for her without hesitation."

"Yes, sir."

"Inform your soldiers of this. Prepare this room's defenses."

"Sir."

"Dismissed."

The lieutenant turns. Carson lets go of Haskell. She doesn't move though—just glances over to where Lynx is being neural-locked by two soldiers. His helmet's off. His back's to her. She notices Sarmax drifting over to where she and Carson are.

 ow's Lynx taking it?" asks the Operative on the one-on-one.

"How do you think?" replies Sarmax.

"The Rain almost fucked us."

"You really think they got to him?"

"No question."

"So now we space him?"

"Probably. But for now they've taken him to where the marines from the ships are setting up the outer perimeter."

"Those guys have brought in some heavy equipment, huh?"

"Nothing that doesn't suit the occasion. Lynx really got strapped to the railroad tracks this time."

"With the Hand driving the shit-train to end all shit-trains."

"And that guy breaks for nothing."

Sarmax looks amused. "If you're pressed for conversation when he gets here, you might consider asking him to go easy on Lynx."

"Are you nuts?"

"It'd look good—you know, plead his case, show some concern and all that."

"Tell you what, man, why don't you start shooting into the ceiling or something just so it's totally obvious to everybody that I have no ability to lead a fucking team whatsoever."

"Maybe they'll even give me back the job," says Sarmax.

"Like you'd want it."

"I'm starting to think I might."

"What's that supposed to mean?"

"What are you guys talking about?" asks Haskell.

They look at her.

"She's quick," says Sarmax.

"She is," says Carson. "We were just talking about the situation."

"Which is?"

"Precarious."

"What do you know about him?" asks Linehan. "Just the usual stuff you hear around the campfire," says Spencer. "The Hand's second only to the president in the Praetorian hierarchy—"

"And responsible for one thing."

"The security of the Throne."

"Meaning the Throne's taking one hell of a risk if he's really sending him in."

Spencer mulls this over—and then sees the captain suddenly signal to the gunnery officers on the left of the bridge. He watches numbers race one another across his screens as the ship's batteries start responding.

"Hey," he says. "They're priming the DE cannon."

"Which ones?"

"That'd be all of them."

• • •

The Praetorians have set up heavy weapons pointed at both windows—two-person gatlings that take about fifteen seconds to configure—and are also boring holes in the ceiling and floor, shoving wires through them to communicate via direct transmission with their brethren who apparently have occupied the adjacent floors. Haskell's assuming it's all still off the zone—that it's all been worked out in advance. She floats near the inner deck with Carson and Sarmax hovering nearby. She counts at least thirty soldiers. She wonders how many are in the structure around her—wonders if the millions who dwell in the city all around have any idea what's taking place within their midst.

More Praetorians enter the room. They're bunched tightly around a single figure who wears the same uniform as they do—but who now separates from them, rockets in toward her and Carson and Sarmax accompanied only by two other Praetorians. Haskell notices that the approaching suit has no rank. It seems like he's moving toward her over some infinite distance; like she's seen him so many times before. Carson and Sarmax come to attention as the man brakes in front of them.

"Sir," says Carson.

"At ease," says the man.

"This is the woman, sir," says the Operative.

"Good," says the man. The face behind his visor is much older than she was expecting. His hair's as grey as his eyes. "Claire, my name's Huselid."

"The Throne's own Hand."

"I need you to remove your helmet."

She complies wordlessly. Brown hair spills out as she breathes in the air around her. The Praetorians standing to either side of Huselid begin pulling material out of their suits, begin to erect what looks for all the world like a tent around them. Walls quickly cut them off. What seemed to be fabric at first is now hardening into something that's more like plastic.

They're in a room within a room. She feels everything closing in around her. She feels the universe billowing out beyond her. Huselid doesn't take his eyes off her.

"Claire, there are a couple of scans we have to run. I need you to remove your suit."

"Don't you fucking get it?" she says, but though it sounds like protest it's really not. It's more like ritual. "There's no time. They might hit us at any moment."

"Precisely why you need to hurry." The Praetorians pull themselves out of the structure, affix its plastic to the larger chamber's walls. One of them steps back in, stands with her weapons trained on Haskell as Huselid continues: "I apologize, but prudence dictates precautions. Gentlemen, if you'd be so kind."

Carson and Sarmax salute and leave, pulling the door-flap shut behind them. Haskell shrugs, opens up her suit, steps out, strips off her shirt and pants. She stands there, noticing that Huselid's noticing the bloody scars wreathed upon her.

"What are those?" he asks.

"Schematics that depict how the Rain might be taking the ground out from under our feet while we sit here chatting."

"I'm going as fast as I can," he says—gazes at her, and she realizes he's scanning on multiple spectrums. She takes him in—soldier of the Throne, playing the hand he's been dealt. Though apparently he's still fully capable of multitasking:

"It wouldn't have worked," he says.

"What wouldn't have?"

"Breaking into the Aerie to confront the Throne."

"Only way to be sure the Rain weren't listening in. Only way he could be sure *I* wasn't Rain."

"But they were trying to follow you in. You almost fell into their trap."

"They almost fell into mine. Once I'd combined with the Throne directly, we could have destroyed them at point-blank range."

"We'll give you the next best thing."

"Remote-junction's too great a risk."

"It's the only risk the Throne will take," he replies.

"Then he's a fool."

Huselid says nothing. But his eyes say everything. She doesn't even know why she's arguing. She's just following the script. Because how she gets to the impending moment doesn't matter. What matters is that it's about to be unleashed. And now a door in the enclosure folds up and two more Praetorians float a small cart into the room. It contains an object: a cube about a meter on each side, covered in a metallic paperlike substance peeling all around its edges. A screen's attached to one end. What looks like a small radar dish exudes from the other. One of the soldiers takes her clothes and pulls her suit from the enclosure. The other adjusts the dish. Looks at her.

"Hold still," he says, and points that dish at her. She feels nothing. She counts the seconds, watches herself reflected in the dish's hazy mirror, watches the scar-maps on her skin distorted by its curves. She feels like she's on the verge of seeing something new within those patterns. She feels as though she's on a river drifting toward the roar of falling water....

"Turn around," says the Praetorian. She does. More seconds pass. "Face me again." She does. "We need a DNA scan," he says. "Hold out your hand." She holds it out. He peels off some of the metal-paper from the cube, touches it to her hand. "Your tongue," he says. She sticks out her tongue. He repeats the procedure with more of the metal-paper. Huselid takes all of this in without expression.

"Are you finished?" she asks.

"Yes," he says. Another Praetorian pulls another suit into the room. It's heavy armor. It's obviously packed with weapons. "This is your new suit," says Huselid.

"What's it do?" she asks.

"What doesn't it," he replies.

The Praetorian salutes, leaves. She looks at the armor. Garments hang off the back of it: light pants and shirt. She puts them on, climbs into the suit, hits the ignition. Lights flare out around her. She feels time starting to quicken.

"Now what?" she says.

"Now we do what I was sent for," Huselid replies. The enclosure suddenly opens up, drapes inward as it reverts back to cloth. A Praetorian holds up one corner. Huselid ducks beneath, gesturing at her to follow. He fires his thrusters, floats down into the basin of the inner room, lands at an alcove set within one side—an alcove cut off from the line-of-sight of both the windows. Wires protrude from its wall, their ends grasped by Praetorians. She scans the alcove, scans those wires, puts her suit through its paces as she does so. It's working like clockwork. She instinctively moves toward the zone for the rest of the routine checks she'd usually run.

And stops.

And waits. She's bracing herself for what's about to happen. She's resigned to it. She's just a tool of the future now, even if it wasn't precisely what she was planning. Because now that the Throne's calling the shots there's no way he's going to let her near him. Not until she's been tested, via a hidden line rigged across the whole of the cylinder, all the way to the Aerie. And Haskell figures what the hell. She's ready to take to the zone to merge with the Throne itself—to integrate her capabilities with his and put her sword at his service. Though she swears to God she won't hand him her mind.

She stops near Huselid. Two other soldiers move in, scan the walls around them. Huselid takes a wire from one of his soldiers, extends it toward her. She feels herself teeter on the brink. He looks straight at her and she struggles to meet his gaze through the contingency pouring in upon her.

"Claire Haskell. President Andrew Harrison asks for your forgiveness for all that you've suffered at the hands of his servants. He asks that you work with him now to save our people from the thing that assails us. When that's done, he'll grant you anything you wish. Anything at all. He asks that you join with him to triangulate the locations of the Rain hit teams throughout the Earth-Moon system."

"What about the back door to my own systems?"

"We'll give you the key."

"Which the Rain already has."

"We know the nature of the game we're playing."

"Do the Eurasians?"

He pauses. She laughs, but only just. "They really sent their leadership?"

"They really did," he says. "But we're talking about two separate zones here. Meaning that the triangulation the Throne's attempting with what we believe to be the Eurasian executive node—in the other asteroid—won't yield results for hours. With you, it'll take a minute to clean out the U.S. zone. Then we can worry about helping the East out."

"Give me that wire."

Huselid hands it to her. She looks at the metal, feels everything tilt around her—and then she shoves the wire into the side of her head. She steps inside the zone, and right before her in that endless grid is something that looks like an endless head and its eyes are like windows and its mouth is time itself and it's the Throne upon the ramparts of the highest firewalls imaginable: the Throne itself blazing light down upon her and then she

      meets

         that

           light

and feels herself swept upward, rising above it, feeling it rise above her as she bears the Throne up on wings of intuition and lets the U.S. zone fold in around her. She sees the bulwark of Montrose's InfoCom flaring off to one side—notices the extent to which it and the Throne have opened to each other—notices, too, that all the strategic weaponry across all the Commands remains accounted for, even in those areas that are slightly darker to the Throne. Much of that terrain's clustered within Space Command—but now that obscurity's fading as she applies the pressure: shifts gears, turns wheels, sweeps her gaze across those grids. Nothing's denied her now. The codes of the Throne slam shut her back doors, augment her own power, carry all before her. The map of the U.S. zone and all its secret corners blazes within her head. The L3 system shines before her. The president has set up the executive node within the Aerie (a crimson orb deep within that asteroid), and configured a portion of the Euro net as a temporary extension of the U.S. zone.

Only it's no ordinary zone. It's layered behind the firewalls of the Euro Magnates, mostly latent within the cylinder, but switched on in full defensive architecture within the Aerie—set up to mirror the Eurasian zone that's been stretched across the farther cylinder and farther rock, looming largely opaque to Haskell, but she suspects that she could penetrate it if she tried. Particularly with the Throne riding shotgun for her. Or is she running shotgun for it? Because she remembers now. Her job. Find the Rain, and let the Praetorians pin them down with snipers while troops emerge from the asteroid and deploy from the disguised warships to finish them. And such forces will be backed up by strategic weaponry set up in layers beyond the Platform itself: the batteries of the warships, the gunnery platforms on the adjacent satellites, and on the periphery of the L3 vicinity, the directed energy projectors rigged upon the ten-kilometer-long Helios Station . . .

She switches on to the primary sequence, takes in the whole of the U.S. zone, sees all the routes where the Rain's been gaining access—sees them as though she's staring at her skin once more. It's as she figured. It's as they've done before—the Rain have been using the legacy routes: paths from before there was a U.S. zone—back in the days of the global net—tunnels that lead through wires that used to be mainlines so many decades ago, before they fell to disuse and secret things began to prowl them.

Only this time they've gone deeper than anyone save she thought possible. She picks up the Rain's scent at those doors, starts to follow the trails, out of the legacies, into the here and now, far out across Earth and Moon. Some of those paths lead along the directions of the Rain hit teams of four days ago.

Some don't.

She attains critical mass—fast-forwards through the last three days in an instant. Everything crashes through her head: she sees the Rain and nothing stands between her and them. She sees every square meter of every scrap of territory the United States controls—as well as the locations of every hit team the Rain have within that territory. All of those hit teams look to be the standard triad model that the Rain uses. There are three of them.

All within this half of the Europa Platform.

One's only a klick off, holed up in a safehouse on the out-skirts of New London. New London's easy. Anything can get in there. Getting past it and out into the rest of the cylinder is the problem.

But the second Rain triad has managed to do just that. It was using the back door within Haskell to move within her zone-wake. That back door's now shut, but the triad's still sidling forward, far more cautiously than before. And the odds of it being detected have been growing the closer it draws to the Aerie. Odds that approach near certainty when it reaches the South Pole.

But the third triad's managed to beat those odds anyway. It's managed to get inside the Aerie itself. By being in that asteroid all along. By guessing right. By not letting anybody see what Haskell's now seeing: right after the failure of their attempt to ignite war between the superpowers, the Rain placed various triads in various places across the Earth-Moon system in anticipation of the next move of the superpowers' leaderships. There were only so many moves. Only so many places. And one triad hit the jackpot.

Though finding the president in a huge chunk of rock filled with Praetorians is a long way from easy. The triad's still trying to pinpoint his exact location, a task that's made all the more difficult due to that triad's immobility, holed up in a chamber that's literally walled off within those corridors. It's waiting for the other hit teams to reach the asteroid. But in the wake of Haskell's disappearance from the zone its members may be about to change up their tactics.

Though Haskell's not about to let that happen. Because now she winds up and lets herself pour forth; she's fire burning through the sky of zone—she swoops down upon them all, merging her wings with those of the Throne and screaming in like a bird of prey. She can't miss.

But she does.

Because next instant they're not there. All three Rain hit teams vanish from the zone.

As does the whole Aerie.

The asteroid's still there in physical space. Her eyes take it in upon the cameras the fleet has trained upon it. But she's lost zone-contact with everything in it.

Including the Throne.

Suddenly there's activity on the bridge around Spencer. The firewall around the Aerie just collapsed. There doesn't seem to be any zone presence behind it either—though seismic readouts monitoring the surface show heavy combat has started within.

"They're sealing the drop-ships," yells Linehan.

His voice is thick with static. But Spencer already knows exactly what the drop-ships are doing, along with the rest of the fleet. His mind's a blur of motion as he works the zone in tandem with the prime razor. In the firmament beyond, he can see tactical command has been activated somewhere on the cylinder. He can't see where, but he can see the result. The *Larissa V* engages its motors; nuclear-powered engines flare, sending the ship surging forward. Spencer feels himself pressed back in his seat. He watches the Platform roar in toward them—watches on virtual as hatches slide back from slots all along the ship and gun-barrels extend out into vacuum.

"What's going on?" yells Linehan. He's almost lost in static now.

"We're attacking the fucking Platform! Get ready to get in there!"

The ship's guns start firing.

The Operative turns toward the window as an explosion rocks the cylinder's interior, several kilometers down the valley. Forest gets torn backward. Flames blast toward the inverted valleys overhead.

"Fuel-air bomb," says Sarmax.

"Nasty," says the Operative.

Not small either. The hole that's now billowing smoke extends for several layers into the cylinder's infrastructure. So far the cylinder's atmosphere remains intact. But shots are ringing out. Sirens are going off. Lasers flash across the cylinder's interior as micromissiles curl in toward their targets. Everybody visible on the streets and ramps and rooftops of the city is heading for doors leading inside. All too many are getting caught in the crossfire.

"This is more than just the Rain," says Sarmax.

"Looks like they've managed to co-opt some of the Euro security forces," replies the Operative, glancing at the Praetorians within this room. Several are watching the developing situation through the crosshairs of their heavy weapons. But most of them are watching the other window and the walls themselves. They have their assignments.

And now the whole cylinder's rumbling as something massive smacks against it.

"What the fuck," mutters Sarmax.

"The cylinder's getting shelled from space."

"By us?"

"Better hope so."

Plan B is now Plan A: cut off from the Throne, Haskell has switched to link up with Huselid, who's coordinating the counterattack. The asteroid remains out of contact, and a pitched battle's clearly going on within. All hell's starting to break loose within the cylinder.

But inside Haskell's head it's calm—a peace such as she's never known. Because there's no more future. Future's here. She's riding the raw moment—and now that the Rain have made their move, she's making hers, countering the sinkhole the Rain were seeking to trigger in the zone, halting the fraying of its edges, preventing them from extending the rot any farther as she takes over executive capacity within the U.S. zone. She's holding steady. She feels the zone creak around her as she shores up its foundations according to parameters that precisely mirror the patterns etched upon her. She's extending her support to the Eurasian zone as well, though nothing seems to have happened there so far. But she's sure the Rain are over there, continuing their infiltration runs. Or just playing for time. Because if the Rain in the Aerie can kill the president, it can take the executive node—rip the software from his skull and use it to wrest control of the entire zone from her.

But Huselid doesn't seem worried. It's almost as though he's been expecting this. He's unleashing a flurry of commands. Tactical battle readouts parade through her skull. The Rain hit teams in the cylinder are back online in combat mode, shielded against her onslaughts now, engaging with several Praetorian special-ops units—and those units are fully active in the zone, fully supported by the Hand and her. The ships outside are swooping in toward the Platform, opening fire, sending DE beams and KE shells streaking into the cylinder's outermost layers to crash in and around the areas in which the Rain units are operating. And now the first of the dropships is deploying marines along the length of the cylinder, the majority of them near the middle where the fighting's heaviest. Two of the ships coming in behind that first one are slated to deploy directly onto the surface of the Aerie. Haskell moves to shift some of the heavy vehicles situated in the levels beneath her closer to where the action's going down.

But Huselid stops her. She sees his point. With the Throne cut off, this chamber has become the command post. And the forces protecting it are substantial—the Praetorians from the ships that docked earlier are massed along the outer perimeter, about a hundred meters out from where Haskell's standing, while the Hand's own shock troops form the inner perimeter, which starts about thirty meters from this room. Haskell can see that Huselid is anxious to maintain robust defenses around his makeshift citadel.

Particularly given the extent to which the security and household robots in the city have been hacked by the Rain. New London's plunging into chaos. But the nearest Rain triad seems to have been trapped in a series of elevator shafts in the city's basements. And the one just south of the cylinder's equator has been pinned down in a construction area. The Rain have seized the bait. The hammer's coming down upon them. And whatever's going on within the asteroid, the Rain team there will have its work cut out for it in making headway against the main force of the Praetorian Core.

"We have them," says the Hand.

Even as she feels the zone writhe beneath her.

The cannons of the *Larissa V* unleash on maximum strafe. Puffs of explosions dot the cylinder—and now the Platform's giving way to space as the ship turns at a sickening angle and rushes parallel to the main cylinder.

"This is it!" screams Linehan—and cuts out as the dropship he's in launches. Spencer watches it go on the screens within his head, watches the other dropships launch, watches as the *Larissa V* blasts past the Platform and engages its rearguns. The targeted areas light up—and then go dark.

Along with everything else.

What the fuck," says the Operative.

His screens are showing static—within his helmet, but also within his head. He looks at Sarmax, who's looking puzzled. The other Praetorians are clearly having the same problem. They're communicating with hand signals. Those within this room are still holding their positions. But as to what's happening to the Praetorian marines in the perimeter that defends this room, the Operative has no idea. He hears no sign of combat.

But the fighting in the cylinder has clearly stepped up several notches. The air's ablaze with laser and tracer fire. Most of it's concentrated some fifteen klicks out, but there's plenty of it that's a lot nearer. Two more fuel-air bombs have detonated. New London is on fire in several places. The Operative gets glimpses of mobs in the streets—tens of thousands of terrified people in full stampede along the ramps. In the far distance, a giant jet of flame gouts out from the southern mountains. Whatever's going on behind them in the Aerie isn't pretty. The Operative moves to where Sarmax is standing, places his helmet against his.

"They've lost the whole fucking zone," he yells.

"Can you reestablish one-on-one?" yells Sarmax.

"It's gone, man!"

"What do you mean it's gone?"

"I mean it's fucking vanished! We could broadcast in the clear, but that's suicide!"

"So what do we do?" says Sarmax.

"Purge the loose ends and get ready for the mother of all slug-outs."

"Loose ends?"

"Lynx. Let's execute him."

"Works for me," says Sarmax. The Operative turns away, fires his suit's thrusters, glides over to one of the Praetorian officers, slams his helmet up against his.

"Kill the prisoner," he says.

"Sir, I need the authority of the Hand for that."

"The Hand's a little fucking busy right now," snarls the Operative.

"Those are my orders."

"Your orders have changed," says the voice of the Hand.

Tsunami's surging out across the zone. Nothing left around her. Nothing—save the implications of what she carved upon herself. What she failed to recognize. The nature of the real trap.

"Both zones," she says out loud.

They let her make the first move. They drew her in, convinced her that they had nothing in reserve, forced her to become the one thing propping up the universe. But now there's no more universe left to prop. The Eurasian and U.S. zones have just gone down. The Rain used the legacies to link them, leveraged the proximity of the executive nodes of East and West.

And set them against each other like opposite charges to neutralize each other.

"What the hell?" says Huselid.

"Every wireless conduit," she says. "Chain reaction."

Autumn Rain's razors just rode their megahack in style, smashing against every exposed razor they could find on the way down. They couldn't damage her, though—couldn't touch the razors under her personal protection, within the Hand's perimeter. All they could do was yank the zone from under her feet.

But not the one within her head. Haskell's the one thing that's not affected—the one thing capable of restoring what's been lost. She's doing her utmost to jury-rig a whole new zone around her. But it's going to be pathetically small. Because all she can reach is the software of those in immediate line-of-sight. Though that's a damn sight farther than anyone else can manage. She beams new codes to the Hand, beams them to his bodyguards—sends soldiers racing out toward the outer perimeter to try to restore some semblance of order. Other soldiers are turning to the outer window of the room, setting up Morse code to signal the ships out there via direct visual.

"Order them all directly onto the Aerie," snarls the Hand. *"Tell them to hit that asteroid and deploy everything that's left."*

But now the Rain make the move aimed at checkmate.

• • •

Spencer opens his eyes. It's not easy. His head hurts. It feels like his nose is bleeding.

He looks around. The bridge is in chaos. Personnel are removing panels, pulling out wires. Trying to find a way to control this ship, which continues to hurtle out into space, away from the Platform. Spencer wanders through his own mind's haze, wonders if there's anything he can do about it. Because it doesn't look like the prime razor's going to do shit. He's sprawled in his chair, eyes staring at nothing.

"He's fucking had it," shouts a voice. "Now get the fuck over here!"

The captain hasn't deigned to speak to his secondary razor until now. But Spencer just got a battlefield promotion—he releases his straps, fires his suit's thrusters, jets over to where the captain's holding onto his own chair. The captain points at the exec-dashboard in front of him.

"Get the fuck in there and give me control."

"Sir." And Spencer does. He finds himself blocked—slides past that blockage, reaches down the redundant wires, bypasses the software to interface directly with the engines. It's not much. Every wireless conduit that might lead to the larger zone beyond this ship is fucked. But it'll have to do.

"I have it," he says. "Give me orders, sir."

"Back to the fucking Platform," says the captain, giving him the vectors—and turning from there to the gunnery officers, starting to gesture at them to get their consoles' wires extended to where Spencer is. But Spencer's got eyes only for the fragment of the ship's zone that's still remaining, a glowing ember amidst scattered ash. The angle along which he's turning the craft is almost insanely aggressive, in large part because he's only got partial control of the steering. He feels G-forces building upon him. He watches people clinging to their straps and chairs. He watches panels that have been torn loose fly into the walls—watches the Platform swing back into the windows and start to rush in toward them once more. Two other ships are out in front of them. They've managed to get back in the game as well. They're running the same race, closing on the same target.

"Landfall on the asteroid," says the captain. "Following coordinates."

Spencer lines up the approaching Aerie. But now one of the ships that's up ahead lights up in a sudden flash—a flash that intensifies as its armor crumbles and its engines detonate.

"Gone," screams someone.

"What the hell's going on?" yells the captain.

"We're under fire, sir," says Spencer.

"I can see that! *What the fuck's shooting at us?*"

"I'm trying to figure that out!" screams Spencer. "Give me a fucking moment!"

"We don't *have* any moments! Evasive action!"

But Spencer's already got that going. Everything that's not tied down starts moving again. A huge bolt of energy just misses their ship, flashes past on the screens. Spencer runs subroutines on what's left of the ship's comps; he traces that energy's strength and direction, looks back along its route, reaches its source.

And finds himself staring across a hundred kilometers at the Helios Station.

⊕ **B**lasts keep on rocking the chamber. The Praetorians have switched back from hand signals to the one-on-one. And now Lynx sails on thrusters back into the room. Sarmax looks at the Operative.

"Thought he was supposed to be dead."

"Divine intervention," says the Operative.

"What the hell are you talking about?"

"The Manilishi. Apparently she purged his skull's software. He's clean."

"Not that it matters," says Sarmax, gesturing at the window. Lynx reaches them, stares out at it—and whistles.

"Christ," he says, "they're going to *town*."

An understatement. The shelling of the Praetorian ships has penetrated the cylinder in several places. And somebody's busy blowing airlocks. People are getting sucked by the thousands down tunnels and holes now laid open.

"Look on the bright side," says Sarmax. "The vacuum'll put out the fires."

"I can't believe what I'm seeing," says Lynx.

"About as bad as it gets," says the Operative. "We could use you back in the game. How's your hand?"

"Fucked," says Lynx.

"He means can you fight," says Sarmax.

"I know what he means, you prick. The answer's yes."

"It's less a question of lost firepower," says the Operative. "More one of—"

"Lost balance?" Lynx's smile is pure ice. "Armor can compensate. Particularly with the download that bitch just gave me. So we've lost the broader zone?"

"Yup," says Sarmax. "The Manilishi and the Hand seem to have managed to get a local connection going. And that's it."

"Where's the Throne?" asks Lynx.

"In the asteroid," says the Operative.

"Still fighting?"

"Who knows?"

The three men amp their scopes, peer out into the cylinder's vast hollow. Most of the lighting is gone now. Explosions flash out amidst the gathering dark. Half the Platform's robots seem to be running programs set in motion by the Rain. Debris flies past the window. Tracer-fire cuts swathes everywhere.

"Let's prep tactics," says the Operative.

"Has the Hand given you scenarios?" asks Lynx.

"He's given me nothing," says the Operative. "I think he and his new friend are trying to assess events."

"They'd better catch up quick," says Sarmax.

But now the Operative's heads-up is giving him more data—directly from the Hand/Manilishi battle management node. Some of the Praetorians are pointing at the exterior window.

"Someone's lighting up the vacuum," says the Operative

"With what?" asks Lynx.

"Oh Jesus Christ," says Sarmax.

They've already processed the implications. Ten klicks long and studded with microwave and laser projectors, the Helios has long served as a linchpin of power-generation for the L3 system. It can divide its energy among its dishes or channel it all through a single one. It seems to be firing through about fifteen of them right now, changing those fifteen up to allow it maximum field of fire upon the targets that it's now engaging. It was never intended for anything but peaceful purposes.

Though its new owners could give two shits.

"We and the East had four special-ops teams apiece up there," says the Hand.

"Not anymore," says Haskell.

"Why the fuck didn't you spot them up there?" he demands.

"Presumably they were hiding in the East's zone."

"Order all our ships onto the attack—"

"Done it already. But—"

"I know," he says. "They don't have a prayer."

"Neither do we," she says. Her mind runs through the inventory. They're pinned down. The Throne's pinned down. The zone's paralyzed, as are all forces throughout the Earth-Moon system. They're confronted by the Rain's elite. And they can only assume that whatever's going on in the asteroid is even more of a nightmare than what's going down in both windows.

"I agree," says the Hand. A scenario flits from his head to hers. "Here's what we're going to do."

She stares at what's turning in her mind. "Are you sure?"

"Only option we've got left."

The ship hurtles in. The bridge-crew can see the odds against them as certain as any number that's left on their screens. That thing out there is basically a directed-energy machine gun. A hundred klicks is basically a turkey shoot.

"Evasive action!" screams the captain.

But Spencer's already giving it all he's got. The Platform veers crazily in the window. Spencer feeds in instructions from the gunnery officer, lets the ship's batteries rip, peppering the Helios with fire while more shots streak in from the few remaining emplacements on the asteroids and the surviving ships.

"Target remains eighty-five percent effective," says the gunnery officer calmly.

"Use the fucking Platform!" shouts the navigator. "Use the fucking Platform!"

And Spencer's trying—doing his utmost to keep the Platform between him and this monster—trying to pop out and fire and then dart back into cover. But those kinds of precision maneuvers are pretty much beyond the capacity of this ship now. He watches clouds of humans starting to billow from the northern end of the Platform. He realizes with sick finality that there's no way out of this. He slams his visor.

Just as a microwave spear impales them.

The Praetorians aren't moving. But the Operative can see they're standing at attention anyway. He can see their eyes shifting in their visors as they cease their private conversations. He's getting instructions now too.

"Relay these to your men," says the Hand.

"Listen to this," the Operative says to Sarmax and Lynx.

The Hand is now moving away from the inner deck. The Manilishi is following him. The Hand's bodyguards cluster about both of them. Soldiers start exiting the room as they receive specific tactical instructions. The Operative hears engines starting up at close range—from the sound of it, the mechanized units of the Praetorians on the outer perimeter. Beyond that he hears only the rumbling of explosions within the cylinder.

But now that changes.

Spencer's aware of some kind of roaring noise. His brain feels like it's been burned to a crisp. He can see nothing but white light. He wishes the afterlife was less painful.

But now that white is fading into the black of space. He focuses, realizes the window's gone, along with the rest of the bridge. Somehow he's been blasted about twenty meters farther back into the ship. He's wedged in beneath some debris, his suit somehow still intact. Dead bodies are everywhere. So are those of the living, clinging to what's left of the walls. Vibration keeps on washing through him. The engines of the ship are going haywire. And now the Platform comes into sight, careening in toward them. Metal surface fills Spencer's view. He braces himself as though it still mattered.

THIS IS THE HAND. THIS IS BEING BROADCAST ON SE-CURE CHANNEL ENABLED BY THE MANILISHI, THE RAZOR NOW AT MY SIDE. YOU'RE TO PROTECT HER AS YOU PROTECT ME. THE DECISIVE BATTLE IS UNDER WAY. OUR THRONE IS TRAPPED BY RAIN COMMANDOS IN THE NEAREST OF THE AERIES. WE'RE GOING TO CROSS THE CYLINDER AND RESCUE OUR PRESIDENT. WE'RE GOING TO DESTROY THE ABOMINATION CALLED RAIN. DE-TAILED TACTICAL OVERLAYS TO FOLLOW.

The Operative receives those overlays for his team, relays them to Lynx and Sarmax.

"This is fucking it," says Sarmax.

"Straight shot to glory," says Lynx.

"Let's move out," says the Operative.

But even as he says those words, the whole cylinder shakes—shakes still harder, shakes like it's breaking apart. About ten klicks distant in that wilderness of dark and tracer lines, one of the valleys ruptures into flame. What's left of a burning spaceship bursts through, pulling ground and metal with it, falling back onto what's left of that ground, shredding itself and everything around it as what's left of its engines keep on firing.

"That's a new one," says Sarmax.

PART II
HEAVEN'S RUNNERS

Waking up. Pain washing against you. Vibration rumbling through you. Visor pressed up against your face, your back pressed up against some wall, your mind feeling like it's coming apart: Where are you? How did you get here?

And what the hell are you going to do next?

Spencer opens his eyes. It doesn't help. Everything's still dark. Everything hurts. But at least he's breathing. Vibration keeps on shaking the surface beneath him. He switches on his suit-lights—realizes they aren't working. He turns on his comlinks, finds only static. He figures he's somewhere in the remains of the *Larissa V*. Which, judging by the gravity, must have crashed onto the cylinder. He tries to access zone, but he can't find a trace of it.

So he starts crawling forward, tracing his way along the wall. He pushes his way through debris, stumbles into something that feels like a shattered suit. He slides through something slick—crawls past it, hits another wall: a corner. He starts tracing his way along the new wall, which ends suddenly, in some jagged edge. Somewhere past that edge is a flickering light. Spencer moves through the hole, crawls carefully toward that light. He's got one hand out in front of him, probing to make sure there's still a floor beneath him.

He's in luck. There is. The light keeps swelling. As he gets closer he can see it's somewhere past the edge of yet another tear in yet another wall. He's starting to see a bit more of the environment he's in. It's one of the ship's interior hangars. The hole's not that far ahead now, a glow framed by metal walls. Spencer crawls off at an angle, gets against that wall, makes his way along it. He reaches it, peers through.

And wishes he hadn't.

He's looking up through darkness toward the central axis of the cylinder—staring at thousands of burning bodies scattered about. Euro civilians caught in the crossfire that's raged through this part of the cylinder—or who just got blasted into limbo from whatever surface they were trying to escape over. Apparently there's still enough oxygen left up there to keep the fires going.

For now at least. But as Spencer pulls himself out of the hole and onto the top of the spaceship's hull, he can see all too clearly that's not going to last very long. It's the biggest fucking mess he's ever seen. Artificial ground's piled up all around where the *Larissa V* plowed through it. Twisted metal structures in the middle distance conceal all function they once had. Past them is more fire—or rather, images of those overhead flames flickering on the remains of some shattered, kilometer-long shard of mirror. Beyond that's only darkness. Spencer's pretty sure that's the direction of the cylinder's South Pole and the Aerie. He remembers the asteroid being on their right as they made their final run toward the Platform.

Meaning New London should be on his left. But if it's still there, there's no sign of it. There's every sign of combat, though. Most of which looks to be several klicks away. It's spread out on a broad front across the width of the cylinder:

flashes of lasers and flaring explosions that cast shadows reaching all the way to the valleys far overhead. It's like some giant elongated cloud, moving toward Spencer at speed. He ponders this.

But then he sees movement that's much closer.

Terrain whipping by. Shots flying everywhere. Tactical overlays adjusting as data pours in from all sides. The view from the Operative's visor is framed by at least a hundred screens. He's moving at just under 200 klicks an hour, streaking through the suburbs of the city that's now fading in the rearview. Above him's a chaos of light.

"Tighten up," yells Sarmax.

"No," replies the Operative, "mind the fucking gap."

They're responsible for a wide swathe of terrain. They're charging through it at street level, dipping into the basements just often enough to stay unpredictable.

"What's past this?" says Lynx.

"You don't want to know," mutters the Operative.

Not that he has much of a clue himself. The usual battlefield intel is nonexistent. Zone's just a function of what the Manilishi's propping up. And he's receiving her signals only intermittently—relayed in by tightbeam laser from what seems to be about a klick or so behind him and somewhere off to the right. But he's not exactly sure. And that's fine by him.

"They're pressing on the rear," says Lynx.

"Trying to get in behind our left wing," says Sarmax.

"They're going to have to catch us first," says the Operative.

Which won't be easy. The Praetorian formation is spread out along a triangular wedge almost two klicks across. The spearhead of that wedge is aimed straight at the far end of the cylinder. The Operative's unit is well out on the left flank. A rearguard's covering the wedge's base. And the Manilishi and the Hand have their own inner perimeter somewhere in the center of it all . . .

"Sniper," says Sarmax.

"Triangulate," says Lynx.

The Operative says nothing, just takes evasive action as shots streak past him. A micromissile unleashed by Lynx rockets past him off to his left, veers downward, disappears among the buildings. Next instant, the flash of a minitactical lights up everything; the Operative's already firing his thrusters, the bombed-out buildings falling away from him as he rises to a vantage point where he can lay down covering fire as Sarmax streaks amidst the streets to where Lynx's missile has just hit. There's nothing there now, just a big gaping hole—and the Operative rains shots into that hole to forestall whatever might be lurking down there. He catches a quick glimpse of targets getting flayed by his suit's minigun—sees very clearly off to his right some of the vehicles in the Praetorian spearhead—and then he's plunging back toward the surface. He drops below the level of the buildings, his path curving as he rockets down those streets. Another explosion flares as Sarmax dumps a microtactical down that hole.

"Drones," confirms Sarmax.

"What else?" yells Lynx.

A lot else, thinks the Operative. As always, Autumn Rain has rigged proxies to do the dirty work. Thousands of miniature drones, hundreds of Euro police robots, scores of heavy-equipment droids—all of it making for one big problem for anyone trying to cross the cylinder as fast as possible. How many of these things were brought in by the hit teams, how many of them were rigged in advance by remote artifice, the Operative doesn't know. He scarcely cares.

"They hacked *everything,*" says Sarmax on the one-on-one.

"So kill everything that's not us," snarls the Operative.

"This is getting *hot!*" yells Lynx.

"So let's get lower!" screams Sarmax.

Sarmax on the right, Lynx on the left, the Operative in the center, scores of meters separating them—they streak forward over those fields, descend into a grove of trees, start roaring up depressions in the ground within them. The whole Platform shakes—and shakes again as microwave bolts smash against it. As long as the Helios is out there, nothing can get off the Europa Platform.

"That fucking *thing*," says Sarmax.

"Reminding us who's boss," says the Operative.

"That'd be the devil," says Lynx.

Flames erupt through the dark, shapes dimly visible through smoke as the Praetorian formation steams forward, keeping low, crushing everything in its path. What's visible through her vehicle's camera feeds is like nothing Haskell's ever seen. Fire lights up the valleys overhead. She can see bodies burning all along the center axis.

But the real data's on the screens within her mind; she's obtaining that data in the most judicious way possible, routing most of the traffic through a neighboring vehicle in order to keep the Rain guessing the same way she's guessing—trying to work out the nature of whatever zone they've got going, trying to work out the location of their triads. Which would be tough enough given Autumn Rain's megahack. But it's even tougher as the electrical systems in the cylinder collapse, along with everything else. Haskell estimates the place is down to about 30 percent oxygen. Millions of civilians are dead. All she can do is write them off as collateral. Because the only casualties that mean anything now are those of the

Praetorians in her formation. A percentage that's already well on its way into the double digits.

"Unacceptable," says a voice.

The man who's calling the shots. Huselid's taken up position in the cockpit. He's scarcely a few meters from where she's crouching with her bodyguards, just aft of the forward gunners, as far away from all the windows as possible. They've already argued about that. She felt she should be in another vehicle altogether—that putting them both together was too great a risk. He pointed out that if one of them got hit the other would be pretty much fucked anyway. And that they were too likely to lose contact with each other in the maelstrom now unfolding. Looking at what's going on outside, she's starting to think he's probably right.

"We've got no choice *but* to accept it," she says. "We're taking fire from every direction."

"I can see that!"

"Then you can also see there's no way out of this save forward."

"Which we're going to lose the ability to do unless we make good our losses."

"With reinforcements," she says.

"Of course."

"Can't go fishing for those without taking a risk."

He laughs. "What the hell would you call this?"

M ovement close at hand. Spencer sees figures climbing up what's left of the spaceship hull. They've clearly seen him and are making straight for him. All he's got is a sidearm.

They've got a lot more than that. They're Praetorian marines in full armor, their guns pointing right at him.

They're almost on him. Spencer's comlink buzzes. He activates the receiver. Uncoded transmission echoes in his head.

"Give us one good reason why we should let you live."

"I suck a mean dick," replies Spencer.

The suit jams a weapon right up against Spencer's visor. "How'd you survive the crash?"

"You're Autumn Rain," says someone else.

Spencer laughs. "If I was, think that I'd be sitting around waiting for you assholes?"

The suit pauses for a moment. The others gesture. It looks like they're arguing among themselves. Spencer can understand their dilemma. They don't know what's going on. Everything's gone wrong. They need information. They suspect everybody who might have it. Spencer decides not to wait for them to make up their minds.

"Look," he says, "I'm a razor from the ship's bridge crew. The Rain brought down the zone and then hosed down the fleet with that DE megacannon outside—"

The marine cuts him off. "If you're a razor, motherfucker, you're definitely Rain. Only way you could be alive."

"Tell him what happened to Petyr," says another voice.

"I can guess," says Spencer wearily.

"He's a fucking vegetable. We left him laying in his own shit about half a klick back."

"The Rain wiped him out."

"They wiped *all* the razors out."

"I wasn't in the primary node," says Spencer. "That's how come they missed me. I was secondary razor—"

"Doesn't mean shit to me, fuckface."

"Enough of this."

"Kill him and let's go."

"Where?" asks Spencer.

They glance at each other. They don't have a great answer for that. And at that moment more vibrations shake the ship beneath them. The Praetorians are looking at what's over Spencer's shoulder. It's clearly making an impression on them. He tries to take advantage of that fact.

"And by the way," he says, "the gang now approaching is going to face the same problem with you as you've got with me. If you start killing survivors from this crash out of hand, you'll just be answering their question for them."

"We should go," says someone.

"Start running from our own side?" asks someone else. "That's going to get old fast."

"How do we *know* it's our own fucking side?"

"Look at those things," says someone. "Those are fucking *earthshakers* coming up that valley."

"And a shitload of cycles on the flanks."

"If that shit ain't Praetorian, we're fucked anyway."

"Jesus Christ," says someone else. Spencer sees flaring reflected in his visor. He turns to face what's coming.

The Praetorian triad's going full throttle, punching out ahead of the main formation. The bulk of the combat's now behind them. Which isn't to say they've left it in the dust altogether. Sarmax starts unleashing his pulse rifle at long range on some wayward drones. The three men roar at ground level up and over a hill.

The crashed ship is just ahead of them, half protruding from the gash it tore through the cylinder's side. There's some kind of activity atop what's left of it. The Operative starts broadcasting on what's left of the Praetorian frequencies.

"This is for anyone who's still in the fight. What's coming up behind us is the Throne's own Hand. We're going to storm the Aerie and rip the Rain apart. Tune into the following frequency and stand by for new downloads. Anyone who doesn't can die right here."

"How do we know *you're* not the Rain?" says someone. Sarmax fires his pulse rifle, takes off that someone's head. The body topples.

"Any other questions?" yells the Operative as he hurtles in.

There aren't. He knows these marines could just open up on him en masse. But he also knows they know they're within range of the long-range guns atop the heavy vehicles. That they're just going to have to roll the dice. The three men roar past the ship's wreckage: the Operative to the left, Sarmax to the right, Lynx straight above. They keep on going, broadcasting that same message. The area of heaviest drop-ship deployment is just ahead of them.

But now the Operative feels something descend through his mind—something that suddenly drops in from above him in the jury-rigged zone, wraps him in its endless folds, commandeering his suit and his brain, propelling the latter out into the minds behind him and wiring over downloads. They've tuned into the frequency he stipulated. Ten Praetorian marines, one Praetorian officer, one Praetorian razor—

Not a Praetorian razor.

Something else. The Operative feels something *click* within his skull. He hears a voice. It's Haskell, along with the Hand's own codes.

"Carson," she says. "Leave this one to me. Keep going. Keep gathering the lost under our banner."

He acknowledges, and accelerates as Lynx and Sarmax keep pace.

. . .

Spencer watches the suits swoop past—watches as those suits are blotted out by a woman's face that expands in from what seems to be some suddenly activated zone. The face curves about him, envelops him in endless eyes. And now a woman's voice enfolds him within some endless hollow:

"Interesting. Wheels within wheels."

"Who are you?"

"*You're* InfoCom," replies the voice.

"Listen, I don't know why they put me here," says Spencer. He's transmitting as rapidly as he can. "I serve Montrose and she serves the Throne and—"

"That's why. The Throne covers all his bases. You were a counterweight against possible treachery within the Praetorian ranks. A conduit to sniff out possible treachery within InfoCom itself. None of which matters now. I need every razor I can get. These marines will stay with you until my vanguard reaches your position."

The voice cuts out. Spencer shakes his head as though to clear it. The marines are looking at him.

"Sir," says one.

"About fucking time," replies Spencer.

"What are your orders?"

Spencer looks around. There's combat on the far left. But the armored earthshakers roaring up the valley seem to have broken through whatever resistance they were encountering. They're making straight for the wreckage on which Spencer and the soldiers are standing. At the rate they're going, they'll be here in less than a minute.

"My orders," says Spencer, "are to do whatever the guys driving those things tell us."

• • •

Haskell disconnects as her mind swoops up to take in the overall situation. It's bleak. Seven of the eight Praetorian ships managed to unload their soldiers in drop ships along the cylinder. Two of those ships were the ones that docked at the New London spaceport. The troops within those were the ones that she started out with. The other five got deployed all along the cylinder, in drop-zone patterns calculated to pin down and destroy the two Rain triads that were lurking there. But the overthrow of the zone has thrown those Praetorians into chaos. They're scattered, their chains of command shattered and their ability to tell friend from foe smashed. With the inevitable result that they're fighting each other, letting the drones and robots of the Rain clean them up piecemeal.

But Haskell hasn't given up. As her shaker gains height, she searches for the zone through which the Rain's orchestrating all this. She's getting glimpses of fragments here and there: clouds of what may or may not be communications flying back and forth. But everything she can discern is well south of the cylinder's equator. She's starting to suspect that the Rain triads are nowhere near the onrushing Praetorian wedge, and that all these drones have been prepped to operate without a zone, deliberately dumbed-down and programmed to just get in there and do as much damage as possible to anything that looks like organized opposition. Haskell knows damn well that by now the force that bears the Hand's standard is the only thing that's even capable of looking the part.

Which is why he's ordered her to take such a chance with the Praetorian stragglers. Integrating their rewritten nodes into the zone she's bootstrapped requires that she make herself vulnerable to hacks from Rain units wearing false colors. And that she risk exposing her physical location. So she's working through proxies insofar as possible. The few razors under her command are now well out in front of the main formation, taking heavy casualties. But she's hoping that the influx of reinforcements they're bringing in is worth the trade-off.

"As long as we keep them on the formation's edges," he says.

"I've cleared them," she replies.

"I don't care."

And she can't blame him. Not when every calculation has fallen short. Not when the Rain has proven the equal of every contingency. Not when God only knows what the next twenty kilometers have in store.

They're hugging the ground, well into the area where the main drops went down. They're broadcasting the codes they've been given—the codes that override the Praetorians' blocked systems, tell them to rally to the Hand. And from the remnants of buildings in which they'd taken shelter, from basements where they'd destroyed the droids within, from armored drop-pods they'd never left: Praetorians are returning the signals.

Not that they need that much convincing. Most of their razors are dead. Their world's been torn apart. They can see the size of the force that's bearing down upon them. They're swarming in toward the Operative.

"Because now they've got a reason to live," he says.

"You mean a reason to die," says Lynx.

It'll have to do. Because there's plenty of fighting to be done. Most of which now seems to be occurring in the center: behind them, far to the right—distant flashes denoting fresh fighting at the spearhead of the main formation.

"Must be a whole mess of the fuckers still in front of us," says Lynx.

"Not to mention the Rain's hit teams," says Sarmax.

"Who are inside the Aerie working out on the Throne," says the Operative. "That fucking asteroid is where it's at. These fucks are just trying to delay us."

"And the Manilishi wants you to send *all* these marines back to the main force?" asks Sarmax.

"She gave me discretion."

"So use it."

"I intend to."

Spencer watches as the earthshakers sweep in toward him. Each is several meters long, covered with guns and turrets. One's churning past the ship on treads. Another's running on legs that are a blur. Another roars past on its jets. Another suddenly leaps; Spencer ducks involuntarily along with the soldiers standing next to him as it sails past them, hits the ground running on the other side of the ship. Another stops close to one of the fissures from which the ship is protruding. Its forward cockpit swivels, tilts upward like some misshapen head. Sensor-clumps that look disconcertingly like eyes regard Spencer.

"You the razor?" says a voice.

"I'm *a* razor," replies Spencer.

"Then get in."

A hatch opens just behind that forward cockpit. Spencer stares at it.

"Better do what he says," says one of the Praetorians standing next to Spencer.

"What about you guys?"

"Never mind those guys," says the voice. "Get down here."

Spencer clambers down from the ruined ship—slides along panels, using ripped cables to steady himself—and grabs onto the edges of holes torn in the ship's side. He soon reaches the level of the shaker, which edges carefully forward until he can step over to it. He reaches out, grabs the hatch, pulls himself inside. The hatch swings shut behind him.

"Hold on," says a voice—and in the next moment Spencer's thrown to the floor as the shaker reverses at speed. He rolls against the wall, activates magnetic clamps as the vehicle starts to race forward. The space he's in looks like the interior of a fuselage. A hatch leads rearward. Most of what's further forward is cockpit. Windows are slits amidst instruments. A man's working the controls. His hands are a blur as they play across the dials. He glances back at Spencer. His hair's white. His eyes are hollow.

"One-way ticket to Ragnarok," he says. "Sit back. Enjoy." Lights flash outside the window. Something crashes against the shaker's left side, bounces off with a dull clang. Spencer's audio feed howls as one of the turrets farther back discharges on full auto. A rumbling rolls through his bones as the earth-shaker's gears shift.

"Protected my Throne against the East for years," mutters the pilot. "Now we fight to save him from demons."

"You mean the Rain," says Spencer.

"I mean the false Christ," says the pilot. Lights streak past the window. Off to the right there's an explosion that lights up torn terrain and shattered mirrors. Several other shakers are visible in the near distance. Those that are flying are keeping low. One's on fire—still surging forward all the same. "God's own messenger leads us through the gates of hell tonight. She's Joan of Arc. She's beautiful. I saw her face, you know."

"So did I."

"So rejoice."

Spencer's not so sure about that. But the pilot keeps on talking, keeps going on and on about the hinge of the cosmos and the fate of the universe and the final judgment. Spencer suspects that he'd be carrying on just as eloquently even if he didn't have an audience. He realizes this man's mind is processing a situation he can't understand as best he can. But Spencer knows he wasn't picked up by this craft to get up to speed on its pilot's metaphysics. So he cuts in as tactfully as he can manage:

"So what'd she want you to do with me?"

"She?"

"Uh, Joan of Arc."

The man curses under his breath, swings his body leftward in his chair. The shaker swerves crazily sideways. Something big slides past the window: massive piles of debris that look to be all that's left of some maglev train that piled up along the valley floor. The shaker roars past, fires jets, gains height. Ground drops away. Tracer rounds curve overhead. The man laughs.

"She told me to take you to limbo's driver."

A grid appears on a screen above him. It shows the Praetorian formation—a wide blue arrowhead slicing forward. A light situated almost at that arrowhead's point—"That's where we started," says the pilot—has almost totally traced a line over to its right. And now that line's drifting out ahead of the right flank, into the ranks of the forward skirmishers.

"That's where we rendezvous," the pilot adds.

"With what?" asks Spencer.

Something flies past the window. It looks like a motorbike, only it's more fins than wheels. Spencer gets a quick glimpse of a figure hunched on its back—and then the vehicle loops backward, just missing the shaker, disappearing behind it.

"Jesus," says Spencer.

"No," says the pilot. "Just one of His servants." He gestures at a screen that shows a ramp opening in the rear of the shaker—the jet-cycle suddenly materializes out of the darkness beyond and cuts its engines, slamming down onto the floor within. The ramp starts lifting back into place.

"Get down there," says the pilot.

But Spencer's already on his way, ducking down, heading through the rearward hatch, moving through a narrow passageway, stepping beneath more hatches that lead to turrets in the ceiling, stepping past Praetorians firing the left- and right-facing heavy guns—and then down a ladder into the cramped cargo bay.

The marine bending over his jet-cycle straightens up, turns around. He's so close Spencer can recognize his face.

"I'm *baaaaaack*," says Linehan.

"Fuck's sake," says Spencer.

The pilot's face appears upon a screen: "Hurry it up and get out there!"

"Shut it, Gramps," says Linehan. "We're outta here."

Spencer looks toward the screen: "Thanks for the lift," he says.

"Go with God," replies the pilot.

"We'll let you know if we see Him."

Haskell's still looking for what she's missing. Because there must be something. There always is. The screens show that she's now lost a quarter of her forces. And that it's unlikely there are that many more wayward Praetorians still out there. She's managed to reassimilate a couple hundred. But most of the rest have been killed. By one another, by the drones, by the Rain ...

No. Probably not by the Rain. Same as it always is: they're using proxies to do their work, wearing down their enemy, waiting for their moment. Which could be here anytime. Because the Praetorian formation is approaching the cylinder's equator and Haskell still doesn't have the slightest idea of what's going on at their ultimate destination: the South Pole mountains and the Aerie that lies beyond them. Anything could be taking place within the corridors of that asteroid. The fighting might be over. The Praetorians within might have been crushed completely.

But somehow Haskell doubts it. The force she's got out here is a fraction of the force the Aerie contained. Meaning that whatever the Rain have deployed within the asteroid is probably even nastier than it is out here. And as intense as the resistance she's encountering, she feels that she's starting to get the better of it. Her attention's riveted on those distant southern mountains. Drawing ever closer for a second time. Only this time she won't be denied.

Take a listen to that," says the Operative.

"Christ almighty," says Lynx, as the feed gets patched in.

"They're getting taken apart," says Sarmax.

The frequency's being used by Eurasian soldiers in the opposite cylinder. Even on the border of valley and window, the sight of that cylinder remains obscured by the mirror hung outside. But the transmission's wafting in anyway, carrying the sounds of Russian and Chinese. Which is the only thing that's even halfway coherent about it. Because really it's just screaming. And cursing. And orders cut off by other orders that in turn get drowned out by somebody shrieking about traitors—becoming ever more hysterical until it all gives way to an earsplitting crunch. Followed by silence.

But only for a moment.

"I think we've heard enough," says Sarmax.

"They're getting creamed in there," says Lynx.

"They can't restore even the semblance of a zone," says the Operative. "They're broadcasting in the fucking *clear*."

"That's how bad we'd be getting it if the Hand didn't have Haskell," says Sarmax.

"And how bad the Throne might be getting it in the aster-oid."

Which is why they've been speeding up. Why they can feel the left flank pressing up behind them. They're accelerating to stay out ahead of it. Along with the marines the Operative's retained under his own command. Two squads in all. Bringing the total under him to almost forty men and women, blasting their way forward, following the Operative, doing whatever he tells them.

Which right now is *heads up.*

Not that anyone really needs the warning. The mirror on their left lights up with such brightness it's like a sun's thrusting through it. Translucence shimmers, starts to liquefy.

"Ah *shit!*" yells Lynx.

"The Helios!" screams Sarmax.

"Trying to bust through," mutters the Operative.

Not just trying. The Helios intensifies the fusillade, sears straight through the mirror, starts firing directly against the plastic window behind it. The one that connects this valley to the next one. That plastic's superhardened. It's ballooning inward all the same.

Spencer sees what's happening on the external cameras: shards of window dripping, disintegrating as microwaves start burning in above them, streaking across the cylinder, smashing against the far wall. What's left of the air starts exiting the cylinder posthaste. The fires that have been blazing overhead start to get snuffed out—even as raw microwaves lacerate the drifting debris and dead flesh that's strewn along the zero-G axis, smash into the valley adjacent to the one they're in—nailing a few Praetorians outriders—but striking well afield of the main force . . .

"It can't reach us," he yells. "It ain't got the angle!"

"You're not thinking!" screams Linehan.

But clearly someone is. Both men are hurled against the wall as the shaker veers sideways, drops downward. The cameras show that the onrushing Praetorian formation's no longer moving forward—disorder's hitting it as those suits and vehicles up in the air start plunging back toward the ground. Those already on the ground start finding a way beneath it. They're looking like animals trying to hit their burrows. They're looking pretty desperate. And suddenly Spencer gets it.

"Christ," he says, "rotation."

"Bingo," snarls Linehan.

Three men plunge toward the valley floor. The Praetorians they've brought back into the fold are swarming after them. No one's got the slightest intention of hanging around to see the Helios light them up with enough wattage to make their corpses glow for weeks. The Operative leads the way through one of the holes smashed in the valley surface by one of the fuel-air bombs from earlier. They streak into tunnels.

And find themselves in combat with still more drones. But the three men are used to close-quarter tunnel showdowns. Sarmax is in the center, his pulse-rifle on near-continuous spray, almost to the point of overheating. Lynx and the Operative have their miniguns blazing. Euro mining robots get in behind them, but are nailed by the marines bringing up the rear—and now the marines fan out on either side, start maneuvering through rooms and corridors, blasting down the walls, getting deeper, wondering all the while just how deep they need to go.

• • •

Haskell watches on the screens as her shaker makes a beeline for the surface. Calculations flash through her head. She'd figured the Helios would be too preoccupied bombarding the northern city-spaceports to bother trying to penetrate the cylinders. But maybe whoever's squeezing the trigger has gotten word of the size of the relief force that's rolling in toward the asteroid. Haskell doesn't know. All she's thinking about now is just the situation: the cylinder rotates every two minutes; each of its three windows is directly opposite a valley—which makes for about twenty seconds during which the Helios will have line of sight onto the valley along which the bulk of the Praetorian force is moving. And now more ground-to-air shots from guns on the ground are rising up toward the Praetorian spearhead. Haskell feels her stomach lurch toward her throat as the shaker climbs, takes evasive action, dodges those shots.

Most of them anyway.

There's a shriek of imploding metal as a wayward shell rips through one of the engines, rips through the tail-gunner's position. Metal shards fly past Haskell's head, eviscerating one of her bodyguards. Part of the wall starts tearing away: a widening crack exposing the bombed-out landscape beyond. Haskell sees other shakers diving past. She feels the minds of her craft's pilots as they wrestle desperately for control; she lends her own mind to theirs, working frantically to try to get the shaker stable. She's holding onto the torn edge of metal, looking out at the flickering lights outside while her remaining bodyguard holds onto her—now tightening his grip as the stricken shaker arcs off at an angle, other shakers scattering to avoid it as Haskell frantically searches for some way to jury-rig its systems. Terrain streaks past. Her life starts to flash past her.

• • •

Spencer and Linehan are hurled every which way, flung against the wall—the shaker's pitching about as the winds of escaping air smash against it. But it's no longer heading downward—no longer making for the relative shelter of the basements. Which makes exactly zero sense to Spencer.

"What the fuck's your problem?" he screams at the intercom.

"All of you shut up!" yells the pilot. Apparently the shaker's gunners are voicing similar concerns. Spencer turns his head as the ramp starts dropping. Nightmare scenery flashes past outside.

"We're outta here," says Linehan, pulling himself from the wall where he's been flung, trying to start up the cycle.

"You're insane!" yells Spencer.

"That'd be the *pilot*," screams Linehan as something hits the roof. "Probably thinks if he kills us all he'll wake up in heaven. Let's get out of—" But he stops short. And Spencer sees why: another shaker's suddenly churning into view, larger than the one they're in, and way too close—blotting out the view of the valley beyond it, smoke pouring from it, half its side staved in. It looks like it's fighting just to stay in the air—like it's about to ram Linehan and Spencer straight through to their own craft's cockpit.

"Make yourself useful!" screams the pilot.

Which basically amounts to leaning out of the landing bay and firing their suits' thrusters, shoving against the damaged earthshaker, aiding its pilots as they attempt to hold it steady. Turrets on the vehicle start opening. Hatches start peeling back. Suits start leaping out, vaulting across and into the landing bay. Spencer can't help but notice that those suits aren't marines. They're members of the Core. Three of them are pulling a fourth out of the damaged

craft, hauling that figure past Spencer. He gets a glimpse of
her face.

Haskell angrily shrugs off her escorts. She doesn't
need their help—they only draw attention to her.
She shoves past the Praetorians in the cargo bay,
moves through into the larger fuselage. She wishes it was bigger. But by the time she regained control of her shaker she was
well to the right of the Praetorian spearhead, leaving her with
no choice but to board the nearest vehicle. She feels the eyes of
its gunners upon her, a feeling she's starting to get used to.
Most of the Praetorian force has already managed to get below. Reports of fighting throughout the basements are already reaching her. She heads through into the cockpit. An
aging pilot glances at her.

And does a double-take.

"My lady," he says.

"The cellars," she snarls.

"At once," he replies—and even as she's strapping herself
in, she's shoved against those straps. Landscape spins past the
window. The shaker she was just on plunges past, bereft of
crew. Somewhere overhead she can see the window far above
starting to glow white-hot as it rotates into the Helios's field of
fire. Remnants of buildings whip by; the shaker starts leveling
out, starts touching down, clawing its way through the
ground, ripping aside landscape to reveal the infrastructure
beneath—and then dropping down amidst the roofless passages, getting in beneath the jagged shards of torn ceiling.

• • •

Roof closes in above the shaker. It's all Spencer and everybody around him can do to hold on. They've entered one of the maglev tunnels. They're following it deeper. Walls keep on rushing by, lit up by flashes from the vehicle's heavy guns.

"Let's close this fucking *ramp!*" yells Linehan.

"The turrets are fucked," snarls a Praetorian. "We're the rear guns!"

He's got a point. Besides Spencer and Linehan, there are four other Praetorians in the cargo bay. It makes for a tight fit. But the construction drones now blasting after them are taking everybody's mind off any problems involving etiquette. Everybody in the cargo bay starts firing. Spencer watches his shots streak down the tunnel, splinter one of the drones. But behind those drones he can see a larger shape overtaking them.

"Christ almighty," says Linehan.

"It's one of the trains," says Spencer.

"Impossible," yells someone. "Maglev's history!"

Apparently not everywhere. High-explosive rounds crash through the train but it keeps on coming. It's military grade. A slight bend in the track reveals six armored cars. The first of them fires torpedoes that streak in toward the shaker.

"Fuck!" yells Linehan.

But now static's pouring over their screens. Tiny sparks of lightning chase themselves down the walls. The guidance systems in the pursuing torpedoes go haywire: they slow, bend in toward the walls, slow still further. The train careens off the suddenly defunct maglev, starts folding up at high speeds, catches up with its own torpedoes. There's a particularly memorable explosion.

. . .

Haskell can see the light of the blast through the cockpit window. And that's pretty much all she's seeing. The Helios is shelling the valley floor up above, disrupting a lot of the environment down below. It's not point-blank—there's a lot of shielding. Meaning the damage is a long way from total. But even temporary damage could easily prove fatal amidst combat conditions. Shots from drones are flashing past the window and Haskell's got no way to do anything constructive. She's leaving that to the man she's partnered with; he's clamped onto the outside of the shaker with his bodyguards, firing at everything in sight. Haskell's trying to think a little more long term. Her mind calculates furiously—no way to stop the cylinder's rotation save firing the retros...and since the Euro zone's down, those would have to be engaged manually, from multiple points. And the Praetorians are already more than halfway through the cylinder. They've already crossed the equator. They've got no time for any diversions.

Meaning that the cylinder's going to keep on rotating. Meaning that the Helios is going to keep on turning each valley into a shooting gallery every two minutes. Meaning that the ones it's trying to target are just going to have to deal until they get beyond the windows and reach the southern mountains. Haskell screams at the pilot to take the upcoming off-ramp—but he's already doing it, his face as rapt as she's ever seen someone look, swerving the shaker expertly, engaging the afterburners, letting the vehicle blast out into the valley overhead.

Which is a total shambles. It looks like a giant flame-thrower just hit it. The fires burning along the center axis have gone out, along with every remaining light. The only illumination left is that of the stars visible between shards of mirror still hanging in place...but Haskell can nonetheless see shakers are emerging everywhere, along with cycles and suits. There are far more remaining than she'd hoped. She's acutely aware they've got about another ninety seconds before they're going to have to do their mole routine again. She's trying to get the formation back into order as they forge onward toward that southern pole.

The Operative's team is way ahead of the main force now. He's not even bothering to resurface— just keeps on blasting forward, streaking through the tangled infrastructure that houses the trains and conveyor belts that serviced the cylinder's southern half. He's getting ever lower. The gravity's slightly in excess of normal now. He wonders if there's some way to stop the rotation. He doubts it. Not at this point. Which is probably the way it's been planned.

But the Operative's leaving the nuances of strategy to others. All he cares about is carrying out his orders, which involve making as much speed as possible. And now he and Sarmax and Lynx and the marines behind them come out into a wider area. One where floors and walls and ceilings have been torn out, along with large chunks of the cylinder's hull. Stars wheel slowly past.

"Fuck's sake," says Lynx.

"Careful with the timing, Carson," mutters Sarmax.

"I know what I'm doing," says the Operative.

He'd better. The hole's the product of the initial bombardment laid down by the Praetorian ships. The trick is to stay clear of such openings when they're facing the Helios. And now the stars are giving way to the cylinder opposite theirs— and then that view vanishes as they all jet back into the tunnel. But not before the three men have had ample opportunity to take in whatever the Eurasians might be broadcasting.

Which turns out to be nothing.

"Not a thing?" The Operative sounds puzzled.

"Nothing I can pick up," says Lynx.

"Not without a fucking spirit medium," says Sarmax.

"They've been wiped off the map," says the Operative.

"At least in the cylinder," says Lynx.

"I doubt it's much better in their Aerie."

"We need to pick up the pace," says the Operative.

⊘ "Time to go," says one of the Praetorians.
Spencer looks at him. Looks at the ground that's sweeping by. Looks back at the Praetorian.

"Fine," he says—starts pushing the cycle into launch position—starts climbing on—

"Not so fast," says Linehan.

"What?"

"Get your ass off that thing," says Linehan.

"Are you fucking nuts?" Spencer's transmitting on the one-on-one. "The fucking *Hand's* aboard this thing. Not to mention his prize razor. These guys want us out of here pronto."

"Sure," says Linehan, "but you've got my seat."

"Jesus Christ," Spencer mutters. He slides backward, turns around so that he's facing rearward—slots the cycle's rear gun into position. Linehan climbs on. The two men strap themselves in. The Praetorians unlock the struts that hold the cycle in place.

"Ready," says Spencer.

"Believe it," says Linehan.

"Later," says a Praetorian, giving the cycle a hard shove. The cycle slides down the ramp—and then they're plummeting away from the shaker. Spencer watches the ground spin in toward them. He catches a glimpse of far-off mountains lit up by nearby explosions. And then there's an explosion that's even nearer, as the cycle's engines come to life and Spencer's flung backward, grabbing onto the straps out of sheer reflex as the vehicle's front lifts and it accelerates forward.

"This," says Linehan, "is where it gets interesting."

Haskell's head is really starting to spin. The constant play of light within her mind is less a function of the explosions flaring in the window and more a matter of the surrogate microzone she's midwifed and that she's just trying to prop up somehow, some way. Any way. It's that much more difficult now that the most powerful weapon remaining in the Earth-Moon system has managed to extend its reach inside this cylinder, forcing everybody to hit the basements at regular intervals. Haskell's compensating as best she can. She's sending out commands regarding the new criteria: draw in the flanks, blow down as many walls as possible, clear out space insofar as can be achieved, choose warehouses over corridors, galleries over tunnels, large spaces over small... and above all, keep the comlinks open—keep the transmissions coming so that everyone's connected to some piece of the formation, and all the pieces ultimately link back to her. No one gets cut off. No one gets left alone.

Save for those who have to be.

The Operative's on a mission to get his team to that rock ASAP. He's guessing he's not the only one who's received orders to get out ahead of the main formation, which can only move as fast as its heaviest vehicles. Grids of the approaching mountains crystallize within his head. He beams them into the skulls of his colleagues, focuses on the conduits that connect mountains to the Aerie. There are fifteen in all. Nine are intended for personnel. And some of those that aren't look a little narrow...

"No way are we fitting through one of those," snarls Lynx.

"Wanna bet?" says the Operative.

"Ain't what you think we can do, Lynx," says Sarmax. "It's what the Rain think that counts."

And the Operative knows all too well that they might run into them at any moment. Maybe the Manilishi is counting on him to do just that, to weaken the Rain a bit before he gets taken out. But somehow he doubts it. He's guessing they're deep in the Aerie, busy with the Throne.

"They're counting on their proxy forces in the cylinder to hold us off," says the Operative.

"Not to mention blowing every bridge to that rock and then some," says Sarmax.

"Now why do you have to go and say a thing like that?" mutters the Operative.

Mountains loom in the distance. Stars gleam between blackened valleys. They're moving out ahead of the main formation, well in front of the right flank, which seems to have drawn level with the center as it overhauls it. Linehan's singing to himself. He seems to be having a blast.

Spencer isn't.

"Will you shut the fuck up," he says.

But Linehan just laughs. "We're both going to shut up forever in a few more minutes," he says.

"The sooner the better," grumbles Spencer.

"Says the guy who's already missed all the fucking fun. You should have seen this place when it all got going, man. We got fucking fried." Shots streak past from somewhere far above them. Linehan doesn't alter course. "Ain't *never* been part of any outfit that got fucked so hard. I think I'm the only one from my dropship left."

"How'd you make it through?"

"You know how, man. By being a chickenshit. We were right on top of one of those Rain triads. We had it pinned down every which way. But when the zone went, I didn't wait. Got the fuck out of there while drones carved everybody up; ended up in that valley while it went from green to black. Sat in a park while the world went to shit: put my legs up on a god-damn bench and watched New London burn like a fucking ro-man candle. Figured that'd be it. It nearly was. Until the Hand showed up with his bitch-queen razor."

"And bailed you out."

"If that's what you'd call this."

Spencer nods. The Manilishi's ordered him to head south as quickly as possible, outpacing the main force. The center vehicles that are aboveground are visible a little farther back, down near the floor of the valley. They've got about forty seconds before the Helios gets the angle on them again.

"Check that out!" yells Linehan.

Spencer turns, sees it: several klicks farther south of them, though not as far on the right flank as they are—flames of thrusters darting in and out of valley forest.

"More of our cycles," he says.

"More meat," says Linehan. "The Throne's *fucked*. The Rain turned his trap inside out. They're butt-fucking him in that as-teroid. We get close enough, we might even hear the squeals."

"You sound like you're getting turned on."

"Only thing that turns me on is the idea of getting out of this fucking shooting gallery."

"We're almost at the rock."

"Hate to break it to you, but we'll never make it."

"You don't think—shit!" Suddenly Linehan turns the bike so sharply that Spencer's almost thrown off, despite the magnetic clamps. It's like the whole of the approaching mountains have come alive with lights. Shots start searing past them. Explosions blast nearby bikes to hell. Debris flies everywhere. Linehan accelerates, dives groundward.

"Guess that answers that question," he snarls.

It looks like the Euro guns situated throughout the southern mountains are still operational. Apparently they'd been holding back. But now they're opening up on the onrushing Praetorians and the foremost units are getting hammered. Everybody's forced to hit the deck, get back into those cellars. Haskell watches as the pilot works the controls and the shaker descends below the curtain of shots, drops down into a riverbed that's been stripped of its river by the vacuum—and from there into subterranean waterways now bereft of any liquid. Other shakers roar in after her: other cycles, other suits. Basement combat starts up again, even as microwaves and lasers surge through the spaces overhead, unleashing fury that's becoming almost reassuring to Haskell. Almost familiar. And why not? The universe has shrunk to nothing save the Europa Platform and the thing that's orbiting it, controlling it, pinning down all those who exist within it. The Helios has attained the status of some kind of inscrutable god.

But its reign is coming to an end. Because once the force gets past the windows and in amidst the mountains it'll just have to gnash its teeth in the vacuum. Haskell's concentrating on those mountains now. They're frozen in her mind's eye even as tunnel walls flash by, even as some kind of awareness builds within her. She feels herself giving way before it.

• • •

Taking corners and roaring past turns and it's all the Operative can do to keep on breaking through. He's changed up the formation a little. He's got the marines out in front of him now. The odds keep on getting steeper: walls that suddenly collapse inward, floors that blast themselves into the ceiling, mines and drones and droids that keep on springing in from out of nowhere . . .

"The terrain's narrowing," says Sarmax.

"I realize that," says the Operative.

But he still hasn't figured out how to handle the implications. They've left the valley behind. The exterior wall of the cylinder is curving in toward the southern pole—letting the defense stack itself up pretty thick, depriving the Operative of room to maneuver. Which is the one thing he can't afford to lose.

"We need more space," says Sarmax.

"The surface," says the Operative.

He signals to the marines around him, and swerves on his jets while everybody follows. They blast through metal corridors and into stone-lined tunnels. Gravity slowly subsides as they catch glimpses of lights flaring up ahead. They accelerate, emerge amidst the foothills.

Can't turn around!" screams Linehan.

Spencer gets the feeling he would if he could.

But any craft or suit that deviates too far from the attack vectors is going to stray into the field of fire of the ones behind it. What's left of the flanks are struggling forward, desperately trying to reach the sloping mountains. Linehan keeps whipping the bike from side to side. Spencer watches valley and window slide past his visor. He catches quick glimpses of the wraparound mountains up ahead, of vehicles flying everywhere behind him. He watches as the guns of the shakers in the center open up against the artillery rigged into the rocks. He wonders how this could get any worse.

They're on the verge of off-world mountains, and Haskell's no longer fooled. It's as though every cell in her is suddenly flaring into life. Her conscious mind's swallowed in the vortex of the unknown—of *her* unknown—and she's not even trying to keep pace. She feels her head tilting back in her seat, feels the pilot glance at her nervously, feels him recede from her along with everything else. She sees the lives of all those around her on some grid from which infinite axes sprout. Space-time's just one piece of something larger: something that's now blossoming through her, shooting her through with rapture, seizing her with ecstasy beyond any she's ever known—life lived between the two singularities of birth and re-birth and skirting all the little deaths in between. Her mind catapults out on the zone, leaps in toward those mountains.

Shots hurtle all around the Operative. Plasma hurtles overhead. Debris is going everywhere. He's seeking whatever cover he can find. Those around him are doing the same. They're right at ground level, smashing through groves of stubby trees, whipping past rocks. Towering overhead are endless mountains, wrapping above them and onto the ceiling, converging upon the South Pole.

"The place of reckoning," says Sarmax.

"Or near enough," replies the Operative—and starts screaming at those behind him to keep up the pace. They hold course, streak in over the foothills.

"Which conduit are we making for?" yells Sarmax.

"We feint *there*," yells the Operative. "We hit *here*."

"And our marines?" asks Lynx.

"Let's play that one by ear," says Sarmax.

"Exactly," says the Operative.

Meaning that maybe those marines will end up just piling in toward that diversion while the three who pull their strings swing the other way at the decisive moment. It's all going to depend on how the next few minutes unfold.

Or the next few seconds.

Because suddenly the Manilishi's shoving herself into the Operative's head, pushing him beyond his skull, making him one with the mountains. The Euro guns that became Praetorian that became the Rain's are blasting past him; the whole cylinder's turning around him as his mind dives deep into the rock, slicing through the wreckage of the Euro zone. There's no zone left in there now.

Only there is. Although he's not even sure it *is* a zone. It's more like the intimation of one. He's got no idea how to hack it. Not even with *her* doing the hacking. He's not even sure that matters.

Linehan's screaming at him but Spencer no longer hears. Guns keep on firing but he no longer sees them. He's bound up in something far stronger than himself. He's the tracks over which the whole train's rolling. His mind's ablaze with the insight of another.

Because Haskell finally gets it—finally sees the pattern she's been searching for. The one that was right under her nose: she triangulates through the eyes of all her razors, all along the battle line, zeroing in on the one thing that only she can. She's looking at the most customized zone in existence. Zone that's probably not even capable of hacking anything outside itself. Zone that's not designed to. It's just a tactical battle mesh. One that's supposed to be invisible—and it has been up until now. But now she sees that the Rain are going to do their utmost to prevent her from crossing to the asteroid. At least one of their triads is preparing to make a stand. Has it figured out a way to hold off the whole Praetorian force? Or is it just going to try to bloody the formation's nose, before falling back into the asteroid, blowing the conduits as it goes? Now she's got the chance to draw some blood herself. She's sending out the orders almost before she's thought of them.

H ow many?" yells Sarmax.
"Manilishi thinks a full triad," replies the Operative.

"Same as us," says Lynx.

Sarmax laughs. "They learned from the best."

The Operative orders the marines forward. They surge in on their thrusters, scrambling up cliff faces and flitting over peaks. Ten seconds, and they're out of sight. They swarm forward, steadily closing in on where the Manilishi believes the Rain to be.

"Nothing like a little cannon fodder," says Lynx.

"What the fuck would you call *us*?" asks Sarmax.

He gestures on the collective heads-up at the main force behind them, now moving out of the valley at maximum speed. The Operative can appreciate that those who direct it are anxiously watching the results of the combat that's about to take place. But what he can't understand is why the Rain's even making a stand here in the first place.

Sarmax's voice is in his ear: "The party in the asteroid's *over.*"

"Wrong," replies the Operative. "It's just begun."

• • •

They've almost left the land of valley and window behind. The mountains fill the screens. Spencer and Linehan are right near the edge of the window. They're not about to get any nearer to it. But even as Linehan eases the bike away from the window, something else becomes visible—out in space amidst the flashes of light, reflected off the edge of a wayward shard of mirror . . .

"Shit," says Linehan.

"Just keep *driving*," says Spencer.

It's just a fraction of the whole thing. It's all they can see. It's all they really want to. It's the asteroid itself: sun-scorched rock to put the faux mountains in the cylinder to shame. What's now known as the Aerie was harnessed by the Euro Magnates, towed across the vacuum, tunneled through, and studded with engines. And at least a few of those motors must be firing right now, because judging from the view in the mirror, the whole rock is swinging steadily in toward the cylinder.

"That's a trick of the eye," says Linehan.

"I don't think so," replies Spencer.

What the fuck was that?" yells Sarmax.

"They're blowing the fucking conduits!" screams Lynx.

"Let's take them," says the Operative—and Lynx moves left while Sarmax goes right. The Operative fires his thrusters, steams up the center, steering toward the peaks in which the Rain lurks. He feels the Manilishi's presence descending in over him. He hears explosions as the Rain triad opens up on the marines. Why the Rain are blowing the conduits when they've still got a presence in the cylinder is beyond him. But he no longer cares. His team's going to turn this triad into mincemeat. After which they'll leap to the Aerie and seize a bridgehead there. The Hand's engineers will be able to get another bridge going. Death or glory—and it's all going down in the next few seconds.

Until another message changes everything.

⊘ G et us the fuck out of here!" screams Spencer. But Linehan needs no urging. He swings the bike leftward, starts roaring away from what's swelling in those mirror-shards like some impossible battering ram. And yet all that's visible is just a tiny portion of what must be about to hit the southern mountains.

"Inform the Hand!" yells Linehan.

"Already did," replies Spencer.

⊕ R everse thrust," screams the Operative. Same thing Haskell's screaming at him. He's pushing off the rock even as he feels that rock hum beneath him. He blasts backward, watches Lynx and Sarmax do the same. The mountains seem to be swaying like leaves in a breeze. The whole landscape's undulating, and then ballooning outward in an awful slow motion. The peaks that conceal the Rain fold in like closing jaws. This whole end of the cylinder is imploding, collapsing in upon itself. The valleys that extend away from it are corrugating like so much cheap metal. Something's shoving its way through the mountain—ripping slopes asunder as it bludgeons through. Something impossibly huge—God's own wrecking ball—pieces of cylinder and mountain slicing into it, sliding off it. Its edges aren't even visible. Debris's flying in from all sides. The walls of the Platform are coming apart and show no sign of stopping.

"Only one way to do this," says Sarmax.

"You got that right," says the Operative.

They reverse direction once more, hurtle toward the on-rushing wall.

The orders flash out from Manilishi: take that fuck-ing rock. The whole of the Praetorian wedge steams straight in even as the ground starts to buckle beneath it. The outlying riders hit their jets, race in through what's starting to look like a full-scale asteroid field.

"No choice," screams Spencer.

None at all. He's got no idea why someone's fired what-ever motors are left on the asteroid, set it to swing against the cylinder to which it's linked. And right now it doesn't matter. They can't swerve any farther to the left lest they risk collision with the nearest bikes. They can't turn around—the only bike to do that got taken out with a long shot from an earthshaker. Two more bikes were just smashed into oblivion by flying de-bris. Linehan's taking the vehicle through evasive maneuvers that owe more to guesswork than to planning. He's going way too fast for much else. Spencer can see mountain flapping in toward them like so much paper. Pushing in behind that mountain is what looks like the surface of some planet: craters and caves and gullies decked out with shorn-off py-lons and ripped-up wire. It seems to Spencer that this world's the one he's been looking for the whole time. He's been yanked all over the Earth-Moon system like a puppet on a chain—and yet all of it was really leading up to the thing that was built to be the sanctuary of the Euro Magnates. He watches a wire snap from a pylon, curve in like a monstrous whip toward them as Linehan steers past it, rockets into the nearest of the caves.

• • •

It's rushing in toward them, a fissure in the rock, crisscrossed by platforms and sprouting the remains of torn-up bridges. The Operative dodges past those bridges, cuts between the platforms, blasts through to find a shaft that's been cut into the bottom of the canyon. Sarmax and Lynx swing in behind him. Walls enclose them on all sides. Debris piles in to fill the opening behind them.

"Made it," says Sarmax.

"Made *what?*" says Lynx.

They race deeper into the Aerie. The walls buckle around them, but don't break. The rock shifts about them. The shaft becomes a corridor, the corridor a labyrinth. Sarmax activates the one-on-one.

"Carson, do we have a plan?"

"End this fucking war."

"Got it."

"The Throne had his best shock troops in here, right?" asks Sarmax.

"Half an hour ago, Leo. God only knows what's left."

"And the Rain?"

"They started out with three triads."

"One of which is now a mountain sandwich."

"Let's hope they've suffered more casualties than that."

"Wonder how many drones they've got in here," says Sarmax.

Way too many, the Operative's thinking as they roar onward. The topography of the Aerie clicks into view within his head; he beams it over to Lynx and Sarmax. Several klicks in diameter, the asteroid is a honeycomb of passages and chambers. Most of it's given over to industry, mining, and R&D, though the private quarters of the Euro Magnates also lie within.

"Fuck," says Sarmax, "what a maze."

The Operative isn't about to disagree. They come through

into a vast gallery—one that must have backup generators nearby, because lights are flickering here and there. Whatever original function the place had is no longer clear, thanks to the firefight that's taken place within it. Dead Praetorians and shattered equipment are everywhere. The three men soar past them. But even as they do . . .

"Hey," says Sarmax. "That's—"

"Look at those bodies," hisses Lynx.

"I see it," replies the Operative.

There's no way she could miss it—it's all coming in straight toward her. Wreckage smashes through vehicles, crushing them like tin cans and turning suited figures into bloody pancakes. Her pilot's hurling his body this way and that, taking the shaker through turns it wasn't designed for, firing jets and motors, even pushing claws off a smaller chunk of metal that's coming in at an oblique angle—and bouncing off with a resounding *clang* that feels like it's shaken her brain loose inside her skull. Scorched earth's behind her and shattered stone's in front. The forward units are either inside that rock or in hell. The main force is heading in to join them. She gets glimpses of the other shakers coming in behind her. Her pilot moves their ship into the spearhead of the formation. The main rock's coming in like a wall. She estimates they've got less than thirty seconds till they reach it.

"One choice, m'lady," says the pilot.

"I realize that," she snarls.

"No point in firing piecemeal," says the Hand.

"I'm syncing the whole formation," she replies. "Stand by."

He acknowledges as the calculations flash through her head.

• • •

Thruster-flames play upon the walls. Their own shadows chase them through the tunnels. Garbled transmissions reach their ears from somewhere deeper within the catacombs.

"Can't hear a word they're saying," says Linehan.

"That's because you're not listening," mutters Spencer.

Or just not processing them properly. Because Linehan's no razor. There's no zone in here to speak of anyway, save the fraction that now resides within Spencer's skull. But that's all he needs to figure out what these transmissions contain. Which isn't much.

"Well?" demands Linehan.

"Death trap."

"What?"

"That's it."

"What do you mean, that's it?"

"I mean that's the message."

"It says nothing else?"

"You think it fucking needs to?"

Everyone in here got *fucked*," says Lynx.

"Stay away from the bodies," snarls the Operative.

"We don't have time for this," says Sarmax. "We need to keep moving."

"What we need is more data," says the Operative. "These Praetorians must have taken out *some* of them. Scan the walls. Scan this place. Has to be some debris somewhere."

"Nanotech," says Lynx. *"Fuck."*

"Not *quite* that small," says Sarmax. "More like micro—"

"Close enough," says the Operative. "The Throne slung

the asteroid into the cylinder to make sure the Rain couldn't blow the conduits. To keep alive the hope that the Hand could get across and bail him out of this mess."

"Hey," says Lynx. "We've got heat signatures—"

"Yeah," says the Operative, "I'm picking it up too."

"Coming this way," says Lynx. "Fast."

Spencer's the first to notice. The shadows cast by the flames of the bike's thrusters are starting to look a little strange. They're flickering in ways they shouldn't. They're . . .

"Linehan," screams Spencer, "step on it!"

Linehan hits the gas. "What the hell's going on?"

"I said fucking step on it!" Linehan floors it; Spencer grabs onto his seat, engages the rear gun, opens up on what's starting to overtake them. He can't tell if he's hitting anything—or if there's even anything to hit. But the flames are shifting in ways that flames don't shift. It's almost as though he's viewing them through layers of static. He stares. He magnifies the view.

And then he gets it.

Let's get out of here," says Sarmax.

"Out as in exit?" asks Lynx.

"Don't be a fucking retard," snaps the Operative. "*Out* as in the place on this rock we need to get to." He gestures at the corpses drifting all around. "Look, these fucks died by surprise. Before we start running, let's rig one of our own—"

But Sarmax and Lynx are already scrambling to take up positions.

• • •

It's unmistakable now, right on their heels, swarming in toward them. Spencer's spraying shots at the onrushing cloud. He's failing to get discernible results.

"Any idea where the fuck we're going?" screams Linehan.

"Just make it fucking faster!" yells Spencer.

Linehan's clearly trying, but they've got neither maps nor plans. All they've got is speed. And that's no longer at a premium. The tunnel walls rip past. Ahead of them are lights, getting brighter. And the intimations of some larger space...

The three men start firing almost before the Praetorian cycle flashes past them. Sarmax's pulse-rifle dispenses plasma on full auto. The Operative ignites the fuel that's floating all across the tunnel mouth. Lynx sprays flechettes like they're going out of style. Nozzles atop their helmets unleash flame. They've got their targets in a crossfire. They keep on firing, making everything as hot as possible, shooting hi-ex up that tunnel for good measure. The tunnel mouth is glowing as though it's in the throes of supernova. The bike is turning, braking behind them as the two men riding it leap off.

"You fuckers stay where you are!" shouts the Operative.

Which is when the room starts shaking like it's coming apart.

The Praetorians' only hope for survival lies in motion—and the massive shape-charges they're now slinging into the disintegrating side of an asteroid at point-blank range. Explosions flare all along the line—and the shakers, suits, and cycles are roaring in behind them, making for the places where Haskell estimates they'll be able to break through. But all those estimations are just guesses— just long lines of probabilities whipping through her head— and maybe she's staying on the right side of those odds because she's still breathing. Space gets cut off on all sides by shattered mountain and blasted rock; Haskell's ship starts maneuvering through tunnels. Cycles whip in ahead of her to ensure that the Hand's ship isn't the one on point. Rock rips past on all sides. Maps click on overlays in her head. Tunnel walls streak past as she dives in among those grids.

The room's rocking like it's in the throes of an earthquake. The Operative pours on the flame, keeping the two who rode that bike in the crosshairs of his rear-screens while he keeps on shooting. Suddenly his enhanced vision is obscured by what looks like some kind of whirlwind: it rips in toward him, patters like rain against his suit.

"Carson!" yells Sarmax.

"Keep firing," replies the Operative, and turns his own flame on his suit. For a moment he's a human torch. He watches the temperature readings climb, compounds their effect by clamping his hand against his chest and extruding acid from the fingers of his suit-glove. He burns off a large chunk of his suit's outermost skin, along with all the material that's managed to cluster on him—and then switches off his burners. Deprived of oxygen, the flame cuts out. The Operative smears acid neutralizers across his suit's front torso.

At the same time, Sarmax and Lynx stop firing, because there's nothing left to fire at. The target area's a total shambles. The tunnel mouth looks a lot wider. Dust drifts through the zero-G. But there's not much of it. And that's all it's doing: drifting.

"Okaaaay," says the Operative as he takes stock. This room's clear. And the seismic readings from the direction of the main force have dropped away to nothing. Suddenly it's all too quiet. Sarmax covers the newcomers while Lynx covers the exits. The Operative does the talking.

"Praetorian cycle serial number X seven three five G. Which must make you . . . Spencer and Linehan. Now how about you transmit the codes and prove it."

He'd already seen Spencer—earlier, back on that ship that hit the cylinder. But the Operative isn't about to give anyone the benefit of any doubt. Not now. Not in here.

"How the fuck do we know—"

"Linehan," says the Operative. "How about you shut your mouth?"

"Or I can do it for you," says Sarmax.

Spencer transmitted his codes almost as soon as the Operative started speaking. Now Linehan follows suit. Both sets of codes check out against the cypher the Manilishi's given the Operative. He syncs Spencer and Linehan with his tactical mesh. Locks them in.

And grins.

"Okay, now listen up. The guy with the fuck-sized gun is Sarmax. The guy with one hand's Lynx. I'm Carson, one of the Throne's bodyguards. The main force is probably about a half a click behind us. We're the advance team. Next stop's the Throne's sanctuary."

"Yeah?" asks Linehan. "How the hell do you propose we get past all the nanoshit?"

"Not to mention the Rain hit teams," says Spencer.

"By redefining the word *stealth*," replies the Operative.

"And you'll never guess who's taking point," adds Sarmax.

• • •

I don't like this one little bit," says Linehan.

"How the fuck do you think I feel?" asks Spencer.

"I wasn't asking."

It's a minute later. They're moving through a narrow crawlspace. They're making as much speed as they can muster without turning on their thrusters. Neither are using active sensors save for an occasional light.

"That fuck of a bodyguard is going to hang us out to *dry*," says Linehan.

"Earth to Linehan: he already did."

The two men are attached to each other by a hyperfine tether, specially designed to avoid snagging and containing a wire that serves as their comlink. Another such tether's attached only to Spencer; it trails behind him, disappears in his wake. Meaning that in theory Carson's no more than fifty meters behind them.

"Gotta hand it to the guy," says Linehan, "he sure knows something about how to play a weak hand."

Spencer laughs. "The problem for the Praetorians is that the better they get at that—"

"The shittier their cards keep getting? I noticed."

They're about seventy meters behind the men on point. The tether is slightly longer than those men were told. It allows the Operative and Sarmax to see the perspective of the ones on point without having to maintain line-of-sight or risk a broadcast. To say nothing of the peace of mind that comes from having somebody else go first . . .

"The Rain have really been pushing the tech envelope," mutters Sarmax.

"They've got a real nasty talent for surprise."

"Speaking of, what's this about you being a bodyguard?"

"Funny, Lynx was just asking me the same question."

"And did you answer him?"

"If *fuck off* is an answer, then yeah, I did."

Lynx is about thirty meters farther back, connected to the Operative via yet another tether, bringing up the rear. He's been instructed to limit all further transmissions to mission-critical developments.

"But I'm not him," says Sarmax.

"No," replies the Operative, "thank fuck for that. I've been one since the beginning of the year."

"So, newly promoted."

"Yeah. I think the Throne was doing a reshuffling in the wake of Zurich. Rethinking who he could trust."

"That's a good one," snorts Sarmax.

"Hey, he's got to trust *somebody*."

"And your handler's the Hand himself?"

"Huselid. Yeah. He's changed it up a little these last few months. He's got about five operatives who never leave the Throne's side and about ten of us in the field riding herd on all the other agents."

"A one-to-two ratio? That's—"

"Risky? That's the point. Best defense's a good offense."

"And it's backfired on him big time."

"Not if I can help it." As the Operative transmits those words, he starts picking up a new vibration coming through the rock. He keys Lynx immediately.

"Lynx."

"Yeah?"

"You got that?"

"Yeah." Lynx sends over the seismic data. The Operative combines, triangulates.

"What's up?" says Sarmax.

"What's up is that the shit's saying hi to the fan."

• • •

It's all Haskell can do to keep up with it. She's got the Praetorian force spread out along about ten interlocking routes, heading in toward the heart of the Aerie. She's got hostiles coming through the walls. She's chewing through them on overdrive...

"No wonder we got fucked," says Huselid.

He's back inside the shaker now, sitting right behind her and the pilot, watching things spray against the windshield. Things that she's just nailed. Smartdust's reliance on a zone makes it pretty easy for a razor to fuck with. Which is part of why it never really caught on for combat operations. But a situation where the defenders suddenly lost their zone is a different story. Particularly if those defenders got caught by surprise, hit from every side in a labyrinth that had suddenly become a killing ground... but Haskell's doing her utmost to prevent a repeat performance. Her mind's dancing among her vehicles and razors, leaping down passages and tunnels she's got no line of sight into, out to the flanks where the small fry's making some headway. And all the while she's taking stock.

And realizing something.

"They're not really trying to stop us," she says.

"They're drawing us deeper," Huselid replies.

"What are your orders?" says the pilot.

"Hold course for the center," says Haskell, as Huselid nods.

More combat," says Linehan.

"Way behind us," says Spencer.

"Somebody's throwing some shit around back there."

It's hard to miss. The walls of the room through which they're moving are trembling again. The pipes that jut out here and there are like reeds in a storm. Linehan shines his light around, starts down the next corridor that Carson's prescribed.

"Way too quiet in our neck of the woods," Spencer mutters.

"Enjoy it while it lasts," Linehan replies.

⊕ "Thanks for the news flash," says the Operative.

"Christ almighty," says Sarmax, "is he still on the line?"

"Spencer? I just cut him off. He's not saying anything we don't already know."

"Those two are just anxious 'cause they've figured out they're bait."

"Probably."

"We could stumble upon the Rain anytime."

"Can't wait."

◖ They're really getting into the swing of things, forging ever deeper toward the heart of this whole damn mess. Microtacticals plow the way before them, taking out smartdust along with mining droids and Euro milbots. Shit's flying everywhere. Walls keep folding up, taking out Praetorians wholesale. But that's the price they're paying to keep moving. And now they're coming out onto the greenhouse levels, though Haskell can see that it's all just burnt-out florae and twisted trunks now. There's not a single living plant left. What happened before they showed up saw to that.

But the real action's on the screens within Haskell's mind. The formation's well into the inner reaches of the asteroid now. The core's not that far off.

"It's a trap," she says.

"Of course it is," says Huselid.

"And yet we're still driving on it?"

"Not for much longer."

"Could you be more specific?"

"Absolutely."

They're starting to feel a little gravity under their feet. They pull open a trapdoor; Linehan's light plays along the corridor beneath. It's ornately furnished. They've clearly come through into some of the living quarters. Carpeting's burnt here and there. Mahogany panels along the walls are largely intact. Linehan lowers himself through, Spencer follows. They move down the corridor, reach oak doors that have been blasted off their hinges. They move through into the room beyond.

"Shit," says Linehan.

They've found some of the Magnates," says the Operative.

"In what condition?" asks Sarmax.

"Minced," replies the Operative.

"But no Throne," says Lynx.

"I thought I told you to shut up," says the Operative.

"I think Leo needs to hear this."

"Hear what?"

"How you're taking us way off the beaten path."

"Yeah," says Sarmax, "was wondering about that— *Hello.*"

He and the Operative have come into the rooms where Spencer and Linehan just were. The tether trails out the new corridor down which the men on point have gone. Gore is everywhere. Two of the Magnates and their families had their quarters in these suites. They were held in custody by the Throne's soldiers. Until the Rain's machinery butchered them.

"Not a pretty sight," says Sarmax.

"Never is when hostages outlive their usefulness."

Which is when Lynx enters the room. And almost gets shot by the Operative and Sarmax. Almost shoots them himself. A general standoff ensues.

"Easy with the guns," says Lynx.

"Why the *fuck* are you leaving your post?"

"You know why," snarls Lynx. "You're taking us away from the main force. They're cutting deeper. Driving on the core."

"So?"

"So I thought you said we were the advance guard!"

"Let me be more specific," says the Operative.

About two hundred meters out from the core of the asteroid, a switch-up's in motion. The left wing of the Praetorian formation slows while the right accelerates, wheels left as it unleashes a barrage of torpedoes into the tunnels that lead to the Aerie's center . . .

"Aren't you worried that'll be too much?" says the pilot.

"We know what we're doing," says Haskell.

At least, the man beside her claims to. Huselid's clearly gambling that the rock's integrity will hold despite the tactical nukes about to start blasting away within its heart. Haskell starts plotting the route away from the asteroid's axis as the pilot starts taking the shaker through a new set of tunnels. Just as shockwaves start tearing through them . . .

• • •

"Jesus," says Linehan.

"Is right," mutters Spencer.

Someone's pulling out all the stops. The walls are shaking like they're going to fold up at any moment.

"That's off to our right," says Linehan.

"Is that the main force?"

"It's time you started talking sense," says Sarmax. "Look," says the Operative. "It's like this." He beams grids into the minds of both men. The view of the Helios covering the north end of the Platform collapses in upon the south end of the cylinder they've come from, closes on the asteroid they're in: a rock that's still rotating around an axis that extends through a core that must have just been completely hollowed out by the blasts. Off to one side—set in a southern-facing overhang along the asteroid's equator—is the Window, the conduit via which heavy mining equipment is moved into the asteroid. Farther south along the asteroid's opposite side is a door that bulges slightly outward.

"The Hangars," says Lynx.

"Which is where the Throne originally landed," says Sarmax.

"Probably," says the Operative. "But to the extent that anyone's still holding out there it's only because the Rain have had bigger fish to fry."

"But that's where the spaceships are—"

"Spaceships aren't what they used to be," says Lynx.

"Neither are presidents," says the Operative. "If the Throne stuck to the game plan, then he set up his HQ at the core, but he didn't stay there when the combat hit. He was supposed to split for the Window as soon as the fur started flying."

"Do the Rain know that?" asks Lynx.

"I've no idea. But what really matters is what they thought *we* thought. And when the main body of the Hand's relief force reached this rock, they immediately drove on the core. So that's where the Rain would automatically figure we still thought the Throne was. They were trying to egg on the Hand, draw the relief force in, and annihilate them accordingly."

"So the Rain haven't found the Throne yet?"

"Let's hope not," says the Operative.

"But now the Hand's steaming up behind us," says Lynx.

"And we're way closer to the Window than the Rain know," mutters Sarmax.

"Too right," says the Operative. "Now how about we move."

They're moving at high speed now, charging in toward the Window. Seismic readings keep rippling in from the way they've come . . .

"Those aren't just *our* bombs," she says.

"They probably rigged the core with their own munitions," says Huselid.

She nods. The Throne's defenses in the Aerie were clearly overwhelmed early. Haskell can only hope that they kept the Rain as busy as possible while she and the Hand were fighting their way across the cylinder. Huselid's indicated that the only two places that have a hope of still holding out are the Window and the Hangar. And the relief force just tipped its hand as to which one of those it deems as more important. Haskell's working feverishly to keep her forces coordinated in the wake of the formation's switch-up. Some of the outlying units have been cut off—swarmed by dust and drones like jungle creatures being brought down by army ants. She can't do anything for them once they fall out of contact. In these tunnels, all she can reach is what's available to her along a chain of vehicles and suits.

But now suddenly her mind's reaching out much farther than that.

The words flash into Spencer's helmet: hurry the fuck up. He passes it on to Linehan. Who laughs. "Easy for them to say," he says.

They're deep into an industrial area, about thirty meters down a very narrow chute. The gravity's intensifying the farther into it they go. Spencer and Linehan are all too conscious of the nature of the tube they're crawling in. And they know exactly what's going to happen if it gets put to use . . .

"Easy or not," says Spencer, "we got to hurry this up."

"No shit."

It's a tough passage. Linehan's got his neck and shoulders against one wall of the chute, his feet against the other. There's just enough room for him to lower his gun arm past his legs. The light on the end of the gun casts a beam that vanishes into the darkness below. But not before illuminating a hatch.

"Okay," he says. "I see it."

"About time," replies Spencer.

They work their way along those last few meters, pry the hatch open. The mass-driver tube they're now exiting extends straight through half the asteroid. It can fling chunks of rock and metal at speeds well in excess of orbital velocity. It's a useful shortcut for anyone who's feeling lucky.

"Now those fucks get to try it," says Linehan.

"They'll probably use their thrusters," replies Spencer. "Now that we've paved the way."

"Pussies."

"For fuck's sake, focus. We're getting close."

They crawl along what looks like a maintenance tunnel built to service the mass-driver. It's very narrow. They move along it, slide a door open, go through into a much wider corridor.

Just as the floor beneath them starts to shake again.

"Ahead of us this time," says Linehan.

"And way too close," mutters Spencer.

It's unmistakable. Huge explosions are going off in close proximity up ahead. Triangulation with Lynx establishes pretty quickly where.

"Things are getting hot at the Window," says the Operative.

"Small wonder."

"The Rain's trying to shatter the Throne before the cavalry arrives."

"The cavalry that's now about five minutes behind us."

"Hold on," says the Operative. He and Sarmax step into the mass-driver chute, ignite their thrusters. They blast down to the hatch that's still open, turn into the maintenance corridor, turn off their thrusters while Lynx descends after them. The explosions are closer, intensifying. Rockdust starts drifting from the walls.

"We've got to get in behind the Rain's assault," shouts the Operative. "Find a way to fuck them up the ass."

"Find a way to get their dick out of ours," mutters Sarmax.

They descend down ladders, move through a series of airlocked hatches that have been blasted open. They head through a cave that's filled with derelict mining vehicles—edge past them, down a corridor that's shaking so hard it feels like it's right inside their helmets.

But then it stops.

"Huh," says Sarmax.

"My thoughts exactly," says the Operative.

He releases the tethers, tells the guys on point to start running. He and Sarmax are doing the same, throwing caution to the wind, taking advantage of the fact that they're now in gravity to sprint. They're still holding off on their suit-thrusters, though, since that would raise their heat-signature to unacceptable levels. They race down a stairway that seems like it has no bottom, head through a series of interlocked galleries, emerge into another passageway. Spencer's voice sounds in the Operative's skull.

"Movement," it says.

"Where?"

"Right on top of us."

It's burning in her fucking brain. She can *sense* the Rain out there, at the Window. Not as precisely as before—she can't detect their zone through all the rock. But she knows they're there all the same. That sixth sense again, telling her that the Rain have done what they came for. But she's just beginning. Her formation's tearing its way through low-G factory levels now, coming in through torn rails and storage units, fighting Euro security robots and mining droids—not to mention things that seem to have been created by the very factories that her forces are now destroying. In her mind, calculations slide together in a dawning realization. She's not surprised in the slightest when Huselid's voice echoes in her helmet. She suddenly realizes that she's been expecting this all along.

"Change up coordinates," he says, reeling off numbers. "Entire formation."

"Away from the Window?" asks the pilot.

"Just do it," snarls Haskell.

• • •

They're pressed up against the walls. They've got their camouflage going. They're looking at some kind of flame down the farther reaches of this tunnel.

"Don't move a goddamn muscle," says Spencer.

That's what Carson's just ordered. And Linehan's obeying. He's already switched off his light. He and Spencer keep their weapons trained on the thing that's now approaching: a suit that's been nailed almost beyond repair, thrusters so gone it's a wonder it's still flying. It hurtles in toward them.

"It's Praetorian," breathes Spencer.

"You mean it *looks* Praetorian."

It's got the Praetorian colors, that's for sure. It sears past them, rounds a corner.

Now!" yells Sarmax.

He and the Operative fire simultaneously as the suit flashes past them. The thrusters on its back explode: the suit skids against the floor, smashes against the wall. The Operative rushes into the blind spot of its weapons, shoves a gun against its visor. A man's face stares up at him. Sarmax risks a tightbeam transmission.

"We're Praetorian," he says. "Same as you."

"It's over," says the soldier. "We're fucked. We're fucked. We're—"

"Shut him *up*," hisses the Operative.

Sarmax lowers his gun, fires, grazes the soldier's helmet with a shot that melts the man's comlink. He shoves a tether into a jack on the soldier's shoulder.

"Now talk," he says.

"And keep it together," adds the Operative. "You're a Praetorian for fuck's sake."

"Not anymore," mutters the soldier.

"What?"

"The Throne's fucking *gone*."

"Bullshit."

"The Rain collapsed our perimeter in nothing flat. They executed him in front of my eyes. Jesus—"

"So how come you made it out?"

"Saw it happen from an observation platform," says the soldier. "Saw only one way out."

"You mean this?" asks the Operative. He fires a single shot through the soldier's visor. Blood and bone churn inside that helmet. Sarmax whirls on the Operative.

"What the fuck's your prob—"

"Shut up, Leo," snarls the Operative. "Anyone who leaves the Throne's side is forfeit."

"The Throne's gone. The executive node—"

"Is up for grabs. Let's get in there and take it."

Spencer's head whips back as Carson starts screaming at him. In the distance he can see Carson's thrusters igniting. He hits his own, yells at Linehan.

"Let's go! This is fucking it!"

They surge forward. Apparently there's no point in stealth now. Nor is there any further sign of fighting up ahead. He and Linehan roar down the corridor, down another tunnel, up another shaft, throttling up to breakneck speeds. He'd like to take it a little slower. But he knows better than to question Carson. Especially when the man's got his guns trained on Spencer's back.

Or maybe he doesn't. Spencer suddenly realizes he can't even see Carson and Sarmax on the rear screens anymore. Apparently they're letting him and Linehan get out ahead. Letting them get in there first. Because—

"We're history," says Linehan.

"In a moment," replies Spencer.

They blast down a staircase, blast past Praetorian corpses, tear past vents that have popped open and out of which something seems to have emerged. Signs of firefight are everywhere.

"The outer defenses," says Linehan.

They charge into an elevator shaft, drop down it like meteors. They break through more doors, streak into a huge chamber where a power plant's been scattered all over the walls, along with too many Praetorians. The tunnels that lead away from here have the remnants of heavy weapons protruding from them.

"The inner defenses," says Spencer.

They roar past the last guns, down the last tunnels, hurtle out into a vast space.

They've sidestepped away from Linehan and Spencer. They're running full throttle—Lynx on rearguard, the Operative and Sarmax on point. They're taking their own route in: a passage that cuts straight in from the tunnels that honeycomb the area beyond the outer defenses. A passage that leads to the edge of the Window. A passage off all the maps.

Or so they hope.

"What the fuck's going on up there?" asks Sarmax.

"We're about to find out," says the Operative.

"Hey, are you picking up anything weird with that relief force?"

"That's one way to put it." He patches Lynx in. "Lynx, are you—"

"Yeah," says Lynx. "The cavalry's changing it up."

"Let's have it," says Sarmax.

The Operative meshes the data, sends it over.

"What the fuck," says Sarmax.

"They're wheeling right. And moving away at speed."

"The Rain's intercepted them," says Lynx.

"Doubtful," says the Operative.

"Especially when the Rain were just here," says Sarmax.

"They've got a way of moving fast," says Lynx.

"So do we," mutters the Operative.

They crash on out into the vicinity of the Window: a mammoth cave carved into the asteroid's side, a quarter-klick wide in places, shards of translucent plastic jutting out across its mouth. Space drifts beyond. Broken bodies and shattered machinery are everywhere. There's no sign of life.

Except for Spencer and Linehan. They're over on the far side, checking things out.

"Glad you could join us," says Linehan.

"Save it," says the Operative. "What've you found?"

"A real fucking mess."

"Split up," says the Operative. "Search this place. Find the president."

The place is in shambles. But the search doesn't take long. It's reasonably clear where the defenses were concentrating. Where the attackers closed in. Where the last stand went down.

"Got it!" yells Sarmax.

"Everyone hold their positions," says the Operative.

He blasts in toward Sarmax while Linehan and Lynx and Spencer vector outward, sweep the vast room on a covering pattern. Sarmax is standing on a ledge that overlooks most of the cave. A smaller cave leads back into the rock. Several of the Praetorians sprawled on the ground wear officers' uniforms.

"Where is he?" asks the Operative.

"Back there," says Sarmax.

All the way back. A man in armor without insignia.

He's been shot repeatedly through the chest. His helmet's been pulled off. His skull's been opened up by a laser scalpel. But his face is intact, and clearly recognizable. The Operative whistles.

"That's Harrison alright," he says.

"Minus his software," says Sarmax.

"They've got the exec node."

"Which will let them control the zone."

"If they can get it to restart."

The two men look at each other.

"*If,*" says Sarmax.

"They're the ones who pulled the fucking plug," says the Operative. "They probably know a way to switch it back on too."

"Hey," says Lynx. The words echo in their skulls. "The relief force."

"Yeah?"

"It seems to be heading straight for the Hangar now."

"Fuck," says Sarmax, "why did they switch directions?"

"Don't know. But it's just as well they did."

"Why? The node's been taken. We need them here."

"To do what?"

"Track down the Rain. Take back the node."

"Don't be stupid," says the Operative. "As long as the Hand keeps his force bunched up, their search-and-destroy capability is for shit. And if they disperse, the Rain will take them apart."

"The Rain may anyway," says Sarmax. "Look what they did to this place."

"Which doesn't add up."

"No," says Sarmax. "It doesn't."

"These guys were dug in. They knew all about the nano. They knew what to expect. How did the Rain take down the perimeter so quickly?"

"They found another way in?"

"Sure," says the Operative. "Where? These guys had every approach covered."

They look at each other.

"Except for one," says Sarmax.

"Shit," says the Operative, and starts screaming orders.

Spencer hears the instructions, hits his jets even as he sees Lynx and Linehan do the same. The wall soars in toward him; the Window wafts away from him. He surges into the nearest cave—the one that Sarmax and the Operative entered. He can see them crouched against the far wall.

And then everything goes black. And white. And all the colors that ever were and might ever be invented: he's hurled against the wall while his screens blast static and his heart surges to the point of explosion. Electricity chases itself across him. He lies there twitching. The Operative bends over him, stares into his visor.

"Still alive?" he asks.

"Unfortunately," says Spencer. He feels like he's been stuck into a socket—like his body just got aged past the point of no return.

"Helios nailed us again," he mutters.

"And how," says Sarmax.

"But I thought—"

"That it didn't have the angle?" The Operative laughs mirthlessly. "You weren't the only one. Looks like the thing's got more mobility than we thought. They must have moved it round to the Platform's south side and opened up." Spencer hears a click as the Operative keys in everybody else. "The party's over here. The Throne's out for the count. The Rain ran off with the crown jewels. If they can restart the zone with that, they win. If they can't—"

"Then they'll need the Manilishi," says Sarmax.

"Who seems to be racing toward the Hangar like her life depends on it," says Lynx.

"Not that it matters," says Linehan. "Carson, no disrespect, but we're *out* of this. We trail them on stealth and we'll never catch up. We fire all jets and we'll get eaten by the Rain."

"Or some nano booby trap," says Spencer.

"That's why we're going to cut some more corners," says the Operative. "Beat them all to the Hangars in one fell swoop."

Lynx clears his throat. "Surely you don't mean—"

"Sure I do."

One final race to go. Shakers and suits and cycles are all surging forward, smashing their way through the resistance, blasting through a series of elevators and chutes—opening up the terrain with the remaining microtacticals. They tear their way into a series of industrial levels, peel back ceilings, carve through floors. The gravity's starting to lessen.

Even as the pursuit's starting to gain. And she knows why. Because the Rain's no longer fooled. They know what they've got. They know what they're missing. They're coming after her with a vengeance. She can feel them as surely as she's ever felt anything. She's content to sit back and let it happen.

• • •

They drop past torn bodies and shattered machines. Drop past the last of the cave walls,
shoot through what's left of the Window.

Space opens up around them. Stars gleam. The Operative
turns in one smooth motion, starts sidling along the side of
the rock. The others follow him through a landscape of impossible contrasts. Horizon crowds up way too close. It seems
like they've reached the end of the world—the world that
streams below them in all its incarnations: hatches, metal
panels, struts, wiring, pylons, all set within the same unend-
ing rock. The Window vanishes in their rearview. They get out
into the thick of the hostile landscape. There are no transmissions between them now. They're just following the Operative
as he darts forward, staying as close as possible to the surface
while detouring as little as possible. Screens within the
Operative's helmet show vectors that trace around the Aerie—
show him, too, the rock's rotation putting ever more mass between him and Helios. He can't believe how bad this has
gotten—can't believe there's still a chance of pulling it off. The
screens show him almost at the edge of the place he's seeking.

But they also show him the last thing he wants to see.

"We got company," says Sarmax, breaking radio silence.

The five men activate conduits, lock in the tactical grid.
Blurring mars the horizon, as though the stars in front of
them are getting swallowed by a wayward nebula. It's swarming in toward them, blocking their way forward.

"On our left, too," says Spencer.

"And the right," says Linehan.

As if they weren't fucked enough. The Operative realizes
too late that he was an idiot to think they could make it across
the surface. That of course the Rain would have everything
covered. The Hangar's probably been overrun anyway.
They're now on the cusp of what should be the outermost of
its perimeters, but the turrets jutting along the horizon show

no sign of any guns, just scorch-marks where energy's been hurled against them, unleashed by the Helios, which is going to get the drop on the Operative's group if they retreat from the onrushing swarm or if they try to hold their positions on the asteroid while it rotates. Though they're being forced to do that anyway: halting, taking up positions, covering all directions.

"Fire at will," snarls the Operative.

The vise is tightening around them. The mined-out areas through which they're passing are alive with dust and drones. And more besides: suited figures are appearing around corridor corners, emerging from cave mouths, opening up on Haskell's force.

"Jesus," says the pilot. "Those are—"

"I know," she says.

Praetorians. Who got swarmed in the initial combat. And repurposed, with a new lease on life. They may be dead, but their suits are fighting on. Haskell catches glimpses of lifeless eyes behind visors as suits hurl themselves at her shaker, go down beneath its treads.

"Not easy," says Huselid.

She says nothing. She doesn't know whether he's talking about the resolution required to shoot at former colleagues or offering a more general assessment of the whole situation. All she knows is that the hunters are overtaking them. She urges her pilot to pour on the speed.

• • •

The five men open up, tearing swathes in the swarms heading in toward them. Explosions rip across the rock. Flashes light up the horizon all around.

But the opposition's playing it like a numbers game, darting out of the blast-radii of the nukes; hugging the surface; getting in between the nooks and crannies of the rock, then rushing forward again.

"Jesus," says Spencer.

"Behind us too," says Lynx.

"We got to get off the surface!" yells Sarmax.

"Agreed," says the Operative.

He's blasting the nearest hatch, which spins off into space. More dust pours out of the opening.

"Shit," he mutters.

"At least let's make 'em pay," says Sarmax.

It's all they can hope to do. The shit's coming in from every direction now. They've got no more hi-ex. The clouds close in on them. Beyond them the Operative can see still more shapes rising from the horizon, wafting into the black above.

And raining fire down on everything below.

Jets of plasma. Whole racks of minitacticals. Light overwhelms the Operative's screens, even as he fires point-blank at what's gotten past the firing zone. As the flashes fade, he sees Praetorian gunships overhead, their engines glowing molten, their guns flaring.

Another hatch pops open. The Operative doesn't hesitate; he starts blasting in toward it, and the others follow him while shredded nano wafts everywhere. The gunships soar past, drop back toward the horizon.

And the Operative knows the reason why. Because the world's still turning. And the Helios is about to come up over the horizon like a demented sun. The hatch swings shut. The five men find themselves enclosed in a tiny elevator-like chamber, which starts moving along an unseen shaft within the asteroid.

But then the chamber stops. An interface in the wall transmits. The Operative hears a voice.

"Carson," it says.

"Yeah?" he replies.

"What the fuck's going on out there?"

"And what kind of street trash have you brought in with you?" asks another voice.

"Fuck you guys," says the Operative. "How about reloading us and letting us go kick some ass?"

"Give us some codes and sure."

"You mean to say you actually have a zone in the Hangar?"

"We brought a cauterized mainframe online. It's a long way from perfect. Now how about those codes?"

"All yours," says the Operative, beaming them over. "Now how about you tell me who the fuck's in charge."

"Us," says the first voice.

"Now tell us who we are," says the second.

"Give me a break—"

"Just do it."

"Murray," says the Operative. "And Hartnett. And I can't believe you guys are fucking *it*—"

"We've taken a beating, Carson. Is that Leo you've got with you?"

"Who the fuck else would it be?"

"Patch him in," says Hartnett.

The Operative wants to argue—wants to tell the two men who are now in command of the Hangar just how urgent the situation is. But he knows they've got to do their due diligence. Voiceprint and retina sampling, not to mention a little conversation—he'd do the same if he were them. Nothing's conclusive. But every little bit helps.

"Hey, Leo," he says.

"Yeah," says Sarmax.

"Remember me?" asks Murray.

Sarmax laughs. "Moving up in the world, huh?"

"More like the world's crumbling down around us," says Hartnett.

"So what's up?"

"What's up is that you're back."

"Don't tell me you didn't know that," says Sarmax.

"Thought it was just a rumor."

"Maybe we should keep it that way."

"Not when you're a living legend," says Murray.

"Or when you kicked so much ass for so long," adds Hartnett. "And I guess the one-handed wonder is Lynx."

"What about these other two?" asks Murray.

"Some cannon fodder we picked up," says the Operative.

"That managed to remain alive?"

"Sometimes it happens."

"So how about you upload their IDs?"

"Sure." The Operative complies. "Steroid-casualty named Linehan, razor calls himself Spencer. They were InfoCom before the Throne overwrote their asses. Linehan used to soldier for SpaceCom back in the day."

"And the Throne gave him a ticket to *this* show?"

"Didn't exactly give him the best seat in the house."

"Ain't getting it here either. You guys ready to get back in it?"

"Open this goddamn door," says the Operative.

The door slides open to reveal a gigantic chamber. Spencer watches Carson and Sarmax move through the doorway, apparently deep in some conversation. Lynx shoves his way after them. Linehan follows him with his eyes, before turning toward Spencer and grinning mockingly.

"After you," he says.

Spencer steps out onto a catwalk that stretches away in both directions. The Hangar is as big as it gets. It's a hub of activity, too. Praetorians are everywhere: crawling over the jagged ceiling like ants, moving along catwalks higher up and lower down, tending to the ships positioned along the gridded floor. Spencer can see three smaller gunships and one ship that's much larger—the same model as the freighter he was riding back when it all began. Soldiers stand upon it, float around it.

"Only one they got left," says Linehan on the one-on-one.

"The Throne's getaway vehicle."

"Too bad he ain't around to use it."

"They'll just have to get a new Throne, huh."

"Or work out what they did with the old one," replies Linehan.

They exchange glances.

"Funny," says Spencer. "Been thinking along the same lines myself."

We move," says the Operative, and fires his motors, letting the others trail him toward the ceiling. One of the hatches in the overhead opens.

"You going to tell them now or later?" asks Sarmax on the one-on-one.

"Tell them what."

"Carson. Everyone in this place thinks the Throne's still alive. If the punks we got with us start ranting on about how he's dead, then—"

"Then what?"

"Bad for morale."

"No one's going to rant about anything, Leo. Not if they value their hides."

They shoot through the hatch and along a chute into a smaller cave carved adjacent to a portion of the Hangar's ceiling. Vaultlike doors close behind them. The walls are covered with cables. Heavy guns are mounted in multiple places along the floor. Each gun is tended by a full complement of Praetorians and pointed at a tunnel mouth on the ceiling. The Operative heads toward one of the tunnels, and the others follow him.

"But surely you owe them the truth?" asks Sarmax.

"Namely?"

"What really happened to the Throne."

"You saw it for yourself."

"Did I?"

The Operative laughs. "What are you trying to say?"

"That you can't fool me."

"Did I ever claim I could?"

The five men roar out into a larger space—a full quarter the size of the hangar that all these defenses protect. The machinery that packed this place has been dismantled to allow for wider fields of fire. Heavy guns are lined along the near walls. The blast-doors on the far wall are at least ten meters a side. Praetorians cling to the walls, point their guns toward the doors.

"I sat at his feet once, Carson. I thought up half the tricks he knows. I'm not fooled by them. And you know what? I'll bet you the Rain weren't either."

"Let's pray they were for long enough."

"How long is that?"

They swoop across the room, swerve past the blast-door gate, perch upon the wall nearby. That gate's starting to shake. Dust floats up around it. Distant vibrations roll in from somewhere beyond it.

"Until a few minutes ago."

"But now they're going to hit this Hangar like they've never hit anything before," says Sarmax.

"I think they've got their sights set on something else first."

More Praetorians hurry into the room, heading out of the tunnels or moving in toward the leftmost of the gates. The rumbling outside is intensifying, resolving into blasts that are drawing ever nearer. Or getting steadily more powerful.

Or both.

"The Manilishi," says Sarmax.

"And the Hand," says the Operative.

"You mean the Throne."

Another vibration churns the room. It's coming from the direction of the Hangar. A whole section of the wall is sliding away; one of the gunships is emerging from the space revealed, turrets extended, Praetorians holding onto its sides. The ship adjusts for Coriolis spin, swans in slowly toward the gate opposite it, which is already opening.

"And he expects you to do your utmost," says the Operative.

She couldn't ask for anything else. They're well into the mining areas that ring the Hangar. They're almost there. But she can feel the Rain closing in from both flanks now. She glances at the man beside her.

"The cat's out of the bag," she says.

"Of course it is," he replies.

"And Huselid?"

"A role I play."

A necessary fiction for the man who's really Andrew Harrison. She wants to ask him who the unknown soldier was. That man in the Window, giving orders in the Throne's name: Did he even know the game he was in on? Was he an actor, or just a puppet? It doesn't matter now. The point is he played his part. Now the ones he died for have to do the same.

"They're pressing," she says.

"Might have thought that chip would have led them on more of a wild-goose chase," he says.

"Not if the Rain's razors activated it immediately."

Which they almost certainly did—tried to run the whole U.S. zone through the fragment they'd pulled from a shattered skull . . . only to find it wasn't capable of switching on a washing machine. That, as complex as it looked, it was really just a maze of dead-ends whose only functionality was pretending to be something it wasn't, creating a zone-node that looked like all the wires led back to it. Even she was fooled at first. Back on the other side of the cylinder—back to what seems like years ago—she'd thought she was gazing at the executive node, and in reality all she was doing was dealing with its reflection, while the vessel of the real one stood beside her.

Just like he's doing now.

"How much strength is left at the Hangar?" she asks.

"We're about to find out," says the president.

Spencer watches as the gunship fires its motors, moves through the opening blast-doors. As it passes beneath, Carson floats onto it. Spencer and the rest follow him, alight on the hull, crouching just behind the forward turret. Walls slide past. Praetorians swarm after them. Carson's words sound in Spencer's head.

"I'll keep this brief. The Throne's still alive. Our victory up to this point has depended on fooling the Rain as to his real location, and on keeping them too distracted to launch an all-out assault on the Hangar. The Throne and the Manilishi are still out there, and hopefully making straight for this gate. We're going to get out beyond the perimeter and bring 'em in. It all comes down to us. Fight like you've never fought before. Over and out."

The gunship comes out into a cave. Its lights splash around the chamber, illuminating the tunnel-mouths dotting the walls. There's no way the ship's fitting through any of them. The walls are trembling with the force of nearby explosions. The craft fires auxiliary motors to keep pace with the rotation of the asteroid—and starts firing bolts of plasma down one of the tunnels. Praetorians start scrambling into the openings adjacent to that one.

"Fucking bait and switch," says Spencer.

"So the Hand was the Throne?" asks Linehan.

"Or the Throne was one of the soldiers with the Hand. Fucking Praetorians. Nothing's ever what it seems."

"You're one to talk."

"Heads up."

"Shit."

Smartdust is swarming from several of the tunnels, billowing into the cave. Everyone on the ship's hull starts firing. The ship opens up with all five turrets: one in front, one in back, one on each side, one set within its belly. The walls are a frenzy of light and shadow.

"So did you know all along?" asks Lynx on the one-on-one.

"Been unfolding in my mind as we went," replies the Operative as he unleashes his minigun. "The Throne plays his cards pretty close to his chest."

The nano is getting lacerated. More Praetorians enter the room via the main tunnel. Several are riding cycles, towing other suits behind them. They swoop past the ship, head into tunnels, while the soldiers remaining keep firing.

"It's a paradox," adds the Operative as he revectors his guns. "The Hand's responsible for the Throne's security. But how in God's name can the Throne delegate such a responsibility? Especially in this day and age—no sane head of state can give a chief of security the power necessary to do that job effectively. Yet taking on the role of the Hand—*disguising* himself as the Hand—increases the ability of the Throne to evade an assassin's first blow."

"But this is nuts," says Lynx. He momentarily ceases firing a gun to let it cool. "You're saying the Throne *deliberately* stepped outside of the asteroid he was doing his best to make invulnerable?"

"Precisely because he knew he *couldn't* make it invulnerable. If the Rain were able to pull off anything anywhere *near* as epic as what they've actually gone and done, the Throne wasn't going to be able to rely purely on firepower."

E specially when the Rain are so adept at forcing their opponent to fight with only a fraction of his strength," says Linehan.

"I noticed," replies Spencer.

Crosshairs and flaring grids: they're both tracking nano racing along the ceiling. Diving from the walls, soaring in toward them, getting chopped into even finer dust . . .

"Then you also noticed that this is it."

"Yeah."

"The Throne and the Manilishi have run out of tricks."

"But if they can reach the Hangar they might be able to make it impregnable."

"What I don't see is why the Throne didn't start out there," says Spencer.

"How could he? He had to start somewhere he didn't think the Rain would be. And the Rain never dreamed he'd leave this asteroid. They thought they'd pinpoint his exact location by watching where in this dump he drew the Manilishi."

"It probably never occurred to them that the Throne would dare triangulation remotely."

"Nor did he," says Linehan.

He stops firing. Along with everybody else. Nano is no longer in sight. Spencer shakes his head.

"You're right," he says. "Too great a risk."

"In retrospect it seems fucking obvious. He'd have had to trust one of his subordinates with the Manilishi. But say one of the subordinates was Rain?"

"Or was just plain disloyal."

"Sure," says Linehan.

"Or was working for that SpaceCom outfit you flew cover on. Christ, when they woke me up on that ship and I learned you were still alive I wondered if the Throne was merely putting you back on the bait-hook in case Szilard or one of his henchmen was still out there trying to nail him—"

"That occurred to me as well."

"—which he probably was, in a sense."

"Meaning?"

"Meaning I doubt you'd have been let inside the Aerie."

"But here I am anyway."

"Because the Manilishi's cleared you," says Spencer.

"But who cleared the Manilishi?"

"If she was going to turn on the Throne, she'd have done that by now. As it is, she's the only reason he's still ticking— only reason he's even got a *hope* of making the Hangar."

"But now they're going to throw their full strength against him before he gets within the perimeter."

"Like I said, been nice knowing you."

Another rumble starts up. This one doesn't stop.

• • •

Orders start crackling over comlinks. Some of it's in the clear. It can't be helped. Everyone starts scrambling from the room—swarming down different tunnels. Only the gunship remains where it is, weapons tracking in multiple directions, a few soldiers continuing to cling to its sides. The Operative leads the way down one of the tunnels. He sends out another transmission.

Linehan, Spencer—you guys get on point again."
"Christ," says Linehan. But Carson's already cut them off. Spencer and Linehan accelerate past him, wending their way into a maze of tunnels using the route that the Operative's given them, making turns so sharp they're pushing off the walls. Vibrations are echoing through those walls from multiple directions. Small-arms fire, heavy shells, explosions, not to mention—

"Someone's busted out some digging machines," says Spencer.

And realizes immediately that his words aren't going anywhere. He's cut off from Linehan. He starts firing with everything except his hi-ex, raining shots past Linehan—who now opens up himself.

The Rain's jamming the point," says the Operative.
"We're right on top of them," says Sarmax.
"Picking up combat all around us," says Lynx. He starts to say something else—his voice cuts out. The Operative makes a turn, away from the route that Spencer and Linehan have been taking. About a hundred meters ahead the tunnel bends sharply.

. . .

Machines of every size and shape are crashing in like waves against the Praetorian formation. The flanks are getting forced steadily in toward the center. The rearguard's pretty much toast. All that's left is just a dwindling core. But the vehicles within it are staggering on regardless.

"Still softening us up," she says.

"I realize that," he replies.

Not that much more's going to be required. Because this earthshaker's in shambles. Smoke's streaming through the cockpit from more than one electrical fire. The side-gunners are dead. All that's left are those few of the Throne's bodyguards still remaining: riding on top of the shaker, firing through the holes torn in its side, moving alongside the crippled vehicle as it keeps on plowing its way through the endless tunnels. In her head Haskell can see the route they've traversed—her mind traces back past the Window, skirting the bombed-out heart of rock, back into the wilderness of smashed stone and metal where the South Pole of the cylinder used to be. All of it keeps on whirling within her, like some siren screaming in her head.

But up ahead is the southernmost point of all. The Hangar itself. The only hope of sanctuary. Ignored by the Rain so far—or so she's hoping. Holding out from the onslaught—or so she's praying. She takes in the combat, watches more swarms billow toward her, more drones popping from the wall, unfolding long legs only to get their limbs shorn off by cycles slashing past her. Rock and debris smash against the cockpit window. Something streaks in behind them.

"Heads up," says the pilot.

Too late: the window shatters. The pilot gets smashed back in his seat. Blood's everywhere. Her suit's been hit. She feels her systems starting to go.

Someone grabs her. She feels herself pulled bodily forward—out of the stricken shaker and into the tunnels. She feels a helmet pressed against her, sees tunnel walls flash by. She hears a voice. It's Harrison. He's got her in his arms. He's telling her to hold on. She sees rock flashing past her. She feels like she's pretty much lost it. She's sending her own mind out all the same.

Spencer and Linehan blast through into a larger chamber. Nano comes swarming in from the other side. They start firing, but it makes little difference—the waves seem endless.

"Fuck," says Linehan.

An explosion punches out an entire wall. Carson and Lynx and Sarmax come through firing, catching the swarms in a crossfire. Spencer roars out of the way of their trajectory, curves off, veers around the cavern's ceiling.

And sees it.

Caught in the light of the explosions, it's the same color as the rock. But it's not rock. It's a suit—someone clinging to the wall. Spencer hits his jets, whirls. Opens fire.

There's a blinding flash.

Explosions everywhere. Not to mention something that looks to be the flare to end all flares. All the Operative's picking up is overload all along the spectrum. He's dampening the inputs toward zero. He's amping up his optic nerves to the limits of what he can take. All he can see is near-total white—and the suit of Sarmax flying past him in reverse, smoking from the chest, smashing against the wall. But now he sees something else: the vaguest outline of some other suit coming straight at him. He whips his arms up, fires.

Spencer's blind. A blow hammers on his back. Something slams against his leg. He gets a glimpse of some landscape shot through with way too many colors, watches his own suit smash against a wall, bounce. Rocks close in from all sides. But past them he gets a glimpse of something he's never seen before . . . overwhelming light . . . the very minarets of heaven . . .

Far too fast: the figure dodges past the Operative's fire, veers crazily toward him, fires at some other target—slams its boots against the Operative with a force that almost cracks his armor. The Operative tries to grab the boots, finds himself holding nothing. All he can see is blur. He fires his jets in a desperate attempt to stay unpredictable, fires his weapons at where he thinks the target is, lashes out wildly with his razor nodes. But he knows he's toast. Something clicks through his skull. He figures it's death.

It's a woman instead. Haskell—and she couldn't be that far away, because she's just made zone contact with him. And suddenly her vision's his; coordinates upload and all at once the Operative can see the suit he's fighting. He whirls in one fluid motion—fires on the now-visible figure that's dancing past him, tossing something in its wake. . . . The Operative ignites his jets, hurls himself onto his nemesis as an explosion cuts through the wall behind him. He grasps onto the suit's back, pulls against its helmet; the figure punches upward, smashes its fists against the Operative's chest, straight through the outer armor—whereupon the Operative starts firing into the figure's back at point-blank range. He unloads his wrist-guns, unleashing his minigun at the same time as the momentum sends him sailing backward. But the figure's already fired its own motors, jetting aside, continuing out of sight down a tunnel. The Operative hits his motors, charges in toward the opening—

"No," says a voice.

From right inside his head. Haskell again. She's flaming through his brain—and now he sees her, sprawled in the arms of the U.S. president as he surges out of another passageway, along with three bodyguards. The last of the emissions-bombs the Rain set off in here are dissipating—the Operative fires his motors, soars toward the center of the chamber. He sees Lynx moving in to join him.

"Where the hell have you been?" the Operative asks.

"Here all along," Lynx replies. "Got blinded. Was about to get the chop when suddenly everything kicked back in again."

"That's because the Manilishi got within range of us before the Rain did us in. They seem to have fucked off."

"Guess they didn't like their odds."

"Or they've got something else planned. Where the hell's Leo?"

"Beats me," says Lynx in a tone that says *hopefully dead.*

Two shakers emerge from the rock-wall like insects boring their way through wood. Jets slung along them ignite even as hatches open in the first one. The Throne pushes the Manilishi within, leaping in behind her. The shakers head for the passage that leads back toward the Hangar. The Operative swoops after them, but spots Sarmax floating near the wall, dips in toward him.

"Leave him," says Lynx. "Too risky."

"What's too risky is thinking we won't need him for whatever's next."

Besides, the Manilishi just green-lighted it. Sarmax's

systems remain intact, despite the pounding his suit's just taken. The Operative grabs him by the torso, vaults in toward the last of the shakers, and settles on its back. Lynx motors in to join him. The two men perch there while the shaker accelerates. The Operative can see more Praetorians coming into the cave behind him.

"Is he still alive?" asks Lynx.

"Like you care," replies the Operative.

"Of course I care."

Just not in the way he's supposed to. But it looks like Lynx isn't going to get his wish just yet. Sarmax's vital signs are holding up. An explosive went off right next to his suit, tore it in a few places, knocked out the suit's systems, and hit Sarmax with a concussion that rendered him unconscious. Automatic backup seals seem to have kept him alive. Whether he'll stay that way will need to await a med-scan. Not to mention the resolution of more pressing problems.

"This ain't over yet," says the Operative.

"No shit," replies Lynx.

Bombs are detonating in their wake. The Praetorians back there are firing at something, getting fired upon in turn. But the turret against which the Operative and Lynx are crouching remains silent. And now the shakers are coming out into the cavern in which the gunship's situated. It's still there—still firing, too, sending salvos streaking into tunnels. Praetorians clustered around the gunship head toward the shakers.

Which is when a voice sounds in the Operative's head. It's not calm. He amps it, broadcasts what it's saying:

"Stay back. Stay the fuck back!"

The Praetorians turn away. The shakers are vectoring in toward the tunnel that leads back to the Hangar. No one's trying to follow it. Which the Operative realizes is precisely what the Manilishi and the president want. *He's* one of the bodyguards. *He's* cleared. The others aren't. And there isn't time for the Manilishi to make sure. Too many variables, too far outside the outer perimeter. And the Manilishi would prefer not to indicate which of the shakers she and the Hand are in. Thus the Operative gets to be the voice. It's okay with him. It means he's at the Throne's side as the shakers power out of this room. Behind him he can see the gunship starting to reverse. Ahead of him he can see the rows of gun emplacements. And more Praetorians, cheering, shaking their fists—and getting left behind as the shakers keep on going, moving on through into the Hangar itself. Soldiers scramble as the shakers head straight in toward the outer wall—and the one remaining large ship.

"Time to fly," says Lynx.

"Not while the Helios is still laying down the law," replies the Operative.

"It's still a factor?"

"Unless you know something I don't."

Hatches open along the sides of the ship. The shakers vector in toward them. The Operative hears a voice in his head, with orders he's been hoping to hear.

"Let's get Leo to the medstation," he says, gesturing at Lynx, who grabs Sarmax's legs. The two men fire their thrusters, carry Sarmax away from the main Hangar and toward a room set into the hangar-wall in which a med-ops unit has taken up position.

"Incidentally," says Lynx, "what happened to those two expendables we picked up?"

"I think you just answered your own question."

But sometimes fate takes a funny turn. Because Spencer's waking up once more. He can see light in the distance. He feels cold all over. He tries to focus. But what's coalescing out of blur is a face he doesn't want to see.

"You still there?" says a voice.

It's Linehan. Spencer doesn't know what the fuck he's doing here. Unless the two of them have finally ended up in hell together. Spencer tastes blood in his mouth. He grits his teeth. Exhales.

"What the fuck's going on?" he says.

"They just dug me out," replies Linehan.

"The Praetorians?"

"No, the Rain."

There's a pause.

Linehan laughs, slaps Spencer's visor. "Dumb-ass. Had to think about that one, didn't ya?"

"Not really," says Spencer wearily.

"The Praetorians have thrown up a new outer perimeter. Turns out we're inside the latest iteration of the defenses."

"They must be feeling their oats."

"Of course. They sent the Rain packing."

"But we're still trapped on this fucking rock."

"And how."

"And presumably that's why they bothered to dig us out."

"Quick as ever, Spencer. Now get up."

Spencer does—pushes himself off the rock, hauls himself to his feet. He looks around. Praetorians are rigging equipment everywhere. A nasty thought occurs to Spencer.

"We're not part of this dump's garrison, are we?"

"Nope," says Linehan. "Apparently they got more plans for us back at the Hangar."

"What kind of plans?"

"Crazy ones, I hope."

PART III
RAIN'S SHADOW

The room is dark, though that doesn't matter to its occupant. She's plugged into everything anyway. She sits strapped into a chair positioned along a wall. The lights of the zone play within her—the one she's concocted to make up for the paralysis of the real one. It's not much of a substitute. But unless she can reverse that paralysis, it'll have to do. Wireless is safe only on short-range line of sight. And wires lead only so far. No farther than the perimeters, in fact.

The perimeters are less than half a klick out, encompassing a tenth of the Aerie. Almost three hundred Praetorians are within. God knows how much firepower lurks without. Haskell's assuming that in the three hours since she got here the Rain have moved most of the rogue weaponry from the cylinder into the asteroid, and have brought up all remaining smartdust. They have the Hangar under siege from all sides, except for space. But that's covered by the Helios. It was laying down a cannonade against the Hangar doors a couple of hours ago, but it failed to break through. Then it fired its engines and fucked off. In Haskell's mind is a grid that shows its current position: eighty klicks off the Platform's north end, no longer in line of sight of the asteroid, but poised to annihilate anything trying to leave...

There's a knock on the door.

"Come in," says Haskell.

The door opens. Light flows in from the corridor beyond. Two Praetorians enter the room. They train their visors this way and that.

"It's been swept," says Haskell.

They pay no attention. Just keep on scanning.

"Twenty minutes ago," she adds. "I've been here ever since."

"Orders, ma'am."

"The Throne's?"

The soldiers say nothing—just stiffen as the U.S. president appears in the door. Still dressed in the Hand's armor, still wearing Huselid's face. Haskell figures he may as well. Given that Huselid never really existed in the first place. She sees herself reflected within the visor: her helmet thrown back, so many wires protruding from her skull she looks like some kind of mechanical medusa.

Andrew Harrison gazes at her. His expression's neutral.

"Any ideas?" he asks.

"The only one I've got is the one I hate the most."

"It happens," the Throne replies.

He's tired. He's bone-weary. But he's still alive. He hurts everywhere. But they've patched him up okay. His body'll keep on ticking. As to his mind: that would need more than just a doctor. That would need something capable of changing the one thing that can't be changed.

The past.

"Penny for your thoughts," says Lynx.

"They're not in the bargain bin just yet," mutters Sarmax.

They're at the junction of two of the catwalks that crisscross the now-pressurized hangar. Their visors are up. Lynx is sipping water from a tube within his helmet. He's sitting cross-legged against the railing. Sarmax is leaning over it.

"Meaning what?" asks Lynx.

"Meaning I'm not in the mood for conversation."

"With me, you never were."

"That's because you talk too much."

"I've heard of worse weaknesses."

Sarmax doesn't reply. Just keeps on staring at the Hangar floor. The gunships have been moved out into the perimeter. The president's ship is the only craft down there now. Sarmax has been keeping an eye on it for almost fifteen minutes—ever since he emerged from the crowded med-unit and climbed out into the catwalks. No one's boarded that whole time. No one's left.

"How long has he been in there?" he asks.

"I didn't quite catch that," says Lynx. "It sounded like you were asking me a question."

"Don't make me wait for an answer."

"Easy, Leo. Carson's been holed up in that ship for almost an hour. Along with the rest of the bodyguards."

"What about the Throne? And the Manilishi?"

"No one's seen 'em leave."

"They're trying to think up a way out of this mess."

"You sad you weren't invited?"

"You sad I shot your hand off?"

"Fuck you," says Lynx.

"I'm going to go stretch my legs instead."

Lynx leans back. "I'm not going anywhere."

"No one is," says Sarmax.

• • •

F ive minutes later he's walking along a platform up in the Hangar's rafters. Gravity's a lot weaker up here. Praetorians pass him, salute, and keep going. He eventually reaches a point where the platform widens into a bona-fide balcony.

A single man's sitting there, wearing a unistretch jump-suit that does little to conceal his bulk. A suit of armor's standing in a corner of the platform. Another suit of armor's in pieces all around him. The man looks up from trou-bleshooting it.

"What's up?" says Sarmax.

Linehan shrugs. "Figure you'd know that better than me."

"Where's your friend?"

"He's not my friend, boss."

"Whatever."

"He went to try to get more ammo. We heard a rumor they were dishing it out on level H."

"You could have asked us for some. We've got connec-tions."

"With strings attached."

"Fair point."

"Besides," adds Linehan, "we couldn't find you. Heard you were out for the count."

"I was. But now I'm here."

"So your man Carson can involve us in another suicide run?"

"He's not my man."

"Then whose is he?"

"The Throne's."

"So what's going on out there, boss?"

"The Rain are massing for one last assault."

"I meant out in the rest of fucking existence?"

Sarmax laughs. He glances at the Hangar ceiling, a scant

fifteen meters overhead. He looks down at the Hangar floor.
Back at Linehan.

"That's a good one," he says. "Life beyond the Europa
Platform. Sheer chaos, I'm sure. There's a lot of jamming going on. But that can't disguise the fact that everyone and their
dog are broadcasting. Though we've no idea who's who. No
one does. The Rain have frozen everything that counts. No
one knows what the codes are. No one can launch shit."

"Including the Eurasians."

"The Eurasians are finished."

"Are they?"

"Blew themselves up in their asteroid."

"Must have been quite a sight."

"It's not like they had much of a choice."

"Because otherwise the Rain would have gotten their executive node?"

Sarmax nods.

"And the Coalition couldn't transfer it elsewhere," adds
Linehan.

Sarmax's eyes narrow. "How do you know so much about
executive nodes anyway?"

"I get around."

"Because you used to run wet-ops for SpaceCom."

"I wouldn't say it that loud."

"Son, they can't bust me, I wrote half the rules. Besides,
it's not like your history's a secret."

"Yours is."

Sarmax stares at him. "What's that supposed to mean?"

"It means I've been listening to the talk around the camp-
fires."

"You shouldn't."

"They say you got out of all this once upon a time."

"Is that a fact?"

"I'm just saying what they're saying, boss."

"What else are they saying?"

"That you came back because of your pal Carson."

"That's not true."

"Then why did you?"

"You ask a lot of questions."

"I'm just trying to build rapport."

"That's not a good way to do it."

"The Throne's going to nuke this whole place, isn't he?"

"Why would he do a thing like that?"

"Same reason the East did," says a voice.

It's Spencer. He's pulling himself up the ladder that leads down from the platform. He looks exhausted. But it looks like he's managed to get his hands on several packs of ammo.

"Lyle Spencer," says Sarmax.

"Sir," replies Spencer, reaching the platform.

"Kissing ass as always," says Linehan.

"Relax," says Sarmax. His gaze shifts to encompass both of them. "The East's sacrifice may be in vain. Just because the Rain can't capture their executive node doesn't mean they can't gain control of the Eastern zone. Or ours, for that matter."

"How else would one do it?" asks Spencer.

"Well, that's the problem. No one knows for sure."

"Or at least they haven't told you," says Linehan.

Sarmax gazes at him without expression.

"Boss, I'm just pointing it out. I'm not trying to be rude."

"You don't have to *try*," says Spencer.

But Sarmax just shrugs. "We're in uncharted waters now. The Rain proved they could freeze both zones without recourse to either executive node. My guess is that they'll ultimately figure out how to control one or both of them too. Somewhere out there a clock's ticking. And if it hits zero, you're going to know it. Because as soon as they restart either zone, they'll launch all weapons at the other side. And destroy this asteroid for good while they're at it. I can't see how much longer we have. No one can."

"None of which makes any difference now," says Linehan.

"We're expendable," says Spencer.

"We all are," says Sarmax.

"It's all relative," says Spencer.

"Too right," says Linehan. "Aren't you slumming it hanging out with us?"

"I go where things amuse me. And you guys should suit up."

"Why?"

Sarmax gestures at a door some distance along the platform. Lynx and Carson have just emerged from it.

"*Shit,*" says Linehan.

"Gentlemen," says Carson. "So glad you made it."

"Wouldn't dream of checking out early," replies Linehan. He and Spencer start to climb into their suits.

"Leo," says Carson, nodding to Sarmax—who raises a hand in mock-salute. He turns back to Spencer and Linehan. "Guys, I've got good news. I'm through using you as cannon fodder."

Spencer and Linehan look at him.

"It's true," he says. "You're off the hook."

"What's the catch?" asks Spencer.

"You mean besides the fact that you'll get croaked anyway?"

"Yeah," says Linehan. "Besides that."

"You get to haul our luggage," says Lynx.

They take a different route away from the center this time. They climb a series of ramps to where gravity dissipates still further—and then wind their way along more passages, back toward the side of sphere. Gravity starts to kick back in. What look like recently strung cables line the walls the whole way. Other Praetorians pass them on numerous occasions. Everyone seems to be going somewhere. Everyone seems to be getting ready.

"Hurry it up," says Carson.

"Easy for you to say," says Linehan.

He and Spencer are almost staggering under the weight of the containers they're dragging. The low gravity was providing some help. But now that it's returning to Earth-like levels, the going's getting tougher. Spencer almost trips, manages to avoid getting crushed by his container, and finally stabilizes it.

"What the fuck's in these goddamn things?" he asks.

"Your mother," says Lynx.

He's carrying a container as well—a decidedly smaller one. Spencer figures that's why he's still smiling. Either that, or he's relishing having someone beneath him on the totem pole. Spencer doesn't plan on giving him any trouble. However...

"What'd you say?" says Linehan.

"He didn't say a goddamn thing," says Sarmax evenly. "Did you, Lynx?"

"Of course not," says Lynx.

"Fucking liar," says Linehan.

"We have those around here," says Carson. He doesn't turn around—just keeps on walking forward with the container he and Sarmax are sharing between them. "Doesn't matter, Linehan. Draw on a member of my team, and I'll toss you through an airlock."

"Are you trying to get yourself killed?" says Spencer to Linehan on the one-on-one.

"Carson's half my size," says Linehan. "I can take him no prob."

"He's a fucking bodyguard," says Spencer. "Even if you killed him, you'd be court-martialed and assigned to orbit the Platform sans spacesuit."

"Maybe," replies Linehan. But he does nothing—just keeps on trudging forward with his burden. Spencer keeps waiting for Lynx to break back in and start baiting Linehan again. But Lynx seems to have lost interest.

I mean it," says the Operative on the triad's closed channel.

"I'm sure you do," replies Lynx. "You can fuck off anyway."

"Say whatever you want to me," replies the Operative.

"Just don't provoke the minions," adds Sarmax.

"A soldier should know how to withstand provocation," says Lynx.

"A soldier should be above dishing it out," says Sarmax.

"Everybody shut up," says the Operative—and now he's broadcasting to Spencer and Linehan as well. "We're here."

Almost on the outer perimeter. Which isn't much. Just a metal grille staircase. The Operative peers carefully over the edge of the railing. Cables are strung down from the platform to a door at the bottom of the stairwell. The Operative broadcasts codes down to the door, which slides open.

"Let's go," he says.

They descend the staircase, go through the door, and find themselves in a room that extends up to a second level. Praetorians stand along the upper railing, regard them through the sights of mounted weapons.

"What do you want?" asks one.

"We're looking for Garrick," says Sarmax.

"He's right here," says a voice. A door on the lower level opens. Another suit enters the room. He wears a major's stripes. Red hair dangles behind his visor.

"Carson," he says. "Been a long time."

"Long time for sure," says the Operative.

They touch gloves. Garrick turns toward Sarmax. His eyes narrow.

"Leo?"

"The same."

"Fuck's sake, man. Didn't even know you were up here."

"That's because you're slipping."

"I doubt it," says Garrick—looks over Sarmax's shoulder. "Lynx, you bastard. Ain't a party unless you're in it. What's happening?"

"Way too much," mutters Lynx.

"And who are these other guys?"

"Reinforcements," says the Operative. He narrows the channel to one-on-one. "Expendable."

"And the rest of us aren't?"

"Seriously, do what you want. I'm finished with them."

"And they're still alive?"

"They've got a talent for survival."

"They'll need it out on the perimeter. What about you guys?"

"Is our vehicle here?"

"It is. And I gotta say, it's pretty fucking weird—"

"Let's go," says the Operative.

 Marines hop down from the upper level, relieving the men of the containers they've been carrying.

"Thanks," says Linehan.

"No problem," says one of them.

"You two," says another. "Come with me."

"But—" Spencer turns, finds Carson trailing Garrick out of the room, Lynx and Sarmax following them. "Hey, what about us?"

"Told you I didn't need you anymore," says Carson.

"See you in Hades," says Sarmax.

The door slides shut behind him.

"Ingrates," says Linehan.

"You guys done whining?" asks the Praetorian who just gave them instructions. She wears a lieutenant's stripes.

"Yes, ma'am," says Spencer.

"Good," says the lieutenant. "Let's go."

They follow her down another corridor, to a room lit by the spark of laser cutters. Praetorians are busy slicing holes along the walls. Spencer notices that those holes are mostly at gun height. He also notices a web of cables intersecting in this room.

"Sergeant," says the lieutenant.

A man leaps to attention. "Yes, ma'am."

"What's the situation here?"

"Situation good, ma'am."

"Can they spare you for a few minutes?"

"Yes, ma'am."

"Take these two to Outpost LK."

"We withdrew from there twenty minutes ago, ma'am."

Her face darkens. "It's been taken?"

"No, ma'am. We just didn't have enough men for some of the forward positions. Lieutenant Crawford felt that—"

"Never mind Lieutenant Crawford," she says. "Have these two reoccupy it."

"Ma'am," says Spencer.

She turns toward him, impatience written on her face. "What?"

"I'm a razor," he says. "Surely I can be of more service to you than this?"

She makes a dismissive gesture, turns away. "Razors aren't worth much now," says the sergeant.

"Not gonna see me complaining," says Linehan.

• • •

S o how's the situation at the center?" asks
Garrick.

"Under control," says the Operative.

"Now ask him to define that," says Lynx.

They're walking down more stairs. The lights overhead stutter fitfully. Soldiers stagger under the weight of the containers. More soldiers walk behind and in front, their weapons at the ready.

"I heard the Throne's got himself a new friend," says Garrick.

"More like a prodigal daughter," says Sarmax.

"Can she stop the Rain?"

"I guess we're going to find out."

They reach a door. Praetorians are positioned on both sides. Garrick flashes codes, confirms by retina—slots back his eye, confirms via the real retina behind it.

"Neat," says the Operative. He lets the light flash across his own retina, gestures at Sarmax and Lynx to do the same.

"Thanks," says Garrick. "But it doesn't remove the problem."

"How to make precautions Rain-proof," says Sarmax.

"Exactly," replies Garrick.

"Don't wander off alone," says the Operative. "That's how."

The door slides open. The soldiers within regard the ones now entering.

"Sir," says one.

"At ease," says Garrick.

A tarpaulin's draped over what looks to be some kind of vehicle—five or so meters long, about the size of one of the smaller earthshakers. The contours are strange, though. So is the tarp: it's wrapped pretty tight. None of its edges are visible. And even the most cursory of glances reveal that it's resistant to all scanning. The soldiers eye it nervously.

"In one piece?" asks the Operative.

"Yes, sir," says one of the soldiers.

"We don't know that for sure," snaps Garrick. "We were told not to remove the cover."

"And I'm glad you didn't," says the Operative.

"Because it's booby-trapped," says Sarmax.

"Tell your men to get out of here," says Lynx.

"You heard the man," says Garrick.

Ever get the feeling you're being stalked? Here's how it works. Everywhere you look there's nothing. Not a thing—just the hollow sound of your own breath echoing through your helmet as you follow the sergeant along a corridor that feels way too empty. Linehan's keeping an eye on the rear. Spencer's keeping an eye on the sergeant. In this fashion they carry on their conversation.

"Tell me about these cables," says Linehan, gesturing at what's strung along the wall.

"That's how we receive the word from center," says the sergeant. "They've been strung all the way from the hangar."

"Primitive," says Linehan.

"Try realistic," says the sergeant. "Anything that could be intercepted is right out. If we can see each other, we signal each other via tightbeam laser, and if we can't see each other, we don't signal. End of story."

"So if you're not in line of sight and you're not near a cable, you're not talking."

"Most of it was pretty tedious anyway," says the sergeant.

"But they're not even trying to deny a zone to Autumn Rain," says Spencer.

"Fine by me," says the sergeant. "I don't need nothing fancy. All I want to do is get those bastards in my sights."

"You'll get that soon enough," says Linehan.

"*You'll* probably get it sooner," says the sergeant. He descends a spiral staircase. They follow him down it. He opens a door. They stare within. Spencer whistles.

"Shit," says Linehan.

"Outpost LK," says the sergeant.

J esus Christ," says Garrick.

"What the fuck is it?" asks Lynx.

"A secret weapon," says the Operative.

One that bears an uncanny resemblance to a miniature brontosaurus. Four legs sprouting off an elongated body that narrows into a kind of head. It seems more organic than mechanic. It doesn't even seem to be made of metal. More like ...

"Is that *skin?*" asks Sarmax.

"Let's not get carried away," says the Operative. "This thing's pretty much a tweaked-up Mark IIB crawler."

"Some tweak," says Garrick.

"Fuck, I hope so," says the Operative. "It's pretty much soundless. And what looks like skin is actually a kind of grown plastic. The latest camo alloys we could dream up."

"Have they put this thing into production yet?" asks Lynx.

"No," says the Operative. "It's a prototype. The Remoraz."

"How did it perform in field testing?"

"Who said it had been field tested?"

"Let's load up," says Sarmax.

They start unloading their containers, slotting pieces of machinery into the machine that crouches before them.

. . .

A lmost makes me wish we were still part of Carson's entourage," says Linehan.

"No it doesn't," says Spencer.

"I said *almost*."

But even when the Europa Platform was running like clockwork, this place probably wasn't a destination spot. It's basically a single room, a bunker that bulges out slightly from the curved edge of the asteroid. Narrow windows slice through the walls on all sides. And in those windows...

"Did you see the expression on his face?" asks Linehan.

"Whose?"

"The sergeant's. He couldn't get out of here fast enough."

"What the hell did you think he was going to do, break out a flask and share it with us?"

"He could have at least said thanks."

"Linehan. We're in a fucking *war*. No one says thanks. All they say is *go here and die*."

"And here we are."

"With the only suspense being whether we'll even see it coming."

Though they certainly have a good enough view. Protruding over one end of the sharply curved horizon are the topmost ramparts of the gun-towers that form the inner perimeter around the hangar. The fact that they're only just visible gives the two onlookers a sense of just how far out on the edge of things they are. The view in the other direction confirms it: a couple of strategically placed mirrors extend the line of sight into the field of fire of the Helios, show the asteroid falling away along a slope of rock and metal. Beyond that's the mammoth hulking shape of the cylinder itself, the nearer parts illuminated by the sun, the farther parts largely in shadow, though visible nonetheless as a gigantic shape carved among the stars.

Spencer blinks.

"Did you see something move?" he asks.

"You're imagining things," says Linehan.

"I don't think so," says Spencer, and downloads the vid-feed he's just taken to Linehan. "Take a look at that."

Linehan does. Frowns. "That's just a shadow—*oh*."

"See what I mean?"

"What the fuck is it?"

"Whatever it is, it's gone now."

"The way it was moving—almost looked like some kind of animal."

"In a vacuum? I don't think so."

"At least it was heading away from us."

"If it comes back this way, we nail it," says Spencer. He makes some adjustments to the control board that's connected to the plasma minicannon mounted beneath their feet. Linehan snorts.

"How many shots do you think we're gonna get off with that thing?"

"One if we're lucky," says Spencer.

Get your foot out of my ear," says Sarmax.

"Sorry," replies the Operative.

"Any way you can move your left arm back a little farther?" says Lynx.

"I'm trying," says Sarmax.

Though he doesn't have much room to maneuver. None of them do. It's a tight fit, especially since they've got a lot of equipment and the Operative has insisted they keep their suits on. He's driving. He's pushed himself forward, into the head/cockpit. Sarmax is ensconced in the midquarter, Lynx in the rear. Screens are slung all around them, showing the corridors through which they're creeping. They started off across the exterior of the asteroid—and then cut back inward, crawled up a long network of elevator shafts. It's heavy going. And conditions inside aren't making it any easier.

"So maybe we should talk about the mission," says Lynx.

"Maybe we shouldn't," says the Operative.

"Don't you trust me?"

"We saw how far that got us earlier," mutters Sarmax.

"Hey man, I'm *clean* now. Superbitch scrubbed me."

"She should have cauterized your mouth while she was at it."

The Remoraz keeps moving. So far they've avoided combat, but not without some close shaves. Once some nano flew by while they sat there, frozen—swirled past them without noticing that they weren't just some lumpy feature of the shaft-walls. Another time they saw some droids hauling what looked like a piece of artillery. They weren't about to put it to a close inspection. But the overall picture's clear enough. The Rain are building up hardware all along the Praetorian perimeter.

But this thing they're in seems to have made it through the siege lines. They're now near the axis of the asteroid, moving through rooms in which the first round of fighting took place. Ripped-apart Praetorians are everywhere. Holes pockmark the walls. The Operative switches gears, transitions into zero-G mode. A faint vibration passes through the craft.

"Normally a little louder inside a crawler," says Sarmax.

"Nothing's normal about this thing," says the Operative.

He's not kidding. Background noise is virtually nonexistent within the Remoraz's cramped compartments. But the movement of the craft keeps humming against them all the same. It's almost as if it's *sidling* along somehow—a loping rhythm that starts to permeate the brain. A rhythm that's getting all the more insistent now that they're making their way through shattered walls and into . . .

"Check it out," says the Operative

"Do you know a way through?" asks Lynx.

"Gonna have to improvise."

Or just get lucky. The asteroid staved in the entire south end of the cylinder, turning a chunk of itself to rubble in the process. Any trail that now winds through that rock probably wasn't a trail to start with. But the Manilishi's been analyzing collision vectors, overlaying them against the blueprints of the asteroid, taking her best estimates as to where the result-ant hollows might be. So now the craft crawls slowly through space that was solid an all too brief time ago.

"Strange that we fought our way through here so re-cently," says Lynx.

"We were heading the other way then," replies the Operative.

"Looks a little different now," says Lynx.

That's for sure. The fissures through which they're creep-ing are strewn with floating rock and metal. The Remoraz probes on a few spectra, stays quiet on most. Twice they reach dead ends and are forced to retrace their route, make different choices. They head into a side tunnel that looks to be what's left of a much larger gallery. From the looks of the walls they're now in the infrastructure that ran beneath the south pole mountains. Or maybe they're still in the asteroid. Everything's so smashed up it's hard to tell. Rocks rattle against the hull. The craft's maneuvering through a narrow space that's thick with dust, though greenery is strewn along one wall. The Operative quickens the speed. The space through which they're moving is getting ever narrower. But their craft's like a cat: it retracts its legs, distends its body to the point where it's almost wriggling. It kicks from side to side. It slides forward—and then it's through. The screens light up with enclosed space that stretches out into forever.

• • •

O kay," says Spencer. "Something's moving again."
It's ten minutes later. They've been floating in
this room for far longer than they'd like. They've seen
plenty of Praetorian hardware being shifted around in the direction of the hangar—breaking the horizon here and there,
then dropping back below it. That's not what's got Spencer
worried.

"Where?" asks Linehan.

"There."

Way out in the other direction. Almost out of the angle of
the mirrors. Spencer and Linehan triangulate. Focus. On—

"That."

"Yeah," says Linehan. "That's definitely something."

"That's what I've been trying to tell you."

"What the fuck is it?"

"Hard to say. It's only just scraping the top of the horizon."

"Is it on the cylinder?"

"It's on this rock or I'm a mountain goat."

"Maybe you are. I don't see it now. Not anymore."

"It's right th— No." Spencer shakes his head. "It's gone.
Fuck."

"Don't know what you're complaining about," says
Linehan. "At least it's not heading this way."

"Yeah, but they're moving something around out there."

"Sure they are," says Linehan. "Probably a lot of stuff too.
But it's what we can't see that should have you worried."

"Meaning?"

"Meaning who the hell's responsible for keeping an eye on
all the corridors that lead into this room?"

"I presume other Praetorians—"

"I wouldn't presume anything, Spencer. We're not *on* the
perimeter, we're *past* it."

Spencer shakes his head.

"And I don't know what you mean by *other*," adds Linehan. "It's not like we're part of that gang—why are you laughing?"

"Because we're Praetorians whether you like it or not."

Emptiness stretches all around them. The fighting's long since over. All the fires are out. There's no oxygen left, just vacuum filling thirty kilometers that were once the pride of the Euro Magnates. Only a fraction of those kilometers are visible. Light gleams in a few places, reflected off the remnants of the mirrors that still hang from the sides of the cylinder. But mostly it's just dark. If there are still survivors out there, they'll be huddled in sealed rooms watching their air dwindle. Wondering what happened. Wondering how soon they'll join everybody they ever loved. They won't be waiting long.

"Hope neither of you owned any property here," says Lynx.

"I shorted the market," says Sarmax.

"You probably did," says the Operative.

Lynx laughs a dry chuckle. "So what's the plan?" he asks.

"Act like we're part of the scenery," replies the Operative.

The craft starts creeping through the rocks that descend into the blackened valley beneath. Though *creeping* doesn't exactly describe it. It's more like a kind of loping. It's super stealthy nonetheless. Camo programs barely off the drawing board are working overtime. The craft's paws are barely touching the surface. There's almost no vibration to speak of. They leave the chaos of the collapsed mountain behind, move out into the valley.

"Carson," says Sarmax on the one-on-one.

"Yeah," says the Operative.

"We need to talk."

"Yeah?"

"She's up here."

"Really."

"You don't sound surprised," says Sarmax.

"You've been acting kind of funny."

"Funny?"

"The way you always act when she's on your mind."

"She's always on my mind."

"Really getting to you, then."

"Because she's up here."

"How do you know that?" asks the Operative.

"I saw her."

"Hey," says Lynx on the general channel, "wouldn't we be better underground?"

"Why's that?" asks the Operative as he puts the one-on-one on hold.

"Surely it'd be harder to see us."

"Seeing's one thing," replies the Operative. "Doing something about it is another."

Meaning it's a judicious balancing act. Anything they run into in the cylinder's basements is likely to be right on top of them. Anything that spots them in the vast interior is going to have a lot more difficulty sneaking up on them. Doesn't mean it's impossible. If this was a normal crawler or an earthshaker, they may as well strap a homing beacon to their ass. Because there's almost certainly plenty of hardware at large in this cylinder. Along with God knows what else . . .

"Yeah," says Sarmax, back on the one-on-one. "I saw her."

"Where?"

"In front of the gate to the Hangars. Right after I got blasted against a wall."

"And knocked your head up pretty bad."

"You don't believe me."

"Because she's dead."

"Is she?"

"You killed her."

"That's what I thought too."

"Holy shit," says Lynx, once again on the general line.

"I see it," says the Operative.

"Jesus," says Sarmax.

The valley above them is even more shrouded in shadow than the one they're in. But the angle of the cylinder's rotation allows reflected sunlight to dribble across its upper reaches. The surface revealed is alive with movement. All of it going in one direction . . .

"The asteroid," says Lynx.

"Going to be quite a slam-dance," says Sarmax.

 Only question now is when it starts."

"It may already have," says Linehan.

"Meaning?"

"They may have already gotten inside the perimeter."

"I guess we'll find out soon enough."

"Maybe sooner."

"What's that supposed to mean?" asks Spencer.

"It means you and I are big fucking asterisks."

"Said the man who used to be a SpaceCom assassin."

"Used to be?"

"You about to tell me something I don't want to hear?"

"Turns out they got in here as well," says Linehan.

"Who?"

"SpaceCom."

"*What?*"

"While you were out hunting ammo, I was talking with some of the marines."

"Yeah?"

"Yeah. They said that SpaceCom managed to infiltrate a

bunch of assholes into the Platform to take down the Throne."

"They were trying to use the Rain *again?*"

"No one uses the Rain. The Com learned that lesson the hard way last time. No, this was a separate plot, aimed right at the president."

"And they didn't make it."

"Didn't get near him."

Spencer's eyes narrow. "And were you part of this?"

"If I had been, I'd *be* dead instead of just thrust out beyond the perimeter about to *get* dead."

"The Manilishi definitely cleared you."

"But the Throne still didn't like the looks of me."

"Can't say I blame him."

"It's enough to make a man paranoid."

"Isn't that your natural state?"

"Paranoid about *you.*"

"You need to relax," says Spencer.

"You need to tell me who you really are."

"Get a grip on yourself."

"Just answer the question."

"I'm Lyle Spencer," says Spencer as he readies his weapons. "Who are you?"

"Seb Linehan."

"What the hell are you on, Linehan?"

"I'm high on life."

"And a damn sight more than that."

"So what if I am?"

"So what are you on?"

"Ayahuasca."

"Getting dosed in South America wasn't enough?"

"Same dose, Spencer."

"What?"

"Same dose, Spencer."

"You're still—"

"Hallucinating. Yeah."

"Three and a half days later?"

"Has it been that long?"

"You don't *know*?"

"I don't even know which way is up anymore."

"There is no up," says Spencer. "Not out here."

They're deep into the valley now. They're sticking to the forests whenever possible, though far too many of the trees have been ripped from the ground, along with all the leaves. It's like the land of endless winter now. There's no sign of life anywhere. No sign of movement either.

"Too dark to see if that shit's still up there," says Lynx.

"We'll dodge it if it is," says the Operative. "They're not looking for us. They're just busy getting into their assault positions around the Throne's perimeter."

"Fucking great," says Lynx.

They move out of the woodlands and start along a riverbed. The water's at one with the vacuum now. Sun glints above them as the cylinder rotates, gleams off the tens of thousands of bodies drifting along the axis as Sarmax starts up the one-on-one again.

"I'm telling you it *was* her," he says.

"You're saying Indigo Velasquez has risen from the dead?"

"I'm saying I didn't finish the job."

"*Oh,*" says the Operative softly.

"Oh. All that time, and all you can say is *oh*? I left her bleeding on the floor of a suborbital. I bailed out. Ship bit Pacific minutes later."

"And her body was never recovered."

"Nothing was," says Sarmax. "*Carson, it was her.*"

"Easy," says the Operative.

"Ten years gone," says Sarmax. His voice is hollow. "Ten minutes I lay senseless in those tunnels. I drifted against a wall and the combat raged around me. I opened my eyes and couldn't move and *she* was moving past me."

"Faces can be imitated," says the Operative. "Just ask the Throne."

"It wasn't just the face," says Sarmax. "It was the way she looked at me. The way her eyes narrowed. She *recognized* me."

"She was the perfect soldier. If she saw you, she would have killed you."

"She was the love of my life."

"Exactly."

"Look—"

"No," says the Operative, "*you look.* You suffered head trauma in that fucking slugfest, and before that you'd been cowering on the bottom of the Moon for a fucking *decade* trying desperately to think of anything but her."

"I'm not going crazy!"

"Who said anything about crazy? You've just been under a lot of stress."

"*Shit*, man—"

"What did your armor's cam-feeds show?"

Sarmax hesitates.

"Have you even *looked?*" asks the Operative.

"They were junked. They showed fuck-all."

"Can I make a suggestion?" says Lynx.

"What the hell are you doing on this line?" asks Sarmax.

"That'd be hacking it."

• • •

 So you're still tripping," says Spencer. "So what?"
"Would have thought you'd be a little more concerned."

Spencer gestures at the view in the window. "It's all relative," he says.

"But after the Jaguars dosed us, InfoCom erased my systems and rebooted me. The Manilishi probably did the same."

"So?"

"So how come I'm still tripping?"

"How the fuck am I supposed to answer that?"

"And why aren't you still flying too?"

"Maybe the Jaguars gave you a heavier dose."

"Fuck, Spencer, I saw the way your eyes looked back in
that goddamn temple. The Jags were trying to interrogate us
both, weren't they? No reason they would have given you the
lightweight version."

"There's *every* reason. You're twice my size, Linehan.
Maybe they were trying to account for it and fucked up.
Maybe you're just highly receptive. What's your normal
dosage on combat drugs?"

"I don't take combat drugs."

"You're kidding me. I thought all mechs did."

"My officers always said I was a natural born psycho."

"No arguments there. Look, I take a lot of shit to let me
run zone. Razors are used to altered states, that's all we're
ever in. No wonder you've been having such a hard time."

"It's getting harder by the moment."

"Why the hell didn't you tell InfoCom the ayahuasca was
proving so persistent?"

"I figured your team wouldn't be that happy."

"We could have given you an antidote."

"Assuming you let me live, sure."

"One rogue factor gets past the conditioning, maybe there
are others?"

"Exactly."

"Not of the sort that would matter," says Spencer. "The InfoCom reconditioning wasn't aimed at any recreational drugs you might have taken—"

"Recreational?"

"Whatever. Point is it was aimed at your *loyalties*."

"That's what I'm worried about."

"Because you no longer feel like fighting for the Throne?"

"Fuck, man, as long as I was *fighting*, I was loving it."

"So what's your problem?"

"There's no combat."

"And?"

"And the suspense is getting to me."

"You never struck me as the type to get scared."

"Precisely why I'm getting so freaked out."

They've emerged from the riverbed, forged on into fields purged of all harvest. Dead valley stretches all around, with two more like it stretching far overhead . . . all three converging on the shattered city that dominates the northern end of this cylinder. Call that city capital of memory, because that's all it holds now. And the men now approaching it have the same problem.

"I'm going to rip your head off," says Sarmax.

"Not so fast," says the Operative.

"He's right," says Lynx.

Of course he is. Combat inside the Remoraz would be insane. Sarmax would have to blow one of the vehicle's hatches to even turn around to face Lynx. But Sarmax seems so angry right now the Operative's not taking any chances.

"Anyone starts anything, I'll take 'em out myself," he says. "Lynx, you've got some explaining to do."

"*I've* got some explaining to do?"

"So start talking," growls Sarmax.

"What's there to explain? Guess Carson's not as good a razor as he thinks he is. I hacked his ass, and got my cock right up in it."

"Or Carson let you do it," says Sarmax.

"Why the hell would I do that?" asks the Operative.

"Maybe some misguided attempt to get us all on the same page."

"Man," says Lynx, "you do not want to tell him *any* secrets. Look, Leo, sorry to hear that you're having problems with your woman, but—"

"Watch it."

"I am. I'm watching you lose it and I think you might be missing the point. You're too wrapped up in it, man. You need to think about this from the only perspective that matters."

"Which is?" asks Sarmax.

"Autumn Rain's," says the Operative.

K"eep talking," says Spencer.

"About what?" asks Linehan.

"About what the hell is going on inside your head."

"You are."

"No kidding?"

"I can see straight through you and you're hollow."

"That's what I called you once."

"What?"

"That's what I called you once," repeats Spencer. "The original hollow man."

"Maybe you were right."

"I'm your handler, Linehan. I'm supposed to be right."

"So tell me what the fuck you think is going on."

"I think the basic core of your personality is probably

disintegrating. Essentially what you are is just an empty shell held together by love of killing. Once you're out on your own for long enough, you'll start coming apart."

"Is this some kind of reverse-psychology to shock some sense into me?"

"It's just a theory about what your brain might be up to."

"You really don't think I'm being fucked with?"

"You *were* fucked with, Linehan. By InfoCom and before that by the Jags."

"And before that by the Rain."

"Maybe you should tell me more about that."

Three men in a room that's no room making passage through the land of the dead. Black landscape stretches away toward the unseen outskirts of the city at the heart of it all . . .

"Don't make me go there," says Sarmax.

"You fucking have to," says the Operative.

"Otherwise we can't break this down," says Lynx.

Sarmax nods. Going head to head with the Rain is going down memory lane—looking into the eyes of the ones he hasn't seen for all these years. They never liked him, of course. Partially because he represented the power that brought them into existence. But mostly because they knew that one of them loved him—and for that the men and women who became the Rain could never forgive Leo Sarmax. So when they fled ahead of the Praetorian axe, the woman who called herself Indigo Velasquez had to make a choice. Her brothers and sisters won out over her lover. Her lover killed her for that. He's had to live with himself ever since.

And that's been getting tougher. He thought getting back in the game would be what he needed to get it all behind him. He should have known better; should have known which way this game was heading—that it would bring him to a place like this, stalking his own memories through a maze that hides far more than one mind ever could. . . .

"Easy," says the Operative.

"Goddamn you both," says Sarmax. "She was real. Christ, I shouldn't have—shouldn't have—"

There's a lurch. The screens show the craft's starting to sidle up hills. Starlight filters in through some fissure far above them, bathes the land in a ghostly light. Past those hills the structures of New London stretch up toward an unseen summit. Sarmax exhales slowly.

It's funny," says Linehan. "Looking back on all of it. Coming up in SpaceCom you start to scorn everything that crawls below. Living and breathing it, right? Working for the cause. Night's when they say it is, and day's whenever the sun falls upon you."

"You're not making any sense, man."

"Is that so bad?" Linehan's smile is almost sad. "What I mean is that I'd never been to Earth before."

"Before what?"

"Before I came to your door in Minneapolis when you were doing time for the Priam Combine. Before I walked the streets of Hong Kong in search of a group called Asgard's Banner."

Spencer stares. "That was the only time?"

"Yeah."

"So how—"

"Did I stand it? How do you think? Had muscle grafts to deal with the pull of the planet. Had lung filters to deal with its stench. Had software to prep me for what it'd be like—but nothing could."

"Nor could anything prepare you for Asgard's Banner."

"Though with a name that gay I should have known, huh? Autumn Rain took our codes, and maybe they took our souls too. But standing in that city, with the mountains of planet towering overhead—I think that fucked my head even more than the ayahuasca. I feel like all of it's still playing out within me."

"Same here," says Spencer.

"Do you see shimmering out of the corner of your eye?"

"Sometimes. Probably not as strong as you."

"Do you see cat-skulls when you sleep?"

"I never dream. I'm surprised you do."

"I don't."

"Dream?" asks Spencer.

"See cat-skulls when I do."

There's a pause. The two men look at each other.

"I see them when I'm awake," says Linehan.

"That's a problem."

"And the rest of this bullshit isn't?"

Creeping through streets filled with fresh wreckage and dead flesh. Stealing past buildings that have collapsed in upon one another to crush whoever was taking refuge within. Took more than fifteen years to build this city and less than fifteen minutes for it to die.

"Indigo always was a survivor," says the Operative.

"Of course she was," replies Sarmax. "I trained her."

"You trained all of us," says Lynx.

"And we all trained the Rain," says the Operative. "And that's why we need to go back to first principles to beat them. They knew the three of us would be up here. And you're the only one of us who let himself get emotional over one of them."

"But you took up with—"

"Do I look like I'm letting it get to me?"

"The man's ice cold," says Lynx.

"Cold enough to realize that the odds of the Rain trying to fuck with you are pretty good," says the Operative.

"Maybe," says Sarmax.

" 'Seize all advantages', that's what we told them. Any of them could be wearing her face."

"*All* of them could be wearing her face," says Lynx.

"Or it could just be combat fever," says the Operative. "You want to see her, and you do. It happens."

"Shit," says Sarmax.

He's staring at bodies. Most of the population seems to have perished as the seals burst. Those who made it into suits and airlocks found their sanctuaries hacked. Those who took their suits offline were shot down by the servants of the Rain. Sarmax clears his throat, swallows.

"I know they could be fucking with me," he says. "I know I could be fucking with myself. It isn't helping."

"This isn't about trying to help," says Lynx.

"This is about trying to get inside *their* heads," says the Operative. "Inside their schemes. The Throne reckons three of their triads hit each cylinder. We think all three of the ones chasing the East got nailed when the Coalition's leaders blew themselves to kingdom fuck. We think one of the three after us went down when the asteroid buttfucked the mountain."

"Still leaves two full triads after us," says Lynx.

"But they'll be wishing it was more," says Sarmax.

"This is coming down to the wire," says the Operative. "They're going to want every advantage they can get."

"And if they can get to you, Leo," says Lynx, "they're halfway there."

"You're the last person I'd expect to say that," says Sarmax.

Lynx shrugs. "I owe you a lot. Doesn't seem much harm in admitting it."

"And without your drugs you'd be perfect."

"That's what *makes* me perfect. How else could I get this city around my fucking brain?"

"Christ almighty. You're high right now."

"That's how he does his best work," says the Operative.

And who the hell can blame him? Not with Hades itself unfurling on the screens. Not with all these shattered roads to keep on reaching up to that wraparound summit so far overhead. But it's what's still moving that's the problem now. It's what's close at hand.

"I see it," says the Operative.

More important, their vehicle does. It gets low, gets crafty, slinks through alleys toward the activity that's up ahead. Toward the new scene that's getting built within the heart of the old . . .

"*Fuck,*" says Lynx.

"Economy on war footing," says the Operative.

He's not kidding. Whole sections of buildings have been torn away. The chasm revealed stretches down through basements, through maintenance levels beneath, and into what was once the spaceport. The light that emanates up from that chasm isn't visible from the rest of the cylinder. But it's certainly visible to the ones peering beyond its edge. The walls are thick with machines of every size. Who seem to be busy slicing up everything in sight: floors, walls, spaceships, launch derricks, equipment. Not to mention . . .

"Yeah," says Sarmax, "those are people all right."

"The meat gets tossed," says the Operative. "The implants get kept."

"Not very efficient," says Lynx.

"Doesn't need to be," says Sarmax.

. . .

Rumbling fills the room, dies away. Spencer and Linehan glance at each other, glance out the window. Nothing's visible, save the Earth dropping back out of sight again. But something's definitely happening out beyond the shoved-up horizon . . .

"Kills you, this waiting," says Spencer.

"Not much longer now," replies Linehan.

"What the hell are they *doing?*"

"Getting ready to overwhelm the perimeters with their hardware."

"Leaving open the question of where they themselves will strike."

"Maybe they'll come straight through our position."

"Maybe they're *in* our position already," says Spencer.

Linehan stares at him. "I hope not."

"Where exactly in Hong Kong did you meet the Rain?"

"Little Sydney district."

"Where *exactly?*"

"Bar at the Hotel Rex. I ordered a coffee, and then handed them the keys to down the Phoenix Elevator."

"How many of them?"

"A man and a woman."

"Or not."

"Might have just been robot proxies," admits Linehan.

"Might have planted anything inside you."

"I used to worry about that. But now I figure if the Manilishi couldn't find it, we're all fucked anyway."

"Well," says Spencer, "at least that story's the same one you were telling InfoCom's interrogators four days back. No one's fucked with it since."

"By changing up my memory?"

"I'm just checking. It's all I can do."

"Not for much longer. The Rain's going to have to fire this

party up before the Throne . . ." Linehan pauses, stares out the window at the Earth.

"Before *what*?" asks Spencer. Linehan looks back at him with a strange expression on his face.

"Before the Throne finds a way out," he says.

"You mean by incinerating himself."

"Sarmax was hinting to me that if he does that, the Rain may take over regardless."

"So what's your point?"

"That the Throne might just try to get out the same way he got in."

A pause. Then: "You're not serious."

"Of course I am."

"He can't do that."

"He sure as fuck can *try*."

They've left that chasm behind. They're moving into the very heights of the city. The gravity's dropping away around them. There are signs of more combat here: buildings flattened like something's plowed through them. The remnants of something lies in the middle of the street in front of them.

"One of our shakers," says the Operative.

"Must have got nailed right out of the gate," says Lynx.

The droids that did it lie in pieces all around. The main Praetorian spearhead exited the city far lower—went through the basements and then surged out into the suburbs. This was one of the flanking formations. Another shaker's laying on its back, farther down the city slope, in the middle of a crushed bridge. The Operative maneuvers round it, takes the Remoraz up stairs that become ladders that lead past some of the more rarefied neighborhoods. Conventional wisdom says that people prefer gravity to its lack. But conventional wisdom ended up playing second fiddle to the law of scarcity. The views up near the axis are exclusive.

Maybe even more so now. The city falls away beneath them like a wall down the side of some dark well. Electric lights stutter here and there—stand-alone generators still holding out against the odds. The valleys beyond are just black, lit up by the occasional streak of sun. Nothing moves in all that gloom. Nothing visible, anyway.

The Operative works the controls. Their vehicle leans off the ladder, leans against a wall, kicks off with its back feet, drops down to a balcony, its front feet extended. Laser cutters set within the feet trace arcs in the window before them. The craft extends its nose, shoves. Plastic gives way. The Operative gestures at the shadowed city on the rear screens.

"Take a good look," he says. "Might be your last."

"Let's hope so," says Lynx.

"Let's do it," says Sarmax.

They start their journey into the interior.

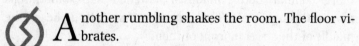

Another rumbling shakes the room. The floor vibrates.

"What the fuck," says Spencer.

"Take a wild guess," says Linehan.

The rumbling intensifies. The gun beneath their feet starts swiveling on automatic. They can feel it sliding back and forth, seeking targets, sensing them close at hand . . .

"Jesus fucking Christ," says Spencer.

"Like he gives a shit," replies Linehan.

The vibrations are relentless now. The sensors show they run the gamut—ranging from almost undetectable to off-the-charts unmistakable. It's almost impossible to discern the exact nature of any one of them. But in aggregation they tell

Linehan and Spenser all they need to know about what's clearly taking place. Explosions ripping apart bulkheads, shakers grinding through walls, shots slamming into everything and then some—combat's under way. The two men eye the windows, the door, the corners. Almost as though they suddenly expect their enemy to spring from the walls. Which may not be an illogical assumption.

A gun-tower off to the side suddenly balloons outward, silent explosion tearing its turret off and tossing it into space. Suited Praetorians are emerging from a bunker nearby, firing at something still unseen. Even as they do so, a frag-shell lands among them, shreds their suits, leaves pieces floating lifeless.

"Getting hot," says Spencer.

"What the hell's that?"

A new rumbling's shaking the room, coming from straight out beyond the perimeter. It bears a familiar vibration signature.

"That was what we heard earl—"

"I know," says Linehan.

And now they're seeing it again too: some strange object protruding just beyond the asteroid's horizon. Something that's not small. And that's rising steadily from the horizon. Not because it's getting any larger. But rather . . .

"It's heading straight for us."

"What the fuck is it," says Spencer.

"I'm not sure it matters," replies Linehan.

The basements of the shattered city that reigned as queen of neutral space give way to maintenance corridors that give way to freight conduits that give way in turn to . . .

"These look familiar," says Sarmax.

"They should," replies the Operative.

Because this is where it all kicked off. The warehouses through which they're moving are the ones from which the shakers set off on their breakneck haul across the cylinder more than twelve hours back. They're empty now. Backup filaments cast a feeble light. The Operative wonders how many of the soldiers who waited here are still alive. He lets the vehicle prowl up a ramp and rise through more trapdoors and into another corridor. A vaultlike door lies open at its end.

"Fucking déjà vu," says Lynx.

They head through, into a familiar double-leveled chamber. The darkness is near total, save for the light of stars coming in from the window facing space. The Operative amps the craft's photo-enhancers, uses the starlight for a close inspection of the room.

Not that there's much to see. It's mostly empty. Though it's obviously been ransacked since the Praetorians took off. Wall panels have been ripped down, tossed aside. Flooring's been torn up. The area where the Manilishi and the ruler of the United States once stood shows signs of special attention.

"Due diligence," says Sarmax.

"They'll have found nothing useful," replies the Operative.

But he understands the thinking. Make sure you're in a position to capitalize on every fuck-up. Or anything that even looks like one. Which is why the Operative has crossed from pole to pole again. Why he's come back to this room. And why he's turning to the men behind him.

"It's time," he says.

• • •

The final stage of the last battle's under way. The Rain's machine proxies are hitting the Praetorians all along the perimeter. They're pressing for a break-through along several fronts. Spencer and Linehan are right in the middle of one such area. They've never been so fucked. Nor have they ever seen anything like what's now bearing down upon them.

"Look at the *size* of that fucker—"

"I noticed," says Linehan.

There's no way he couldn't have. It's three stories high. It's like a medieval siege-tower on acid. Guns are mounted all along it. Magnetic treads drive it forward. It's some kind of modified construction robot. It used to dig out chambers in this asteroid. Now it's going to plow like hell all the way to the Hangar, racking up a fuck-sized body count as it does so.

"We've got to get below," says Linehan. "We stay here, we're just a speed bump."

"Someone's got to stop it," says Spencer.

"No reason it has to be us."

Plasma starts streaking past them. Guns mounted atop the behemoth are firing. Shots are striking home along the in-ner perimeter. Their bunker's own gun is firing back. And be-ing targeted.

"We're outta here," says Linehan.

"Agreed," says Spencer.

They haul open the trapdoor, pull themselves into the corri-dor beyond. Rumbling cascades through it. But it's still empty.

"Back the way we came," says Spencer.

"Fuck," says Linehan, "the Praetorians'll shoot us if we run that way."

"What would you have us do?"

"Admit we're out of options."

"Meaning what?"

"Meaning get unpredictable."

• • •

The three men get busy getting ready, pulling their stashed equipment out of the vehicle, snapping pieces together, soldering others, configuring what's taking shape before them.

"Faster," says the Operative.

They're trying, but it's tough work. Not to mention tense. At any moment something might streak into the chamber and crash their little party. They keep on pulling pieces from compartments, unloading the cargo they've brought with them.

"Looking good," says Sarmax.

So far. The composite structure is almost the length of the Remoraz. But it's still taking shape. And they're pretty much out of things to add to it. The cargo they packed is almost gone. In fact—

"We're out," says Lynx.

"Somebody fucked up," says Sarmax.

"Relax," says the Operative. "We got everything we need."

They look at him.

"*Oh,*" says Sarmax. "Got it."

"Knew you would," says the Operative.

So what the fuck are you suggesting we do?" yells Spencer.

"I'm making this up as we go!" screams Linehan. He fires his suit-jets, starts heading out beyond the perimeter, down a corridor that seems like it's going to buckle at any moment.

"Linehan! Come back!"

"Come with me!"

Spencer curses—but heads after Linehan. Who he figures has finally lost it. Or just bowed to the inevitable. Because the shit's hitting from every side. And Linehan's right. Everyone who retreats is going to get run down or else be butchered by their own side. Spencer's on the point of trying to do exactly that to Linehan. But instead he just keeps on racing after him, even as he realizes what the man's up to.

The Remoraz," says Lynx.

"Yeah," replies the Operative—and ignites a flamer, starts getting to work. Their vehicle's skin looks so real he almost expects it to start screeching in pain. But it doesn't. It just sits there, gives itself up to one last service.

"Did they build it like this?" says Sarmax.

"They built it with all ends in mind," replies the Operative.

Because there are only so many reasons to do the infiltration run. You're either taking a closer look or busting up the china. If it's the latter, then you need to make sure you can pack a punch. Their vehicle's got rear and aft KE guns, not to mention micromissile batteries. But sometimes you need a lot more than that.

"Tap its generators," says the Operative.

"Tapping," replies Lynx.

"Load the nukes."

"Loading," says Sarmax.

"Target sequencing," says the Operative.

"Initiated."

They're stumbling forward as the floor shakes beneath them. The walls are buckling. Vibration churns within their suits. Repurposed police droids are appearing at the end of the corridor. Three of them. One looks like a large spider; it clambers down the walls toward them. The others rev their treads, close in. But Spencer and Linehan are already firing: letting their armor absorb shots, spraying KE into those treads, dissecting legs with a fusillade of fire. They charge past the wreckage, keep on going.

"Fuck yes," says Spencer.

"We'll break on through," says Linehan.

Not that there's much of a plan beyond that. Apparently Linehan's just figuring that they might be able to get into an area of the asteroid that's less trafficked. Somewhere they can await events. But those events have caught up with them anyway. Smartdust's swarming into the corridor on both sides. Spencer's suit is flinging out thousands of flechettes. He's pumping hi-ex down the corridor. Linehan's doing the same. The microshit disappears in sheets of light. The corridor crumbles under the blasts. The two men are knocked sprawling. The floor starts rising up behind them.

"What the fuck!" yells Spencer. He's trying to get to his feet, gets tossed off them yet again. Linehan is firing his thrusters. He rises, grabs onto the shaking wall. Just as the floor bulges—and breaks. A huge tread smashes through it.

"That bitch is right on top of us!" yells Spencer.

"Below us," screams Linehan.

"Whatever!" Spencer fires his thrusters, only to switch them off again as minidrones start pouring into the corridor's far end. They're a fraction of a meter in length. There are hundreds of them. They roar in toward Spencer and Linehan, who fire bombs down the corridor toward them. Explosions start tearing targets apart. But...

"Not enough!" yells Spencer.

"Only one way out of this," says Linehan.

He gestures behind them, where the tread's still slicing through the floor, leaving torn metal in its wake. Through that gaping hole Spencer can see stars. Linehan hits his thrusters, blasts out toward them.

• • •

Their vehicle's looking more than a little skeletal. Strips have been torn from its sides. Half its head is gone. But the power plant in its belly is still intact. Cables run from beneath it to the multibarreled contraption that's taken shape alongside.

"Stand by," says Lynx.

"Scanning for target," says Sarmax.

He's looking down a barrel five meters long: straight out the window that looks out into space strewn through with stars. Some of which aren't stars. Some of which have shown up a little more recently. Some of which are proving to be a real pain in the ass.

"At power threshold," says the Operative.

"Main target acquired," says Sarmax.

The Helios is only eighty klicks away. It's far too big to miss. Nailing it is going to be a piece of cake. The real problem is nailing what counts within it.

"Acquire nexus," says the Operative.

"Scanning," says Sarmax.

Which is when lights suddenly start filtering into the room through the open door—lights of something coming their way. Something that's not in the mood to be stealthy.

"Acquire nexus," repeats the Operative.

"I'm working on it," hisses Sarmax.

The two men shoot through the rift in the asteroid hull, surge on out into space—and total chaos. The spectrums are on overload. Directed energy's flying everywhere, all too much of it aimed at the thing that's towering above them. Linehan darts in toward it.

And Spencer follows. Because he sees the logic, mad though it may be. The only thing this thing can't hit with its guns is itself; he charges after Linehan, thrusters flaring, as the surface beneath him erupts anew. The charges Linehan tossed down there are detonating. The drones are getting shredded. But the two men have bigger things to worry about.

One giant thing, in fact. Whose lowermost rear guns are lowering still further, unleashing plasma that's spraying over their heads as they dart past it, grabbing onto metal paneling and . . .

"Get in there!" screams Linehan.

G ot it!" yells Sarmax.

"Preliminary burst," says the Operative.

Energy streaks from one of the barrels of the gun, strikes the room's window, melts a hole in it, melts the edges around the hole. Plastic drips. The light in the doorway's growing brighter.

"Zero margin," says Lynx.

"So take the shot," says the Operative.

"With pleasure," says Sarmax.

Energy streaks from the main barrel out into space.

They've got their laser cutters out, ripping away at the metal in this beast's side. Linehan's almost gotten a whole panel off. Spencer's halfway through another when the panel suddenly slides aside— he moves with it just in time to evade the burst of KE rounds from the minigun that's extending from the space within. In the next instant he's slicing the barrel in two and pivoting past it, cutting through the metal beyond to reveal an opening. He and Linehan crawl through it as fast as they can go. As if sensing their intentions, the vehicle starts speeding up, trundling along the surface toward the hangar. More shots slam against it. Spencer and Linehan pull themselves up a narrow chute. A clawed drone leaps at them. They waste it, keep on climbing as the behemoth in which they're riding accelerates.

F irst shot's away," says Sarmax.

"And we're still alive," says Lynx.

Meaning the Manilishi called it. Their laser just struck one of the antennas along the Helios, sandwiched between a solar panel and one of the microwave guns. Codes devised by the Manilishi and enclosed within the wavelengths of the laser are going to town, moving straight to the primary targeting system and paralyzing it. It won't stay that way for long. Whoever's aboard will find a way to beat it. Or else they'll cut the wires and jury-rig the targeting.

But the Operative doesn't intend to give them the chance.

"Round two," he whispers.

And triggers the gun's third barrel. This one isn't a laser at all. Coils touch; electromagnetism surges; nuclear-tipped projectiles sail off into space. Even as machinery bursts into the room: three hunter-killer droids. The Remoraz's rear guns start firing, lacerating targets. The three men spread out as they blast the intruders, trying to maximize cross-fire. Two of the droids are down. The third retreats.

"After it!" yells the Operative.

But Sarmax is already putting micromissiles down the corridor. There's a large explosion.

"Scratch one metalhead," he says.

"Let's get the fuck out of here," says the Operative.

"And leave those?" asks Sarmax, pointing at the laser cannon and the vehicle.

"Along with some souvenirs," says the Operative.

• • •

"The control room," breathes Linehan.

Only nothing human's at the helm. Whoever was running the show before this thing got commandeered has been turned into sliced meat. It's on autopilot now, with a very specific set of directives. The room's shifting from side to side like a boat in an angry sea. The screens show carnage: bunkers getting burned, Praetorians getting laced, metal getting smashed.

"So much for the outer perimeter," says Spencer.

"Shut up and burn it!" yells Linehan.

They lower their arms, start firing. Screens shatter. They start spraying the computers behind the screens. The floor's tilting—Spencer and Linehan are firing their thrusters, trying to stabilize themselves as the monster they're in revs up to speeds well beyond its safety margins. The screens that still remain show it's no longer making for the Hangar.

"Going fucking haywire," screams Linehan.

And then the screens go blindingly white.

Electromagnetic pulse washes across them, but only barely. The warheads weren't designed to spray massive amounts of radiation everywhere. All they were designed to do was annihilate several klicks of target.

"It's gone," says the Operative.

They are too. They've left the room behind, and are now blasting through the gutted chambers of the ultrarich. They can see bodies everywhere. But it's what they can't see that's worrying them...

"Pursuit," says Sarmax.

"No shit," says Lynx.

Shots are streaking past them. Machinery's surging after

them: droids, dust, minidrones, the works. They're turning on their afterburners. But this place is a maze. They can't hit full thrust. They're heavily outnumbered. Meaning they'd better do something fast.

"Back to the cylinder," yells Sarmax.

"Fuck no," screams Lynx. "Let's hit the hull!"

"Neither!" yells the Operative—and explains as they go.

They're setting off nukes!" yells Spencer.

"Can you see where?"

"The direction of the cylinder! Can't tell beyond that!"

Their sensors are overloaded, but their vehicle is still intact. Still running amok, it lurches across an uneven area of the hull—almost tips into a crevasse, but somehow finds the far side. The remnants of the screens show Praetorians and droids scattering, doing their utmost to give it a wide berth. It steams past the main fighting, starts to leave the Hangar behind.

"Let's get out of this fucking thing," yells Spencer.

"Why?" asks Linehan calmly.

Spencer stares at him. They're both clinging onto the walls. "Because we could tip over at any fucking moment!"

"Which means that nothing sane's getting near us!"

"Because we're going to fucking crash!"

"It's still a damn sight safer than *that*," says Linehan, gesturing at a rear-facing screen. The ravaged Praetorian bunkers look like some pockmarked lunar landscape. Drones of all description are waging a full-on assault. Praetorian shakers and crawlers are emerging from hatches farther back in what looks to be some desperate counterattack. But it's clear that the inner perimeter's about to get overrun.

"See what I mean?" says Linehan, turning back to Spencer.

"Yeah? Well, what about *that*?"

And gestures at the same screen. Linehan turns back toward it.

"Shit," he says.

The Rain's machinery is in hot pursuit of the Praetorians who just blew their ace card. Lasers and bullets streak out in search of targets that keep on making turns that leave them one step ahead of the hunters. Carson and his team are coming back into the domain of gravity. But they're not letting that slow them.

"We need some fucking margin," mutters Sarmax.

The Operative says nothing as he leads them down corridors that have seen more than their share of firefight already. Looks like a battle went down here between the Euro cops and their out-of-control droids. Looks like the cops got busted for keeps.

"Nasty," says Lynx.

They shoot through housing levels where ceilings and floors have been carved out with what looks to be an industrial-strength laser. They surge through what might have been a park, come back into more housing levels. The drones are catching up.

"Now!" yells the Operative.

Their bomb racks start spewing out disruptor grenades while their helmets discharge smoke. They toss hi-ex over their shoulders for good measure, swivel their jets, turning and surging out into what's left of a school. Explosions start going off behind them. They hit the ventilator shafts, start searing through them.

"I think we lost 'em," says Lynx.

"Not for long," says Sarmax.

"All we need's ten more seconds," says the Operative.

• • •

The carnage on the screens has to be seen to be grasped. But the onslaught of machinery hasn't reached the Hangar yet. At least not on the surface. It's getting held up by the last stand of the inner perimeter. And back at the Hangar itself . . .

"The fucking doors—"

"They're opening!"

And something's becoming evident on top of the shaking of the machine they're riding. Something that's reverberating through the vibration that's all around.

"Damn," says Linehan, "they're going for it."

They're through into a tube about five meters wide. There are rails running through it. It looks familiar.

"The Magnates' private railway," says Lynx.

"We've been here before," says Sarmax.

"Not this section." The Operative hits his jets, blasts up the tunnel. It bends along a gentle curve. The curve grows sharper, and then dead-ends.

"We should be going the other way," says Lynx.

"I don't think so," says the Operative. He touches the wall, applies pressure, works a manual release—watches as the wall swings back to reveal more rail.

"Nifty," says Sarmax.

"And off every fucking map," says the Operative. He hits the jets.

"Let's hope so," says Lynx.

They cannon down that tunnel. Five seconds, and they reach another dead end.

"End of the line," says the Operative.

He turns to a fusebox, starts throwing switches in a

sequence. A wall starts folding away. The men stare at what's behind it.

"Shit," says Sarmax.

"Now we're talking," says Lynx.

They're in a control room, but they're controlling nothing. The off-the-leash war machine they're riding is rolling away from all the fighting. All the men within it can do is check out the latest thing to hit their screens.

"The Throne's fucking launching!"

"I realize that, dipshit!"

It's hard to miss. It's fifty meters long, the last ship remaining to the man who's desperate to avoid becoming the last president of the United States. It's powering out upon jets of flame, rising above the Hangar and the fighting, lashing out with its gunnery in all directions.

In the cockpit Haskell's presiding over all of it. Grey of walls giving way to black of space; vast doors quivering as the blast of engine hits them; rockscape beginning to recede; Praetorians trying to buy the ship some margin. . . . Myriad images swirl through her head as she monitors the moments after main engine start. The hands of the pilots fly over the controls. Her two bodyguards are staring straight ahead, at the windows past which the Earth is reeling. The ship's accelerating.

And then shuddering as something smashes into it.

. . .

*M*ove," hisses the Operative.

But Sarmax and Lynx are already leaping onto the ship that's their ticket off this dump. It's small. No larger than a jet-copter, it was intended by the Euro Magnates as an escape craft, though they probably never figured on a getaway under these circumstances. The wall beyond starts folding away to reveal the glimmering of space. Sarmax and Lynx vault into the two pilot seats. The cockpit canopy hisses shut, though there's neither time nor need to pressurize the ship. The Operative grabs onto straps at the back, shoves aside the spare Euro suits that take up most of the space remaining. Sarmax powers up the craft.

*H*e's hit!" yells Linehan.

By a KE hurler mounted by the Rain upon the cylinder: a laser aboard the president's ship takes it out even as it fires, but the damage is already done. The ship's gyros just got nailed, locking the craft into an arc that's way too tight. It's veering crazily back toward a point on the asteroid about half a klick from most of the fighting, coming in virtually on top of a certain wayward vehicle . . .

"We're gonna get tagged!" yells Spencer.

"So don't just stand there!" screams Linehan, who fires his thrusters and rockets along the rungs that lead through the hatchway in the control room's ceiling.

• • •

Haskell's just sitting there, visor down and suit sealed. Fear's some sensation far away. She sees rock coming in toward the window, sees the lips of one of her bodyguards moving in silent prayer. She knows she's the only one worth praying *to*. Her mind's surging out through wires throughout the ship as she runs end-arounds, bulldozes a secondary route to prop up what's left of the rudders. It wouldn't mean a thing if the pilots weren't so good. But the deep-spacer flight crew strapped in before her possess intuition of their own. Born of life-or-death moments way past Mars. Moments like this one now. Pilot and copilot and navigator: she gathers their minds into hers as the ship staggers toward the asteroid.

Sarmax hits the gas. Hits it again. Nothing's happening.

"What's the problem?" says the Operative.

"The problem is I can't get this bitch started."

"Keep trying," says the Operative, and extends razorwire, starts getting in on the systems. Lynx is doing the same. Only to find that there's some kind of lock on the ignition. Some kind of Euro code that's still holding out. Something they'd better hack fast.

"We got company!" yells Sarmax.

Two trapdoors blasted aside, and Spencer and Linehan come out onto the siege-engine's roof. The ship's almost on them. It's like some asteroid all its own now: blotting out the sky, engines flaring, nose lifting . . .

"It's gonna miss!" yells Spencer.

"But we can't!" screams Linehan, and fires all his thrusters on full-blast, streaking upward. And suddenly Spencer gets it, sees in a sudden flash what Linehan's doing, sees why—and hits his own jets, sears in toward the metal that's rushing past. A turret whirls toward them; he hits evasive action, knows himself for dead, watches as though in a dream as the turret disintegrates, the cylinder-based DE cannon that nailed it flaring on his screens as onrushing metal fills his visor . . .

"They're crippling it *deliberately*!" screams Linehan.

They crash against the hull.

Screens and windows within a woman's mind: the asteroid falls away even as the last of the exterior cameras show suited figures leaping onto the ship. More shots strike the ship as it hurtles past the asteroid, straight toward the cylinder—and then it somehow straightens, roaring parallel to it. The ship's gunnery teams are exchanging fire with cannons on the cylinder. The ship's cameras are getting taken out. The pilots are relying only on the cockpit window. The ship starts using the last of its batteries to fire missiles into the cylinder—into both cylinders. The batteries are going blind. The missiles are anything but. They crash home.

Minidrones streak into the Euro launch chamber, start opening fire. But the issues their target is having don't extend to its guns. Sarmax starts unleashing the escape craft's flechette cannons on full auto. Tens of thousands of pieces of metal start tearing the minidrones to pieces. What's left of them retreat.

"They'll be back," says Sarmax.

"We're through!" yells the Operative as he finds the key, reverses the ship's codes in a single stroke, locks them in under a new imprint. Sarmax ignites the motors. The ship lifts off from the floor, turns its nose toward the tunnel, fires a bracket of torpedoes.

W hat the hell do you mean?" yells Spencer. It's not the best time for a conversation. They almost missed getting a foothold. They're right at the back of the ship, where the hull narrows around the engines. Plasma pours past them. The asteroid's dropping away; the surface of the cylinder whips by. The other cylinder's coming into view as well. But Linehan seems to be intent on getting his point across anyway.

"I mean the Rain could have *destroyed* this ship! They didn't! They were picking off the monitors! Taking out the guns! They were hitting us to wound! Hitting it to send us on this course!"

"They weren't trying to crash us?"

"Acceptable fucking risk," screams Linehan. "So they could fucking *board it*. Jesus Christ!"

He can't point. All he can do is stare. At the Platform rocketing below. At shards of mirrors. At fragments of debris. At the blackened cylinder.

And at more suited figures rising from it.

T he ship curves away from the Platform. The pilots are getting it back under control. They're flooring it. The Platform's being left behind. In Haskell's mind a countdown's closing on a zero that's precisely calibrated. A voice sounds within her head.

"Situation," says the Throne.

"Ship stabilized," she replies. "Warheads away. They're lodged in the cylinders. But we may have company."

"Beyond the ones we picked up at the asteroid?"

"Don't know."

Though she's got a nasty hunch.

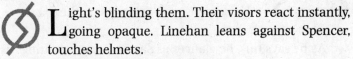 The torpedo blasts start ripping the tunnel apart. The roof of the station's starting to collapse. But Sarmax is hitting the auxiliary jets, letting the ship swan sideways from the minihangar—and then firing the main thrusters. The cylinder starts to recede, along with its twin and the rest of the battered infrastructure that comprises the Europa Platform.

"Good fucking riddance," says Lynx.

Both cylinders suddenly shine as though suns have ignited within them.

Light's blinding them. Their visors react instantly, going opaque. Linehan leans against Spencer, touches helmets.

"You called that one," mutters Spencer.

"They had no choice," replies Linehan.

"But the Rain got aboard anyway."

"Think they'd miss the endgame?"

. . .

Cockpit sensors pick up the gamma rays. The nukes that just ripped apart the cylinders and tore chunks off the one remaining asteroid were far more powerful than those that shredded the Helios. The Rain's machinery just got annihilated. Along with every last Praetorian at the Hangar.

Haskell feels she's about to join them. Because she can't evade the truth. She can see all too clearly how the Rain have played this—that they prepared for the eventuality of the Helios getting nailed. That they were willing to risk crashing the presidential ship in order to get aboard it. The ones she saw leap on were the InfoCom operatives. Who *could* be Rain. Who could have been turned since, or replaced. But it seems unlikely. She checked them out already. And she's got footage of their suicidal assault on the siege tower. She feels she's seen them. Seen what they're up to.

It's what she can't see that has her worried.

Scratch one Platform," says Lynx.

"Those were our soldiers," says the Operative. "Give respect."

As he says this, he glances at Sarmax, who's gritting his teeth, gunning the ship, sending it streaking forward.

"Easy," says the Operative.

"What?" asks Sarmax.

"Focus on the now."

"I'm there," says Sarmax, gesturing at the screens. The blast's fading from them, to reveal empty grids up ahead.

And the president's ship.

• • •

We gotta get forward," says Linehan.

"I'm working on it," replies Spencer.

They're crawling along the side of the ship like mountaineers whose slope keeps shifting like it's trying to throw them off. And while they're moving forward they're scanning as best they can. But all they can see is metal up ahead. As well as...

"Behind us," says Linehan. "Stars—getting blocked."

"By what?"

"Pursuit."

They're hurtling out of the L3 vicinity, and everyone's fingers are on the edge of the trigger. Every airlock's booby-trapped. Haskell watches it all on her screens while her bodyguards watch her, eye the bridge's only door.

"Rearward hull breach," says the pilot.

"Confirmed," says the navigator.

"Combat," says the voice of the Throne.

The metal walls shudder as an explosion passes through them.

We're catching up," says Lynx.

"No way we couldn't," says the Operative.

The ship they're in is the fastest the Euro Magnates could configure. And the craft they're chasing is wounded. They're overhauling it quickly.

"Suits," says Sarmax. "On the rear of the hull."

"Blast 'em," says Lynx.

"Not so fast," says the Operative.

• • •

A signal echoes in Spencer's helmet. The codes check out. Spencer takes the call.

"Yeah?"

"Spencer," says the voice of Carson. "You reading me?"

"Jesus," replies Spencer. "That Carson?"

"You guys turn up in the strangest places."

"So do the Rain. They've boarded."

"Thought you'd say that."

The ship is caught in an agony of reverberations as explosions slam against bulkheads somewhere farther back. The speakers are a cacophony of voices and shots. It sounds like all hell's breaking loose back there. Haskell's bodyguards have their guns out, pointed at the cockpit door. One signals for her to huddle in the corner. She does.

"Rear units no longer reporting," says the copilot.

"Cauterize," says the Throne.

Haskell obeys, sending out the signals. The ship shudders. And diminishes.

Smooth move," says Sarmax.

"Ain't gonna be enough," says Lynx.

Close enough to be visible in the windows: the rearmost sixth or so of the president's ship has suddenly been jettisoned, along with the two men desperately clinging to it.

• • •

Jesus Christ," says Spencer.

"That's a new one," says Linehan.

They're still hanging on—just barely. The engines next to them have shut off. The newly visible engines of the newly shortened presidential ship have switched on, powering the craft away from the derelict that's now drifting through space.

"Guess they thought we were Rain," says Spencer.

"Or else the Rain's inside this piece of tin."

"Which could be about to detonate."

"Which is why I'm bailing," says Linehan, and he hits his jets, swans away from what's now a floating island. Spencer looks at him receding and lets go, follows him. Stars glimmer all around.

"What now?" he says.

"Now we give you a lift," says the voice of the Operative.

The combat's intensifying. More explosions. More shooting. More speakers falling silent.

"They're cutting through the perimeters," says the voice of the Throne—tense, taut. "Can't stop them."

"Fall back," says Haskell. "We'll cauterize other sections."

Which is when her bodyguard is suddenly slammed against the wall. He pitches over even as the other bodyguard's whirling and getting shot through the chest by a nasty-looking heavy pistol wielded by the ship's navigator. The pilot and copilot are drawing weapons, too, vaulting from their chairs. Haskell hits the ship's zone and is pushed back: someone's activated a point-blank jammer. The conduit to which she's connected has been switched off. The pilot yanks the razorwire from her head.

"The Manilishi," he says.

"Which one are you?" she asks.

"You forfeited the right to know."

"You're Iskander. Right?"

"Enough of this," snaps the navigator. "We're here for the Throne. Not her."

"I'll cooperate," says Haskell.

The navigator sneers, kicks off a wall, reaches Haskell. Shoves his gun against her visor.

"Cooperate with *this*," he says—starts to pull the trigger— just as the windows of the cockpit explode and shots start riddling the space within. The navigator crashes into Haskell, gun firing wildly as they both go over. Haskell grabs the hand that holds the gun, turns it toward its wielder, only to realize that there's no resistance. She seizes the pistol, shoves the navigator's body away from her. The bodies of the pilot and copilot are floating lifeless, suits shredded. The windows of the ship are gone. But in that space float more suited figures. They fire their jets, enter the cockpit. She recognizes them.

"Hi guys," she says.

"Here's what's going to happen," says Carson to her and everybody else. "Claire, you're going with Leo. Lynx and I are going to bail out Harrison. Linehan and Spencer: stay here and hold the cockpit."

"Splitting up?" asks Haskell. "Is that a good idea?"

"We need to get you away from the Rain," says Carson. "You can work this ship's zone from the next ship over."

"There's not much of a zone left," she says.

It's true. In the moments after the Rain jacked her, they hacked the microzone aboard the ship. She's reversing the hack now, but the damage has already been done. The ship's defenders are no longer reachable. Carson pulls open the cockpit door and Lynx goes through with his guns at the ready. Carson turns, follows him. Linehan hovers in the doorway covering them. Spencer takes the ship's controls while Sarmax gestures at Haskell.

"Let's go," he says.

⊕ Through the cockpit doors and they're off. The ship is large enough to make that complicated. There's combat going on across both decks. The internal monitors are fucked. Everything's being jammed. The Operative doesn't know where the Throne is. He doesn't know the exact location of the Rain. He's only got one thing going for him.

"The Rain think they've got him caught between them."

"They'll be driving him toward the cockpit," says Lynx.

The Operative has no intention of waiting for them to get there. He and Lynx charge through another doorway, through a chamber, through an engine room . . .

"How many fucking engine-rooms *are* there on this bitch?" asks Lynx.

"Nowhere near enough," replies the Operative.

◖ Haskell follows Sarmax up through the shattered windows and out onto the ship's roof. The Euro interceptor sits atop it, tethered just aft of the cockpit. Its canopy is up. The back's packed with weapons and extra spacesuits.

"We need all those?" says Haskell.

"The Euros were into redundancy," says Sarmax.

"For all the good it did them."

Sarmax nods, then starts the motors as Haskell straps herself in.

• • •

Linehan's crouching at the side of the door, ready for whatever might come through it. Spencer's at the controls. He's watching as the Euro craft sails past the cockpit, engines glowing. It hurtles out ahead of the ship they're in, swings off to the left. As soon as it's out of range of small-arms fire, it matches speed. Sarmax's voice echoes through the cockpit.

"We'll hold here," it says. "Maintain open comlink by laser. Give us the heads-up if you see anything."

"You'll be the first to know," mutters Linehan.

The Operative can guess what's happening. A Rain hit team on the warpath is virtually impossible to stop. Especially in a situation where an opponent can retreat in only one direction. The Praetorians outnumber the Rain by at least ten to one. But with the makeshift zone gone, they can't coordinate with one another. They'll be going down like ninepins. The Operative and Lynx crash through a wall, past more engine blocks, through another wall, through a weapons chamber from which all the weapons have been stripped. They crash through into the chamber where the Throne briefed his senior officers so recently. Two of them drift there now.

"Fuck," says the Operative. He leans toward them while Lynx covers him. "*Fuck.* Both dead."

One of the men he's looking at opens his eyes. The Operative leaps backward, his arms up, guns at the ready.

"No," says the man. He's barely whispering. "Carson... save... save..."

"Where is he?"

"They... cut us off."

"Murray. *Where the fuck is he?*"

"Engine block," says Murray. "Third," he adds—coughs. Chokes. Dies.

"Engine block number three," says the Operative.

"What the fuck's he trying to do there?"

"Stay alive," says the Operative—hits his jets.

Sarmax gazes at the screens. The president's ship is down to three of its six segments. It's hurtling toward the Earth. But by the time it gets there, this'll be long over.

"How can two men succeed where a whole shipful of Praetorians couldn't?" asks Haskell.

Sarmax looks at her. "I doubt they can."

"In which case?"

"We nuke that ship and head for Earth."

"To see if I can reconfigure our zone there?"

He nods. Something on the screens catches her eye. She gestures at it.

"Hello," she says.

Sarmax stares.

And starts screaming orders.

Spencer! Cauterize and go!"

Spencer needs no urging. Titanium doors slam shut two rooms back. Engine block number one blasts to life. The new ship starts roaring forward. Though it's not much of a ship. It's basically the cockpit and the engines, speeding away from what's left.

"What the hell's going on?" asks Linehan.

"The Throne's on the hull," says Spencer.

• • •

Jets and minds racing, the Operative and Lynx hit the engine room, which has just gone silent, surge across the chamber, past the turbines and into the crawlspace that's still warm with the heat signatures of the armor that just passed through. The Operative leads the way, finds the point where the engine shaft's been melted through with thermite. He goes through, rockets down it and into an adjoining vent. Lynx follows him. His voice crackles in the Operative's ears.

"We're sitting ducks in here!"

"Shut up and get ready to fight!" screams the Operative.

Sarmax floors it, starts piloting the craft along an arc that turns it back toward the bulk of the presidential ship. It's shooting headless through space. Ten more seconds, and he can start bringing the forward guns to bear. Haskell works the cameras, adjusts the magnification.

"What we got?" asks Sarmax.

"Two assholes after the Throne."

Fuck," says Linehan, "can't you hold us steady?"

"It's tougher than it fucking looks," hisses Spencer.

He's got his work cut out for him, that's for sure. The truncated cockpit-ship's maneuverability is for shit. He's trying to bring it round and back toward the scene of all the action. The debris that constitutes what's left of the Europa Platform is a speck upon the screen. Spencer's getting the ship under control, turning it . . .

• • •

The Operative and Lynx blast out of the vent to find themselves in a wilderness of panels and struts and wires. No one's in sight.

"Spread out," says the Operative.

Lynx knows the drill. The two men get some distance between them. They're keeping low, keeping each other in sight the whole time. And now the voice of Sarmax echoes through the Operative's ears.

"Carson," it says, "they're on the other side. We've got visual on them. We've— Shit!"

"Talk to me, Leo," snarls the Operative—even as he sees what Sarmax is talking about.

He must have stashed it out there," says Haskell. A man who thinks ahead: the rocket-sled that's now streaking from the ship's hull is piloted by the president himself. It's scarcely bigger than his own suit. It's making good progress all the same.

"Let's get in there," says Sarmax.

"I don't think so," says a voice.

Haskell whirls along with Sarmax. One of the suits in the back is stepping forward, reverting from its Euro trappings to its real ones in a swirl of shifting hues. A minigun's sprouting from its shoulder. A woman's face smiles mirthlessly behind the visor. Her face isn't familiar. But Haskell can see that Sarmax is shaking anyway.

"Indigo," he says.

"You've forfeited the right to know," says the woman.

"For fuck's sake, talk to me."

"Sure, I'll talk to you. Take us thirty degrees left or I'll blast you both into that dashboard."

. . .

Ⓢ H e's veering away," says Spencer.
"So ask him why."
"He just cut off contact."

"Christ," says Linehan, "that's a fucking *sled* out there."

"What?" asks Spencer, and suddenly feels something smack against his shoulder and lodge there. He turns in his chair, sees that he's been hit by a strange-looking gun. It's held by the ship's navigator, who's still slumped against the wall, blood clearly visible behind his visor—but he's turning the gun on Linehan all the same. Spencer dives from his chair, bringing his own guns to bear.

Even as his armor freezes, shuts down as a hack pours from the projectile now embedded within it. Spencer tries to fight it— gets shoved back into his own skull. He floats against the floor. Out of the corner of his eye he can see Linehan drifting helpless, fury on his face. The navigator pulls himself forward to the in- strument panel. Blood's dripping from his mouth. He starts working the controls. His words sound in Spencer's head.

"I'm dying," he says. "But you're already dead."

⊕ T he Operative gets a glimpse of metal falling away, feels himself being hauled out into space. Lynx is about ten meters behind him. They're both hanging onto tethers they've fired at the president's sled.

Problem is, they aren't the only ones.

"Light them up," snarls the Operative.

But that's tough when the ones you're targeting are be- tween you and the sled's rider: two members of the Rain are about twenty meters ahead, clinging onto tethers, one firing at Harrison, the other firing back at the Operative and Lynx— who ignite their suit-jets, dart aside, return fire. The Operative can see Harrison slashing out with a laser, slashing at the tethers—and then sprawling against the sled's controls as shots from the Rain strike him. The sled accelerates. Light fills the Operative's visor.

A white flash from the direction of the presidential ship. It's disintegrating, breaking apart. Pieces of it are flying everywhere.

"What the hell," says Haskell.

"The Throne's last card," says the woman.

Haskell stares at her—is met by an expression of pure resolution.

"It won't save him," the woman adds. "Ships beat suits any day."

"Depends who's wearing them," says Sarmax.

"Enough," she snaps. "Here's what's going to happen."

The wayward cockpit accelerates again. Spencer slides across the floor, drifts against the wall, turns his head within his helmet to behold the navigator putting the ship through a series of maneuvers. Spencer hurls himself against the hack once more, practically gets brain-fried for his troubles.

"Take it easy," says the navigator. "It's almost over."

Contingency planning: the Throne had set charges over his ship to detonate after he'd gotten clear—though *clear* is a relative concept. Debris is flying everywhere. The Operative feels like he's heading through an asteroid belt. It's all he and Lynx can do to shoot at the Rain while they're dodging. Shots whip past the Operative: he reels in the tether, sees the sled rushing closer, sees that one of the Rain's just had his suit perforated by ship fragments. The lifeless suit flies past the Operative, almost knocks him off. But the other member of the Rain has slid forward, reached the sled several suit lengths ahead of the pursuit, and slashed a laser through one of the tethers.

"Fuck," says Lynx.

And tumbles past the Operative. Who can see all too clearly that he's next.

The Euro interceptor gives the expanding field of debris a wide berth. It starts turning one more time along vectors laid down by the woman with the guns.

"How many of you are there left?" asks Haskell.

"Tell this whore to shut up," says the woman.

"What did she do to you?" asks Sarmax.

"Betrayed us, Leo."

"And you betrayed me."

"You've lost it. You don't even know—"

"I know you're Rain," says Sarmax. "That's enough."

"So shut the fuck up and prime this ship's weapons."

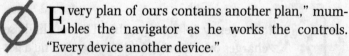

Every plan of ours contains another plan," mumbles the navigator as he works the controls. "Every device another device."

Spencer's hardly listening. He's just thinking furiously. If he could find a way to trigger one of his suit's weapons on manual . . . if he could explode his suit's ammo . . . if he could do fucking *anything*. He hurls himself back and forth against his suit in a vain attempt to move it. He exhales, tries to pull his arm into the space reserved for his torso. But it's way too tight a fit. Out of the corner of his visor he can see Linehan struggling through similarly unsuccessful contortions.

"Thus it is with humanity," says the navigator. "Trapped in a cage while we gaze between the bars."

They hurtle toward the wreckage of the Throne's last ship.

R ain is cutting off the competition. Or trying to—but the Operative fires his jets, surges from his tether, streaking off at an angle as he fires a burst from a wrist-gun at the sled. Shots slam into its motor in precisely calibrated points, knocking its nozzles sideways, sending it careening from its course, straight onto that of the Operative—who reaches out and leaps on to grapple with the suit within.

B ring up the targets," says the woman. "Lock them in."

"Lynx is easy enough," says Sarmax. "He's going nowhere. But Carson's hand-to-hand with your own—"

"Gun them both down," snarls the woman. "It's the Throne's skull I want."

"Don't do it," says Haskell.

"One more word and I'll do you."

"You're going to kill us anyway!"

"At least let *her* live," says Sarmax.

"Long enough for a little brain surgery."

"What the fuck are you talking about?" snarls Haskell.

"Back on Earth, we'll find out what makes you tick."

"Never in hell."

"My minigun's quite the surgeon too. Leo: lock in the targets."

Sarmax complies.

"Crossfire time," mutters the navigator.

Spencer can't see what he's looking at. But the tone of triumph in the navigator's voice is unmistakable. He can see that the man is priming the ship's weaponry, getting ready to fire.

But then he sees Linehan.

Who's hit his suit's manual release. Who's holding his breath. His face is already blistering in the vacuum. His expression's one of total mania. He's hurling himself upon the navigator.

Who turns—

The sled's turning in circles. The Operative pivots against his foe's armor, smashing the other man's helmet. For his trouble, Carson gets a boot to his face, falls backward across the limp figure of Harrison—who's sprawled out unconscious against the steering equipment, barely breathing, his suit holed and cauterized in the lower back. But the Operative's got other things on his mind, like fending off the laser cutter that's slashing toward his face. He ducks in under it, fires his suit-jets, slams head-on against the man, grabs onto his arms and tries to bring his minigun to bear. But they're both too close. Over the man's shoulder the Operative can see the dwindling figure of Lynx, opening up on ships that are closing in . . .

• • •

Shots streak past the cockpit.

"Waste them," says the woman.

"First tell me Indigo's still alive."

"She is."

"You're lying."

"You're stalling."

"You're her," says Sarmax.

"So what—" The woman triggers the minigun, just as something hits the ship. Something that's not small. Velasquez is hurled against the wall, her shots ripping through the ceiling. The other wall's tearing to reveal space—and the cockpit of the president's ship, jammed right alongside theirs. An unsuited man's leaping though the tear, his face more burn than face.

The Operative's letting rip with his flamer, but the other man turns his helmet to avoid the fire, letting it boil off into space, shoving against the Operative, and then firing augmented wrist-jets to suddenly pin him against the sled's rear. The Operative fires his own jets, but to no avail. He's being pushed against the sled's engines—against the reaction-mass still churning from them. His suit's temperature's starting to rise. He lets razorwire extrude from his suit, plunge into his assailant's, feels his mind slam up against the other's even as he starts to smell smoke. But the other man's got razor capabilities too. He's holding his own, keeping the Operative at bay while he shoves him against the heat searing from the sled. In the distance the Operative thinks he can see spaceships colliding. Worlds imploding. His suit's going critical. His failsafes are overloading.

. . .

Sarmax hits the jets, knocks Linehan aside, crashes into the woman, knocks her into the rear of the ship. Haskell gestures at Linehan, pops the canopy, goes through it with Linehan hanging onto her foot—

—holding on for fucking life as cosmic rays lacerate him. Everything's going black. But the hardware that augments his heart keeps chugging away even as his oxygen levels plunge—even as Haskell he's just saved hauls him back into the ship he's just left. His suit's floating where he left it. His field of vision collapses in upon it. Everything spirals in upon a single point—

—as the woman shoves against Sarmax, pushes him away from her.

"It doesn't have to be this way," says Sarmax.

"Oh yes it does," she replies, and starts unloading the minigun at him. He fires his jets, roars under the trajectory, cannons against her, rips the gun from her shoulder. She whips up her legs, kicks him in the chest, vaults backward, then raises her hands and starts firing with her wrist-guns. He does the same. They pour shots into each other. Neither's trying to dodge. Neither's trying to evade. They're just soaking up each other's munitions. The outer layers of their armor are getting shredded. Their visors are starting to crack.

• • •

The Operative's helmet is pretty much at one with the rocket flame. He's seeing stars for real now. He can't budge his opponent. Can't hack him either. At least not with his own mind—he reaches out, extends more razorwire; his assailant shifts slightly to dodge it and the Operative plunges the metal into the prone figure of Harrison. The president may be out of commission, but his software isn't—and now the Operative's running codes given him by the Manilishi, drawing on that software, sending the merest fraction of the executive node surging out and through his own suit and into the suit of another.

And from there into his brain.

The man convulses. The Operative kicks him off into space—and then leaps up to see what's hurtling toward him.

Any second now," mutters the woman.

"We'll hit Valhalla together," says Sarmax.

"Not if I can help it," says Lynx, streaking past the ship and tossing a shape-charge through the gap in the wall and onto the woman's back.

"Fuck," she says.

The charge explodes, blasting clean through her back and chest, knocking her forward toward Sarmax. He grabs her in his arms. But she's already dead. He shoves the body away, starts broadcasting how he's going to kill Lynx and leave him to rot in vacuum. But now Carson is vaulting into the ship, grabbing him, remonstrating with him. Sarmax switches back into business mode.

"Where's the Throne?" he snarls.

"Haskell's on it. With Linehan and Spencer. She restarted their suits. Which the Rain fucked."

"So that's why that nut job was running around without one."

"Apparently he's pretty fucking enhanced."

"I'll say. What happened to the other Rain guy?"

"Dawson," says the Operative. "It was Dawson. Though I didn't know it till the end."

"He's dead?"

"For sure."

"It's finished," says Lynx.

"But we aren't." Sarmax's voice is dangerously calm. "And you'll get it too, Carson. For stopping me from nailing him."

"Jesus Christ," says the Operative, "you seriously want to go head to head with us *now*?"

"There'll be another time," says Sarmax.

It's another time. An hour later. A very jury-rigged ship is starting its journey back toward the Earth. It consists of the remnants of two ships held together by bolts and wires.

"Precarious," says the Operative.

"But functional," says Sarmax.

The two men are sitting in the pilot seats of the Euro craft. The Operative is at the controls. He glances at Sarmax.

"It wasn't her," he says.

"What?"

"That wasn't Indigo who Lynx killed."

"What the hell are you talking about?" asks Sarmax softly.

"I did a DNA test on what was left."

"Ah, *fuck*," says Sarmax.

The Operative opens up a channel. "How's it looking back there, Claire?"

"He's still stable," says Haskell. "He might even make it." She's sitting beside the president. His sightless eyes stare past her. Wires run from her to him.

"And Linehan?"

"He'll be fine," says Spencer. He and Linehan are sitting in their suits, in the remnants of the presidential cockpit. Spencer's at the controls while Linehan siphons oxygen from the heaped-up Rain suits from which the bodies have been stripped.

"You know," says the Operative, "if you hadn't pulled that stunt we'd have been fucked."

"Who the hell are you talking to?" asks Lynx.

"I'm talking to Linehan."

"What was that?" asks Linehan.

"He said without you our asses would be grass," says Spencer.

"Guess you could look at it that way," says Linehan.

"You *guess?*" The Operative laughs. "It's a fact, man. A fundamental fucking truth. You saved us all. The whole fucking planet, maybe."

"Maybe I'll have to visit it again sometime," says Linehan.

Up ahead that world draws closer.

PART IV
GRAVITY
AND RAPTURE

M y fellow Americans."
It's four days later. The U.S. president is on the screen. Short-cropped grey hair above grey eyes. Mouth set in that familiar, reassuring way. Words that say everything his people need to hear.

And nothing that they don't.

"It is with a heavy heart that I address you tonight. But also with fresh hope. The paralysis of the worldwide nets by the terrorists who called themselves Autumn Rain is over. We have defeated them. In attacking the Europa Platform, they hoped to expand their war of terror to neutral targets—targets that lacked the defenses necessary to withstand the Rain's assault. It is my duty to inform you that the Europa Platform has been entirely destroyed, along with the cities of New London and New Zurich. The loss of life was catastrophic. May God help me to tell you the death toll is numbered in the millions.

"But in striking at L3, the Rain overreached themselves. In the aftermath of that terrible crime, we were able to trace the routes of their hit-teams back to the bases from which they struck. We were able to penetrate their lairs and eliminate them wholesale. We have ended the menace of Autumn Rain. Their leaders have been destroyed in the bunkers from which they were planning the world's demise. Their strike forces have been cut down while still en route to their targets. This war is over.

"Our nation has borne the primary role in ending this threat, but we were not alone. Eurasian forces cooperated with ours in bringing the Rain to justice. The East's data was invaluable in building up a full picture of the Rain's location, making our triumph all the swifter. They are our partners, and they should be honored as such. Let the rumors that they were in any way connected to the Rain be laid to rest, along with all talk of a return to the dark nights of cold war. Those days are gone forever.

"Even as I speak, our diplomats are meeting with those of the East in Geneva. Not out of some misplaced fear that the pact of Zurich is on the verge of becoming a dead letter. Nor out of some futile need to seek remedial action to bolster a fragile peace. Mark my words: the peace of Zurich is as strong as it ever was. Even stronger, now that the Rain have vanished from the scene. But we shall not miss this opportunity to consolidate our friendship still further.

"And we cannot ignore the reality before us. The Rain hid behind the borders of neutral nations for a reason. They knew that trying to base themselves within either superpower was an impossibility. Knowing the neutrals' military weakness, they used their territory, first as staging grounds and then as targets. Nor can we be tempted by the Rain's destruction to deceive ourselves into thinking that future elements opposed to civilization and all it stands for will not follow the same strategy. The course before us is clear.

"We are thus coordinating with the Eurasian Coalition to extend our protection to the neutral territories. In doing so, we contemplate no violation of sovereignty. We shall not force ourselves upon any unaligned nation. However, we have every intention of offering aid to those neutrals who wish to secure themselves from future onslaughts like the one that engulfed the Europa Platform. It would be the epitome of injustice to deny intelligence data, military training, and advisers to countries that wish to protect their own citizens.

"Our initial efforts have focused on the Far East, where the Governing Council of HK Geoplex has already invited the superpowers to replace the local police and security units that were destroyed in the anarchy that the Rain unleashed. Rather than allow that city to continue to suffer, we have accepted the invitation. Our troops have taken up residence across one half of Hong Kong; the Coalition occupies the other. While this arrangement is merely a few hours old, we have already brought that great city a peace that its inhabitants had despaired of ever seeing.

"It is inevitable, of course, that there will be some in the neutral nations who disagree with our course of action. To them, we can only say that we hope to have the chance to prove ourselves worthy of your trust. But should anyone attempt in any way to harm our soldiers, we will treat them the same way we did the Rain. Let there be no mistake: if attacked, we will retaliate with a force that will ensure *our* blow will be the last.

"And to the American people, I say we are not about to underestimate the gravity of the course that we are now embarked upon. We must extend our shield across the world for the good of all. We must render sterile all ground from which the seeds of a future Rain might spring. And we must cement our partnership with the Coalition so that we may enjoy the fruits of a lasting peace.

"These last few days have witnessed the greatest trials faced by our nation since the signing of the Zurich treaty. We have paid a heavy price. But we have withstood adversity.

Those voices who called for the unjust punishment of the Coalition have not been heeded. Those voices who said we could not defeat the Rain have fallen silent. As have the Rain themselves. We shall not hear from them again. May God be thanked for that. May God defend the United States—"

Linehan switches the vid off. The reflection on the empty screen shows Lynx standing in the doorway.

"Anything interesting?" he asks.

"The usual horseshit," says Linehan. "Are we outta here?"

"Believe it."

The room is lavishly furnished. Mahogany everywhere. The rugs are practically knee deep. Paintings hang along the walls. Set between two Flemish masters are several screens. The woman on the topmost one looks like someone caught between duty and fear:

"—that this is the latest shooting this morning. The victim, Shuryen Ma, was an outspoken critic of the Chinese leadership. We believe that his parents died in a camp in Burma in the 2080s and that he arrived in HK in 2095, but have yet to confirm this. According to our sources, Eurasian soldiers burst into his home without warning and shot him. Several witnesses were arrested."

"How's it looking?" asks Spencer. His voice echoes through the room from an adjacent one.

"So far, so good," says Sarmax.

He's sitting in the corner of the room behind a table. He spares scarcely a glance at the news. His attention's almost totally monopolized by the camera feeds that show what's going on in the rest of the city. His eyes dart among them as the broadcast continues.

"—and we must advise our viewers in the strongest possible terms not to attempt to cross from this part of the city into what's now American territory. Again, we have confirmed reports that Eurasian soldiers have adopted a shoot-to-kill policy toward anyone trying to move between the sectors. And we have reports of mass arrests now under way in the American sector."

"All depends on whose list you're on," Sarmax mutters to himself as he looks around the room. The body that's sprawled on the rugs seems to have stopped bleeding.

"You done with this guy?" he yells.

"Not yet," says Spencer as he emerges from the other room. His hands are covered with blood. So is his shirt. Razorwires hang from his head. Sarmax looks at him. Spencer shrugs.

"Turns out he's got some kind of spinal backup," he says—turns to the body, extends a laser scapel, scoops out the chip at the base of the spine.

"How much longer?" says Sarmax.

"How about telling me who I'm dissecting?"

Sarmax looks at him. Says nothing.

"Have it your way," says Spencer, "but you're slowing us down. The core data structures are a really weird hybrid. In fact—"

"A traitor," says Sarmax.

"What?"

"The man was a traitor. Alek Jarvin. The main CICom handler in HK."

"CICom? As in Counterintelligence Command—"

"Sure."

"But the Throne had CICom annihilated when he locked up Sinclair."

"All of CICom he could get his hands on, sure. Jarvin cut loose and hit the streets."

"The streets? This is his fucking *house*."

"No," says Sarmax, "it's his fucking *safe house*. From which he was building up as large a stockpile of data as possible in the hopes that he could stay alive for as long as possible. And maybe even win his way back into our good graces."

"Guess that last one was a bit ambitious," replies Spencer as he walks back into the room and shuts the door behind him. Sarmax shakes his head, turns his attention back to the screens where the action's starting to pick up.

"—we're getting reports now of shooting outside the studio." The newscaster's voice is edging toward panic now. Noises are coming from somewhere off-camera. "No, *in* the studio." The woman's standing up now. "I apologize but—"

Her body convulses, drops. She's been hit by a taser. A suited Eurasian soldier steps in front of the camera, grabs the kicking woman by the legs, drags her off-screen. For a moment the camera's focused on an empty chair.

And then a man enters, sits down where the woman was sitting. He looks like any normal newscaster.

"We apologize for the interruption," he says. "We are pleased to resume normal service. The attacks against the Coalition's liberating forces will continue to be dealt with severely. We are compiling a comprehensive list of all enemies of the people believed to be in residence in this city's sector. There are substantial rewards for any information that leads to an arrest. Tune in to the following site for more information—"

Sarmax switches the screen off. "We're out of time," he yells.

"Five more minutes," says Spencer.

"Try one."

"I need more than that to make sure there's nothing else in Jarvin's files."

"Bring 'em with us."

• • •

She's waking up again.

Or at least, she thinks she is.

She thought she was awake awhile back too. But then fire flared against her. Lava fell across her. She was dreaming. She was glad of it.

But now she's in a metal-walled room. Strapped into a chair, in what feels like zero-G. She's wearing civilian clothing. She tries to move—and can't. She tries to access the zone, only to find that she's cut off. The room's clearly been sealed to wireless access. She's not going anywhere. Nor can she remember how she got here in the first place.

All she knows is that something's very wrong. She tries to think back to something . . . anything . . . grasping to remember something that feels *real*. But it's like reaching for land in a world of endless water. Nothing's solid.

Except for the Rain.

She remembers now. After she and the Throne and his operatives reached Earth, she restarted the zone, and the Eurasian zone restarted with it.

That made him angry. She remembers the expression on his face as he lay there with his doctors attending to him. She told him it wasn't her fault the two zones rebooted at the same time. It was just the way the Rain configured the whole thing, though she didn't like the expression on the president's face. It was one of missed opportunity. It was a question in her mind: who knows what he would have done had he been confronted with the temptation of an undefended East? She hates to even ask the question. But Harrison had to be content with settling with the Rain—and even before he could walk again, she was merging her mind with his once more in that strange congress, using the amplified executive node to finish the job they'd started together back at the Europa Platform.

Only this time the Rain had no counterplans ready. They

were caught. They knew it. And there were so few of them left. A triad in Zurich, a triad in London, another in HK . . . she helped the Praetorians wipe them out. She wept while she was doing it. She knew all their names, remembered them all too well. But she didn't trust her memories of them. And she'd already chosen sides.

Or so she thought. Now she's a lot less certain. She stares at the room around her, tries to remember what she's missing.

So what's the story?" asks Linehan.

"The story is you get to stop watching the vid."

"I mean what's up with your hack?"

"I know what you meant. Now get in here."

Linehan doesn't move; he keeps on gazing at the city in the window while the ayahuasca keeps on crackling in his mind. It seems to have intensified now that he's on the Moon. He feels so gone it's almost as if the city's gazing in at him: the heart of lunar farside, the translucent dome of downtown Congreve shimmering in the distance. The L2 fleet's a blaze of lights in the sky beyond. The city beneath it has managed to slip through the events of the last several days. It's been left unscathed.

So far.

"How are we getting in?"

"I'll tell you as we go," says Lynx. "Help me out with this."

"With what?"

"In here, you moron!"

In the other room, Lynx is pulling material out of a rather large plastic container. Material that looks like—

"Those are suits," says Linehan.

"No shit."

"Just making sure we're on the same page."

"You're really getting on my nerves," says Lynx. He pulls

the suit out farther, his new bionic hand hissing softly as he does so. He hands the edges to Linehan, starts pulling at the second suit.

"So where did you get these?" asks Linehan.

"Special delivery. They showed up while you were watching the vid."

"I would have thought I'd have heard the door."

"There was no knock."

"I still would have noticed," says Linehan.

"Alright, asshole, you win. They were here all along."

"Where?"

"Behind that panel." Lynx gestures at a panel in the wall. One that's ever so slightly askew.

"How'd they get there?" asks Linehan.

"You ask way too many questions."

"It's how I stay alive."

"But somehow you keep ending up on suicide missions."

"That what this is?"

"Take a good look at those suits, Linehan."

Linehan does. And then takes an even closer look.

"Wait a sec," he says, "it's not even—"

"But you're wearing it all the same," says Lynx.

The streets are a total mess. Everyone went to work this morning thinking it was just a normal day, only to realize it was anything but. Now they're all trying to get home, or just trying to find a place to hide. Vehicles are jammed everywhere. Everyone's honking. Everyone's yelling.

"What do you think?" says Spencer on the one-on-one.

"I think we need to get a little lower," says Sarmax.

They're on a two-seater motorbike. They're wearing civilian clothing. Sarmax is driving. Spencer's just looking—at the data in his mind, at the chaos on the streets. Sarmax takes the bike up along the sidewalk, weaving through the crowd. People leap out of the way—he steers past them, and down a covered alley. The vaults of the city overhead vanish. They roar through the enclosure and out into more traffic. The city-center ziggurats glimmer in the distance. Eurasian flags fly atop some of them. American flags have been raised on others.

"Divide and conquer," says Spencer on the one-on-one.

Sarmax says nothing. He's lost in thought. Or maybe he's just trying to avoid thinking. He's been acting strange this whole time. When Spencer realized he was being paired with Sarmax he was grateful to be getting away from Linehan. But a day and a half with the new guy, and he's feeling a little nostalgia for the old. Linehan may have been nuts, but at least he was hell-bent on avoiding hell. Whereas Sarmax has been running this mission like a man who's tired of life, as though the one thing that mattered to him in that life is gone. Spencer doesn't know what's up with that. He's pretty sure he doesn't want to. He's got enough on his hands dealing with what's in his head anyway. And now a wireless signal reaches his brain.

"Ignition," he says.

"Good," replies Sarmax.

The only thing that gets Sarmax to talk is something that involves the mission. In this case the news that the thermite they rigged at the handler's safe house has just ignited and is probably busy spreading to adjacent buildings. Nothing back at Jarvin's place is going to be found intact. The only evidence of the mission that's left is on this motorbike.

Which Sarmax is now sending down another alley. It slants downward, turns into a tunnel too narrow for larger vehicles. People jump out of the way as the motorbike roars past them, and then the bike pulls out into a larger concourse-cavern where buildings reach from floor to ceiling. The road here is much wider. Only it's got even more traffic on it. The wrong type of traffic too . . .

"Shit," says Spencer.

"Relax," replies Sarmax.

And stops the bike. To do anything else would attract attention from the Eurasian convoy now steamrollering its way down the center of the road. The two men wait by the sidewalk with the other bikes and mopeds while the drivers of the vehicles trapped in the path of the juggernatus flee past them. The heavy Eurasian crawlers crunch the civilian traffic into so much wreckage. Spencer stares at the power-suited soldiers sitting atop those crawlers.

"The fucking East," he says.

"Better stop thinking that way," says Sarmax.

"Why's that?"

"Because we're here to look the part."

Spencer's been doing his best to make sure that's the case—to make them into Russians who are part of this city's vibrant émigré community—and who fortunately never did anything to get onto the list that the new bosses of this half of HK compiled in advance of their arrival. These two particular Russians have been living here for more than a decade.

Even though they arrived only yesterday. About five hours before Russian and Chinese soldiers showed up, in fact. Infiltration's a lot easier if you arrive before a perimeter gets established. So now Sarmax fires up the motorbike again, takes the vehicle out of the cavern and through a long series of service tunnels. At one point they bump down stairs. Sarmax stops the motorbike just past the stairs and leaps off the back. Starts rigging things onto the wall.

"What's that?" asks Spencer.

"Hi-ex."

"To use on who?"

"Nobody."

"What's up with that?"

"Shut the fuck up."

Spencer obliges. Sarmax finishes what he's doing and gets back on the bike. They keep going, wind along the passage, onto still wider streets, with buildings crowding up the walls along both sides. Cyrillic logos are everywhere. This is an area that's nowhere near as crowded as some of the ones upstairs.

"I'm surprised it's not bedlam," says Spencer.

"It was," says Sarmax, "when it got cleaned out."

"Which was when?"

"This morning. This was one of the first places the 'liberators' hit. I'd estimate half the population got rounded up. Everyone who's left is keeping a low profile."

"Like us."

"Just act natural," says Sarmax. He turns the bike down a side street, hits the brakes, and slides off. He leans the bike against a wall and turns to Spencer.

"Let's go," he says. "Remember, only Russian from now on. I'll do the talking."

Spencer's downloaded the requisite software. But Sarmax has known the language for years. Theoretically that puts them on the same level. But in practice, the edge goes to the man who's actually run missions against the East before. He and Spencer walk farther down the side street past several storefronts. Nearly all are boarded up. The only one that isn't has no signs. Noise can be heard from within, along with music and singing.

"Sounds like a whorehouse," says Spencer.

"Because it is."

A well-appointed one too. With a madam to greet them before they get much farther. She speaks to them in Russian.

"Do I know you gentlemen?"

"I hope not," says Sarmax.

• • • •

She hopes this isn't what it looks like. Because it looks like the Throne's stabbed her in the back. Like he's got her imprisoned. And it doesn't do anything for her peace of mind that the only other explanations she can think of are even worse. Perhaps the Rain got to the Throne after all. Perhaps they were waiting for him in his bunker. Perhaps they'll be here any minute.

But the minutes keep on ticking past, and the only door to the room she's in remains closed. No sound emanates from beyond it. All she's got is the vibration that's coming through the walls, the low humming of some engine. She wonders how long it's been—wonders how long she's been drifting in and out of consciousness.

Wonders whether she's even awake right now.

The thought that she's not continues to be the most optimistic scenario she can think of. But it's not one she takes seriously. She thinks back to the Throne talking to her in the wake of her destruction of the Rain. Telling her he wasn't sure they were all gone.

Or was that her saying that? That they needed to execute the original strategy: needed to combine with the Eurasians to sweep the globe and achieve certainty that the Rain were finished. But then Harrison said he was no longer sure that was the right strategy. That he wasn't even sure the Eurasian executive node had been reconstituted yet. That he needed better data on what was going on in Moscow and Beijing before he renewed his overtures to the East. That he needed her help in obtaining that data.

And she said no.

She remembers now. She said no. And when he asked her why not, his voice wasn't in the tone of a man whose life she'd saved. It was in the tone of a man who had never been denied. Who had learned nothing, as though the hours on the Europa

Platform had happened to somebody else. She'd answered him—said she couldn't play power games. He merely blinked, asked her what she meant. She tried to tell him, but she couldn't explain.

Or maybe she can't remember her own explanations. Because she's having trouble piecing together what happened after that. Something about her begging him to finish what he started. Something about taking détente to the next level. But he'd just smiled—almost sadly, it seemed to her—just smiled and said that détente was a balancing act, that he was the only one who knew how to walk that line. That he couldn't turn back the clock. That he wouldn't want to. That he couldn't rely solely on the advice of a computer...

She'd stared at him. She'd said, *you mean me?* He shook his head. Said—

But now she hears something. On the other side of the door. It's unmistakable. It's electronic locks sliding away.

"Who's there?" she says.

There's no reply. She hears manual dead bolts being slid from their grooves.

"Who's fucking *there?*" she yells.

But there's no reply.

The door opens—

"You been here before?" asks Linehan on the one-on-one.

"What makes you say that?"

"You drive like a man who has."

But Lynx just shrugs, keeps on maneuvering through the traffic on Congreve's outskirts, toward the dome that's rising in the distance. That traffic's pretty light. It ought to be—it's the middle of the graveyard shift. The sun is visible in the sky, but Congreve runs on Greenwich Mean Time. Totally arbitrary—but it has to run on something. And the sun's cycles are of limited aid to those who dwell upon this rock.

"Like I said," says Lynx, "you ask too many questions."

"And you give nowhere near enough answers."

"What exactly do you want to know?"

"I want to know about the fucking mission, Lynx."

And why the fuck they've got no armor. All they've got is workers' suits. They're sitting in the cab of a truck loaded with ore. They got the ore from a train stopped in the rock fields outside of Congreve's suburbs. Normally such a train wouldn't unload until it reached its destination in central Congreve. But apparently there's some problem with the rail downtown. Meaning that now lots of trucks are going where lots of trucks usually don't go.

"I already told you about the mission, Linehan. We're going to deliver this ore to Congreve's citadel."

"Ore that we've rigged with something."

"We just picked it up. I've been driving the whole time since. How the hell could I have rigged it?"

"Maybe it was rigged already."

"Linehan. We were two hundredth in line. There were at least two hundred trucks behind us. The moonscape back there looks like a fucking drive-in theater. How the hell would anyone know what chunk of ore was going to get dumped in the back?"

"You're a razor, Lynx."

"Meaning?"

"Meaning stranger things have happened."

Lynx laughs. "Surely it would have been easier for me to just rig the truck?"

"Did you?"

"No."

"Why not?"

"Because we haven't been ordered to blow the heart of SpaceCom power in Congreve to kingdom come."

"So you *do* know what our orders say."

"What gave you the idea I didn't?"

They're at the city dome. They get scanned, waved through. They halt inside a massive airlock with two other trucks. The instruments show air and pressure manifesting all around them. The far door opens. They drive on through and into downtown.

"Let me put it this way," says Linehan. Possibilities swirl within his head, and he struggles to make sense of them. "What the orders *say* and what we're expected to *do* may be two totally different things."

"Where you going with this?"

"This could be a setup."

"Sure," says Lynx.

"You used the term *suicide mission* earlier."

"That was just a figure of speech."

"You sure about that?"

"I guess we'll see."

"How much do you know about me, Lynx?"

"I know you used to be SpaceCom."

"And?"

"And I'm guessing that's why someone thought you'd be useful in infiltrating your old gang."

"Someone?"

"The Throne."

"Who seems to be intent on mixing things up," says Linehan.

"Meaning?"

"Meaning why aren't you with the rest of your triad?"

"You missing your boyfriend?" asks Lynx.

"You're missing the point. Your triad was hell on wheels. You guys were the fucking elite. And now you've all gone in different directions. Why would he break up a winning team?"

"It wasn't exactly a winning team, Linehan."

"It saved the Throne."

"Who I don't think wants to be reminded that he had to be dragged through two days of space like a diapered baby."

"Oh," says Linehan. "I get it. You're *happy* to be away from those other guys."

Lynx raises an eyebrow. Says nothing.

"You're *happy* to be away from Sarmax and Carson because they never treated you as an equal and—"

"Shut up," snaps Lynx.

"Why should I?"

"Because I'm in charge here, asshole!"

"And could your hard-on about that be any more obvious?"

"Go to hell," says Lynx.

They're coming into the center of the city now. Multiple road levels are stacked above theirs. Buildings tower above them. The dome's sloping up toward its height. Stars shimmer through that translucence. Linehan feels it all pressing in upon him. He shakes his head.

"Look," he says, "all I'm saying is that we saw the Throne in action. We got a sense of how that guy thinks. His paranoia puts ours into the goddamn shade. He's separating everybody who might be a threat to him—throwing them off balance by sending them off in new directions."

"Get a grip, man. He's got bigger fish to fry than fretting over us."

"Exactly," says Linehan. "And now we're one less thing he needs to worry about."

"And you really think it's a one-way trip."

Linehan's brow furrows. "So you really *don't* know what our orders are."

"Did I ever say I did?"

"About a minute ago. Yeah."

"I may have given that impression. But I think I managed to avoid being explicit about it."

"Why the hell are you playing these mind games with me?"

"Do I have to give you a reason?"

"Is it because that's all anybody's done to you?"

"Hardly," says Lynx. "Those pricks are gone. I'm free of them."

"We're about to try and sneak into the most heavily guarded fortress on the Moon's far side without knowing the reason why."

"I'm sure it'll come to me," says Lynx.

O nce upon a time, there was a city on the edge of Asia. A city that didn't like where the twenty-first century was headed. A city that could read the writing on the wall as China emerged from civil strife. A city that embarked upon the impossible and moved a thousand klicks to the east: Hong Kong became HK Geoplex, sprawled across the eastern half of New Guinea. By the early twenty-second century, that sprawl is the largest neutral metropolis on the planet.

Though it doesn't feel so neutral anymore.

The soldiers now shoving their way into the brothel are behaving like a conquering army. Which is pretty much exactly what they are. They hit the Little Moscow district this morning, cleaned out the enemies of the state who thought they'd escaped that state, sent them to makeshift interrogation chambers, or just shot them on the spot. The lucky ones got sent back to Mother Russia for special treatment.

But that's no concern of the soldiers now carousing in this brothel. Get their armor off and get enough vodka in them, and they almost feel like they're on leave back home. But back there they can't get their hands on women like these. These girls come from all over the world. They'll do just about anything. And the soldiers now taking them don't even have to pay. Better yet, they can make the girls pay. And some of them are doing just that.

There are two in particular who are really going to town. Two soldiers who are less interested in sex and more interested in simple violence. They've got some girls in a room all to themselves. They're tossing them all over the place. The screams of the girls can't be heard over the noise of the party that's going on in all the adjacent rooms. And even if they could be, it's not like anybody gives a shit. Not when the madam's getting gang-raped and at least one girl's been shot for resisting.

"Hey asshole," says Sarmax.

The naked man turns round, his eyes widening as he sees the pistol and silencer protruding from under the bed—and then he pitches backward as a bullet crashes through his skull. The second Russian turns around casually from where he's about to bring his fist down against the woman's face— but even as he starts lunging toward his weapons, Spencer's emerging from a closet and shooting him through the face. Both men lie there. Both girls start screaming.

"Shhhh," says Sarmax, emerging from beneath the bed. The girls ignore him, keep on screaming. Sarmax fires quick shots into each of their heads. Bodies tumble while Spencer rounds on Sarmax.

"What the *fuck* is your problem?" he snarls.

Sarmax looks at him. "What's yours?"

"I didn't sign up for this."

"You *got* signed up for it, asshole. And I'm not leaving any witnesses. Now how about you do what you're here for?"

Spencer's about to protest further, but the look in Sarmax's eyes stops him. He kneels next to one of the Russians, stabs razorwire into his eye socket. The head wound his victim received was calibrated to avoid key circuitry. And now Spencer's in that circuitry, dropping in amidst all the software, running the hacks he's been preparing, siphoning off the codes and uploading them into his own head. His new ID clicks into place: he locks it in, turns to the second Russian, repeats the procedure. Only now he downloads the ID wirelessly to Sarmax—who accepts the codes and starts putting on one of the light armor suits that's standing in the corner.

Spencer kneels on the floor and closes his eyes while he lets his mind waft out beyond the two nodes he's just co-opted, out to where a broader zone awaits. It's a zone he's never seen before, save in the training modules through which his brain's been prowling for almost two days now. Ever since they got their new orders from the Throne. Ever since they got sent to HK to do what Spencer's doing now: making an incursion into the Eurasian zone.

And looking around.

At difference. Different colors, different lettering, different symbols—a whole new universe of net. Grids of light billow out all around him. Spencer sees the way those grids overlay against the prostrate HK zone. That net's been commandeered at key points by Eurasian razors—and sliced down the middle too, cut off by what looks like an impenetrable wall, behind which the Americans are presumably up to pretty much the same thing the Eurasians are.

"Hurry it *up*," says Sarmax.

Spencer's working on it. He's climbing up the ladder from the two Russians he's just offed. Ascending a long stairway of codes: to the squad sergeant . . . the platoon lieutenant . . . the regimental colonel . . . the divisional general. Who's at the level that Spencer wants. He reaches in, hacks into the staff plans that give him access to the troop deployments throughout the city.

"Time's up," says Sarmax.

Spencer jacks out, opens his eyes. All the bodies are gone, though patches of blood are still visible on the walls.

"Where did everybody go?"

"The closet," says Sarmax.

"Not gonna help. This place looks like an abattoir."

"I've also got this," says Sarmax. He holds up another thermite bomb. Tosses it under the bed, turns back to Spencer: "By the way, question me again and it'll be the last thing you ever do. Now get that armor on."

"Jesus," says Spencer, "relax." He starts putting on his new armor. He's almost finished when a blast shakes the room from somewhere close at hand. He looks back at Sarmax.

"That what you rigged back along that passage?"

"No, that was my bike."

Another blast shakes the room. It seems to be much larger than the previous one. Much farther, too.

"*That* was the passage," says Sarmax.

But it's all the same to the soldiers in the rooms all around theirs. They're getting the hell out of the brothel. They're hitting the streets. Someone hammers on the door.

"I'm on it," yells Sarmax in Russian. Turns back to Spencer. "Got some assignments for us?"

"I'm starting by having us ordered away from everybody who might know us."

"And then?"

"I'm working on it."

"Works for me," says Sarmax.

They lower their visors and exit the room.

I figured it would be you," she says.

"Naturally," replies the Operative.

He pulls himself into the room. He's not wearing a suit. He closes the door behind him and she hears it lock. He smiles a smile that's almost shy.

"I'm sorry about all this," he says.

"What the hell's going on?"

"It's for your own protection."

"Bullshit."

"I wish it were."

"I can protect myself just fine."

"And therein lies your problem."

She stares at him. He gazes back at her in a way that makes her realize he's running some kind of scan. She feels the prickle of spectra upon her skin. He reaches around to the back of her chair, types in codes. The locks that bind her release. She floats free.

"Thank you," she says.

"Has anybody been here?" he asks.

"Here being where?"

"This room."

"Since when?"

"Since you got here."

She looks at him incredulously. "You mean to say you don't know?"

"Don't you?"

"No," she says. "I don't."

"Why's that?"

"Oh you bastard," she says. "You fucking bastard."

"I'm not sure I follow, Claire."

"Then follow this, asshole. I've been drugged. Someone got to me. Someone fucked with me. And I'm thinking that someone's you."

"Why's that?"

"Because you're the one who's standing there laughing."

"Do I look like I'm laughing?"

"You look like you're fucking with me."

"I was following orders."

"Whose orders?"

"Whose would you think?"

"I was thinking the Throne. But that was before . . ." Her voice trails off.

"Before what, Claire?"

"Before you started asking me whether anyone had been here before you."

"Don't you think the Throne would want to know that?" he asks.

"I would think the Throne would be aware of that already."

"I figured it couldn't hurt to ask," he says.

"Well, the answer is, I've no idea."

He looks around. He seems to be scanning the rest of the room now. He turns back toward her, frowns.

"In any case, you're right. The Throne ordered you placed here."

"Here being where?" she asks again.

"This ship. We're eight hours out from moonfall."

"We're going to the *Moon?*"

"Why so surprised? You've been sent this way before."

"But we never made it that time."

"This time you will. We're almost there. We left Earth a day and a half ago."

"But why the hell are we going in the first place?"

"The same reason you're confined within this room."

"I don't understand."

"You will in a moment."

The city center rises to the very ceiling of the dome. Most of it is off-limits to anyone lacking the proper credentials. Lynx and Linehan are showing what they've got to one of the innermost checkpoints. Guards wave them through.

"That was easy," says Linehan.

"That was just the warm-up," says Lynx.

He's nosing the truck up a ramp that's about ten stories

off the ground. Congreve sprawls below. Platforms and elevators are all around. They're in the outer sectors of the city's citadel. There's a lot of construction going on. A nice chunk of dirty fission released right here would blow the whole thing clean to hell, taking them down with it. Something that Linehan's all too aware of. He can virtually feel the blast ripping him apart already. He wonders if that's what people mean by premonition.

"We're getting into the thick of it," he says.

"Don't think I don't know it," replies Lynx.

They brake, dump the ore onto a conveyor belt, watch as the belt takes their cargo around a corner and out of sight. Ostensibly there's no further purpose for them here. Another truck gets in behind them, starts honking.

"Let's get out of here," says Linehan.

"Maybe," says Lynx.

He eases the truck along, starts heading down another ramp. Razorwire extrudes from his bionic fingers, slides into the instrument panel. The truck's engines splutter. They're still running, but only barely.

"Oh dear," says Lynx.

"Don't think I didn't see that."

"Doesn't matter what *you* saw," replies Lynx, and eases the truck down a smaller ramp. He stops the engine, gets out. A power-suited SpaceCom soldier on an adjacent platform fires his jets, blasts over to where Lynx is standing.

"What the hell's going on?"

"Breakdown."

"What's wrong with it?"

"Don't know."

"Hold on," says the suit—he steps off the platform, drops away. Linehan and Lynx watch him disappear.

"So we just wait here?" asks Linehan.

"No," says Lynx. "We walk."

"Sorry?"

"You heard me. Get out of the cab."

Linehan hops out. Looks around.

"Isn't he gonna be back any moment?"

"Probably. But we've got orders."

"What?"

"Let's *go*, asshole."

They proceed to the side of the ramp and hop down to the one immediately below. It leads beneath a ceiling overhang, ends in a door. Linehan glances around.

"*No*," says Lynx. "Just act like we belong here."

Because according to the zone they do. Lynx reaches out to the panel adjacent to the door, keys in access codes. The door slides open. He and Linehan enter and the door shuts behind them. They're standing in an elevator, which starts to rise.

"What about the truck?" asks Linehan.

"What about it?"

"We're just leaving it there?"

"Does it look like it'd fit in here?"

"What's the suit gonna think when he gets back to find us gone?"

"He'll think whatever he's told."

"And what's he being told?"

"That we got ordered to get the hell off the premises."

"And the cameras at the exit? What are they gonna show?"

"Nothing. Hate to break it to you, Linehan, but we don't exist anymore."

"You mean we've exchanged one false set of pretenses for another."

"Linehan, nothing the zone says is ever *false*."

The elevator doors open. They walk out and find themselves in a different part of the base. This section looks pretty complete. They go through another door, find themselves in the midst of a lot of activity. Power-suited soldiers are everywhere. So are workers.

"Here we are," says Lynx.

"We being who?"

"Workers who enjoy a lot more trust."

Who never leave this base. Who have their quarters within its endless corridors. Whose loyalty is beyond question. Who are able to come and go into the most secure areas.

Which is what these two are doing now. Seems that some of the fuel lines up on one of the flight decks are low on pressure. They've been ordered to help out. They climb up a grilled staircase, get in another elevator—emerge from that into hangars within which sit shuttles getting a working over. A soldier steps in front of them.

"Sir," says Lynx.

"Auxiliary hangar D," says the soldier, gesturing at a doorway. "Get moving."

"Sir," says Lynx.

"That's on the roof," says Linehan on the one-on-one.

"What's wrong? You afraid of heights?"

"No."

They step through a door, look down a flight of stairs at a massive platform that extends out across the dome's summit. Spaceships and smaller hangars are strewn across it. The curve of Moon is easily visible from up here. The L2 fleet hangs like a starfield in the sky above them.

"Cool," says Linehan.

They walk down the staircase, start moving across the platform toward the farthest of the hangars. As they do, a vibration shakes the surface beneath them. Movement from the corner of their visors: one of the ships is ascending, its engines glowing white-hot. They keep going, enter the hangar.

Within that hangar is a single craft. A transport shuttle. One large enough that it's being serviced at multiple levels.

Lynx and Linehan are standing on the highest one. They head over to the fuel lines, get busy. No one pays much attention.

"Funny," says Linehan, "these fuel lines look pretty good to me."

"What do you know," says Lynx. "You're right."

"So do we keep working?"

"Sure we keep working. On something else."

"Got anything in mind?"

"I do," says Lynx. He pats the side of the ship. "We need to get inside and join its crew."

"To go where?"

"Only destination worth the name."

They're getting the hell out of Little Russia. The news that two soldiers have gone MIA reaches them about ten minutes after they split. Which is fine by them. They've turned over a whole new leaf by then: switching identities, switching regiments, and transferring from there to special assignments that will keep them as far away as possible from anyone they're supposed to have served alongside.

"Nice one," says Sarmax.

"There are times I impress myself," says Spencer.

Times like now. He's maneuvering through the Eurasian zone while he and Sarmax sit on the back of a crawler that's busy running down anything in its way. The other members of the squad they've been assigned to are sitting all around them, making small talk, taking in the sights—and hanging on while the crawler roars after two others, climbing up roads toward the height of the Owen-Stanley Range. The city spreads out below them.

"This is Seleucus sector," says Spencer.

"So what if it is?"

"I heard something really nasty happened here."

"Nasty being what?"

"Some kind of AI demon."

But whether it was as bad as what's going on right now is open to question. Because at least that demon fucked off. Whereas the Eurasians seem unlikely to leave anytime soon. Spencer's window on the Eastern zone indicates that a full five percent of the city's population is slated for arrest. And another ten percent is scheduled for reeducation camps that will be so extensive that several districts are going to get bulldozed to build them. The populace is selling one another out as fast as they can. Partly to settle old scores. But mostly just to try to save themselves. Though it doesn't seem to be working that well.

"They should rename this place Purge City," says Spencer.

"They may yet," replies Sarmax.

One of the other soldiers chooses that moment to start up a conversation. He starts asking Spencer where he's from. Spencer tells him Irkutsk. According to his files, that's the truth.

It's also bad news. Because it turns out this man's from Irkutsk too. Before he can ask another question, Spencer asks him which neighborhood—thereby buying himself time to manipulate his own answer. One that's on the other side of town from the one that the soldier's mentioning.

But it turns out the soldier knows someone in that neighborhood anyway. He starts playing the name game with Spencer. Starts asking awkward questions.

"Let me handle this," says Sarmax on the one-on-one.

"Sure," says Spencer.

Sarmax leans over to give the soldier a little friendly advice. Tells him that the man he's talking to served a little too long in Africa. That he had a violent disposition even before he was tortured by Ugandan rebels for twelve hours straight a few years back. That it's impressive how together he is now that he's been transferred out of there. How it's a shame that the only thing that still sets him off is talking about the past.

The soldier takes the hint. He and Sarmax talk about other things. Sarmax has done enough missions behind the walls of the East to hold his end up. He knows what's expected of him—knows how to stay on the right side of the line that separates casual bitching from treacherous muttering. He knows how to elicit information too; the kind that may not be readily accessible in the databanks. After a while Sarmax leans back and disengages, starts up the one-on-one once more.

"Apparently there were some pretty severe border riots earlier," he says.

"Yeah?" asks Spencer.

"Yeah. Everyone was trying to get out. Trying to cross to the American sector. Turns out they ran into a crowd trying to get away from the Americans."

"And let me guess—there was a massacre?"

"Of course there was a massacre. During the course of which East and West exchanged some shots."

"Fatalities?"

"The East lost at least fifty."

"Is that what they're claiming, or what this soldier's been told?"

"This soldier saw it."

"But it didn't escalate."

"Seems that cooler heads prevailed."

"Meaning more senior."

"Both sides have orders to keep the peace."

"But the rank-and-file's straining at the leash," says Spencer.

"Yeah. These guys seem to think the day of reckoning is right around the corner."

"Maybe they're right."

"Only one way to find out."

The crawler rounds a corner. HK's new border comes into sight. Barbed wire's everywhere. Tops of buildings have been torn off, used to erect walls that block the roads. Soldiers on either side watch their counterparts warily. The crawlers roar parallel to the barricades.

They enter a complex that was obviously a school until very recently. Now it's been turned into some kind of strongpoint. The vehicles come to a halt in a courtyard. An officer barks orders; soldiers start to bring out captives in electrocuffs and eyeless helmets.

"You called it," says Sarmax.

"Nice to know I haven't lost my touch."

He and Spencer watch from atop the crawler as the captives are shoved through a door in the vehicle's side. Spencer runs through the dossiers in his head: arrested HK scientists, with a special destination. The engines start back up. The crawlers get moving again, away from the border and the checkpoints and back toward the center of the brave new city. He and Sarmax are on escort duty now, charged with carrying out the one rule of such assignments: stick close to what you're trying to protect.

"We've got company," says Sarmax.

"I noticed," says Spencer.

There's no way he could have missed it. The vehicles now swerving in behind theirs are accompanied by new developments on the grids of the Eastern zone. Developments that underscore all too clearly the tensions within it. Spencer extrapolates along those tensions—follows them as they branch out along the fault lines so cunningly concealed from low-grade razors. Fault lines that are all too obvious to him. Because, in reality, the Eastern zone isn't just one zone.

It's two.

"The fucking Chinks," says someone.

"Stow it," says the officer.

But the point's been made. The sentiment's been voiced. The vehicles behind this one are Chinese, as are the soldiers atop them. Spencer can't see what those soldiers are saying to one another. For all he knows it's something nasty about Russians.

Not that it really matters. The Eurasian alliance isn't built on mutual love. It's built upon a common foe. Standing up against the Americans will call for sacrifice. Thus the integration of the zones and the merging of the war machines. Thus a partnership that has endured for decades—a partnership whose watchword is joint ownership. And whose golden rule is keeping your ally apprised.

As far as anyone can tell.

"Makes sense," says Spencer. "We're riding shotgun on some big-time shit."

"So now they are too," says Sarmax.

That's just the way it works round here. But it's useful confirmation for Spencer as to the value of the cargo he's snagged. Even though he was never really in doubt. The custom hacks furnished him by the Throne were just too good. If they're going to get caught it's unlikely to be here. It'll be somewhere deeper.

"Here we go," he says.

The crawlers are emerging from between buildings, rolling through a cleared area carved out of mountain slope. One of HK's airports is up ahead. The civilian craft have been shunted aside. The vehicles of the new order are everywhere. Some are lifting off from runways. Some are landing. Some are disgorging equipment.

Some are waiting.

"That's the one," says Sarmax.

"Looks that way," says Spencer.

"And we've got tickets?"

"Christ I hope so."

They roll toward the waiting jet-copter.

• • •

Two people in a room bereft of windows. The man seems far too calm. The woman's struggling to remain so.

"Is this about the Rain?" asks Haskell.

"The Rain are finished," replies the Operative.

"We can't be sure of that."

"They're finished," he repeats.

"How do you know that?"

"You destroyed them."

"I destroyed all the ones I could find. I need the president to link with the East to—"

"He can't do that, Claire."

"Why not?"

"Because the East can't be trusted."

"It's not a matter of trust. I can monitor—"

"But who monitors you?"

She looks at him like she's just been slapped. She starts to speak. Stops. Starts again.

"So it's me the Throne fears."

"Why else would you be his prisoner?"

"His prisoner? Or his property?"

"Do I look like a lawyer, Claire?"

"I've been naïve," she mutters.

"There are worse crimes," he replies.

"Such as?"

"Treason."

"Is that what you're accusing me of?"

"Technically, you're already guilty of it."

"For what?"

"Aiding and abetting the traitor Matthew Sinclair."

"Jesus Christ," she says. "I was a CICom agent. I was acting under his orders!"

"Are you still?"

"If you're serious about that question, the last thing you deserve is a fucking answer."

"What about what you did before it all started up at the Europa Platform?"

"I'm not sure I follow."

"Isn't it true that you spoke with Sinclair?"

"What makes you say that?"

"I'm not just saying it. I *know* it. You hacked into the L5 fortress. That alone could get you tossed out an airlock."

"So go ahead and toss me."

"I'd rather you told me why you made the call."

"I wanted to talk to him."

"And what did you discuss?"

"I needed to find out if he was guilty."

"But you already knew he was."

"Oh?"

"Why else would the Throne arrest him?"

She stares at him. He laughs. "That's a joke," he says.

"You're really funny."

"But Sinclair really *was* guilty."

"But I had to put that question to him. I had to see how he'd respond."

"And did he admit it?"

"Yes," she says.

"Then?"

"I guess it was what I needed to hear."

"But not what you wanted."

"I don't know what I want."

"Then let me help you," he says. "What you want is to see things from the Throne's perspective. You must realize how it looks if you converse with an enemy of the state. You can hardly blame the Throne for being slow to attribute your actions to some inner need of yours."

"If I really was a traitor, why in God's name would I have saved the Throne's ass?"

The Operative doesn't reply.

"Because that's what's really going on here, isn't it? Why I've been chained up. Why he won't face me. Why don't you just admit it, Carson: Harrison can't forgive me because I remind him of just how close to the edge he came."

"The Throne's above such petty rationales," says the Operative.

This time she laughs. "What makes you so sure?"

"Because of what's afoot outside this room. Within the next few hours all will be decided, Claire. The Throne has set in motion the final strike against his enemies."

"So now we come to the real reason you're here."

"We do."

"And are you my executioner?"

"Would you like that?"

"Just shut up and do me if that's what you're here for."

"I'm just trying to remind you that you're not beyond reproach. That you've got to understand the Throne's fear that his enemies might use you against him."

"How can they do that when I'm here—"

"In this room? Exactly. No one can touch you now. You're off-limits. Offline."

"So what's the hell *is* going on?"

"We're on the brink of war."

"With the East?"

"Who else would be worth the fight?"

She laughs again. But only just. Shakes her head.

"Haven't we been down this road before?"

"We haven't. This isn't like the last time, Claire. That was fleets being mobilized and threats being exchanged. That was out in the open. This isn't. It's behind the scenes. As far as the population is concerned, everything's fine. But in reality—"

"How did things get so bad so quickly?"

"Because things were never good to begin with."

"But the peace summit—"

"Got crashed by the Rain."

"But we *beat* the Rain."

"We being the U.S., sure. The Eurasians didn't fare so well, did they? They lost key leaders. They've passed the torch in Moscow and Beijing, Claire. The hardliners are taking control. The moderates are on the verge of being purged. Those who wanted to join Harrison's alliance have been utterly discredited."

"Utterly?"

"Sufficiently. Enough to render anyone advocating détente suspect. After all, look where it got the East. Almost fucked by the Rain on the edge of the Earth-Moon system. Almost made into a slave-state overnight. The Coalition's generals are gaining power by the minute. The war machine could slip the leash at any moment."

"The Rain must be in the mix somewhere."

"Must they?" The Operative laughs. "Do you really think we need the Rain to fuck up our world? We did it so well for so long before they hit the scene. Why should everything be so rosy now they're gone?"

"The two sides aren't even talking?"

"Oh, they're talking all right. One more reason why the public's in the dark. Officially, everything's going like clockwork. The neutrals are being dissected wholesale. The joint infrastructure keeps getting built. The committees in Zurich and Geneva keep on working. But higher up it's a different story. The hot line's off the hook. The president can't get anyone to call him back. We don't even know who's in charge. *If* anyone's in charge."

"So let me find out, Carson. Let me jack in and recon the East and—"

"You told the Throne you wouldn't do that."

"Maybe now I would."

"Relax, Claire. You've made your choice. Besides, we're already on it."

"You're going to find out who's running the place?"

"Sure, but that's not the main focus. Not now. We're assuming the worst at this point. It's all we can do. What matters is their ability to win a war. We can't leave anything to chance. So we've sent agents in search of the thing we most fear."

She looks at him. "The thing we most fear?"

"Think about it, Claire."

"What the hell are you—*oh.*"

"Exactly."

"If you're going to look at your opponent's cards—"

"—what you're interested in are the aces."

"The secret weapons," she says.

"More than one of them, perhaps. Maybe none at all. We don't know. What we *do* know is that reports from our agents behind the Eastern wall—and Lord knows there's precious few of them these days—all point to the Eurasians feeling like they're in much better shape now than during the height of the crisis that followed the Elevator's downing. Which could just be symptomatic of a shift in ideological currents. Or it could be the result of material factors."

"And our evidence regarding the latter?"

"We've got a whole industry devoted to studying what we can glean about their black budgets. We've believed for a while that something big started its way down the R&D pipelines about a year before Zurich."

"Which doesn't mean that—"

"Two days ago one of our sources in Moscow got ahold of a fragment of a Praesidium memorandum waxing poetic about a breakthrough that would ensure victory in a showdown with the West. And in the wake of your restarting of the zone, we bought information from a rogue CICom handler in HK—"

"Who I met," she says suddenly. "Alek Jarvin. Right?"

"Right."

"What's he up to?"

"Busy being dead. We eliminated him once we had the goods. Which we're inclined to regard as genuine. Particularly with all the other signs pointing the same way. Jarvin had been doing a *lot* of digging, in some very specific directions. He believed there to be a black base beneath the Himalayas that's been cauterized from the rest of the Eurasian zone to prevent net incursions from breaching it. A black base that's only just been upgraded from R&D status to active operations. It's too specific a lead to ignore. Spencer and Sarmax took out Jarvin and now they're going to check this out and destroy whatever they can find without leaving evidence that points back to us."

"That's a one-way trip if ever there was one."

"That's how we intend it. Sarmax has a death wish anyway. And Spencer—"

"I thought Sarmax was your friend."

"—has gotten out of so many no-win situations he can't recognize his luck's finally hit empty. The divvying up of HK is giving us the leverage we need. The Eurasians are seizing all key assets in their sector and pulling them out of the city, with a particular emphasis on top scientists. Spencer and Sarmax have managed to pull escort duty on some physicists who are being sent to some sort of base beneath the Tibetan plateau where they're going to be put to work. We don't think that base is the one we're looking for. But we're pretty sure it's not far off. The hope is that the two of them can take it from here."

"And if they can't?"

"Then we continue to live with uncertainty. War might be averted anyway. War might occur regardless. We don't know. But we have to do everything we can to prevent the Eurasians from bringing disruptive technology to bear against us. And we have to keep the knowledge of such technology from our own hardliners. Who—"

"They still exist?"

"Of course they still exist. And they're all the more dangerous now that the president's lost the lion's share of his Praetorians."

"But the SpaceCom plot to trigger war between the superpowers—"

"Was destroyed before it could strike. But the puppet-masters escaped."

"The puppet masters were Autumn Rain!"

The Operative grins mirthlessly. "As you'll recollect, there were two sets of puppet masters. Autumn Rain was pulling everyone's strings. But even at the time it seemed pretty clear that the SpaceCom general Matthias was reporting to someone else within Space Command. Someone we've been working to identify this whole time. And it turns out the Rain weren't the only ones to crash the Europa Platform. SpaceCom sent a team in, too. With orders to waste the president."

"That's impossible."

"Why?"

"I never saw them."

"You're giving them too much credit, Claire. They went out *early*. The Rain got wind of them first and you know how the Rain feels about competition for the executive node. We found what was left of SpaceCom's finest in a New London sewer. They weren't a factor in what happened subsequently. But someone in SpaceCom is still trying to take down the Throne."

"And we finally know who that someone is?"

"We do. The rot goes straight to the top."

She mulls this over. "He dies tonight?"

"That's the idea," says the Operative.

"That won't be simple."

"Neither is our plan."

. . .

Congreve drops away as moonscape expands out on all sides. Linehan checks out the view. It's been a long time since he's seen it. Yet somehow it's been with him all along.

"How many you think we're carrying?" he asks.

"Those holds are equipped for a hundred," replies Lynx.

"There's more than that in there."

"I doubt we're going to hear any complaints."

The men and women on this ship have done their time in every mine from here to Imbrium and back. But they've all acquired enough clearance to get assigned to more sensitive tasks. Which doesn't mean they're unmonitored. There are cameras all over the cargo holds in which they're sitting. Supervisors too—not that there's much for them to do during the transit. As long as they've got access to the camera feeds from which they can monitor the rest of the ship, they're free to just find a room.

And wait.

"What happened to the two we replaced?" asks Linehan.

"We didn't replace anybody," says Lynx. "There are just a few more supes on this ship than usual."

"But nothing outside the norm."

"Not according to the zone."

On a large transport shuttle a lot can pass unnoticed. A lot can go unseen. Though the view outside shows everything a man could ask for. The curve of the Moon is getting ever more distinct. Stars are starting to fill the window. There's a rumble as the ship's main engines engage.

"How long's the haul?" asks Linehan.   .

"A few hours. You may as well get some sleep."

"I'm not tired."

"Suit yourself, as long as you're not planning on talking."

"What's gotten into you?"

"I've got a lot of shit to prep before we reach L2. How about you back off and leave me to it?"

"At least tell me whether we even know where in the fleet he is."

"I'll know more when we get there."

"You can't hack it from here?"

"Hardly. We're sixty thousand klicks out. We've got to get a lot closer before I can start doing that."

"So you think we've got a chance?"

Lynx sighs, stares out the window. "Sure we've got a chance," he says.

"Of taking Szilard out."

"Yeah."

"But not of living through it," says Linehan.

"Can't have everything."

"We've got a lot in common, don't we?"

"How do you figure?" asks Lynx.

"We both keep getting set up by our bosses."

"That's the truest thing you've said so far."

"Maybe I should quit while I'm ahead."

"But you won't—"

"I can't. Don't you resent Carson for making you do this?"

Lynx laughs. "You've got it wrong, man. I'm loving it. Chance to make history."

"By stopping the head of SpaceCom from starting a war?"

"Nah. War's inevitable. Everyone's got too big a hard-on for it. Whether or not Szilard's got something up his sleeve, someone's going to light the fuse. All we can do is hope it doesn't happen before we can make our mark."

"This tin can—"

"Would be toast. If it kicked off right now, the Eurasian gunnery at L4 would send us tumbling back to Congreve. Assuming we weren't vaporized right off the bat."

"Cheerful, aren't you?"

"Just realistic." Lynx pulls his wall straps tighter. Leans

back. Pulls wires from a wall panel. "But if you've got a god, you might want to settle up before we get there."

"I'll settle with God once I've settled with Szilard."

"I'm starting to wonder if you know the difference," says Lynx.

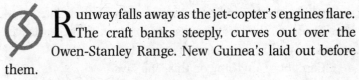

Runway falls away as the jet-copter's engines flare. The craft banks steeply, curves out over the Owen-Stanley Range. New Guinea's laid out before them.

"And we're off," says Spencer.

Sightless helmets staring: they're sitting across from two of the captives. One of whose lips are moving silently as he mouths prayers.

"Hack this craft and find out everything you can," says Sarmax.

"Already did," says Spencer.

"What about Jarvin's files?"

"I'm still working on it."

"So hurry it up."

He's been too busy keeping their identities afloat to worry about the files he and Sarmax ransacked at the handler's safe house. He's starting to multitask as best he can. But so far the most valuable thing he's gotten was in the jet-copter's computers. And it's not much. Just a route—and a destination, a hundred klicks southwest of Lhasa, in the Himalayas. Everything else is denied this craft's pilots.

But Spencer's working on the angles. The whole Eurasian zone seems to be turning in his head now. Over the last few minutes it's been getting ever louder. Now it's like a siren screaming through his mind. He's never felt so wired. And yet the Eastern zone isn't telling him too much about the base-ments and corridors on the maps he's now accessing. He can see the blueprints. But he's missing key data. He's pretty sure that's how it's been designed. He won't know for certain until they make landfall, which won't be for several hours.

So he does what he can in the meantime—continues to make inroads on Jarvin's files, and while he's at it, double-checks the cargo the ship's carrying. He focuses anew on the dossiers. Three of the physicists on board defected from the East awhile ago. Now they're on their way back, to face some new employment conditions. Spencer scans their files, analyzes those of their colleagues—tries to read the tea leaves contained within, but doesn't get very far.

"Can't base anything on this," he says.

"Lot of nuclear expertise," says Sarmax.

"Means nothing."

"Why not?"

"Because we're riding one of Christ knows how many cargoes. All going to the same general area. We just happen to be on the nuke bus."

"Go on."

"And no way were they gonna leave this kind of talent back in HK. They'll grab them as a matter of course. Along with anyone with expertise in nanotech, directed energy, stealth—you name it, they'll have it. Trying to deduce what we're looking for from what they're vacuuming out of HK is an exercise in futility."

"You're probably right," says Sarmax.

"Of course I'm right. And it looks like most of the really sensitive stuff under those hills is cauterized from wireless, if not cut off altogether. We're going to have to wait till we get a little closer to find out for sure."

"Works for me," says Sarmax—turns toward the window.

• • •

A clean sweep," says Haskell. "Against enemies within and without."

"That's the idea."

"The Throne's making a mistake in keeping me out of this."

"I don't think so."

"There's too much at stake, Carson."

"That's why we can't risk you being compromised."

"You really think the Throne's enemies might get to me?"

"Can you guarantee otherwise?"

"Why the hell would I have destroyed Autumn Rain if I was plotting against the Throne?"

"It's a good point."

"So the Throne shouldn't be keeping me stowed away like this." She's disturbed to find how angry she's getting. "He should be bringing me online."

"Unless."

"Unless what?"

The Operative just stares at her. She stares back.

"What are you getting at, Carson?"

"I'm hoping you can answer that question for me."

"You think that someone might still have a back door to my mind."

"Can you rule it out?"

She shakes her head.

"We know those doors exist, Claire. We used one on the Platform. So did the Rain. We'd thought they were all accounted for. But we have reason to believe that some of the original CICom data on you might have wound up in the hands of Szilard himself. Meaning that as a weapon you'd be worse than useless. You'd be turned against us by SpaceCom."

"Not necessarily. It all depends—"

"On what sort of back doors we're talking about. Exactly."

"Where's your evidence?

"Call it a hypothesis."

"A pretty specific one. Why do you think Szilard—"

"Never mind what we think about the Lizard. What matters now is you."

"I can find out," she says.

"Find out what."

"If there's a back door."

"Really?" He moves toward her.

"Given enough time," she says. She draws away.

"We don't have that time," he says.

"What are you proposing?"

"I'm not *proposing* anything."

She starts to lunge aside. But he's already driving the needle into her flesh.

It's as though she's falling down some long tunnel where there's no light and no darkness save what's already in her head—swirling all around, solidifying into fragments of mirror that reflect everything she's ever dreamed straight back into her eyes . . . blinding her, spinning her around to the point where it's like the universe is nothing but rotation and she's the only constant. But everywhere she looks it's the same: the face of Carson and all he's saying is *labyrinth labyrinth labyrinth that's all you are and all you'll ever be—*

It all snaps into focus.

"What are you doing?" she asks.

"I'm operating," he replies.

He's not kidding. He's got her strapped back into the chair, her blood filled with painkillers so she can't feel a thing. She can see through only one eye. The other one's dangling in the zero-G beside her nose. He's plucked it out. The optic nerve is hanging there, along with tangles of circuitry that lead back inside her eye socket. He's got his razorwire extended from one hand into the circuitry. But she sees something else, too: droplets of blood floating in front of her, and she suddenly realizes that—

"You've cut through my skull," she says.

"Trepanation," he replies. "Of a sort."

Messing with her brain. She can't see what he's up to there. But she can feel it. Colors surge against her. Landscapes churn past her. Some moon's hovering somewhere out in front of her. It starts to swell ever larger.

"Have you found the door?" she mutters.

"You're the door," he says. "You always were."

"I never wanted that."

"That never mattered."

Everything goes black.

⊕ **P**rowling through corridors of dark. Climbing up stairways filled with light. Watching from behind the screens as the clock keeps on ticking and the ship keeps on moving away from the farside toward the only libration point invisible to Earth. The fleet that's deployed there is the largest in existence. It's the ultimate strategic reserve. If the war to end all wars begins it'll lay waste to the Eurasian bases on the farside even as it duels with the L4 fortresses— even as its squadrons scramble left and right around the Moon to envelop the Eurasian nearside operations.

Or maybe not. Maybe it'll just stay put. There are so many battle scenarios flitting through Stefan Lynx's head, and none of them really matter: they're just the projections from which he's reverse-engineering the actual composition of the fleet and mapping out the vectors via which he's going to penetrate to its heart. That fleet stacks up in Lynx's mind like some vast web. The only thing that counts now is confronting the spider at its center. Whether or not Szilard is guilty is incidental—there's a larger game afoot. The ultimate run's under way. Lynx has never felt so high. Beneath him engines surge as the ship keeps on taking him ever higher.

She wakes again. She's in a zeppelin. She's been here before. She's looking out a window at a burning city far below.

"Hello Claire," says Jason Marlowe.

She whirls. He's sitting cross-legged against the far wall. He's smiling like he did right before she killed him.

"You're dead," she says.

"And you should know," he replies.

"Why are you here?"

"I was hoping you could tell me that."

"I'm being fucked with, Jason."

"By who?"

"By Carson. He's inside my head."

"Was wondering why it's feeling so crowded in here."

"You've been here all along?"

"I wish you'd joined us, Claire."

"I wish I had too."

"We were Rain."

"Maybe we still are."

"No," he says. "You killed us all."

"There's really no one left?"

He replies. But as he does so his voice is drowned in static. Even as his mouth blurs.

"What'd you say?" she asks.

He speaks again. The same thing happens.

"You're being blocked," she says.

"No," he says, "*you're* being blocked."

"Try it again," she says.

"I said you're blocked, Claire."

"Am I?"

"Why is it so hard for you to admit? Is it because you always thought I was the weak one?"

"You weren't weak. I was just stupid."

"It's not too late to save the world."

"I can't even save myself."

"Carson might do it for you," he says.

"I doubt it."

"You should have joined us."

"You said that already."

"Because it bears repeating."

"If the Rain had won, it wouldn't be any better."

"Why not?" he asks.

"They didn't even have a *program*, Jason. They had no idea what they were going to do once they'd taken over."

"Yes they did. Take humanity to the next level."

"What does that mean?" She points through the window at the sky. "Huh? Other than more fucking spaceships—*what does that mean?* They were divided among themselves. They couldn't decide whether they should rule humanity as cattle or raise the race to some kind of posthuman status. They would have fought among themselves as soon as they took power."

"Christ, Claire. They already *were* fighting among themselves. That was their genius. They were at war with one another the whole time. They stabbed their leader in the back—"

"You mean Sinclair?" She feels some kind of pressure building in her head.

"—and then they fell to bickering. They fell apart even as they had it all within their grasp."

She feels like her skull's about to explode.

"And I could say the same of you," he adds.

The pain goes nova.

. . .

Clouds whip by. The islands of Indonesia flit past. Sarmax watches the world reel below, and it's a world that's dead to him. His mind feels the same way. There's no light left in it. His Indigo's gone. He knows she must have died long ago. And even if she didn't, she's dead now that the Throne's destroyed what's left of the Rain. Yet somehow Sarmax feels like he killed her twice. He wishes he'd made sure of her the first time.

But nothing's ever sure. And the dead have a way of refusing to stay that way. She's still burning in his head.

It's all he has. It's fine by him. Asia creeps closer as he readies for one last run.

She's in some room making love to Jason and it's so long ago. She's fifteen and so is he. She's riding him for the first time and she's wishing she could stay this way forever. He's telling her he loves her. Telling her this really happened. She's telling him she believes him—telling him that she wants to live with him forever in that long-gone country of the past. She feels as though she's never getting out of here, that her mind's a cage and she's never even going to see the bars. And now she's on top of Jason and her hair's dangling across his face and he's gasping and she's crying and begging him not to grow any older and he's moaning *the future's already here* and then he shimmers and fades and vanishes and she's weeping and telling him she'll find him but all there is to find is the note under the pillow that says *you know I know you lie.*

• • •

Hatchet man with too much downtime. Man of action who's unaccustomed to the undertow of his own mind: it's hauling against him in ayahuasca rhythms as he watches the Moon dwindle and stares at the lights flickering off Lynx's spaced-out face. Linehan knows he was never supposed to get this far. He should have been nailed once he'd helped bring down the Elevator. He was a loose end that should have been snipped. In a way, he was. It's almost like everything that's happened since has been part of some fucked-up afterlife. As though the tunnel beneath the Atlantic was really the journey to the underworld.

And back. Because four days ago he made it through the temple of the Jaguars and out into a whole new world. And yet it's ended up being a lot like the life from which he'd been spat. New bosses, old bosses—makes no difference in the end. The higher you get, the more dangerous you are to those you serve and the more lethal your missions become. Living on the edge—and Linehan has been there so long he wonders if he was ever anywhere else. It's all he has, this crazy game where the rules change as fast as you can make them up. He's had his mind blown these last few days. He never knew how good he was until he went rogue from SpaceCom—never dreamed he'd be capable of pulling it off with no cards to show and even fewer to play.

And now he has to go and do it one more time. He remembers the Throne's briefing. The president said the Rain were gone, but that they'd so shaken up the world it was about to go over the cliff anyway. He looked at Linehan and said *soldier, you're a hero.* He said, *I need you on the moon.* Linehan remembers saying *sir, yes, sir.* Remembers asking where was Spencer.

Which is when the Throne told him he'd be working with Lynx this time, that Spencer's one hell of a razor, but

that Lynx is even better. Linehan just shrugged. He liked
Spencer. Loved him, even—loved to hate him, really—and he
worries that with the guy gone maybe his luck's run out at
last.

Which would be a shame. Because coming back to L2
is coming back to where it all began. He trained there, came
up through the ranks there. And it was the machinations
of L2 that left him on Earth running for his life. Now he's
back to take the life of the man who once controlled his.
The Throne said he can retire once that's happened. Linehan
has some vague notion of what such a life would be like: a
life without someone to pursue, a life without someone to
run from. He has some idea of just heading out to Mars—
just rigging a hab halfway up some mountain and spending
his days watching red sprawl below and universe cruise by
overhead. He knows that'll never happen. He knows what
happens to those who live by the sword. He wants it no
other way.

O No way out: she's running through the burning
streets of Belem-Macapa and the burning
Elevator's plunging from the sky toward her. She can't
remember how she got here. She can't remember what happens next. She thought it involved Jason. But Jason's dead.
And she's about to join him. Because there's no way out of
this. The mob's in full cry after her, screaming for her blood,
screaming that they've found themselves a Yankee razor. It's
true. She's American. She can't help that. She can't help what
her people have done. She can't give these people what they
never had. She's got only one thing left to give. She turns a
corner.

And finds she's reached the river. The Amazon stretches

away on both sides, winding through the city. There's so much smoke now that she can barely see the pier that stretches out into the midst of the river. She runs along the pier, reaches its end.

A boat's sitting there. It's small—pretty much a gondola. Carson stands in its rear. He's leaning on an oar, gazing up at her.

"Which way?" he asks.

She leaps in, tells him any way will do. But he tells her she has to choose. Between upriver and downriver. Between jungle and sea. She stares at him. She can't speak. The mob's storming onto the pier behind her. Carson glances at them, smiles. Looks back at her.

"Choose quickly," he says.

But she can't. She can't choose at all. Even as the mob closes upon her. Even as she realizes her mind's not her own. It's as though someone's pulling her strings. As though someone's about to cut her loose.

"Take her apart," says Carson.

Men wielding machetes leap into the boat.

Sarmax is off in his own little world. That suits Spencer fine. He's not interested in dealing with that guy's issues. All he's interested in is what's in his own mind.

Which is intricate beyond belief. Now that they've crossed the coast of Vietnam, more of the Eastern zone's becoming visible. He's got access to a lot more data than he had previously. Things that were blurry are becoming clear. Things that weren't even visible are coming into sight. Most of those things have locks. But that doesn't matter, because he's starting to make inroads anyway. The files of Alek Jarvin float be-

fore him: onetime handler of CICom and fugitive for the last
few days of his life. Spencer still hasn't cracked them.

And he's growing increasingly sure they contain
something he needs. Something he'd better figure out quickly.
His mind's operating on multiple levels now. His thoughts
are accelerating. He's starting to feel like he's tripping
again. Faces dance on the edge of his zone-vision, but every
time he looks, they're gone. He feels like he's become a
ghost, like he's been summoned from some world beyond to
haunt this one for all its sins. His view into the cities of
the East keeps on growing. He's finally got the access he's
always wanted—he looks in upon those lives and streets
and cities and knows himself for the voyeur he always was.
He gets it now—sees that those lives were always more
interesting than his own. That what's inside a screen was
always more compelling than whatever might appear within
a window. By far. He's come so far too—doesn't want to
stop now as his mind races toward the mountains, drops
through shafts, darts in toward all the secret chambers that
lie beneath.

Now she's in a room without windows. Or doors.
She's sitting at a table. The U.S. president sits at
the table's other side. They look at each other.

"Are you really Harrison?" she asks.

"Does it matter?"

"I think it does."

"Indeed," he says. "Have you been granted an audience
under the deepest of truth-serums or is this just Carson rum-
maging through your subconscious, using this face as a filter?
I'm afraid I'm not in a position to give you absolute proof
either way."

"But we can talk anyway," she says.

"I suppose we can."

"Why'd you do it?"

"Do what?"

"Betray me."

"I can't betray anyone, Claire. By definition."

"You really think it all revolves around you."

"I'd be a fool to believe otherwise."

"I don't understand," she says.

"I'm responsible for our nation's future."

"You think I stand in the way of that?"

"I think our partnership was unnatural, Claire."

"Unnatural?"

"Temporary, then."

"Ah."

"The product of a common purpose. We had a common enemy. When that enemy was beaten, what was I to do?"

"Trust me."

He laughs in a way that's not unkind. "I'm not a normal human being, Claire."

"You think I am?"

"I think you genuinely wished to help me."

"Then why—"

"It wasn't a case of what you wanted in the present moment. It was a case of what might happen next. Do you really think you'd have been happy carrying out my orders?"

"I could have given you advice—"

"And you really think I'd need it? I know what I'm doing, Claire. I've ruled this country for more than two decades. I led our people out of chaos. Out of cold war."

"But now war's right around the corner."

"We'll avert it yet."

"And if we don't? My battle-management capabilities—you'll need me—"

"Perhaps. Perhaps not. We'll see where matters stands when Carson's finished."

"You fucking bastard," she says. "You're trying to turn me into a bunch of *programs* that you can copy. You want to own what's in my head without having to deal with me."

"You speak as though you were your own creator."

"Jesus fucking Christ—"

"We built you. We paid for you. We're not in a position to negotiate with you every time we want to take a step you might disagree with."

"You mean like launching an all-out strike against the Eurasian Coalition?"

"You have to admit that if there was some way to just wipe out the East's military at no risk to ourselves—just take them out and take their cities, let the population live beneath our guns—things would be a hell of a lot simpler."

"But there's no fucking way—"

"No," he says. "There isn't. War would be insane. That's why I've done everything possible to preserve the peace. The only window of opportunity for striking the Coalition would have been if you'd been able to restart our zone without restarting the East's. But since that wasn't possible—"

She looks at him. She tries to stop herself from what she's about to say. But she can't.

"It *was* possible," she whispers.

"And you didn't tell us because you guessed I was contemplating a preemptive strike against the East?"

She says nothing. He shakes his head.

"You see what I mean? You're too dangerous, Claire. Too many ideas of your own. Wouldn't be long before you started wondering why the executive node was in my head instead of yours. Or wondering whether you could build a better one to supersede mine. You're Rain, Claire. They wanted to rule the Earth-Moon system. Why should you be any different?"

"I never wanted to rule anything."

"History is littered with leaders who said exactly that. Some of them even believed it."

"You never did."

"And I never said it."

"You're missing the point—"

"No," he says. "You are. Because it doesn't matter what you *want*. What matters is what you're *capable* of."

"Since you're inside my fucking head, why don't you tell me."

"Anything," he says. "You're out of control. You've already gone beyond everything you were designed for. Why are you laughing?"

"Because that's exactly what Sinclair said to me a few days back."

"So why *did* you talk to him?"

"He—he was the closest thing to a father I ever had." She's surprised at how steady her voice sounds.

"Don't you realize how black a mark it was against you when we found out?"

"You weren't supposed to. It was a private matter."

"My prisons aren't some opportunity for therapy, Claire."

"What will you do with him?"

"Execute him. Eventually. Once it becomes clear we've no further need for him. Once we can. Why are you crying? He would never have shed a tear over anybody."

"I know," she mumbles. "I know. He was cold and heartless. So are you. You all are. I'd sweep you all away if I could. I'd—"

"You see? You can't hide anything from us." He gets up, walks around to her side of the table. Looks down. "Not when we're right here with you."

"Fuck you," she says.

"It's a tragedy that you've so much power and so little idea of how to use it."

"*You're* the tragedy," she says. "You'll strangle yourself in your machinations yet."

"You first," he says.

And puts his hands around her neck, starts squeezing. She kicks against him. But his grip may as well be iron.

"It's time," he mutters.

She fights for air. There's none. Everything goes black.

PART V
RIPTIDE

"Claire," a voice whispers.

But it's an eternity before she can process it. She's dwelling in some darkness far beyond all pain. She hears her own name dripping down across some sky, some sound in a world where all that lives is silent. She drifts in toward the voice.

"Claire," it says. "Can you hear me?"

She can. But she's not sure what she's supposed to do, save to keep on forging toward it. But now she's being buffeted by hurt that slams against her. She stumbles onward, upward, toward the light.

"Open your eyes," the voice says.

She tries to. Fails. Tries again—manages to get one of them open. Through a blur she can see Carson's face. She groans as headache engulfs her.

"That's it," he says.

She opens both her eyes. It's agony. But she's keeping them open all the same. She's back in that room, still strapped to the chair. Carson's floating in front of her. His legs are crossed.

"How do you feel?" he asks.

It's a good question. She struggles to come up with an answer. Only to find she can't.

"I found everything I needed to," he says. "I'm done."

"So am I," she whispers.

"No," he says. "You've just begun. Go back to sleep."

She drifts away.

Drifting in toward the heart of SpaceCom power: the transport's passed through four parking orbits, each one tighter than the one before. It's now well within L2's outer perimeter. Stars fall past the window. Ships are everywhere.

"Welcome home," says Lynx.

"Looks like it did when I left it," says Linehan.

"You've only been gone a couple weeks."

But that was all it took to come full circle. L2 set him in motion. L2 has pulled him back into its maw. He seals his visor in place, grabs onto the wall as the ship fires motors, leaves its latest orbit.

"So what's the first step?" he asks.

"We do some honest work," says Lynx.

The ship's turning. A webwork of metal scrolls past the window, so close that Linehan can see numbers and lettering painted upon it.

"Jesus," he says. "We're right up against it."

"Try inside it."

"What the hell?"

But as he stares through the window, he sees that Lynx isn't kidding. The transport has entered the hollow of a much larger, half-built ship. It stretches all around them, like the bones of some vast animal. The rest of the L2 fleet flickers beyond it. Linehan whistles.

"One of the fucking colony ships," he says.

Lynx laughs. "That's a strange thing to call them."

"That's what they are."

"That's what they're *registered* as."

"That's what they're built for, man. Straight shot to Mars."

"By way of Moscow," says Lynx.

"Meaning what?"

"Meaning *look at those guns*."

Which don't look small. They also don't look like they'd be visible from beyond the construction.

"That's why they're building them in here," continues Lynx. "Armaments to augment the L2 fleet, unreported to Zurich or anybody else. Soon as the shit hits the fan, they can blow the hatches and start laying down the law."

"Don't the Eurasians have some of these things, too?"

"Over at L4, yeah. Ours and theirs make for one more piece of glorious joint infrastructure in the wake of Zurich. The next great pioneering fleet. How much do you want to bet that the East is working to rig its behemoths with similar enhancements? Who knows, they might blow the top off Mons Olympus. But I'll bet you the real target's a damn sight closer."

"I don't take bets I can't win."

"Then you've come to the wrong place," says Lynx. The ship's speakers start barking orders. "Let's go."

"We've got everything we need?"

"We'll pick it up as we go."

Linehan shrugs. They open the interior hatch of the room they're in, climb through into a corridor, pull themselves along it and into the transport ship's spine. Right now there's a lot of traffic. Supervisors are herding the workers out of their quarters, into the spine, and then out through where the nose has been peeled back. Lynx and Linehan head the other way. Crew members pass them. So do supervisors. But no one challenges them. They exit the spine, proceed through more hatches, exit the transport.

They're moored against some of the more complete parts of megaship infrastructure. Two other transports are tethered alongside. Workers and supervisors are everywhere. One of the supervisors challenges them.

"Who the hell are you guys?" she asks.

"Engineers," says Lynx. "Who the hell else would we be?"

Linehan doesn't see the codes get transferred. But it must have occurred. Because the supervisor turns away—and he and Lynx keep on going, alight on the interior of the giant craft. Scarcely ten meters away is the nearest of the cannons: what's clearly a medium-grade particle beam. Heavy lifting's easy in the zero-G—workers are maneuvering the weapon into place by hand. Lynx and Linehan move past it.

"Those guys had better pick up the pace if they want to make a difference," says Lynx.

"You seem so sure it's gonna happen."

"Lightning doesn't strike twice, right? It was a fucking miracle we evaded Armageddon back when you were going head-to-head with the Jaguars. We're not going to beat the bullet this time."

"Even if we take out Szilard?"

"That's all I want to do, Linehan. Take him out. After that, the whole of this can go to hell."

They head into the enclosed portions of the colony ship's interior. No one pays them the slightest attention. Lynx leads the way through a labyrinth of weightless corridors and half-installed machinery.

"Let me guess," says Linehan. "Szilard's somewhere in here with us."

"Yeah right. Far as I can make out, he's on the *Montana*."

"He went back to the flagship?"

"Apparently."

"And how exactly do you propose we get from here to there?"

"*We* won't. Someone else will."

"And we'll be that someone."

"And how."

The jet-copter streaks in amidst snowcapped peaks. Valleys drop away at impossible angles. Slopes are like walls that are way too close. The craft is buffeted as it hits turbulence.

"Getting close," says Sarmax.

"We're pretty much there," says Spencer.

"You've found what we're looking for?"

"I've found where we're going to look."

Abruptly, the jet-copter slows perceptibly, banks. Spencer finds himself staring straight up toward some higher peaks. He sees something stretching between two of them. Something that's clearly man made. The craft arcs up toward it, decelerating all the while. There's a rumble as the landing gear lowers.

"We're landing on that bridge?" asks Sarmax.

"Not exactly," says Spencer.

Because he can see things that Sarmax can't. Like what's really going on. They're not the only vehicle about to hit this bridge.

"A rendezvous," says Sarmax.

"Roger that," says Spencer.

The jet-copter soars above the level of the bridge just as a train emerges from one of the tunnels that the bridge connects. The train's maglev. But it's operating at almost a crawl—scarcely thirty klicks an hour. Freight cars fill the bridge, slowing all the while. The copter settles down toward them. Sandwiched between freight cars, an empty flatcar slides from the tunnel—the copter wafts in, touches down upon it. No sooner has it done so than the train speeds up. Mountain disappears as tunnel wall kicks in. The jet-copter's engines die. Only stone's visible outside the windows now.

But there's a lot more than that going on inside Spencer's mind, now that there aren't a thousand tons of rock separating him from this train's systems. Now he can see where this thing's going. The train accelerates, racing ever deeper into the mountain. Spencer sees the rail it's on as one smooth line of light. He becomes aware of more rails sprouting off from this one—and of still more rails sprouting off from those . . .

"Jesus fucking Christ," he says.

"What's the story?" says Sarmax.

"The story is this place ain't small."

The train's slowing again, coming through into a gigantic railyard-cavern. Electric lights hang from a ceiling far overhead. Activity's everywhere. The far side of the cavern lights up in the zone in Spencer's mind. As do vast grids of light beyond that . . .

"We're close," he says. "We're real close."

"Are we trying to get to where this train's going?"

"I have no idea where this train's going."

"Well, try hacking the drivers."

"Already did. They don't know either."

"This place is that compartmentalized?"

"It's not just one place. They've dug out half the goddamn mountain chain as far as I can tell."

"What's down here?"

A better question would be what isn't. It's almost like a series of cities. There's that much activity. It stretches on for scores of klicks, all the way beneath Tibet and then some. Spencer can see why he had so much trouble getting a fix on it. Because the infrastructure he was getting a glimpse of beneath the Himalayas is actually above what they've now reached. And the way this place is organized, it's as though the whole thing is . . .

"Counterforce," he says.

"What?" Sarmax glances at him.

"This place is counterforce. It's intended as reserve. We barely know about *any* of it. Which is the way they want it. They'll commit it in the later stages of a war."

"Which could be ten minutes after it kicks off."

"Sure." Spencer's downloading more data into Sarmax's head. "But the point is that even if the Eurasians strike first, I'll bet they don't strike with any of the shit that's in *here*."

Sarmax says nothing.

"How else would you explain it?" asks Spencer.

"I wouldn't," says Sarmax. "You're right."

"We need to get word of this back—"

"No we don't."

"What?"

"They already know it."

"They do?"

"That the East has hidden reserves? Absolutely."

"But they don't know the extent of this."

"If you send word back to the U.S. zone, you risk compromising our position."

"It's worth the risk."

"Not if there's something else in here we haven't found."

"Maybe this is what we're looking for," says Spencer.

"And maybe it's not."

"You know something, Leo."

"I know a lot of things."

"Including what was in the book you found at Jarvin's safe house?"

Sarmax stares at him. Says nothing. Just smiles.

"So you *do* have it," says Spencer softly.

"Of course I have it."

"What's it say?"

"I don't know."

"You don't *know*?"

"That's why we're having this conversation," says Sarmax.

"But where the fuck did you hide it?"

"I didn't. I burned it."

"But not before you scanned it."

"Can't afford to be as risk-averse as Jarvin was."

"Christ, Leo. Not filling me in is a risk in itself."

"Not at all. If you were going to be of any help, you'd have been able to figure out the file's existence from the rest of what you've got. Which apparently you've done."

"Which was easy enough once I knew I was looking for what *wasn't* there. Jarvin's files are littered with coded references to an overall master file. One that was written down on *paper*. Making it impossible to hack."

"He was the last CICom handler in HK. Every intelligence organization on the planet was hunting him. He had good reason to be paranoid."

"Said the guy who killed him. So where was it?"

"Under his floor."

"And how'd you know it was there?"

"I didn't, Spencer. I just tore the place apart while you were ransacking his data."

"You got a tip."

"So what if I did?"

"You *were* going to let me know eventually, right?"

"Depended how frustrated I got with it."

"How much progress have you made?"

"Nowhere near enough. All I can make out is the first section. It talks about the Eurasian secret weapon being an ultimate one, Spencer. It leads straight into several layers of cyphers. It's—"

"Something you need to give me right now."

And Sarmax does. Spencer stares as the data clicks through.

"Jesus Christ," he says.

"Yeah," replies Sarmax.

"This is more than a thousand pages."

"Yeah."

"What the hell are all these *symbols*?"

"I don't fucking know."

"And where the hell did he have this?"

"On a microfiche. He must have burned the original paper."

"And you burned the microfiche."

"And something's getting ready to burn us. We're not looking for a bunch of tunnels, Spencer. We're looking for something specific. Something that's down here. I should have given you this earlier. I admit it. But I need you to start figuring this thing out."

"While I simultaneously hack this place."

"You think you're so good, now's your chance to prove it. How much access have you managed to get to what else is going on within this labyrinth?"

"A lot."

"But not enough."

"It's too cauterized."

"Deliberately so," says Sarmax. "We need to get deeper."

"That's where this train's going."

"So we ride it."

He leans back. The train keeps on rushing into the root of the mountain.

This time she comes awake in a single instant. Carson's still floating cross-legged before her. The ghost of a smile flickers on his face.

"How do you feel?" he asks.

"Like shit."

"But better than you did previously?"

"That wouldn't take much, you prick."

"I apologize."

"It's a little late for that."

"Indeed," he replies. "I found the back doors."

"Who put them there?"

"We're still figuring that out. Maybe the Rain. Maybe Szilard. Maybe Sinclair. Maybe all of them."

"Maybe none of them."

"Who else would have done it?"

"You."

He smiles. "You're not making sense, Claire."

"I'm making far too much sense, Carson. Since it wasn't the back doors that you were after."

"I never said they were our only motive."

"So let's talk about the most important one."

"You have a hypothesis?"

"I'm on more solid ground than that."

"Go on."

"You were searching for a way to figure out how the Rain almost fucked the president at the Europa Platform."

"We already know how they did that."

"Do you?"

"Sure. They took out the zone by sabotaging the legacy world nets and—"

"No," she says, "not enough. It wasn't enough for them to do that. What really almost nailed us was that they were preventing him from transferring the executive node as well."

"Precisely. Because they'd taken out the zone."

"Don't play the fool," she says. "I know what happened. The Rain collapsed the zone, sure. But they also had a little something in reserve, in case the zone *didn't* go down. In which case they knew they'd have to jam the executive node itself, to prevent it from being transferred to the Throne's successor."

"They *did* prevent it from being transferred. They were jamming the whole fucking Platform, Claire. Getting a signal off that place was virtually an exercise in impossibility—"

"That's not the kind of jamming I'm talking about, and you know it. That kind of jamming wouldn't have worked. The president could have just sent the code in a laser, and even if he hadn't had the chance, the zone's structured so that the successor's software activates the backup executive node in the event of the destruction of the Throne's—"

"Right, but—"

"But the Rain deployed a far more specialized hack in advance of their grand slam, didn't they? One that undermined the executive node itself, and prevented it from being transferred to Montrose under any circumstances—"

"What makes you think she's his successor?"

"I *know* she's his successor, Carson. That was the price she exacted for InfoCom's support of the Throne back when SpaceCom made its big move after the Elevator. In fact—"

"You're assuming a lot."

"I'm assuming *nothing*. I was practically in the Hand's head—in the *president's* head—all that time. And we both saw the node-freezing hack hit just before the zone collapsed. Once the zone went down it no longer mattered—but if the Rain's universal ass fuck hadn't worked, they had plan B already activated. As the Throne knows all too well. And he knows I know it too. I showed him how the Rain pulled the rug out from under the zones of East and West. But I never showed him how the exec node paralysis worked."

"You told him you didn't know."

"And he didn't believe me."

"And he was right not to. Why did you withhold it from him?"

"I wanted some kind of counterlever if the Throne tried to turn on me."

"Which is why he sent me here," he says.

"But he didn't have to send you very far."

He says nothing. Just looks at her and smiles.

"So now we get to the heart of the matter," she adds.

"Was wondering when you would."

Outside again: they've crossed the entirety of the colony ship and reached the docking facilities that occupy the space where the ship's nose has yet to be built. Several small shuttles hang like bats around them. The doors of the nearest one are open. Lynx and Linehan enter.

The pilot within is sprawled in his chair. The expression behind his visor's one of intense boredom. It doesn't change as he regards them.

"Yeah?" he asks.

"We need to get to Redoubt G16," says Lynx.

"What do you think this is, a fucking taxi service?"

"Pretty much," says Linehan.

"My orders are to sit tight until—"

"You got new orders," says Lynx. He beams code to the pilot, who grimaces in annoyance—and turns, starts up the engines.

"You guys ain't even officers," he mutters.

"No," says Lynx, "we're engineers. Who do what the officers tell us. So back the fuck off."

"Relax pal," says the pilot. "We're all in this shit together."

"You can say that again," says Linehan.

He's staring out the window at a wilderness of lights and shapes. Craft of every description are strewn against the crescent Moon that dominates the sky beyond. But one of those lights is swelling by the moment—fragmenting into several smaller lights, set against a larger shape. The shuttle vectors in toward it. Linehan watches as it wafts in.

"You've got to be kidding me," he says.

"At least it's a lot smaller than that Eurotrash rock," replies Lynx.

It may be nowhere near as large as what was once the pride of the Europa Platform, but it's still an asteroid, about fifty meters long, studded with guns and mirrors and the occasional shaft opening. The shuttle drifts in toward one such opening that's been drilled along the axis. The pilot's hands fly across the controls as he lines the ship up with the rotating rock.

"Fucking redoubt," he says. "What the hell're you guys doing here anyway?"

"Telling you to land this bitch," says Lynx.

The pilot mutters something inaudible. Rock walls replace space as the ship glides into the shaft. They emerge a few moments later into a cave that's been carved within.

"Here we go," says the pilot.

But Lynx and Linehan are already hopping out, firing their thrusters as the pilot starts reversing back the way he's come. The cave itself is empty save for mechanics working over another shuttle. They ignore the two newcomers, who continue along the shaft and into the labyrinth that honeycombs the asteroid. They encounter no one else. Linehan feels like he's walking into a tomb.

"Don't tell me there's no one else in here," he says.

"Wouldn't dream of it," says Lynx.

Linehan knows he's not kidding—that there's got to be enough of a crew on this rock to make Lynx's scheme work. No shuttle runs from the ships in the outer perimeter directly to anything that's even *near* the *Montana*. Shuttles reach the flagship only from places that are almost as secure. Meaning that the plan to infiltrate L2 depends on seeing SpaceCom's fleet as an archipelago. Linehan knows that Lynx is playing the game called island-hopping: moving from ship to ship toward the heart of it all. But each locale he selects has to be big enough to allow him to lose himself amongst its garrison. Linehan follows Lynx off the axis and into the domain of gravity.

And now they've got company. Workers squeeze past. They reach an intersection, turn down one of the tunnels. A power-suited soldier blocks the way.

"This is a restricted area," he says.

"I know," says Lynx. "Here's our clearance."

The soldier's expression doesn't change. "Clearance for what?"

"Sorry?"

"So you've got the codes. So what? I can't just let you through here without you telling me where you're going."

"Oh," says Lynx. "Sorry. We're going to the armory."

"To do what?"

"Got a report that some of the suit-batteries were on the fritz."

"How come I didn't hear about this?"

"Feel free to check," says Lynx. "But we're behind on our schedule and really need to hurry it—"

"Cool your jets," says the soldier. His eyes seem to lose their focus as he transmits via zone. And gets his answer.

"Fine," he says. "Let's go."

"Great."

"But I'm coming with you."

"Then who'll stand watch?"

"They're sending down a replacement."

"I'm telling you we're running late already—"

"You don't have to wait. Let's go."

"You're leaving this place unguarded?" Lynx looks nervous. "Is that standard procedure?"

"Shut up," says the soldier, and turns, leading the way down more tunnels. In short order they reach a dead end. The soldier shifts against the rock, swivels a piece of it aside. They proceed through into the armory as the door closes behind them.

The place looks like it's been wallpapered with weapons of every description, from suits to small arms and everything in between. Chances are if this place sees combat they won't get used. But that's what war is these days—a question of contingencies. This asteroid is mainly intended as a KE strongpoint. And yet there's more than one scenario in which it might need to shelter soldiers who have been moved from more vulnerable nearby ships. Soldiers whose own battle capabilities might have been degraded. Soldiers who might need the things this room contains . . .

"So get on with it," says the soldier.

"So we will," says Lynx. He heads toward the diagnostic panels set beside the door. Checks it out. The door slides shut.

"And hurry it—" The soldier's voice suddenly cuts out. Along with the power in his suit. Lynx turns back toward the now-drifting figure.

"What was that? I didn't quite catch that."

The soldier's yelling at him. It doesn't take an expert in sign language to get the gist of what he's saying.

"Yeah," says Lynx, "sorry about that. Linehan, can you help out?"

"With pleasure," says Linehan as he extends a drill from his suit and plunges it into the soldier's back. The man's defenses aren't up. He can't dodge. It's over pretty quick. Linehan basks amidst the rush.

"Enjoyed that, did you?" Lynx looks at Linehan, hits buttons, starts pressurizing the armory. "Well, don't let your sadism cloud your grasp of the big picture. This just became a clusterfuck now that there's no one at that guard post."

"I thought they told him there's another sentry coming along—"

"That was me he was talking to, you dipshit!" Lynx is

pulling off his suit. Linehan starts doing the same. "He was too curious. Too great a risk. He would have done some extra checking. So he had to come with us. But we haven't got long before they figure out a sentry's gone missing. We gotta get off this fucking rock and fast."

"In what?"

"Well, as luck would have it another shuttle's departing in three minutes. And by a strange coincidence, it's en route to our next stop. So you've got thirty seconds to get *that* on." He points. Linehan follows his gaze to two suits. He stares at the insignia on them.

"I like it," he says.

"Thought you might," replies Lynx.

Tunnel walls surge past as the train charges ever deeper into the world beneath the mountains. On the zone, Spencer's watching grids dance within his head. He's pulling strings across the Eurasian zone, closing in on the moves that will take him and Sarmax to the next level within this place.

But he's also trying to make sense of a whole new factor. He's realizing just how out there the man who called himself Alek Jarvin was. The handler's book consists of hundreds upon hundreds of pages of symbols, grids, numbers. And letters, of course: Spencer reckons he's dealing with at least six different alphabets. None of which are even remotely discernible. The only thing he can make out is the initial section that Sarmax spoke of. Which seems to serve as a preface. Written in a low-rent cypher that was easy enough to crack, probably because all it does is make promises.

Though threats might be a better word. It goes on and on about a Eurasian weapon that will change the face of war. A device so revolutionary that nothing the Americans can put into the field will stand against it. Spencer wonders whether it's for real—wonders if Jarvin transcribed what he's reading from Eurasian propaganda. He wonders why he didn't sell the details to the Americans if he really had them. Was CICom's rogue handler killed by Sarmax before he could? Or was he playing his own game? Did he give up on America because he'd been declared a traitor? Did he send his nation's agents on a wild-goose chase? Spencer knows there's only one way to find out. He sets his own software upon the cyphers— even as the software continues to run patterns on the place around him too—and on the train that's now moving in on parallel rails behind the one he's on. It's a lot shorter, gaining steadily on the flatcar and the jet-copter that sits upon it. Within the jet-copter, one of the officers starts giving orders. Spencer and Sarmax get to their feet, open the copter door, and hop out.

As they steady themselves upon the flatcar, more freight cars haul alongside theirs. The door of one of the cars is open. Suited soldiers are standing there, extending some kind of makeshift bridge. Spencer and Sarmax grab it as it reaches them and secure it to the flatcar. More soldiers are leaping from the door of the jet-copter, pulling prisoners along with them—past Spencer and Sarmax, onto the bridge and into the arms of the soldiers who wait on the other side.

Fifteen prisoners later, and the bridge retracts. The freight car's doors slide shut, and the train beside them accelerates. Cars stream past Spencer's visor, leaving tunnel wall flashing in their wake.

"Any idea where they're going?" says Sarmax.

"Probably where we want to be."

"But you don't know where."

"When I do, you'll be the first to know."

"You're saying we're high and dry?"

"Actually I think we're under arrest."

"What?"

Looks that way. The other soldiers on the flatcar are pointing guns at them. One of the officers steps forward. The sergeant flanks him.

"Spies," he says in Russian.

"That's a lie," says Spencer in the same tongue. But he and Sarmax are getting worked over now by their fellow soldiers, who start stripping ammo from their suits, disengaging their guns, detaching and then removing their helmets.

"What the hell are we guilty of?" says Sarmax.

"Being American," says the officer.

"Sir," says Spencer, "that's not true."

"It's total rubbish," says Sarmax.

"You're the rubbish," says the sergeant.

"And you can take it up with *them*," says the officer, gesturing at the rail. Something else is emerging from the darkness, moving along the train's cars, catching up with the flatcar, matching speeds. It's a single gun car, running sleek and low to the rail, not much higher than the flatcar. Another bridge extends.

"Get them in there," says the officer.

Soldiers start hustling Spencer and Sarmax onto the bridge. The anxious look on the soldiers' faces isn't due to the narrowness of the bridge they're on. It's the dreaded military intelligence insignia upon the gun car. The soldiers shove Spencer and Sarmax inside and hastily retrace their steps.

The door closes behind Spencer and Sarmax. They're standing in a railcar, a cockpit at each end, and a turret hatch in the ceiling. A driver's sitting in the cockpit that faces forward. He doesn't look round, just hits the throttle. Spencer grabs onto the wall to steady himself, looks at the driver's back.

"Uh . . . hello?"

Legs emerge from the turret. A man drops down to face them. He wears a Russian captain's uniform and a scruffy beard. He looks at them.

"Your codes," he says.

Spencer transmits codes. The man salutes.

"Sir," he says. "What now?"

"Now we root out the state's enemies," says Spencer.

"Any news from HK?"

"Those scientists are a poison pill. We've got a traitor on the loose."

"As we feared."

"Worse than that. The West's involved. They're trying to take advantage of the scientist roundups to infiltrate some of their agents. And someone in this place is turning a blind eye. We've got to proceed with utmost caution."

"We'll have to," says the captain. "This place is moving onto full war footing. It's like we're expecting an attack at any moment."

"Or else we're going to launch one," says Spencer. "Something the traitors might be counting on. I need your data, and I need it quickly."

"Take the rear cockpit," says the captain. "Access whatever you need from there."

Spencer turns. The captain goes up to confer with the driver. Sarmax joins Spencer in the rear cockpit, activates the one-on-one.

"What kind of a fucking plan is *this*?" he demands.

"I figured we might not have enough leverage on escort duty," replies Spencer. "So I've been running some scenarios to get us a better view."

"By working with this guy?"

"The captain's just an errand boy, Leo. Albeit a discreet one. He thinks our infiltration of the escort was part of our cover. That our arrest will make any traitors rest easy."

"But there aren't any traitors."

"If there are, more power to 'em. Now how about we start the investigation?" Spencer leans forward, starts punching commands into the terminal.

"How about you keep me in the loop going forward?"

"You're one to talk."

"I outrank you, Lyle."

"Look," says Spencer. "I had to be sure they weren't hacking our one-on-one link. Anything we said there had to be chalked up to part of the cover."

"You are playing one dangerous game."

"I'm just getting started," says Spencer, who jacks into the dashboard, starts running code from a whole new vantage point. He doesn't doubt that Sarmax is on board with the logic—that he gets that the best way to infiltrate an impregnable fortress is to make like you're here to stop the infiltration. Because the East is just like the West: purging its own, divided against itself, compartmentalized to the point where the right hand has no idea where the hell the left one was last night. Infiltration works on the same principles. Which is why Spencer's been less than forthcoming with Sarmax.

Though that sort of thing can cut both ways.

"I guess it's time I gave you this," says Sarmax. He's pulled something from his mouth. Something that looks like—

"Your tooth?"

"Just take it," says Sarmax.

"What am I, the fucking tooth fairy?"

"Not unless you're into cross-dressing. This contains a chip. Which contains—"

But Spencer's already grabbing the tooth from him—loading it into his own data-socket, scanning the information revealed.

"This is some kind of hack," he says.

"Yeah. I need you to upload it."

"I need to know more about it—"

"Upload it and you will."

"I'm getting really sick of these surprises, Leo."

"This is the last of them."

"Where the hell did you get this?"

"Where do you think? The Throne."

"He could have handed me this to begin with."

"He trusts me more than you."

"Fuck's sake—"

"Don't take it personally, Spencer. If we'd been busted in the opening rounds, you might have tried to bargain with the East. Might have tried to sell this for your hide."

"And now?"

"You no longer have that option."

"I'm not following."

"Run the program and you will."

I'm still dreaming, aren't I?" she asks.

"Not exactly."

"But I'm still trapped inside my head."

"More like a zone-construct I'm creating with your help."

"My *help?*"

"However involuntary."

"You're in here with me," she says.

"Yes."

"We're both still on this ship."

"Yes."

"And the Throne is on board too."

"Of course," says Carson.

"He wants me close at hand."

"He needs you for what's about to happen."

"He's going to start a war," she says.

"He's going to finish one. One that's been going on for decades. One that's torn our planet at the seams."

"I thought he believed in peace!"

"There'll be peace, sure. When the East lies in wreckage at our feet."

"And détente?"

"Failed at the Europa Platform. As I said."

"But you also said the Throne was still hoping to avert war."

He shrugs. She snarls.

"Goddamn it, Carson, why the hell didn't you tell me earlier? Why this charade?"

"Because I'd never have gotten so far inside you otherwise."

She cradles her head in her hands. Says nothing.

"Your conscious resistance accounts for only so much," he continues. "It's your unconscious resistance that's the bulk of the challenge. Had you known that we intended to harness you as the primary node in a first strike against the Coalition, you would never have let me get to the center of your mind."

"But now you're here."

"And now the time for hiding's over."

"Someone should tell the Throne that."

"We've crossed behind the far side of the Moon," says Carson. "In mere minutes we—"

"Land outside Congreve," she says. "Go to ground in the Throne's bunker beneath the city suburbs."

"You're guessing."

"It's not that hard. Tell the Throne to come in here and face me."

"You've got it all wrong," says Carson. "You're the one who's going to face *him*. Once the last of your resistance has dropped away. Once you wonder why you ever wanted to call him anything besides *sir*."

"You can't make me do anything."

"Can't I?"

On the wall beside Carson appear two vid screens: two sets of grids. One depicts a cross-section of the Himalayas and the labyrinth beneath them, the other the L2 fleet. Each grid shows coordinates of something moving through it.

"The missions," breathes Haskell.

"Now approaching their last phases. And ready for a little nudge from you."

"Right now?"

"Can't you feel it?"

And suddenly she can. Even though she can't do anything about it. Dashboards light up within her mind and it's like someone else is hitting her controls. She looks at Carson.

"So you really *did* give it to me backward," she says.

"That's always the best way."

"You don't want to do a surgical strike on the Eurasians to stop them from starting something. You want to do it so *you* can."

"And we will."

"And Szilard? He's not really trying to unleash war?"

"Does it matter?"

"Sure it does."

"It doesn't. What matters is that when the shit hits the fan the president can't have someone running the L2 fleet he can't depend on. If Szilard didn't personally organize the SpaceCom conspiracy to hit the Throne, then he gave it the green light. And if he didn't even do *that*, then he should be executed for incompetence. For allowing treason to sprout under his nose. He's dead regardless."

"And so am I."

"Not at all. You'll be the Throne's prime razor."

"But I won't remember anything before that."

"You'll remember everything you need to."

"That's all I've ever been allowed to do!"

"But don't you want to know the reason why?"

"What?"

He says nothing. Just gestures. A door's appeared between the two wall-screens. Haskell stares at it. It seems familiar. She wonders where she's seen it before.

And then she remembers.

"No," she says.

Grey, metallic. It's just a door. But she can feel the presence of what lurks behind it. Something she hasn't felt for so long. Something that reminds her how much mercy there is in being able to forget.

"Don't do this," she says.

"I already have," Carson replies.

The door starts to open. Light pours in from the void beyond.

The view from the shuttle window shows machines of every description. Their shadows practically blot out the stars. Their lights are like some minigalaxy. The shuttle's heading toward where the lights clump thickest.

"Ever read Dante?" says Lynx.

He and Linehan are sitting behind a pilot who's maneuvering their shuttle toward a medium-grade war-sat that's part of L2's inner defenses. It's swelling steadily within the window.

"What?" asks Linehan.

"The *Inferno*. Ever read it?"

"Never heard of it."

"That's too bad."

"Why?"

"Because it's the only way you can understand what we're heading into."

"What the fuck are you talking about?"

"The circles of hell, man. We've run the outer ones. Now we've got to beat the ones that really count."

"And let me guess: Szilard's the devil."

"Except he's not. He's just a man. Which is why we're going to nail him."

"But we're men too."

Lynx just laughs. Because he knows that's no longer true. Because the download that's suddenly reaching him has made him far more than what he was a few seconds back. The Manilishi's codes surge through his brain, right on time, right as Carson assured him they would. Close at hand, too—coming from the ship now closing in on the farside. Lynx's mind writhes in the rush of power he's never known. He feels himself building up to heights he's never dreamed of. He's got all the leverage he needs and then some.

So he makes his move, seamlessly reaching out into the mainframes of the shuttle's destination, rigging them so they don't even know they've been rigged. He steals right under the eyes of all the watching razors. He's got them so beat it's as if their eyes were his own. He's almost frightened by how much better he's suddenly gotten—suddenly realizes that all his razor prowess has been mere show beside the real master of the game. All those moments searching through the corridors of the Moon for keys and clues and fragments of some greater knowledge that's finally rushing through him—he struggles to control the rush that sends his heart beating faster than it ever has before. He takes a deep breath.

"You okay in there?" says Linehan.

"Can you feel it?" mutters Lynx.

"Feel what?"

"Crosshairs."

"What?"

"All those . . . crosshairs. Tens of thousands of them. The Eurasian lunar batteries. Their guns at L4."

"Aimed at us?"

"And everything else that's up here, Linehan."

"What are you talking about?"

"The average DE cannon's not firing, you think it's just sitting there and you'd be wrong because it's cycling through a thousand different targets a second, making itself unpredictable, right?" Lynx is talking so fast he's pretty much babbling. "Keeping those who might try to hack it out of the mix. There's no one war plan, man. There's infinite plans. Infinite scenarios. In the time since you last spoke, hundreds of guns have flicked their sights on and off this fucking shuttle. The only weapons tracking us without interruption belong to our own side."

"I'm not following."

"Because you're not listening. There's a difference between war scenarios and in-fleet security, right? This crate we're in is getting close to the SpaceCom flagship. It's thus a threat of the first magnitude. Along with all the other craft that are doing the same thing at any given moment. Normal transport, right? But nothing's normal up here. So they designate certain guns to do nothing but track stuff like us so that the lion's share of the gunnery can worry about the East. Right?"

"Sure," says Linehan. "Whatever you say."

"That's what I thought. Two particle-beam cannons, one microwave gatling, three high-energy lasers: they've got our number. At point-blank range."

"Are you going somewhere with this?"

"Are you a fucking moron? They're the back door to reach the ID configurations with which we're getting inside L2's inner perimeter. Got it? The guns that are tracking us can be hacked, and then it's just dribble and shoot to figure out what their computers think we are, and then we get in there and change their mind so we can get clearance to get to the *Montana* itself— Jesus, will you look at *that*."

The war-sat's swelling through three-quarters of the window. Turrets jut out in every direction. The shuttle drops toward huge doors that are opening to receive it—floats into the landing bay, touches down. The pilot springs the hatch.

"Have a good 'un," he says.

"Sure thing," replies Linehan. He and Lynx get up, pull

themselves out of the shuttle and into the landing bay—only to find themselves surrounded by SpaceCom marines who aren't intimidated in the slightest by the officer insignia on the suits of the men they've got their weapons trained on.

"Sir," says the squad's sergeant, "we need to run a few checks."

"We're running late," says Lynx.

"Orders, sir," says the sergeant. "This way." The marines escort Linehan and Lynx to an airlock. The sergeant and two marines step within, motion the two they're escorting to join them. Doors close. Atmosphere pressurizes.

"Remove your helmets," says the sergeant. Lynx and Linehan comply. "We need DNA swabs," he adds.

"Since when?" asks Lynx.

"Since new regulations got handed down twelve hours back. Sir." The last word seems like an afterthought.

But the DNA scan clearly isn't. The marines take it from the inside of each man's mouth. They also do a retina scan. Not to mention—

"Sir," says the sergeant, "we need a voiceprint."

"Don't you already have that?" says Linehan.

"He means keyed to a lie detector as well," says Lynx on the one-on-one. "Plus a covert brain scan."

"Great."

"Shut up."

"Sir," says the sergeant, "what's your name?"

"Stefan Moseley," says Lynx.

"Position?"

"Major. Intelligence."

"And your business on the *Montana*?"

"A meeting with my boss."

"Who is?"

"Rear Admiral Jansen."

The questions continue, but there's nothing that Lynx hasn't expected. It's all getting relayed to the *Montana*, into databases that Lynx has already hacked, and from there back to the war-sat. It's the same with Linehan's questions. He's less polite than Lynx is, but just as responsive. Two more minutes, and the sergeant salutes.

"Where's the shuttle?" says Lynx.

"We'll take you there," replies the sergeant.

They leave the airlock room behind, proceed through the corridors of the war-sat. The atmosphere definitely seems pretty tense. Everyone looks like they're going somewhere quick. Everyone's averting their eyes.

"Feeding me those answers in real time," says Linehan. "Jesus Christ, you were cutting it close."

"How about you cutting me some fucking slack? I only just figured them out myself."

They reseal their helmets, pass through another airlock, reach another docking bay. This one's even larger. The marines hustle Lynx and Linehan into a shuttle—which starts its motors, floats from the bay and out into the heart of the L2 fleet. One shape in particular looms ever closer.

"That's the *Montana* all right," says Linehan.

"And I can't fucking wait."

"So what the fuck's up here? How the hell did you snag a meeting with the acting head of SpaceCom intelligence?"

"By being Com intelligence ourselves. Obviously."

"Yeah? When did you switch our IDs?"

"About ten minutes ago."

"And the guys who really had a meeting with Jansen?"

"Got carved up in a Congreve alley behind a seriously nasty bar. This was one of several ways in, Linehan. I was playing a couple of other angles, but when we got to the war-sat this was pretty much the only way to keep moving."

"So you keyed the SpaceCom comps to recognize the faces we're wearing."

"Yeah."

"And if Jansen took a look at the camera feeds?"

"He'll see just what he expects to."

"And when we're standing in front of him? Won't our faces be an issue then?"

"Not if we skip that meeting."

On the loose beneath the Himalayas, the train streaks unmonitored through the hollows. Spencer's watching rocky walls whip past. Data flashes by far faster. Something's taking shape within his head.

"I've never seen anything like this," he says.

"It's just a logic bomb," says Sarmax.

"No," says Spencer, "it's not. It's a logic *nuke*. It'll open up a link to the U.S. zone and bring this whole place down around our ears."

Sarmax shrugs. "Shit happens."

"What the hell's going on here, Leo? This is an àct of war."

"And sabotaging a superweapon isn't?"

"This might collapse the whole Eurasian net."

"And that's a bad thing?"

"That's a *crazy* thing. For all we know, the Eurasian weapons will fire if their zone gets disrupted."

"Not if that little fucker does its job."

Spencer keeps staring at the data that's flitting through his head. He's breaking down all its layers, all the way to binary. Those 1's and 0's look so innocuous on the screens within his mind. But put enough of them together in enough sequences and they're capable of anything. Spencer's starting to think that so is he.

"We're not here to *stop* a war," he says slowly.

"We're here to make sure it's as one-sided as possible." Sarmax's face breaks into a half-smile. "Now how about you figure out where we're gonna set this thing off?"

A tricky question. Especially because Spencer is still unsure whether he's found everything in these catacombs. He certainly has access to more than he did. The maps roll through his brain, which takes them apart in all their detail: floor space, transport, logistics, wiring. The scale of the place beggars description. It's even larger than he thought. Several hundred ground-to-space directed-energy batteries and about fifty heavy launching pads; yet so far it's just standard stuff. There's no sign of any one thing that's particularly special. The scientists got shipped to the complex's control center. But according to the readouts they're just being held there. It's unclear what for. A voice sounds in Spencer's head.

"How's it looking, sir?" It's the captain.

"Not good," replies Spencer. "Can you get me some files from Moscow?"

"I can try, sir." The captain sounds nervous. "What do you need?"

"The comprehensive dossiers on the chief of this place. General Loshenko. And his five subordinates. And quickly."

"And his Chinese counterpart?"

"This is an investigation, captain. Not an instigation of civil war. Now move your ass."

"Sir."

The captain disconnects. Spencer imagines he's guessing that Spencer's got his own sources to scope out the Chinese. But the truth of the matter is that Spencer's just trying to keep the captain busy. He doesn't need any official requests to Moscow to figure out what they've got on the men they've sent to run this place. He's already tapped into Moscow's files to get to where he is now, reached out across the long-gone steppes to that city he'll never see, slipped through its streets and basements while he pulled together everything he could find. He's back beneath those streets now, looking for the key to the place he's in.

And not finding it. Maybe his clearance just isn't high enough. Or maybe everything's just that compartmentalized.

"What's the story?" says Sarmax.

"The story is I can't find a goddamn thing."

"What about the handler's mystery file?"

"The book's divided into three sections."

"And?"

"And that's it."

"That's what you call progress?"

"It's what I call a start."

"You're not funny."

"Easy, Leo. The first part deals with this base. The second part deals with the weapon that's in here."

"And the third?"

"I haven't a fucking clue. And I'm not even that sure about the first two. It's just pattern-recognition algorithms I've been running. The first part contains at least a few disguised maps. The second part seems to be technical descriptions. The third's Christ knows what."

"So you're stonewalled."

"So I am."

"So let's do this."

Spencer shrugs, closes a circuit in his head, connects the logic bomb's software to the Eurasian zone. Only there's no detonation. Just lightning racing out onto the zone—and Spencer's riding that lightning, getting hauled up along a new path, up through the mountains and into one of the hidden wireless aerials that the Coalition has secreted in the peaks. The signal churns out into space. Out toward a point just behind the Moon.

But the answer comes back long before it arrives.

It's the Manilishi. There's no doubt. It's her face, her touch. And Spencer gets it now—sees that he's been prepping the ground this whole time. He and Sarmax are the inside guys. Though he wonders why the Manilishi wasn't in on this from the start; why it wasn't just her and Sarmax. Perhaps the Throne figured he'd hedge his bets with a razor physically on the scene. But then why wasn't she running cover from the beginning? Or was she? Spencer wonders what he's missing. He wonders if the answer's bound up in the thing he's seeking.

Or whether it has something to do with the Manilishi. Because there's something strange about her. Maybe it's just the pressure she's causing in his head. Maybe it's because he doesn't have the bandwidth to accommodate her. But there's something almost . . . *tentative* about her movements. Not that that makes her any less hell-on-wheels. She starts using the bomb like a missile homing in on its target: straight into the heart of this complex, straight out to its edges. Coordinates flash into place. A new grid locks in to replace the old. The presence fades.

Spencer is breathing heavily. His heart feels like it's about to explode. He's covered with sweat. He's almost shaking.

"You okay?" says Sarmax.

"I think so," he replies.

He's lying. He's more than okay. He's never felt anything like this. For one moment he was the most powerful creature in existence. And he can still feel her somehow lingering back there within his mind. Though according to his screens there's no live connection. Which makes no sense.

And the map of the place he's in makes even less. Because it seems to have shifted. He's trying to put his finger on precisely how. He can't see anything tangible. It's just more of the same: endless corridors and chambers and munitions posts and barracks and fuel-dumps and guns and soldiers and trains.

Trains.

Suddenly he's scanning the handler's book with new insight. Suddenly it's all starting to make sense. Some of the tables in the first section—numbers packed into as-yet-undeciphered column headers—he'd thought those numbers were disguised coordinates. But now that he's ablaze with fresh insight, it's all too clear: he realizes that factoring those figures in certain ways means they line up a little too neatly with some of the historical data in the logistics mainframes of this base. Because they're really inventories. That contain schedules.

Of trains.

Like the one he's in now . . . *no.* Larger than the one he's in now. Much larger. Like the one he and Sarmax came in on. Those trains are everywhere. They're the main conduit for supplies coming in. They come from underground and aboveground railways that stretch for hundreds upon hundreds of kilometers, all the way to the Ural and Altai mountain ranges. They're all accounted for.

Except they're not.

"What the hell are you talking about?" says Sarmax.

"There are *way* more freight cars coming into this place than there are leaving."

"So they're doing a mega buildup." Sarmax looks unimpressed. "That surprises you?"

"You don't fucking get it."

"Get *what?*"

"Those trains aren't *accumulating* anywhere. They're disappearing."

"To where?"

That's what he's trying to figure out. Some of the excess is getting piled up in plain sight. The entrances to the base are getting pretty jammed. But not all of the rolling stock is accounted for. There are a lot of locomotives that are just vanishing. Which ought to be impossible. But now Spencer's seeing how it's been done. Because the Manilishi's hack is wiping away the false camera feeds and showing Spencer the real views into this base's chambers. Focusing him in on a series of rail yards on the western extremity of the complex where several trains are waiting.

Only problem is that those rail yards are empty.

Spencer double-takes. Double-checks: these trains are there on the screens. They're there in the base's databases. They're crystal clear on zone.

Just not in real life. That yard's empty. Spencer's checking out the last forty-eight hours of actual footage and it's showing him that the trains have gone west from there, into tunnels where there aren't any cameras. Tunnels that supposedly dead-end almost immediately. Tunnels not wired for maglev, either. He mentions this to Sarmax.

"That makes no sense."

"It makes way too much sense," replies Spencer.

"Meaning what?"

"Meaning let me show you something I've just realized about the schematics for these trains." Spencer beams Sarmax the data. But even as he does so, the Eurasian captain suddenly turns toward them:

"Sir. I just got the Moscow data—"

"Thanks," says Sarmax. He fires at the captain and the driver in quick succession, strikes each man in the head. Bodies sprawl in their chairs.

"Can't trust anyone these days," says Sarmax.

"Tell me about it," says Spencer.

L ight transfixes her. Faces surround her. She's shaking, coming apart amidst the maelstrom of impressions. Marlowe and Morat and Lilith and Hagen and Indigo and all the others these last few days, all the years before that into which so much has been crammed and all of it could just be—

"False memory I'm triggering right now," says Carson. "That's all it was. It all stats now. You've been sitting in this room the whole fucking time dreaming of being something you're not."

"Not?" Her voice is weak. She can barely hear it.

"You're not Manilishi, Claire. You're just human." He says this last word like it's a curse.

"That's not true," she says.

"It's true to you," he says. "Because it's your fantasy. That's all it is."

"Then why are you devoting so much attention to me?"

"I'm not," he says. "I'm not even here. You've gone insane."

"Bullshit," she snarls.

"So fucking prove it."

Specific words, couched in a specific tone, heard in a specific emotional state. The moment she hears the trigger phrase she turns the lock within herself, opens the door in her mind—the one that leads to the lost country of the true past. Though at first it seems so familiar. She steps past the missions on which she's riding shotgun behind the Moon and beneath the Himalayas, moves through all the events she already knows. The last week stretches out before her in all its fucked-up glory, the Europa Platform, the Rain's base beneath HK, the spaceplane, Morat, Sinclair, Jason. Jason.

Jason.

She remembers him as the years streak by—remembers being with him so long ago. She misses him so much. She sees the members of the Rain once more: sees herself as a child at play with them. She remembers a garden at night. There was nothing then. No sense of destiny. No sense of mission. No sense they'd ever get old. They were just children. They were just there.

And then they weren't. She was separated from them. She never saw them again. She and Jason are the only ones left. They're brought up, trained as CICom agents. The others get pushed beyond the brink of memory. Replaced by a man who she's forgotten until now. But there's no such thing as forgetting. Particularly not this man.

Who calls himself Carson.

"No," she says.

"You made it," he says.

"Fuck you."

"Is that all you can say to an old friend?"

"You weren't my friend."

"No," he says. "I wasn't. Tutors don't befriend their pupils. They can't. They—"

"You taught me nothing."

"I taught you how to forget."

"Fuck you," she repeats.

"How to keep out of sight from yourself," he continues. "How to build up your talents till you were bursting at the seams and didn't even know it."

"I didn't even know I wanted it."

"But you did."

"And I'd trade it all for—"

"You were a trojan horse, Claire. One that contained yourself. We didn't even know what you were becoming."

"You still don't know."

"We're still finding out."

"And thus you're here."

"You've got your missions, I've got mine."

"The Throne ordered you to—"

"Get right up inside you."

"Fuck *you*."

"I wouldn't be averse. Especially now that you've broken all your chains."

"Except the one you're holding."

"Guess I'd better hang onto that one, huh? At least until the runs are over."

"You mean until the war's finished."

"The war will end in a single strike."

•   •   •

The SpaceCom flagship *Montana*. The first permanent structure established at L2. Forty years ago it was little more than a glorified tin can. But that was before decades of near-continuous construction. Now it's a little more impressive.

"The hub of it all," says Lynx.

Three massive metal wheels are rigged around a central structure that's larger than any of the colony ships will ever be. It bristles with gun-platforms. It shimmers with lights. The shuttle starts its final approach toward a landing bay that's opening like some giant mouth.

"How's it feel to be back?" asks Lynx.

"What makes you think I ever got inside *this* thing?"

"You never did?"

"Christ no. I was strictly outer perimeter material."

"So you're moving up in the world."

"So?"

"So congrats."

The landing bay engulfs them. The shuttle slides into its dock. The hangar that's revealed is a flurry of activity. Ships are getting prepped, worked over. An airlock tube locks against the shuttle's hatch, which then slides open.

"Leave your suits here," says the pilot.

"What?" asks Linehan.

"Standard procedure," says Lynx on the one-on-one.

"But this is a fucking officer's battlesuit—"

"And you really think they're nuts enough to let you run around in here with it?"

Linehan grimaces. Starts to take off his suit. Lynx does the same.

"Don't worry," he says. "I'll get you another one."

They leave the suits behind, exit via the docking tube, which leads through the hangar wall and into a room that's clearly intended as a waiting area. The hatch to the docking tube slides shut with a hiss.

"Now what?" asks Linehan.

"Now I shoot you."

"Very funny."

"No, really," says Lynx—and flicks the dart gun that's set into his wrist, sends a dart flying into Linehan's forehead—even as the man launches himself at Lynx, who steps lightly out of the way, lets paralyzed flesh drift past him.

"Don't fight it," he says.

Linehan definitely is. He's trying to speak. He's not succeeding.

"I'm serious," says Lynx. "You just said hi to a curare derivative. One that plays hell with your software interfaces *and* your voluntary muscle functions. People get aneurysms trying to be heroic. Everything'll be fine."

Linehan clearly has his doubts about that. Or else he no longer gives a fuck. He's foaming at the mouth. Garbled transmissions on the one-on-one reach Lynx's brain.

"Ahh shut up," says Lynx. He fires a second dart into Linehan's back, turns to the two suited marines now entering the room. "Was wondering when you guys would get here."

The marines salute, say nothing—just start strapping Linehan onto a gyro-powered gurney. They fire the gyros up. One pushes the gurney. The other gestures at Lynx.

"After you, sir."

Lynx smiles, starts moving. They leave the room, proceed down a corridor, transition into one of the *Montana*'s rotating areas. Gravity kicks in. They step inside another room. Sensors sprout from every corner, along with what are presumably weapons. Lynx feels the prickle of spectra probing him. He feels the software in him going dormant. He stretches. Yawns.

"Looks like you got them all," he says.

"Sir," says one of the marines. He gestures. The sensors switch off. One of the walls slides away.

The office that's revealed looks like it could have been ripped straight out of any modern corporation. Lavishly appointed furnishings center on an oversize desk. A man's got his feet up on the desk. The name on his uniform says JANSEN. He claps slowly. Almost mockingly.

"The prodigal son returns," he says.

"Just in time for the mother of all parties," says Lynx.

Somewhere beneath the largest mountain chain on Earth is a tunnel. Just one among many. Only this one's much darker than the rest. It's off all the maps. No wires are strung along the walls. The maglev doesn't go down here.

But something a little more primitive does.

The train now rushing down the tunnel was built to ride magnetic current. But it was also configured for old-fashioned rails—and the wheels that have extended out along each side are making for a far more bumpy ride than any modern mode of transport. Though the two men who just got aboard aren't complaining.

"And here we are," says Spencer.

"But where's that?" mutters Sarmax.

It's a good question. They've dropped from the tunnel ceiling. They're spread-eagled in their suits, on the roof of the third car back. They're worming their way into the gaps between the cars.

"Somewhere off the zone," says Spencer.

But somehow the Manilishi's still with him all the same. He's trying to figure out how she's doing it. He's guessing that she's staging in from the end of the maglev rails—broadcasting via wireless down the tunnels. But that seems more than a little risky. Not to mention increasingly difficult as the tunnel steepens and the descent continues...

"The Eurasians rigged a classic tech barrier," says Sarmax.

"Only way to beat the zone is to end it," says Spencer. "But where exactly are we going?"

The last of the lights overhead are gone. They're in total darkness now. The train's accelerating. Spencer's not even sure anyone's really at the helm.

"Where indeed," says Sarmax. "Any thoughts?"

"I've got lots of thoughts. The question is—"

"What the hell the handler wrote down," says Sarmax.

And Spencer's making progress. The second part's definitely a technical treatise. Of that much he's now sure. Or rather, the Manilishi is. She's cranking away behind the scenes while he's struggling to keep up. The specifics are still holding out. But he's ready to make some guesses.

"There are only so many things it could be," he says.

"Right," says Sarmax. "Let's list out possibilities. Work from there."

"Well, for a start, how about another breed of nano."

"Christ, let's hope not."

"They'd have had to solve the hack vulnerability."

"Which won't have been easy. But I think we're thinking along the right lines."

"With nano?" asks Spencer.

"Actually I meant with some kind of zone breakthrough. Look at the sort of hacks that the Rain unleashed. What if the Eurasians were working on similar lines?"

"Then they wouldn't have let themselves get buttfucked in their Aerie so easily."

"Maybe," says Sarmax. "Maybe not. But we're heading into something that's been cauterized from the rest of the zone, right? That's not online, right? Maybe studying the

Rain's incursions allowed the East to put the finishing touches on their own stuff. Or maybe this lot just got caught napping."

"You could be right," says Spencer.

"You don't agree."

"I think we ignore the physical at our peril."

"Got something in mind?"

"I've got *too many* things in mind," says Spencer. "Fifth-generation nukes. Tesla disruptors. Weather control. Anti-matter bombs. Gamma ray pro—"

"Half that shit isn't even possible."

"Leo. We're riding a train going Christ knows where beneath the Himalayas precisely because we don't *know* what's possible."

"But we're about to find out," says Sarmax.

And gestures at the faint light that's growing up ahead.

So what the hell *are* they heading for?" says Haskell. "Don't know," says the Operative.

"And how the fuck am I even seeing this?"

"The zone," he replies.

"But Spencer's cut off from zone."

He and Sarmax vanished beyond its edges five minutes ago. There's been no sign of them since they took the train into the dark. But now this image is wafting through her head. She doesn't know where it's coming from. She can't see why it should even be here. Unless she's somehow found a way into whatever shard of zone Spencer's now in. Or—

"You'll figure it out soon enough," he says.

"None of this adds up."

"Not everything does."

"And the fact that you don't know what the fuck they're making for doesn't make you think twice about starting a war?"

"It doesn't even make me think *once*. Because whatever it is, we're about to take it out."

"And I can't do anything save fly cover."

"Not as long as I'm right here with you."

She looks at him. He's just like the Carson she remembers. He's the man whom time never seemed to age. He's been with her all this time. Ever since the day when he first came to her. Ever since she asked him how he could possibly teach her anything.

Ever since he told her.

"Why did you sell out to Szilard?" she asks.

He laughs. "You really think *that's* what's going on?"

"You're saying Lynx isn't under your control?"

"You think he ever was?"

"You think I can't see through the game you're playing."

"Maybe you should spell it out for me."

"Your team's gone rogue. You're going to hand the Throne over to the Lizard."

"Along with my fucking sanity? Fuck, Claire. I practically lost my life battling the SpaceCom conspiracy on the Moon."

"Not the SpaceCom conspiracy, Carson. *A* SpaceCom conspiracy. One among many that Szilard maintained outside of normal command channels. Only this particular network got infected by Autumn Rain. Szilard tried to use the Rain, and they just ended up playing him. He knew when to cut his losses."

"He still wants to be president, though."

"God only knows what contortions he's going through to keep his game afloat."

"Nothing anywhere near as contorted as the logic twists you're putting your own mind through."

"But that's what you want, isn't it?"

"You think so?" he asks.

"You're testing my capabilities even as you try to figure

out what makes me tick. You *want* me running new theories through my feedback loops, so that you can study me all the closer."

"Keep talking."

"Oh you bastard. Why did you sell the Throne out?"

"I haven't. I'm still loyal."

"You don't know the meaning of the word."

"I'm the one guy who's stuck with him through everything."

"You're the one guy capable of this kind of treachery. Harrison's a fool to have trusted you. And for that matter, so's Szilard."

"Though it certainly made it a lot easier to finish the job against SpaceCom small-fry like Matthias."

"So you're admitting it."

"What?"

"That you've been working for the Lizard."

"In this game, the more bosses you have, the more leverage you get."

"But sooner or later you've got to prioritize."

"Well," says Carson, "that's the art."

"So you made it," says Rear Admiral Jansen.

"So yeah," says Lynx.

Jansen stretches, comes out from behind the desk, walks to where Linehan's strapped to the gurney. Looks at Linehan, who stares up at him helplessly. Jansen laughs, nods to the marines who stand in front of the door.

"Wait outside," he says.

The marines salute, exit the room. The door slides shut behind them. Jansen walks back behind the desk. Looks back at Lynx.

"It's about fucking time," he says.

"I got here as fast as I could. A more direct way wouldn't have been safer."

"Don't I know it. The fleet's riddled with traitors of every stripe."

"And the *Montana*?"

"Far too quiet."

"What about Szilard?"

"He sees no one."

"Not even his bodyguards?"

"You mean his *latest* bodyguards?"

"Guess I just answered my own question."

"You bet your sweet ass. Christ, fuck the bodyguards: that's how the Rain got in the last time. That's how the Lizard beat the Rain's hit team—purged his bodyguards and everybody else while he was at it. And then he ripped the head off the intelligence apparatus and placed me atop the bleeding stump."

"He's lucky he had his own private network to draw from."

"Not lucky. Farsighted. Now, tell me what's going on."

"What's going on is that the Praetorians sent me in here to kill Szilard."

"That's as predictable as it is funny."

"They're coming apart at the seams. They'll do anything to hang onto power."

"Like setting off a war?"

"How do you know—"

"You're not the only agent we've got in the field."

"Yeah? Got anyone aboard the president's ship?"

"You've got the location of his fucking ship?"

"For you, anything."

Jansen gestures at Linehan. "And what about him?"

"The last piece of the puzzle," says Lynx. "The key to stopping the Rain once and for all."

"Aren't the Rain history?"

"I'm sure they'd like you to think so."

"Go on."

"This man Linehan—they met with him. They *rigged* him. In HK. He's still got their software in his head. Reverse-engineer that and we can figure out how they ran rings around Matthias. How they brought down the zones. How they got into the Platform. How they got in *here*."

"You're going to be moving up in the world," says Jansen.

"You too," says Lynx.

They look at each other.

"You really think they're still on the loose?"

"I don't think it," says Lynx. "I know."

"What makes you so sure?"

"Call it a hunch," says Lynx—just as a sentinel beam on the wall spits fire, strikes the acting head of SpaceCom intelligence in the back of the head, knocking him face first onto the desk. The smell of seared meat fills the room.

Lynx looks around. He gets up, turns as the door slides open and the two suited soldiers enter the room; next moment, they're sprawling on the floor as their armor malfunctions and electrocutes them. The door slides shut.

For a moment Lynx stands there. Then he steps over to one of the dead soldiers, opens up the suit, pulls out the body, climbs in to take its place. The sweat of the man he's just killed fills his nostrils. He pays it no heed, turns to Linehan, injects him. Another moment and Linehan has his bare hands around Lynx's armored neck.

"That's not constructive," says Lynx.

"You twisted *fuck*."

"Look, I've got this room in lockdown but I don't know how long I can keep it that way."

"What the fuck was that about me being rigged by the Rain?"

"Total bullshit. And by the way, while me and Admiral

Dead were talking, the queen-razor Manilishi has been shut-
ting down the *Montana*'s defenses. So how about you get in
that other suit and let's go waste the Lizard."

Linehan releases him. He stares through the visor at
Lynx's face. He's so angry he looks like he's about to lose his
mind.

"And then I'll waste you," he says.

"And then you can try."

Ø   "This is just demented," says Spencer.

"Tell me something I don't know," says
Sarmax.

The train's bending right, along a curve. The angle of
descent has steepened. Immediately to the left is a wall.
About ten meters to the right is an edge. And past that
edge . . .

"Christ almighty," says Spencer.

"It's at least a kilometer across," breathes Sarmax.

They're in a cavern that redefines the word *vast*. The railway runs along a route carved into the cavern's edge, descending in long circles along a spiral. Sarmax and Spencer
can see all the way to the other side of the cavern, to where
another train that's farther ahead has descended to the level
beneath. Rows of lights line the cavern ceiling above, illuminating what lies below. Whatever's down there isn't visible
from the current vantage point. The train keeps on rumbling
downward.

"Let's get out and take a look," says Spencer.

"I'm guessing all we need to do is wait."

"We need more data before we ride this thing all the
way in."

"Good point."

Though either way it's a risk. They adjust their camouflage, leap lightly from the train, roll along the ground, stop just short of the edge. The camo makes minute refinements. They peer over. Vertigo kicks them in the face.

"Holy *shit*," says Sarmax.

But Spencer's saying nothing. He's just looking down what must be at least half a kilometer. He feels like his eyes are rebelling at what they're taking in. As if he's lived all his life to see something so completely gone.

"What in God's name is it?"

"Christ only knows."

If that. It's some impossibly mammoth structure—the top of a huge dome, curving down to where it's swallowed by a webwork of platforms and catwalks. The exact size is impossible to discern. But if the curve of what's visible is any indication . . .

"Fucking insane," says Sarmax.

"It must be at least a klick high."

"Sure, but what the fuck *is* it?"

"I think the better question is what does it contain?"

"You still can't access zone?"

"There's clearly one down there. Lot of wireless activity."

"But the answer's no."

"The answer is I'm working on it."

"We need to get inside."

"I realize that."

"Any ideas?"

"How's this for starters . . ."

"This is bullshit," she says.

"Is it?"

"It's something you're projecting."

"You don't think it's real?"

"I think you're making me hallucinate."

"Or maybe . . ." says Carson.

"Or maybe what?"

"What else would account for what you're seeing?"

"Don't do this to me, Carson."

"Think about it, Claire."

"It's fucking real, goddammit!"

"Of course it is."

"You're fucking with my mind."

"Of course I am. But not with that image."

"But what the hell am I seeing?"

"The Eurasian superweapon. Obviously."

She keeps on staring at the image in her head. It's a structure that would be regarded as large were it standing on the Earth's surface. The fact that it's beneath the ground makes it pretty much unprecedented. Haskell looks down toward it. She takes in the platforms that jut out to encompass it, the doors here and there along its vast sloping wall . . .

"No," she says. "Spencer's right. That's not the weapon. That's a fortress. Which contains the weapon."

He stares at her. Almost as though he expects her to continue. Yet she's got nothing more to say.

But then she realizes she does.

"And the Rain," she whispers.

Alarms are howling, but Lynx can barely hear them. Vibration's pounding through the walls, but he can barely feel it. All he's got is his own mind, lancing out in all directions and gathering everything in under its sway. The mainframes of the *Montana* are giving up the ghost. The ship's defenses are going down before him.

And Linehan as well, who's blasting his way through strongpoint after strongpoint and none of the defenders even see him coming. All their sensors show the threat's coming from some other angle. They show Linehan as friendly. By the time they realize otherwise it's way too late. Linehan's leaving only mangled flesh drifting in his wake.

Though he's getting more than just a little help. Lynx has unleashed viruses through the armor of everyone who's standing in Linehan's way. The only thing that's out of reach is this station's own inner enclave. Which is where Szilard's holding out. Linehan's heading there as fast as he can shoot. Lynx is doing the same, along a different route. He's taken off his armor. He's taking one hell of a risk. But that's the only way he's going to be able to squeeze through the spaces he needs to.

Though it's still a tight fit. Even the larger maintenance shafts aren't intended to be serviced by humans. They're accessed instead by a whole taxonomy of robots that double as sentinels. Clawed drones, welders, moving drills—they're hurling themselves from out of the dark and onto Lynx, doing their best to cut him to ribbons.

Only they can't. They're getting stopped just short of him. They're getting out of his way. It's not their fault. Lynx has reached into their brains, giving them a little twist, making them forget just why the hell they were getting so agitated. He's the one thing in these tunnels that's managing to stay focused. He keeps on moving.

And now he's in the inner area. He can see the blueprints of this section stretching all about him. All twenty levels of it. All of the *Montana* beyond it, and the whole fleet stretched out beyond that. The word's spreading among the closest of those ships that something's going down on the *Montana*. But they're also getting word that the situation's under control. That any attempt to land forces on the *Montana* will be seen as insubordination. An attempt to seize Szilard's power. It's all playing out as Lynx intended. All he's doing is taking advantage of the underlying contours. This fleet is as divided against itself as the whole fucking country—as the whole fucking world. Leaving the game wide open to those who can play every end against the middle. Lynx crawls down one last shaft, wedges down one last vent. He kicks a metal grille aside.

And leaps feet-first into the *Montana*'s control center.

They're dangling on a tether that's feeling ever more precarious, descending toward a sheer wall of metal that drops down into eternity. Their camo is put to the ultimate test as they close in on the structure's summit. Neither man says anything. They're preserving absolute radio silence.

Though Spencer can sense the Manilishi in his head anyway, echoing through his software. He still has no idea how the fuck she's doing it. And he's got other things to think about anyway. Because the curve of the dome wall's stretching in toward him. They're close enough to make out lettering painted upon it. Cyrillic and Mandarin, telling the ones who read it absolutely nothing other than where the doors are. There aren't that many. They're so airtight they're almost impossible to spot. Spencer's praying he is too. Most of the activity he can see is confined to the labyrinth of catwalks that obscure the foundation of this gigantic building. But there are eyes and sensors everywhere. Spencer's pretty confident about the ones out here. He's far less certain about whatever lies inside. He's managed to get a tentative grip on the zone within—managed to pry his fingers through a crack in the defenses. But only barely. He can't make out what's going on. He's figuring he's going to get busted at any moment. He's figuring he needs help.

And suddenly he's got it. From the Manilishi. She's showing him what he needs to see—exactly what pressure to apply as he alights on the surface of the structure, right at the point where the dome starts to really slope toward the vertical. He activates his magnetic clamps, starts crawling down the metal like an insect toward the nearest door. Sarmax is right behind him. And the Manilishi's right beside him, encroaching through the circuitry of the door, toward the comps that crouch within. The door is barely discernible, but it seems real enough. As is the hack he's now running on the pneumatic equipment on its other side. He's streaking through endless wires, forestalling fail-safes, fending off countless counter-commands from deeper within the building. He's ignoring the commands without them even knowing it. He's sending in his own instructions.

The door slides open.

Spencer slides in. Sarmax follows. The door shuts behind them.

"Weirder by the second," says Spencer.

They're standing in a chamber. Each wall contains another door. One of them is open. Sarmax starts toward it, just as it slides shut and a panel in the wall beside it swivels aside. A wicked-looking barrel protrudes from within. It's aimed directly at Sarmax's visor. Sarmax leaps to one side. The gun tracks him.

"Fuck," he says.

"It's okay," says Spencer. "I got control."

"So tell it to point somewhere else."

"Tell me what the fuck's going on and I just might."

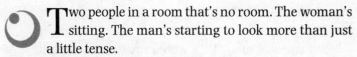

Two people in a room that's no room. The woman's sitting. The man's starting to look more than just a little tense.

"Don't you control Spencer?" he asks.

"You tell me."

"I thought—"

"You thought wrong. Someone got to him."

"You don't know what I was about to say."

"Oh yes I do."

"How's that?"

"I'm reading minds now, aren't I?"

And even as she speaks, the room fades out. To be replaced by the room she started in. She's back in that chair, strapped in again. Only now she's encased within a suit, staring at Carson through a sealed visor. He's dressed in battle harness. The room's shaking as the engines of the president's ship fire. The forces of acceleration are pressing against the walls.

"All you've got is all I want you to see," says Carson.

"We're landing," she says.

"We've started our final approach into Congreve."

"And you're going to kill the president."

"And I'd want to do that why?"

She says nothing. She's too busy testing the barriers around her. What she's wearing is no normal suit. It's more like a cage whose bars are wires that extend into her nerve endings. She can see how it's been done—can see how this thing has been rigged to give whoever's running it every advantage. It's like it's a well and whoever's wearing it is at the very bottom . . .

"Because you've gotten what you came for," she says.

"How to hack the Throne himself to forestall the transfer of the executive node. And now you're going to take him out and take it for yourself."

"Actually I had in mind giving it to someone."

"Who's that?"

"You."

She stares at him. "Why would you want to do that?"

"Because I'm still in love with you."

She laughs. "That is *so* much bullshit."

"You say that without even hesitating."

"You don't even know the meaning of the fucking *word*—"

"I tried to warn you, Claire." He shrugs. "Tried to tell you just how beyond the range of ordinary definition you are. Transhuman in a way that the rest of us can barely *fathom*. Think: your intuition, what does that really mean?"

"Ability to compute in advance of stimuli," she says, almost automatically.

"And how the fuck could *that* be taking place?"

"Retrocasuality," she says. "That's the only way."

"Signals from the future."

"I've felt them."

"I'm sure you have."

"God help me, Carson."

"If you think you can reach Him, let me know."

"Only thing I can reach out there is Lynx and Spencer. And Lynx is on the zone only—"

"And what about the Rain?"

"I think they're inside that building beneath Eurasia."

"And they've turned Spencer?"

But that's not true. She suddenly remembers what she's done, remembers what she's apparently just communicated by some kind of telepathy to Spencer, telepathy that interfaces with both flesh *and* zone: she's told him to keep that gun pointed at Sarmax and stand by for further orders. Because the Rain aren't in that Eurasian structure after all. And the person who tampered with Spencer was—

"Me," she says. "*I* turned Spencer. Just now."

Carson smiles softly. "So now you see."

She does. All those nights with Carson all that time ago, energy going through her body and across her mind and out into the universe beyond her. She suddenly gets where Carson's been coming from all these years. He looks like a man. He's really something more. The leader of the last Rain triad looks at her and she meets his gaze and doesn't turn away.

• • •

At the heart of L2 is a ship around which all rotates. Somewhere in that ship there's a room set apart from all else. Somewhere in that room's the truth.

If only you can find it.

"Don't fucking move," says Lynx.

The man he's got his pistols pointed at stiffens, raises his hands in the air. Which makes him even taller—he turns around, looks at Lynx.

"How the fuck did you get in here?"

"By being unstoppable."

"Whatever you're getting, I'll double it."

"This isn't about cash," says Lynx.

Though it looks like plenty has been blown on this room. It's not small. The Moon floats in the window that comprises most of the ceiling. A massive map of the lunar surface covers the center of the floor. The walls are lined with console banks and the occasional door, one of which now slides open. Linehan enters the room. His armor's been scorched in several places. Smoke's still drifting from his guns.

"Did I miss anything?" he asks.

"We were just getting started."

The door slides shut.

You got the short end of the stick," says Spencer. Sarmax doesn't turn around. Spencer's viewing him through several crosshairs. Getting the drop on a man in powered armor isn't easy. It helps to know your target's suit inside out. It helps to have the Manilishi as a guardian angel upon your shoulder. Spencer monitors the voiceprint as Sarmax speaks.

"How do you mean?"

"I mean did you guys draw straws or something? Lynx hits the SpaceCom fleet and you get inside the Eurasians and meanwhile Carson gets his hands on the Throne?"

"Something like that. So—"

"So your luck's run out, Leo. Carson's going to rule and you're going to die."

"I'm not going to die," says Sarmax. "And neither will you if you manage to grow some brains in time."

"Thank fuck I wised up when I did."

"You didn't. I'll bet it was the Manilishi telling you what was what."

"She thinks you and Lynx and Carson got created in the same moment."

"She's right."

"But that's bullshit. You're all different ages. You were born separately."

"And reborn together."

Y ou no longer control Spencer," says Haskell.

"That'd be all you," says Carson. "You're doing great."

"He's got ahold of the trigger in that room."

"Let him keep it."

"And if he tries to kill Leo?"

"Let him."

"You haven't changed a bit."

"Sarmax hid Jarvin's file from me, Claire. It wasn't Spencer he didn't want to share it with, it was—"

"You."

"Us," says Carson.

"You mean that?"

"You're lucky," he says. "You flew from the start. I had to adapt. Had to deal with it. I was only twenty-eight—"

"That's how old I am now."

"Except you're not. Accelerated growth in the vat—"

"I know that, Carson. You don't need to tell me. Let me out of this suit."

"I can't. Until it's done."

"The missions?"

"Everything. The battle for the world and moon goes down tonight. And then you'll be at my side."

"I need you to let me out of this."

"And I will. But right now I have to let you steer yourself as you activate your powers. You have to ride the raw wave of moment, Claire. Your memory—tell me what you remember."

"Everything."

"Go on."

"I know it all now. Where the implants start. Where they stop. What lies beyond them. I remember my sixth birthday for real and the counterfeit birthdays before that. Six days after being decanted and here I am thinking I'm a normal fucking kid."

"And you weren't even a normal member of the Rain. Just the capstone on the whole project—"

"You need to tell me exactly what you mean by that."

"I'd rather have you show me everything instead."

The head of U.S. Space Command has the look of an animal that's been brought to bay. He's staring down the barrel of the minigun mounted atop Linehan's suit. But he's maintaining his composure.

"The chickens have come home to roost," he says slowly.

"That's for sure," says Lynx. His voice wafts out from behind the consoles he's busy working on. Everything aboard the *Montana* has gone haywire. None of Szilard's marines can get anywhere near this room. Half of them are dead due to suit malfunctions anyway. The lights of the L2 fleet flicker in the window.

"You bastard," says Linehan. "Do you recognize me?"

"Should I?" asks Szilard.

"I was a member of the team you sent to help the Rain take down the Elevator."

"An interesting theory."

"I was *there*, asshole. In the heart of HK, meeting with those fucks. They fucked me good. So did you. And now I'm going to rip your fucking heart out—"

"So what are you waiting for?"

"Me," says Lynx. "I might need to ask you a question or two about how you've wired this ship's inner enclave."

Szilard's expression doesn't change. "So you can control it."

"I already control it, asswipe. I'm talking about the rest of your fucking fleet. To deliver to the president."

"You mean Matthew Sinclair," says Szilard.

B ecause that's who we're really talking about, isn't it?"

"Have it your way," says Sarmax. "But he—"

"Did it all through Carson? I know. Carson came to you and dragged you out of retirement and explained Sinclair's whole scheme. Poured honey in your ears and—"

"You've got it all wrong."

"Yeah?

"We almost killed each other first."

"And I'm supposed to be surprised? When the whole MO of the Rain was to devour each other? Dysfunction junction from the word go and—"

"Fuck, Spencer, I *know*. Jesus Christ, that's why I got the fuck out of all that."

"I heard there was a different reason."

"Don't even go there."

"The conditioning may have backfired on you. But the rest of it didn't matter. You and Lynx and Carson were the originals: three Praetorians who'd kicked ass together for so long you could practically complete each other's sentences. What better subject matter for the initial experiment? What better prototypes for the world's most dangerous hit team?"

"The Manilishi's telling you this?" asks Sarmax.

"Yeah. And I'm pretty sure the third part of the handler's book says the same damn thing. Along with all the specifics."

"The crown jewels, huh?"

"The exact nature of the Autumn Rain experiments, Leo."

"The compiling of which drove the handler mad."

"That may be its basic condition."

"We were flatlined," says Sarmax. "All those years ago. That's all I know. They took out our lights together: meshed us on the zone, crashed our systems, and then woke us at the same fucking time and after that we were fucking linked in some way. I don't think it worked out quite as well as they wanted, though. I think they were thinking they were going to get some kind of group-mind effect, and it wasn't anywhere near that precise. But our reflexes were off the charts. And we could sense when the others were near. I know that Lynx and Carson are heading toward each other behind the Moon right now. I know they know I'm back here. I know that—"

"It has to do with consciousness."

"Yes. Obviously."

"It was a specific process."

"Or more than one."

"Was it used on me?"

But Sarmax only smiles.

"Or am I Rain myself?" asks Spencer. "Goddamn it, Leo—"

"You're just a guy who ended up running with the big dogs. Far as I know, anyway. Carson managed to hook you up to the Manilishi, but that was only thanks to software the Throne gave him to implant in you."

"Rain software."

"Presumably."

"From the original tests?"

"Who knows? I'm just telling you what I was told. But the master process—whatever it was—was refined with the second team. They weren't like us. They weren't modified. They were—"

"—*created*. For that purpose."

"They were hell on bloody wheels, Spencer. They put us in the fucking shade."

"And now they're in the shade forever."

"She told you that?"

"And more besides."

The final descent is under way. The last of the engines are firing.

"You shouldn't have trusted Sinclair," she says.

But Carson just grins. "Who said I trust him?"

"Then why the fuck are you carrying out his orders?"

"Sinclair came to me two days before the Elevator went down. He restored what the Praetorians had stripped from me. My memory of those times. The training I'd received. The training I'd given. Said he was worried that his protégés were getting out of hand. Said he might need me to run some interference. Sarmax had left the service with his memories intact. His little secret. Arranged by Sinclair without the Throne's knowledge. After the Elevator blew, I went to Leo. We struck a deal. We dealt Lynx in on the way back to Earth."

"And after the naughty little children were defeated, why didn't you just seize everything on that ship on the way back?"

"Because we needed you to find and destroy the rest of those fucks. Seizing control of everything with them still out there would have made *us* the target."

"If Sinclair's in prison, then how are you in touch with him?"

"I don't need to be."

"What?"

"You still don't get it, Claire, do you? Sinclair's sitting in his fucking cell watching the universe spin around him."

"He's reading minds too?"

"Have you sensed him? On any level?"

She shakes her head. "Not as far as I know. All I've got is Spencer's and a shade or two of yours. Have *you*?"

"I don't think it works that way," says Carson. "It works like this: when he restored my memory, Sinclair explained to me *exactly what would happen.* Exactly what levers I would need to pull—and when. He laid the whole thing out— said how it would go down if I gave it the right set of shoves. Said it all led up to something that's coming up, some- thing past which he can't see. He's on a whole different level, maybe even *your* level, and I don't even pretend to understand—"

"That's why you're so crazy to be dealing with him."

"That's why I need your help."

"He went through the Rain process himself. He must have."

"I'm convinced he saw it as the best way to get the drop on Harrison," says Carson.

"Is he *really* on this ship?"

"Harrison? Absolutely. And by the way, he's going to re- main president, no matter what the head of SpaceCom thinks."

"As a figurehead."

"As an expedient."

"A temporary one?"

"*Everything* is, Claire."

They look at each other.

"Because that's the core of it," says Carson. "Harrison and Sinclair. Lifelong partners, lifelong rivals, and the guy you thought of as the old man always had to play second fiddle. He and the president cooked up the Autumn Rain scheme together, back when they were both admirals."

"*Before* they ruled the country."

"Why so surprised?"

"Morat told me it was after Harrison assumed power."

"Second-generation team—*your* team—sure. Not the first. Not us. Besides, Morat was a low-grade punk. He never knew the half of it. How the fuck do you think Harrison and Sinclair took over? Me and Lynx and Sarmax took out everyone opposed to them. But Sinclair was keeping his own options open the whole time. And by augmenting *himself,* he must have figured he'd be ready if the shit ever hit the fan."

"But why did he let them put him in the L5 prison?"

"I'm pretty sure he thinks that's the safest place to be."

"I'd rather be within some kind of rock when the shooting starts," she says.

"Makes two of us," he replies.

She nods. The ship drops toward the Moon.

We were seduced," says Szilard.

He steps away from Linehan, steps out onto the lunar map that dominates the floor.

"That's far enough," says Linehan.

Szilard stops. Looks back at him. Holds up his hands in what looks almost like a protest. "But we were," he says.

"Perhaps Sinclair was, too. Because it wasn't just their lack of inhibition. Any sociopath can do as well. What made the Rain so lethal was a radioactive creativity. Seeing patterns where ordinary people see only chaos. An ability to grasp opportunities invisible to anyone else. It wasn't just the telepathy either. Look at the games they've been playing. So twisted you can't even follow the threads. They've got all of us wrapped up in the same fucking web and all they need to do now is suck out the goddamn juice."

"Why are you telling me this?" asks Linehan.

"Because you're just one of the victims," says Szilard.

"Yeah?" asks Lynx. His voice echoes from an open hatch in one of the mainframes. "Is that a fact, Jharek?"

"It is. You're using this man."

"I'm giving him the chance to kill you."

"And I wish you'd let me go ahead and do it," says Linehan.

"You're just a jackal on a leash," says Szilard.

But Linehan only laughs. "I'm riding shotgun on history, and I'm about to put the head of my original boss all over that *wall*. It doesn't get any better than this."

"Maybe you should ask your drug-snorting Rain razor what he intends to do with you once I'm dead."

"Hey Lynx," says Linehan, "what's next?"

"We unleash the war."

"And what's my rank?"

"My bodyguard."

"And what's yours?"

"I thought I'd start with commander of the L2 fleet."

"Fucking cool," says Linehan, "let's do it."

• • •

Ⓢ Two men sit in a room in some structure beneath the Himalayas. The pieces of that structure are like a grid within Spencer's mind. He's trying to grasp the nature of this place. He's trying to focus on the face of Sarmax, but it's as if the walls are blurring around him—as if the floor is undulating beneath his feet. Everything's starting to swirl inside his head.

"Fuck," he says.

"Don't fight it," says Sarmax.

"Ayahuasca," says Spencer. "It's resurging—"

"Is that what it feels like? Being mind-melded with the Manilishi can't be easy—"

"Fuck's sake—"

"—especially now that bitch has been trying to pull your strings. And all the while we've been pulling hers."

Spencer stares at him. But he can no longer speak. Pressure keeps on growing in his chest. The images of the pages of the book pulsate within his head. The face of the Manilishi blazes like some dark sun inside him.

Ⓞ W hat the hell are you doing?" she mutters.

"Having my way with you once more."

Though really he's just holding onto the wall right in front of her while the ship shakes about them, dropping through ten thousand meters. The dome of Congreve is visible below. Haskell's struggling to remain calm. Carson's smile isn't helping. Nor is what he's doing to her mind.

"You miss the essence of the problem," he says. "The Rain weren't some mythical force. They were just men and women who had been engineered to think without fetters. The solution to an equation no one had even dared to postulate. Not a question of ends—"

"But means. Carson, I *know* this. But—I—*fuck*!"

"Sure you do. But you were never asked to prove it. You were kept within the system and everything stayed nice and simple. And all the while the ones with whom you were bred were out in the cold thinking like normal humans never could. Putting together a plan more convoluted than a god-damn Gordian knot."

"Which was *nothing* compared to what you were doing."

"Which just proves the point," he says.

"Even though none of it was your fucking idea."

"At least I know a good one when I see it."

"Christ, Carson, you're hurting me."

"Someday you'll forgive me."

"I'm damned for ever having known you."

"But let's try to make the most of it, anyway," he says. "Some kind of process, right? But what? What was it that the Rain were made of? Sinclair knows it all, and everyone else is in the dark. But somewhere in you—"

"*No one* besides Sinclair? Not even the Throne? Or you?"

"I know only fragments."

"What did you use to bind me to Spencer?"

"Death."

"*What?*"

"We killed you. When we got back to Earth."

"That was a risk."

"The Throne said you'd have to be executed anyway unless we could find a way to harness you. And the Praetorian med-teams know what they're doing: simultaneously flat-lined you and Spencer and then shocked you back while your minds were wired together on the zone. Sinclair had already given me the sequence and Harrison was the one who gave the order but I've no idea how he—"

"And why not Lynx?"

"Too risky. It had been done to him once already, right?

And Spencer's mind had been dosed with ayahuasca, which made him particularly receptive. But the real question isn't what was done to him a few days ago or what was done to me and Lynx and Sarmax more than two decades back; the real question is what was done to you and the rest of the Rain when you were in the fucking *incubator*. The first team was jury-rigged and the second was created wholesale. And only Sinclair knows *that* formula—"

"And Harrison—"

"—*thinks* he does, but his files are rigged with false data."

"You really think you've beaten the Praetorians?"

"You're the one who's done that. It's what you were designed for. Though finding out how much of you goes beyond anybody's planning is what I'm setting in motion tonight."

"I'll tell you what I know," she says, and she can't help but say the words. She can't help but tell him everything she can and then some. She has no idea what he already knows. She has no idea how she knows what she does. It doesn't matter. Her mind twists and turns and it's all she can do to hang on . . .

"I was to be the key node in the Autumn Rain massmind."

"Go on."

"The one that the second generation became. The one that Marlowe and I were shorn from."

"The one you detected traces of at the Europa Platform."

"And that I killed every last member of."

"You sure about that?"

She stares at him. "What do you mean?"

"You sure you got them all?"

"Are you saying that—"

"You know exactly what I'm saying."

"Don't—fucking *do this*—"

But he's already pulling more levers somewhere deep

within the canyons of her skull. Everything blurs around her—

"For the love of Christ, stop fucking with my—"

And suddenly her vision's burning white.

L et's get this show on the road," says Lynx. He emerges from an open hatch in one of the mainframes, wires trailing from it to multiple places in his skull. He looks at Szilard.

"Kill him," he tells Linehan—but Linehan's already opening up on Szilard, even as his target dives away, starts rolling across the floor. But he's got no chance against a suit of armor. Linehan turns, catches up with Szilard in a single stride. Laughs.

And stops. For a moment he's balanced on one foot. And then he topples over. His armor hits the floor with a crash. Szilard's on his feet, leaping Linehan's toppled suit, running straight at Lynx. Who's fumbling for his pistols, raising them, opening up as Szilard hurls himself to one side once more and darts behind the mainframe to which Lynx is attached. Just as the back of the armor that's sprawled on the floor opens and a very pissed off Linehan climbs out.

"What the hell's your problem?" he screams at Lynx.

"What the fuck's yours?"

"My armor just got hacked, and you didn't stop it!"

"I never even saw it! For fuck's sake, this is a live situation! He's behind this console! He's fucking with it and I'm losing control!"

"Give me that," snarls Linehan, snatching one of the pistols from Lynx's grasp. He turns toward the consoles, starts firing, advancing on the place where Szilard vanished.

"Does he have a way out of this room?" he yells.

"Back there? There's nothing."

"You hear that?" shrieks Linehan. "Szilard! This is it! You're dead!"

"Don't just tell me about it," screams Szilard, "come over here and fucking *do it*!"

With an unearthly cry, Linehan starts forward.

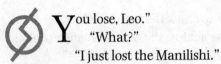 "You lose, Leo."

"What?"

"I just lost the Manilishi."

"She's—"

"Not calling the shots anymore. And neither's Carson."

"Where the fuck did they go?"

"How the fuck should I know? I'm my own man now."

And he is. The waters of his life roar around him and he lets himself get caught in the rush. His mind's still ablaze with static, but now it's all insight that he's gathering into himself. He focuses on Sarmax, wonders whether he should pull the trigger.

"One last chance," says Sarmax.

"You're one to talk."

"I'm serious. Join us."

"*What?*"

"Fuck man, we're inside the Eurasian superweapon. No reason you can't have it once I'm ruling bigger empires."

"You'd put one through me as soon as you saw an opening. I'm not one of your fucking trinity."

"I hate both those fucks, Spencer. Don't—"

One of the doors slides open. A suitless Russian soldier enters the room. His eyes go wide with astonishment.

"It's not what it looks like," says Spencer.

"Drop your weapon," says the soldier—and tries to signal backup. But Spencer's hacking the signal. The soldier's backing up through the door, but Spencer gets his mind around the door, slides it shut with full force, smashing the soldier against the doorway, crushing his rib cage—but not before the man's gotten off a shot. Spencer leaps aside as the projectile sears past him—even as Sarmax whirls to face him. Their guns are right up against each other's visors.

"Shoot and you'll lose your zone coverage," says Spencer.

"Shoot and you'd better believe I'll get a shot off," says Sarmax.

"I'm your only hope to crack the handler's files."

"I've done more runs against the East than anyone alive."

"So? You still need me more than I need you—"

"To do what?" yells Sarmax. "To do fucking *what*? Are you going to try to take down this place or are you going to take this all the fucking way? Don't you get it? The secret of the Rain is out there and whoever finds it can *build more of them*. And you really think you can get to the next level of this fucking game when you're flying solo?"

"I think we should see what the hell's in here with us."

"I can think of worse ideas," says Sarmax.

Spencer nods.

"What the fuck," says Haskell.

"What are you seeing?" says Carson.

"You just overwrote half of Lynx's hacks! And God knows what you just did with my link to Spencer!"

"Never mind that," snarls Carson, *"tell me what you're fucking seeing!"*

She knows damn well what he means even though she doesn't know how the fuck it's happening. All she knows is that there's a new light burning out on the edges of her awareness—a light that's like a cross between a star and fire, that can only be one thing—

"Another mind," she whispers.

"Not Spencer's either."

"Rain—"

"Yes," he says. *"Go on."*

"It's—Autumn Rain—someone—"

"Who?"

"I—can't tell—"

"Who? How many?"

"I can't tell—it's blurring—"

"Location," he says, and his voice is very calm.

"L5," she answers without hesitation. Vast mental geographies loom around her. "But—that's where Sinclair—"

"That's no coincidence."

"But it's not him—"

"Of course not."

"He's got someone else up there."

"Maybe more than that."

"Not all the original batch went rogue," she mutters.

"And not all of the Praetorians who guard Sinclair are who they seem."

"So I see."

"Sinclair told me you'd read it loud and clear."

She nods. Her mind is blasted open. She's draped in the glow that lights up the no-sky of no-zone. She can't communicate with whoever's out there—doesn't even know who the fuck it *is*—but it's Rain, of that much she's certain, because the mere *presence* in her head is more vivid than anything she's ever known. And yet it's all a mere fraction of how it was all supposed to be. Horizon sets within Haskell's mind even as realization dawns. Lines align within her head, and it's all she can do to keep up with them. Someone she was *born with* is still *alive*—she's weeping and she's conscious of almost nothing else.

And then there's nothing she's *not* conscious of. Reality *clicks* around her and something just folds. She gazes at Carson and it's like his face is falling away from her down some endless shaft . . .

"What am I really?" she asks softly.

"Something that's come unstuck in time."

"That Sinclair can't predict."

"Presumably."

She exhales slowly. "And the rest of the Rain?"

"May be related to that fact."

"I can *feel* the Moon out there," she mutters. "It's hauling against me like a fucking lodestone."

"It may yet drag you under."

"What the hell's happening?"

"You're changing."

"Thanks a lot."

"You're welcome. I've been doing my best to crank you up across the last few hours. That suit I've rigged you with is worth the price tag. Overstimulating your system with electric shock and circuit overload and—"

"Fucking bastard."

"We're still not sure what we've got in you, Claire. And maybe it doesn't fucking matter: off-the-charts AI or ESP gateway or crack in the fucking cosmic egg—doesn't matter what we call it as long as we can use it. And with the East about to bring its own superweapon online we'd better make sure we're maxing out on ours."

"So why the fuck did you just shove both missions off the goddamn rails?"

"Getting exciting, isn't it?"

"Because you fear Lynx and Sarmax more than anything else?"

"Because I'm giving up on breaking you open. For now."

"You're—"

"Out of time. And remember what I said about multiple bosses? I got *way* too many assholes on line one."

"Christ almighty, Carson. Are you obeying Sinclair's orders or have you sold him out too?"

"I like to think I'm carrying out the spirit of them."

"And all your talk of love?"

"Just talk. But there'll be time for action later."

"I swear to God I'll destroy you if I ever get the chance."

"That'd be by boring me to death with your threats?"

The door slides open. Armored Praetorians enter the room. They're wearing the uniform of the Core. They fan out, take up positions. Carson looks at them. One of them salutes.

"Sir," he says.

"Half of you come with me," says Carson. "The other half stay here. Seal this door. Don't let anybody in until we've landed." Soldiers head back through the door. Carson follows them—and stops as Haskell starts screaming at him.

"What the fuck are you doing?"

"Like you even need to ask," he says.

The door slides shut behind him.

L aughing like a maniac, Linehan fills the air with fire while he strides toward the console. Lynx has his last pistol trained on the only other exit from behind the equipment. He's waiting for Szilard to come running out to get shot down like a dog. He's desperately trying to bolster his disintegrating zone position through the wires that sprout from his skull. His connection with the Manilishi has been severed. He has no idea why. But something's obviously gone wrong. And it's rapidly getting worse. Szilard's marines are right outside the door, trying to burn their way through.

But it's not too late to salvage the mission. Linehan leaps forward, just as Szilard springs out from behind the console, dodges under Linehan's gun, starts grappling with him. Staff officer versus wet ops veteran: it's no contest. Linehan seizes Szilard, tosses him out toward the center of the room. Szilard mutters something.

"Finish him!" screams Lynx.

"Or you," says Linehan—and turns, grabs Lynx, knocks the pistol out of his hands, hauls him bodily away from the mainframe. Lynx screams as the wires extruding from his skull snap. Linehan hurls him against the console.

And shrugs.

"I'm a conflicted man," he says.

"Christ," mutters Lynx. Blood dribbles from his mouth. He stares up at Linehan. "You've been rigged."

"By us," says Szilard.

"But InfoCom wiped all that—"

"You've made your last assumption," says Szilard. "Soldier, kill this traitor."

"Gladly," says Linehan who whips up his pistol at Lynx, fires. The shot goes over Lynx's head. Linehan fires again. The shot flashes past Lynx's face. Linehan's face is starting to twitch.

"I said fucking kill him!" screams Szilard.

But now Linehan's convulsing. He's pitching forward. Szilard's standing open-mouthed behind him. Lynx starts running. He's got no weapons. He's got nowhere to go. He's heading there as fast as he can.

They're getting the fuck out of that room at speed. They did their best to hide the body of the soldier who crashed their chat—pulled a panel aside, stuffed it in there. And that's about all they've got time for. They're climbing down ladder after ladder, descending through shafts, seeking out the depths of this place, since that's where the heart of its zone activity seems to be. And Spencer's riding toward it. Though without the Manilishi he doesn't dare to try and hack the core. Not until he understands more about what's going on.

Because it's pretty clear *something's* going on. There's a lot of activity under way—a lot of soldiers and technicians going about their business. Spencer and Sarmax are doing their best to look like part of the scenery, hiding behind doors, concealing themselves within shadows, keeping equipment between them and the other men and women within this place.

But it looks as if they might have been detected anyway. Sirens start going off everywhere. Activity's suddenly cranking up to a new level of intensity. Shouting echoes down the corridors. They crouch behind some stowed equipment and wait to be found. Soldiers race into the room.

And keep going. It looked like they weren't searching for anything—just getting ordered into position. Spencer and Sarmax slink out, find more ladders, climb down. The ladders start to get shaken by a distant rumbling, like something's starting up. Spencer's got a feeling that something probably is.

The Operative leaves the interrogation quarters behind, fires his suit's thrusters. The soldiers wearing Praetorian colors swarm in behind him. He lets the Manilishi's hack carve out ahead of him. He's got control of her as long as she remains within the suit. He has no intention of letting her outside it ever again.

He rounds a corner and starts firing. As do all those with him. Their targets' suits are getting shredded. Walls start to buckle under the fusillade. Shots whip past the Operative's head. But he's got the advantage. The fact that his team's maintaining zone integrity allows them to coordinate their shots with deadly precision. He blasts through the dying Praetorian defenders and smashes through into the ship's forward areas.

But now the president responds. The executive node roars out to do battle, bulldozes straight into the Manilishi. Two titanic forces strain against each other. The president has the resources of the whole zone to draw from. The Manilishi is the most powerful razor in existence. Penetrating the U.S. zone is no problem for her. She's already inside it anyway. But assailing its very core is something else altogether.

Which is why the Operative's not counting on her to finish the job. He's planning on doing that the old-fashioned way. He surges forward, tearing his way through more Praetorian defenses. He's not surprised to feel the ship accelerating, surging toward landfall and the president's forces in the base at Congreve. But unless the forces within the ship can stop him, the Operative is going to reach the president before they hit the Moon. He's picking up the pace, too—blasting his way through wall after wall, taking Praetorians by surprise for just the fraction of a second long enough to allow him to destroy them. He's almost at the threshold of the bridge. He can feel the ship's descent quicken toward plummet. He wonders how the hell they're going to stop in time.

And then he realizes they're not.

Haskell's trying to brace herself but there's nothing left to brace. She's already strapped in. The soldiers around her are grabbing onto the walls. The ship's coming in at lethal speeds. She can feel Carson somewhere in the back of her mind. Clarity's bursting on her far too late. She understands that Carson knows that his real enemies are his fellow plotters—that he's riding some deeper scheme.

But apparently he's been too devious by half. Because the president's so desperate to reach the Moon he's going to crash them all. Haskell feels her stomach lurch as the craft accelerates still further—feels herself involuntarily gasp. She feels her whole life start to flash before her eyes—and it's really her own life this time. She understands it all. She gets it—sees her mind caught in the jaws of Carson's trap, sees how he's turned her against herself. How there's no way out.

Not in this world anyway.

Howling heat and burning light . . . the universe opens up around her, rises in her like some voice she's never heard, yet sounds exactly like her own. The minds of everyone she's ever known and everyone she never will flare through her head, pour past her like some runaway torrent. And in that flood she can see it all: the grids of zone and the reins of power that end in the man who holds them within the bridge of a ship that's a blip of light above the horizon that's cutting across a million watching screens—and the woman who's watching all of them knows it'll be the last thing she'll ever see. She's finally free. Retrofire's slamming through her. The ship's firing its brakes. It's way too late. They hit.

There's an explosion. The doors burst open. Szilard's marines hit the room. But Lynx is already gone, through the duct and into the shaft he used to enter the room. Shots streak after him but they're way too late. He's running on all fours like some kind of hunted animal. The mechanized guardians of the *Montana*'s crawlspaces swarm toward him—and scoot away as he uses what's left of his crumbling zone position to talk them out of it. He keeps on moving past them.

He knows he's reached the end of the line. He's out of options. Save whatever's available to him inside all this crawlspace. He's got a feeling he's going to know this place all too well before he dies. The maps gleam within his mind. In their stacked grids he catches glimpses of deeper patterns—how triumph turned so swiftly to debacle, how nasty what's about to happen is going to be. He wonders if it's already begun.

• • •

But if it has, it's news to them. Because down in the lower levels everything's silent. It's as if they've stumbled into the domain of ghosts.

"We've gone too low," says Sarmax.

"I don't think so," says Spencer.

He's starting to evolve a theory about what's really going on within this place. He and Sarmax descend through several more levels, pass through several open hatches.

And arrive in a strange chamber. One where metallic conveyor belts drop from the ceiling, run along walls, pass through slits in the floor. Spherical objects are slotted within the belts. They look like metallic eggs. Sarmax walks over to them. He stares at the objects. He studies one of them in particular.

"Is this what I think it is?" he says.

"I think so," says Spencer.

"Probably five-kiloton yield."

"Probably."

The room has two more exits: a hatch in the floor and one in the ceiling. Spencer does a local hack on the ceiling hatch. They climb a ladder and head on through.

"Hello," says Spencer.

A room that looks to be filled with what must be thousands of those nukes, stacked from floor to ceiling, ready to slot onto the conveyor belts. Spencer breathes deeply.

"Weirder by the second," he says.

"I'd say we're getting close," says Sarmax.

The presidential ship plows into the landing pad and then through the underground hangars stacked beneath, disintegrating as it goes. The base through which it's now spearing comprises about twenty levels. The ship makes it through half of those before momentum peters out. Stars are visible through the hole the ship's just bored . . .

The Operative opens his eyes to find himself staring at those stars. He's lying on his back. He's lost contact with the zone. His armor's taken a serious beating. But it's still functional. He activates its backup comps, surges to his feet.

Wreckage is all around him. As are plenty of bodies. But not the one he's most interested in. He can't see Harrison anywhere. Worse, he's lost contact with the Manilishi. He reactivates his links to zone, hoping it'll have some answers.

It does. The Manilishi's nowhere in sight. But the executive node is clearly visible, still intact, still moving, very close. The Operative fires his thrusters, blasts away from the wreckage and in between the gnarled remains of floors and ceilings. He quickly reaches the more intact areas of the base. He can't see any Praetorians anywhere.

But he can see the president, right ahead of him. Crawling on his hands and knees, in a suit so fucked it's a wonder it's still pressurized. The Operative blasts toward him, just as more figures emerge from the far end of the corridor. The Operative hits his brakes, starts to engage his weapons. But then he stops.

And relaxes.

There are five of them. None are in Praetorian colors. They hit their thrusters, reach the president a fraction of a second before the Operative does. He looks at them. Four are men. One's a woman. She steps forward. He salutes her.

"Ma'am," he says.

"At ease," she replies.

"Stephanie," says a voice, weakly.

The Operative looks down. The president is looking up through a bloodied visor—looking past him, at Stephanie Montrose, the head of Information Command. Her bodyguards stand around her. She looks down.

"Andrew," she says.

"Carson is—this man's a traitor."

Montrose laughs. "On my payroll," she says.

Harrison stares at her with the expression of a man in whom understanding's dawned way too late. "You too, Stephanie?"

"Kinda looks that way."

"You were my fucking *successor*."

"Until now," she says—nods to the Operative. Who places his boot on the president's chest, fires a single shot through his visor. Looks at Montrose.

"Consider the torch passed," he says.

The look on Montrose's face is the look of someone who's just received the software upload that comprises the executive node. The software that holds the reins of the U.S. zone. A transition that's occurred automatically now that Harrison's dead. Montrose turns to the Operative.

"The Manilishi," she says.

"Missing," he replies.

"You're shitting me."

"I wish I was."

"She's dead?"

"Or escaped."

"I thought her suit prevented her from—"

"It might have been damaged in the crash."

"Or shattered altogether. You've fucked up."

"I know."

"If she really has broken loose—"

"We'll find her."

"The tunnels beneath this base are endless."

"We'll find her."

"They say the Rain themselves were down there before we burned them out—"

"I said we'll find her."

"Let that be your next task."

"I'll need soldiers."

"You'll have my best."

Carson salutes, turns away. Montrose turns, too, gets rushed by her bodyguards down the corridors of the base. It used to belong to SpaceCom, before the Praetorians cleaned them out. But InfoCom assisted with that takeover, and it was child's play to lay the seeds of yet another one. Now Montrose's soldiers control this whole place.

And more besides. Montrose gets hustled into one of the underground trains that connects the various military bases scattered beneath Congreve. The train she's in is heading out of Congreve, out beneath the crater perimeter, toward the walled plain of Korolev, dropping ever deeper beneath the surface the whole while. Its destination is the largest command center beneath the lunar farside.

But Montrose doesn't need to get there to make the call she's now making. Szilard's face appears upon a screen within her head. The left side of his face looks like one big bruise.

"Stephanie," he says.

"What's the situation?"

"Harrison almost fucked me," he replies.

"But he failed."

"And I guess I have you to thank."

"I guess you do. He's dead."

"Then we've won."

"Except that the Manilishi may have broken loose."

"Fuck," he says. "Your man—"

"Did the best he could."

"Then we need to wait until—"

"No waiting," she says. "We'll recapture that cunt within the hour or else we'll dig her out of wreckage. Our forces are primed. We're at total readiness. We'll hit the East without mercy and I swear to God they'll never rise again. It's now or never."

"And our latest diplomatic overtures—"

"Are worth whatever we make them. There's no reason to delay."

"Twenty seconds prep?"

"But no prep that'll tip our hand."

"So give the order," he says.

"With pleasure."

Somewhere else below the lunar surface, someone's listening. Someone who feels like she should start fucking with the commands Montrose is giving. But she's not. And she won't. Partially because she's got pursuit hot on her tail. But mostly because she can't see any way around what's about to happen. And because she's sick of being played. She's getting in this game for real now. She's riding the moment that's breaking like a wave throughout the U.S. bases. The moment they've all been waiting for. Her eyes roll back in her head as it begins . . .

With sirens sounding throughout the bases of Earth and Moon and space. Pilots and gunners are sprinting to their stations. Launch codes are flashing down the chains of command. Failsafes are releasing. As one, the directed energy weapons power up, ride astride current capable of lighting every city and then some. Hundreds of thousands of hypersonic missiles slot through the silos. The electromagnetic rails on the mass-drivers surge. The battle management nodes lock in.

The satellites take the range. The warheads prime.

The shutters on the zone close.

And then the sky—

TO BE CONCLUDED

ACKNOWLEDGMENTS

Special thanks to . . .

    James Wang, éminence grise
    Brian De Groodt, for the jailbreak blueprints
    Jerry Ellis, for canoe rides
    Michelle Marcoccia, for bike rides
    Cassandra Stern, for two decades now and counting
    Marc Haimes, for not growing up either
    Rob Cunningham, for reminding me where the shore was
    Paul Ruskay, for outweirding the competition
    Rick Fullerton, for light all those years ago
    Andrew Silber, copilot on the strangeways
    Zakharov Sawyer, for (not) knowing me in a past life
    Jason Marlowe, for his name
    Sanho Tree, for pure octane
    Mitch Engel, for the best line of 1990
    Peter Watts, for debts I'll just have to pay forward
    Jennifer Hunter, may she fly always

And thanks also to . . .

Local D.C. writers: Tom Doyle, David Louis Edelman, Craig Gidney, Jeri Smith-Ready

Not-so-local writers: John Joseph Adams, Jon Christian Allison, Stephen Baxter, Jack Campbell, Jeff Carlson, Erin Cashier, Roz Clarke, Doug Cohen, Richard Dansky, Kelley Eskridge, Neile Graham, Nicola Griffith, Leslie Howle, Dave Hutchinson, Simran Khalsa, Amy Lau, John Scalzi, Stacy Sinclair, Maria Snyder, Melinda Thielbar, Lilah Wild, Bruce Williams, and Mark Williams

The Industry: Jenny Rappaport for representation; Juliet Ulman, David Pomerico, Chris Artis, and Joseph Scalora at Bantam Spectra; Jason Williams and Jeremy Lassen at Nightshade

The Bookstores:
—Duane Wilkins at University Book Store, Seattle
—Alan Beatts, Jude Feldman, and Ripley at Borderlands Books, San Francisco
—Maria Perry at Flights of Fantasy, Albany
—everybody at Borders @ BaileysXRoads

The Artists/Web Maestros:
—Randall MacDonald
—Josh Korwin and Don Zukes at TSA
—Paul Youll
—Stephen Martiniere

The Bloggers:
—Annalee Newitz and Charlie Jane Anders at io9
—Mike Collins at Rescued by Nerds
—Patrick St-Denis at Fantasy Bookspot
—Graeme Flory at Graeme's Fantasy Book Review
—Jay Tomio at Bookspotcentral
—Eric Dorsett at Project: Shadow HQ
—Glenn Reynolds at Instapundit
—Robert Thompson at Fantasy Book Critic
—UberJumper at Relic News